THE HEART OF
THE LION

JEAN PLAIDY

ROBERT HALE · LONDON

© Jean Plaidy 1977
First published in Great Britain 1977

―――――――――――――

ISBN 0 7091 5283 3

Text decorations by
B. S. Biro, F.S.I.A.

Robert Hale Limited
Clerkenwell House
Clerkenwell Green
London EC1

Printed in Great Britain by
Richard Clay (The Chaucer Press) Ltd, Bungay, Suffolk

CONTENTS

A King is Crowned 11

Alice and Berengaria 42

Joanna 57

The Sicilian Adventure 71

The Wedding is Postponed 98

The Fruits of Cyprus 122

The King and the Sultan 152

On the Walls of Acre 176

Philip's Farewell 179

Joanna and Malek Adel 185

The Old Man of the Mountains 208

Farewell Jerusalem 211

The Royal Fugitive 221

The Jewelled Belt 242

Longchamp and Prince John 251

The Return of Eleanor 275

Blondel's Song 287

Release 297

The Reconciliation 305

Reunion with Berengaria 316

The Saucy Castle 323

The Crock of Gold 327

BIBLIOGRAPHY

Aubrey, Wiliam Hickman Smith	*The National and Domestic History of England*
Aytoun, William E.	*The Life and Times of Richard the First*
Brooke, Christopher	*From Alfred to Henry III*
Bryant, Arthur	*The Medieval Foundation*
Davis, H. W. C.	*England under the Normans and the Angevins*
D'Auvergne, Edmund B.	*John, King of England*
Guizot, M. Translated by Robert Black	*History of France*
Hampden, John (edited by)	*Crusader King. The Adventures of Richard, the Lionheart on Crusade, taken from a Chronicle of the Time*
Hill, Lieut. Colonel W.	*Our Fighting King*
Holbach, Maude M.	*In the Footsteps of Richard Coeur de Lion*
James, G. P. R.	*History of the Life of Richard Coeur de Lion, King of England*
Johnston, R. C.	*The Crusade and Death of Richard I*
Lloyd, Alan	*King John*
Norgate, Kate	*John Lackland*
Norgate, Kate	*England under the Angevin Kings*
Pernoud, Regine Translated by Peter Wiles	*Eleanor of Acquitaine*
Pittinger, W. Norman	*Richard the Lionhearted, The Crusader King*
Poole, A. L.	*From Domesday Book to Magna Carta*
Rosenberg, Melrich V.	*Eleanor of Aquitaine*

Stephens, Sir Leslie, and Lee, Sir Sidney (edited by)	*The Dictionary of National Biography*
Strickland, Agnes	*The Lives of the Queens of England*
Wade, John	*British History*
Warren, W. L.	*King John*
Wilkinson, Clennell	*Coeur de Lion*

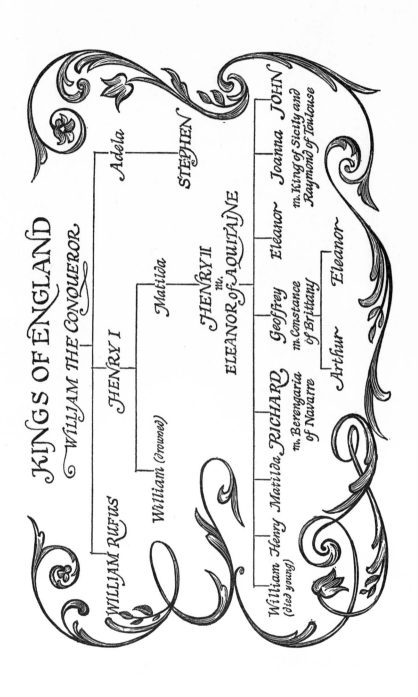

KINGS OF ENGLAND

WILLIAM THE CONQUEROR

- **WILLIAM RUFUS**
- **HENRY I**
  - William (crowned)
  - Matilda
    - **HENRY II**
      m.
      ELEANOR of AQUITAINE
      - William Henry Matilda **RICHARD,** Geoffrey Eleanor Joanna **JOHN**
        (died young) m. Berengaria m. Constance m. King of Sicily and
        of Navarre of Brittany Raymond of Toulouse
        - Arthur Eleanor
- Adela
  - **STEPHEN**

A King is Crowned

THE Queen, having dismissed all her attendants, sat alone in the King's chamber at Winchester Palace. The King was dead and with his death had come release from the captivity in which he had held her for so many years. She was sixty-seven—an age when most people would have been content to retire from life, perhaps enter a nunnery where, if they had lived such a life as she had, they might think it expedient to spend their remaining years in penitence. Not so Eleanor of Aquitaine, widow of the recently dead Henry Plantagenet.

She studied the murals on the walls. It had been a fancy of the late King to have the walls of his palaces painted with allegories representing his life, and this was the room of the eaglets. She remembered an occasion when he and she had stood in this room together. It must have been during one of the periods when there had been a lessening of their antagonism towards each other, for there had been such occasions. One had been at the time of their eldest son's death when sorrow had brought them together—but briefly. She could never forgive Henry for his infidelities; he could never forgive her for turning their sons against him. And there were those sons represented as eaglets waiting to peck their father to death. How bitter he had been when he had pointed them out to her.

'Your just deserts, Henry,' she said aloud. 'You old lecher. Do you expect me to be afraid of you now you are dead? For that matter, when was I ever afraid of you ... or anyone?'

It was morbid of her to come to this room, to think of him

even; yet how could she help it? He had been the most significant man in her life—and there had been many. He had been a great king, she granted him that. If he had been able to curb his lechery, if he had understood how to treat his sons, perhaps he would have kept the devotion of his family.

But he was dead and she must forget him. She had never been one to look back, and there was work to be done. She had been fond of all her children but Richard had always been her favourite. There was a bond between them such as she could feel for none of the others—not even young Joanna, her youngest daughter. And Richard was now the King of England, although his father had done all he could to prevent his inheriting the crown. He had wanted to give it to John. Had he realized in his last hours how foolish he had been to dote on John? How stupid could shrewd men sometimes be when befuddled by their emotions! In his heart he must have known that John was a traitor to him and yet he had stubbornly refused to accept the fact. John had betrayed him as Richard had never done, for at least Richard had been open in his condemnation of his father, whereas John had fawned on him, flattering him while all the time he had been plotting against him.

Henry knew of course even as he deceived himself. What had he said to her when they had stood in this room?

'The four eaglets are my sons who will persecute me until I die. The youngest of them, my favourite, will hurt me most. He is waiting for the moment when he will peck out my eyes.'

'Oh, Henry,' she said softly, 'what sort of a fool were you?'

She chided herself for the softness of her feelings. He had been her enemy. It was weakness to feel gentle towards him just because he was dead and could harm her no more. She had to stop thinking of him; she must shut out of her mind memories of their youth when although she had been nearly twelve years older than he was, and married at that time to the King of France, passion had flared up between them. Then no other would do for her and she had loved him single-mindedly until he brought his bastard into her nursery and she discovered that he had been unfaithful to her in the first year of their marriage. Then had begun the violent quarrels, the recriminations. She smiled faintly seeing him pulling the cloth of his jacket apart in his rage, lying on the floor and gnawing the filthy rushes, throwing some article of furniture across the room...

'You had your weaknesses, my husband,' she murmured. 'But you had your greatness too.'

There had been a time when he was regarded as the invincible warrior throughout England and the Continent of Europe, when men trembled at his name. He had been a brilliant strategist and had made England prosperous after the reign of weak Stephen. Yet how low he had fallen at the end! The account of his death moved her in spite of herself. He had turned his face to the wall and said, 'I care no more for myself or for the world' and in his delirium, 'Shame, shame on a conquered King.'

'Poor Henry,' she murmured. 'And am I as foolish, as sentimental? What am I doing in his chamber? Why am I thinking of the past? My enemy is dead and his dying is my freedom. I shall brood no longer. There is work to be done.'

Resolutely she rose; she did not glance back at the picture of the eagle with his eaglets.

Firmly she shut the door.

When Richard arrived everything must be in readiness for him.

*   *   *

A new dignity had fallen upon her. Her son's first act had been to release her from her prison. She had not been disappointed in him.

And her great aim would be to hold his kingdom for him. It should not be difficult. The English had a sense of fair play and Richard was the late King's eldest living son. That Henry had favoured John carried little weight with them. In fact, John had not made himself very popular with the people, but the main point in Richard's favour was that he was the true heir to the throne.

There was a regality about her—she had been born with it. People recognized it immediately and were ready to pay homage to her, and she could make sure that Richard should find his subjects waiting to welcome him when he returned from Normandy, which must be soon. That was important. His English subjects must not be allowed to think that he cared for other possessions more than he did for England.

There was one whom she had for many years longed to confront—the girl Henry had seduced when she was a child, and who had continued to be his mistress to the end: the Princess Alice. What was Alice thinking now that she had lost her powerful protector? The desire to discover was irresistible. Eleanor would send an order to the Palace of Westminster where Princess Alice had her apartments. How amusing to be able to send for the girl and to know that she dared not refuse to come.

Alice stood before her.

She was comely enough though not outstandingly beautiful as Eleanor herself had been. There was something meek about Alice, and now of course she was afraid because she did not know what was in store for her and she would doubtless have heard rumours concerning the vindictive nature of the Queen.

Alice, betrothed to Richard, mistress of the King his father, must now face her lover's wife!

'I have *sent* for you that I may question you with regard to your future,' said Eleanor.

She stressed the word 'sent'. She, who had been a prisoner, was now the one whose word was law. There had been a time when little Alice only had to express a wish and her infatuated elderly lover would be eager to grant it. Now he was gone and Alice must stand alone to face the fury of the woman he had wronged. Wronged! Eleanor wanted to burst out laughing at the thought of this meek girl setting herself against a great queen. But she had had a great king behind her then. Alas for you, you little fool, she thought; you have lost him now.

'You do not hope of course that there can be any betrothal between you and King Richard now,' said Eleanor.

'I ... I did not think so,' said Alice. She was fair and fragile. Eleanor could understand how she had appealed to him. She would have been clinging and admiring, adoring him, giving him that which he sought in all women. His Rosamund Clifford—that other great love of his—had been the same. They had some inherent femininity which for all her voluptuous beauty Eleanor had never possessed.

'Nay and you do right, having been debauched by the father you could hardly expect the son to take you to his bed.'

Alice blushed. A King's mistress and managing to look so

coy! What a deceitful creature she was. The odd quirk was that she was Louis' daughter. Louis to whom Eleanor herself—when she had been his Queen—had born two children, her daughters Alix and Marie.

Eleanor could see her father in her—she would be good if she could, for she wanted to be, but fate had been too much for her in the form of her lecherous prospective father-in-law who had come into the schoolroom where she was being brought up with his children since she was to marry one of them, and when she could have been no more than twelve years old had made her his mistress. She would have been shy, reluctant and malleable—everything that was needed to stimulate his jaded senses. She could well imagine how it had started and angry jealousy swept over her. He had wanted to marry Alice and divorce Eleanor to do so. It was not so easy though to divorce the heiress of Aquitaine even if it was for the daughter of the King of France.

And now he was dead and Alice was past her first youth; she had already borne him a child it was rumoured. The child had died though, which was one complication removed.

Sly silly girl—so meek, apeing the virgin, when all the time she had indulged with him, and the Queen knew from experience what such occasions would be like.

'So here you are,' said Eleanor, 'a whore no less, though a King's whore. It ill becomes the sister of the King of France.'

'We ... we ...'

'I know. I know. You loved, and he would have made you his Queen. That was if he could have rid himself of his existing Queen. You know who stood in your way, my little Princess. How you must have hated me!'

'Oh, no ...'

'Oh, yes! I'll swear he talked of me. What did he tell you of me, eh?'

'He rarely spoke of you.'

'You are afraid to say. You are a frightened little thing, Alice. You are afraid of me and you'll be afraid to face your brother when he sends for you. What will you say to the King of France when you are taken back to him, when he hears of the games you played in the bed of the old King of England?'

'I must ask you for what is due to his memory ...'

'You silly girl, do you think I am afraid his ghost will haunt me? Let it! How I should enjoy to tell it what I thought of the fleshly Henry. I never feared him in life where I doubt not he was more powerful than he could be in death. Nay he was a lecher. A woman had but to take his fancy lightly and he would have her in his bed—as he did you. Think not that he held you in any special regard.'

'Oh, but he did. He always came straight to me when he was in England...'

'Straight from the rest and swore he would marry you I doubt not, and laughed at you and the son he was deceiving.'

'It is untrue. His conscience smote him. He often talked of Richard.'

'How noble of him! So you talked of Richard and how you were deceiving him and you think that exonerates you from your just rewards for what you have done?'

'Richard didn't really want to marry me.'

'His father prevented his doing so.'

'There are stories of Richard.'

'What do you mean?'

'Of the life he leads.'

'With women?' cried Eleanor. 'Who should blame him, deprived of his bride as he has been? He is no boy. He is more than thirty years of age.'

'And with my brother,' said Alice boldly. 'It has been said that he shared his bed when he was at Philip's court.'

'A custom when one monarch wishes to honour another.'

'It is said that there is great love between them.'

'It is said! Who has said this? Are you, the royal slut of a lecherous king, in a position to judge the conduct of others? Have a care, my little whore, or you could find yourself under restraint.'

'My brother will not allow that.'

'You are not in your brother's court yet. You are in that of King Richard and until he comes to claim his kingdom, I am holding it for him.'

'What do you intend to do with me?'

'Keep you here for a while.' Eleanor came near to Alice and gripped her by the arm. 'While you were sporting with your lover, I, his true wife, was a prisoner here in this castle. There were guards outside my door. When I walked out they accompanied me.'

'You took up arms against the King. You led his sons to revolt against him. It was just punishment.'

'Just to imprison a wife! Think you so? All he suffered he deserved.'

'And you too,' said Alice boldly.

'Have a care. You are in my power now, you know.'

'Richard will treat me well.'

'So you think he will have you now? You are mistaken, Alice. You will be sent back to your brother I doubt not. But no man will want you now.'

'It is not true.'

'Certainly not the King of England who can take his pick from the world. So a life of boredom awaits you, at the best. You will sit over your needlework in one of your brother's castles and brood on the past and remember how Henry sported with you and that such adventures are behind you for ever more. In the meantime you will stay here. You will learn what it was like for me to live here as a prisoner. The same apartment which was allotted to me shall be allotted to you. The same guards shall be at your door. Yes, you shall learn what it was like to be a prisoner. The only difference will be that you will be *my* prisoner and I was that of your lover. Now come, my Princess. You have had enough easy living. You have sinned and must repent. You will have time to do so in your prison.'

The Queen summoned the guards whom she had had waiting.

'Take the Princess Alice to her new apartments,' she said.

*　　　*　　　*

She was wise enough to know that she could not linger in the castle merely to gloat over Alice's fate. She knew too that it could not be of long duration. Philip would never allow it and it was not a matter of which she would wish to make a political issue. Still, she could not resist giving the girl a taste of the humiliation she had suffered.

She must prepare the country for Richard's arrival and make the people ready to receive their new King, so she announced that she was going on a short tour of the country and she set out from Winchester having given orders that if any news of the King's imminent arrival in England was received it must be brought to her without delay.

As she rode along she contemplated the fact that there was

always danger when a king died. It could never be certain how the people would feel towards his successor. To the Conqueror's descendants England had been an uneasy inheritance largely because the possession of lands overseas had demanded their presence abroad. The English naturally did not like to be neglected. Henry's life had been spent between England and France and because his possessions in France had been so much more difficult to hold owing to the presence of the Franks on his very borders, he had been more often there than in England.

The people must accept Richard. She had few qualms that they would. If ever man had the appearance of a king that man was Richard. How different he was from his slovenly father who had thrown on his clothes in a disorderly way and looked like a peasant, who never wore riding gloves and because he was out in all weathers had skin like leather. Yet he had won the respect of his people. But how much more readily would they follow a man who looked like a king.

Riding into the cities she sent for the leading citizens. She knew that the greatest resentment which was held against the late King and his predecessors was due to the infliction of the old forest laws. The Norman kings had been fanatical about their hunting grounds. Henry Plantagenet had been equally fierce. So great was their passion for hunting that they had spared nothing nor anyone in the pursuit of it. On the whole Henry had been a popular king but in the forest areas he had been hated. He had set up officers in forest regions to act as custodians and no one living near was allowed to cut down trees or to keep dogs or bows and arrows. Anyone discovered disobeying these laws was punished in such a dreadful manner that death would have been preferable. Hands, feet, tongues, noses and ears were cut off and eyes put out. The punishment for performing any act which might detract in the smallest way from the King's hunting pleasures was mutilation.

Yet Henry, shrewd as he was, eager to placate a people who must be left under a substitute ruler for long periods of time, knowing that these measures were the source of great unpopularity, would do nothing to repeal them. Hunting was one of the major passions of his life and like his forebears he intended to indulge it in ideal conditions.

Contemplating that passion now Eleanor reflected once

more that although her late husband had been a man of great ability he had had many weaknesses.

'The game laws,' she announced, 'are harsh and cruel. The new King will wish to change them. To begin with in his name I shall release all those who are awaiting punishment under those laws. There is one thing I ask of those who have regained their freedom and that is: Pray for his soul.'

Those who had been saved from a terrible fate, those who had been living as outlaws and could now return to their families were very ready to do as Eleanor asked.

'It must be understood,' she said, 'that this clemency comes from King Richard and while he wishes those who have been condemned under unjust laws to go free, he cannot countenance the release of those who have committed crimes against other laws.'

A great cry of approval went up and Eleanor knew that the freeing of those who had offended against the game laws had been a wise move.

'I command now,' she said, 'that every freeman of the kingdom swear that he will bear faith to King Richard, son of King Henry and Queen Eleanor, for the preservation of life, limbs and terrene honour, as his liege lord, against all living; and that he will be obedient to his laws and assist him in the preservation of peace and justice.'

The new King was hailed with enthusiasm.

Eleanor had done her work well; and when news was brought to her that Richard had arrived in England she hastened back to Winchester to be ready to receive him.

* * *

She had assembled all the nobility in Winchester. Perhaps the most important was Ranulph de Glanville who had been her custodian in the castle during the years of her imprisonment. She bore him no ill will; he had always treated her with due respect and the fact that he had guarded against her escape meant that he was obeying his master. As the chief Justiciar of England and a man of immense talents Eleanor believed that his support would be of help to the new King.

Each day people were thronging into Winchester as Richard's arrival grew imminent. Eleanor was not sure whether her son John would come with his brother. They had been in

Normandy together but it was possible that they might take different routes home. This proved to be the case.

What a wonderful moment it was for the Queen when she beheld her beloved son riding at the head of his entourage, a magnificent sight, enough to delight any mother's eyes.

The meeting was an emotional one and when Richard embraced her she knew that this was one of the happiest moments of her life. She was free after more than sixteen years of captivity; her son—the best loved of her children—was King of England and his first thoughts on coming to the crown were for her. She loved dearly and was loved with equal fervour.

'Mother!' he cried.

'My son, my King,' she answered, her voice shaken with emotion.

There could be no doubt of his kingliness. He excelled in all manly pastimes. It had been so since the days of his boyhood. He was very tall, having the long arms and legs of his Norman ancestors as well as their blonde good looks; his hair was auburn, his eyes deep blue and he had more than mere good looks; his grace of carriage, his kingly air were unsurpassed, and in any company of men he would have been selected as the King.

She was weak with pride—she who was usually so strong and rarely a prey for her emotions! This was the son whom she had reared and she had recognized his superior qualities from his babyhood; they had been the allies and had stood together against his father and the bastard Geoffrey who had been brought into the royal nursery. He had been her boy from the day he was born and the bond, she fervently prayed, would be severed only by death.

'How my heart rejoices to see you here,' she said.

'There was much to be done across the sea before I could come.'

'Your subjects have been prepared to welcome you.'

'Mother, I know you have done good work for me.'

'I trust I shall never do aught but good work for you, my son.'

He scowled when Ranulf de Glanville approached to pay the homage, which he received coldly. Eleanor smiled realizing that Richard was thinking of this man as his mother's jailer. She must make him understand the importance of

Glanville. He must not make an enemy of such a man. There would be much of which she must warn him, and she hoped he loved her enough to let her guide him.

'Let us make our way to the castle,' she said. 'There shall be such feasting and revelry as is becoming to the arrival of the King.'

'There is much we must talk of.'

'Much indeed.'

'How it rejoices me that you are here beside me. It will lighten my lot. You will care for matters here while I am away.'

Her happiness was tinged with apprehension. When he was away? But of course he would have to be away. His dominions were widely spread. That must be what he meant.

She dismissed her fears and gave herself up to the pleasure of seeing homage done to him as he entered the castle. How nobly he accepted it! She noticed how people looked at him.

There never could have been a man who looked so much a king.

*   *   *

To be alone with him, to talk to him of secret matters, to share his confidences, that was a great joy to her.

'Your coronation must take place immediately,' she advised. 'Once a king is crowned he is in truth a king; before that...' She lifted her shoulders.

'I have decided it shall be on the third day of September.'

'Isn't that an unlucky day?'

He laughed aloud. 'Mother, I take no heed of these superstitions.'

'Others may.'

'Then let them. I shall pass into London on the first day of the month, and there I shall be crowned King.'

'So be it,' she said. 'The important point is that the ceremony takes place without delay. Richard, I must speak to you of Alice. She is here.'

'In this castle?'

'Under restraint. I thought that as I had suffered it so long it would do her no harm to have a little taste of it.'

He nodded but he was frowning. 'What must be done with her? I'll not have her.'

'We must not forget that her brother is the King of France.'

A shadow passed across his face. How did he feel about Philip now? There was no doubt that they had once been very close friends. Was that due to love or expediency on Richard's part? He had once needed the friendship of the King of France when his own father was his enemy. Now that he was King of England—and all Kings of England must be wary of Kings of France—had his feelings changed? The one time friend ... lover ... was he now a deadly rival?

'I care not who her brother is,' said Richard, 'I'll have none of my father's cast-offs.'

'Your father never cast her off. He was faithful to the end they say ... faithful in his way that was. No doubt he sported merrily when she was far away but, as with Rosamund Clifford, he visited her in great amity over many years.'

'My father is dead now, Mother; let us forget his habits. The fact remains that I'll have none of Alice.'

'She will have to go back to France. She will not like it. She has been in England for twenty-two years.'

'Nevertheless she must go.'

'Yet you will marry. It will be expected of you.'

'I have a bride in mind. Berengaria, daughter of the King of Navarre, he whom they call Sancho the Wise. We know each other, for I met her when I was taken to her father's court by her brother who is known as Sancho the Strong to distinguish him from his father. We have even talked of marriage but Alice of course stood in my way.'

'That girl and your father have a lot to answer for. Though I doubt we should blame Alice; she is a feather in the wind blown this way and that.'

'Then, by God's mercy, let us blow her back to France.'

'What will Philip say when he finds his sister sent back to him?'

'What can he say of a sister who lived with the man who was to be her father-in-law and bore him a child?' Richard clenched his fists and cried: 'My God, when I think of his taking her from me, using her as he did and all the time deceiving me ...'

'It is done with. As you remind me, he is dead. He can do you no more harm. You are the King now, Richard. You can go with a good conscience to Berengaria.'

'If there is to be a marriage this is the one I want. I feel firm friendship with Sancho. Remember it was he who pleaded with my father concerning you when I requested him to. It was due to him that your imprisonment was less rigorous than it might have been.'

'Yes, I remember well the good he did me.'

'For this reason and because I could trust no other with such a task I want you to go to the Court of Navarre and to bring Berengaria—not to me ... for I cannot ask for her hand until I am seen to be free from Alice. But I wish her to be taken where she can wait until I am free.'

'It shall be so,' said Eleanor. 'But first there must be your coronation. What of your brother John?'

'I left him in Normandy. He was to sail from Barfleur. He hoped to land at Dover.'

Eleanor nodded. 'It will be well for him to be here.' She looked steadily at Richard. 'It is unfortunate that your father should have made so much of him. I could never understand why he did that.'

'It was to spite me,' retorted Richard vehemently. 'You know how he hated me.'

'I could never understand that in him either. You ... all that a king should be, surely a son of whom any father should be proud ...' She laughed. 'You always took my side against him, Richard. Even in those early nursery days. Perhaps you forfeited his goodwill in so doing.'

'It seems so, but I have no qualms about John. He knows I have first claim to the crown. I shall give him honours, treat him with dignity and respect. He must understand that he can never be King except in the event of my failing to get an heir.'

'Yes, we must make him realize that. It would seem to me that he finds greater interest in his dissolute companions than he would in governing a kingdom.'

''Tis better to keep him so. What of Ranulf de Glanville?'

'I doubt not that he will serve you as he served your father.'

'I like not one who was your jailer.'

'A task which was forced on him. He could not disobey your father, you know.'

'Yet a man who has humiliated you, my mother!'

She smiled at him tenderly.

'We must not allow such matters to cloud our judgements, my son. He has been in charge of the treasure vaults at Winchester. It would not be well that he should withhold any secrets of those vaults from you.'

Richard narrowed his eyes. 'I shall find it difficult to give my friendship to a man who acted so to you.'

'I can forgive him. I shall not think of any past wrongs I have suffered, but only what good may come to you. You must take him into your service. You need good servants.'

'More than most,' he admitted, 'for I shall need to leave the country in good hands. I have pledged myself to take part in the Holy War as you know . . .'

'But now that you are King will that be possible?'

'I could never come to terms with my conscience if I broke my vow.'

'You have a kingdom to rule now, Richard. Does not your duty lie with that?'

'Philip and I must go to the Holy Land together.'

'So . . . that friendship still stands.'

'We shall see,' said Richard. 'In all events I intend to honour my obligations to my father's son Geoffrey.'

'The bastard!' cried Eleanor.

'He was with my father at the end.'

'For what he could get.'

'Nay, Mother, I think not. Geoffrey served him well and was with him when all others had deserted him. John had left him. They say that broke his heart and that when he heard that John's name was at the head of the list of those lords who had turned against him he had no will to live. It was his last wish that Geoffrey should not suffer for his fidelity. Nor shall he.'

'Nay, Richard, he would take your throne from you if he had a chance.'

'You do not know him, Mother. You hated him because he was living evidence of my father's infidelity to you, but that is no fault of Geoffrey's. He was loyal to my father to the end when there was nothing to gain and everything to lose from it. As was William the Marshall. I shall always honour such men.'

'But Richard, this whore's son . . .'

'Is my half-brother. I beg you, put him from your mind, for mine is made up concerning him. My father wished him to have the Archbishopric of York and that I shall bestow on him.'

'It is a mistake,' said the Queen.

'It is my intention,' replied Richard; she saw the stubborn line of his lips and knew that it was no use trying to dissuade him.

Lest she should think that this was due to a softness in him he told her of his treatment of Stephen of Tours, the Seneschal of Anjou, who had been treasurer of the late King's overseas dominions.

'He refused to yield to me my father's treasure so I threw him into a dungeon and loaded him with chains. Such treatment soon set him begging forgiveness and what was more important rendering unto me all my father's possessions. Never fear, Mother, I shall be strong. No man shall delude me with his sly behaviour, but there are some men who are bright stars in any kingly crown—those who can be trusted to serve their king with honour—and if that service was given to my father because he was the King and now is offered me, I shall take it.'

He took her hand and kissed it. Although he would go his own way, he was telling her he would listen to her; but if he did not agree with her advice he would not take it.

In her heart she would not have had him otherwise.

'We must now give our thoughts to your coronation,' she said. 'There must be no delay in that. John will soon be with us.'

'He must be at my coronation. I want him to know that if he is a loyal brother to me then the future lies bright before him.'

'He will be with us soon,' said Eleanor. 'I long to see my youngest son. Rest assured, dear Richard, that I will impress on him the need to serve you well.'

'I know it,' said Richard; and in spite of the fact that she deeply resented his showing favour to her husband's bastard Geoffrey, there was complete accord between them.

*   *   *

John had watched his brother embark at Barfleur. 'It would be well for us to travel separately,' Richard had said.

The meaning of those words was evident. They were the two remaining sons of the dead King. If they were both to become victims of the sea—which they could well do if they travelled in the same ship—the next heir would be a boy, no more than a baby, the son of their dead brother, Geoffrey of Brittany. Little Arthur was of no age to govern.

A dark mood seized John as he watched his brother's ship sail away. This was not what his father had intended. He, John, had been promised England. He longed to be a king ... and King of England.

He would never forget that when he had been born his father had nicknamed him John Lackland—Jean sans Terre. That was because his elder brothers had prior claims to his father's possessions and even a great king with overseas dominions could not comfortably provide for so many sons. His brother William had died before he was born, but that had still left Henry, Richard and Geoffrey. Henry and Geoffrey were now dead. So only the two of them remained—Richard and himself.

How secretly he had exulted over the bad blood between his father and Richard! That had seemed to make the way clear for him; and his father had talked to him often of his inheritance. Now this elder powerful brother, known throughout Europe as one of the greatest fighters of his time, claimed the throne. Their mother stood for him and so did the people. What could he do to prevent Richard's becoming King?

The maddening part about it was that Richard would now marry and if he did and there was a child that would be the end of John's hopes.

Once he had been promised a crown as King of Ireland. How delighted he had been then, but when his father had sent him to Ireland there had been trouble. He and his young followers had ridiculed the Irish whose manners seemed so odd compared with their own; the girls were pretty though and being young and full of high spirits they had made good sport with them; but the Irish had resented the rape of their land and their women and John had been recalled. His father had been lenient with him, doting on him until the end. He had sent for a crown of peacock feathers set in gold from the Pope with his consent to make John King of Ireland. What ill fortune had been his! Trouble in Normandy (when was there not trouble in Normandy?) had intervened to prevent the ceremony and he had never received the crown.

He cursed the ill fortune which had made him a younger son, but he had had the foresight to know when to leave his father. In fact he had never cared a jot for the old man; he had deceived him all along, and he had gone over to Richard before his father died; and for this reason Richard was now accepting him as his good brother and ally.

He laughed slyly, thinking of his elder brother. Richard Yea and Nay. That was good. He was predictable. There was little guile in Richard. To Richard an enemy was an enemy, a friend a friend. Richard said No and meant No. He was frank and open. But he could be ruthless and when his anger was aroused against an enemy none could be more cruel. But he had what he called a sense of honour and this would not permit him to dissemble, which made it easy for such as John to know how to act towards him.

Now John must pay homage to the new King; he must make his brother believe that he would be loyal to him; and so must he be—until the opportunity arose to be otherwise.

He was young yet—twenty-two years of age; Richard was ten years older. There had been rumours about certain debaucheries in which Richard had indulged. Sometimes women were concerned in them; but did Richard really care for women? John was unsure. There had been rumours about Philip when Richard was in France; but then a man could spare the time from those he loved to get a child, particularly when that man was king and the child could be the next King of England. It was amusing that Richard's betrothed was the Princess Alice who had been their father's mistress. He could hardly marry her; and the fact that he was betrothed to her would naturally mean some delay before he could marry anyone else. Delay was to be welcomed; for who knew, in the life of such a fighter, when an arrow or some such weapon might not put a speedy end to that life.

And then the way would be open for John.

So he must return to England; he must kneel at the feet of his handsome brother; he must swear to serve him with his life while he waited patiently for his death.

He reached Dover and went straight to Winchester.

There his mother received him warmly. She was fond of him, although of course none of her children could be to her what Richard was. He was delighted when, after he had been formally received by his brother, she took them both to her private chamber and he was allowed to talk with them.

Richard said that there must be no more conflict in the family. It had been his father's downfall and had brought no good to any of them. Let them have done with it and work together.

'Aye, aye,' said John fervently.

His mother eyed him with approval.

'I know that you were once with our father against me,' said Richard. 'I know that he offered bribes to you ... even this kingdom. That must be forgotten.'

'It *is* forgotten,' John assured him seriously.

Richard grasped his hand and John forced tears into his eyes.

'It is well that you understand each other,' said their mother.

'Our father, I know, granted you the County of Mortain, but did not live long enough to give you possession of it. That shall now be yours.'

'You are generous to me, Richard.'

'And intend to be more so. You have been granted certain lands in England and there is a revenue I believe of some four thousand Angevin pounds which comes from them.'

John's eyes glistened. He would indeed be rich. If the Gloucester lands were his he believed he would be the richest man in England—next to the King.

He said: 'There is one other matter. It concerns my marriage. I am no longer a boy. I need a wife.' He did not add: And I need her fortune. But neither his mother nor his brother would be ignorant of the size of that.

'Our father betrothed you to Hadwisa of Gloucester,' said Richard; 'I often wondered whether it was wise. There is a close relationship between our families.'

Wise! thought John. The richest heiress in the country! Of course it was wise!

'I would marry her tomorrow ... if you gave your consent,' said John; and he thought: Aye, and without it, for I would risk much for Hadwisa's wealth.

Eleanor said: 'The Gloucester lands and wealth should be brought into the family. Let John marry Hadwisa and then it will be too late for the Church to do much about it.'

Richard was thoughtful but John's eyes were glistening with avaricious delight.

Rich lands in Normandy and wealth from England and now marriage with its rich heiress.

* * *

From a turret of Marlborough Castle Hadwisa of Gloucester watched anxiously for the cavalcade at the head of which her bridegroom would be riding.

Her father had told her that she must be prepared. There would be no delay. As soon as the party arrived the marriage must take place.

It was not a very romantic wedding, she had complained to her attendants. She wondered what John was like.

'Suffice it,' said her old nurse, 'that he is a king's son. And he is young too. It could have been that an old man was chosen for you. At least you have one who is young and by all accounts not ill-favoured.'

'Tell me what you know of him,' Hadwisa had begged.

Tell her what she knew? Tell of the stories of the wildness of Prince John? Better not. It might be that they had not been true ... not entirely that was. By all accounts the bridegroom was young in years and old in sin; and Hadwisa was not experienced of the world. The child would never understand. Therefore she must discover gradually and for herself.

'It is not an easy position,' said Hadwisa, 'to be half royal as it were. Kings should think of that when they have sons outside their marriage.'

' 'Tis my belief it is the last thing they think of in the heat of their passion.'

'But my grandfather was a great good man.'

'Ah,' said the old nurse. 'I remember him. A fine gentleman, an honourable man. His father respected him, and his father was King Henry I.'

'I know my grandfather Robert was one of his natural sons.'

'And the King loved him dearly. He was the great champion of the King's daughter Matilda in her fight against Stephen.'

'She was a difficult woman but he believed her cause was

the right one and I know that he was partly responsible for helping Henry II to the throne.'

'You know your family history, my child. That is good. It helps you to bear your lot.'

'Why should it, nurse?'

'To talk to those who are long ago dead and to remember that troubles beset them makes you feel your own are not so important.'

'You think *I* have troubles?'

'You, my love! About to be married to a handsome prince!'

'I trust he will like me.'

'He'll not be able to help himself,' the nurse assured her.

If only it were true, thought Hadwisa. She knew she was not beautiful. Her sisters—all married now—had been far more attractive than she was. She was not a fool. She knew that her father was one of the richest men in the kingdom and it was for this reason that she had been affianced to the King's brother.

Now she could see the riders in the distance. There was the royal standard and at the head of the band would be her bridegroom.

Her mother was at the door.

'Hadwisa, are you ready? You must be at the gates to greet the Prince.' She noticed her daughter's anxious looks and thought: It's a pity the poor child is so plain. Nervously Hadwisa went out to greet her bridegroom.

He was of medium height and like all the sons of Henry II and Eleanor of Aquitaine he had some claim to good looks. But although he was young yet and his character had not yet drawn lines on his face there was that about it to strike a note of warning in the heart of his bride.

Cruelty peeped out of those eyes; the mouth was hard yet weak; to some extent he disguised his true nature but it could not be altogether concealed. Lust, envy, greed—yes, every one of the notorious seven sins could be detected there.

He took her hand and kissed it. His eyes gloated but not on her. The richest lands in England! When they were his he would have possession of a goodly part of that country.

'Come,' he cried. 'Let us get the marriage done with. My bride and I will need a little time together before I go to my brother's coronation.'

'My lord,' said her father, 'a banquet is prepared. We had thought tomorrow might be the best day for the marriage ceremony.'

'Nay,' cried John. 'We'll have it tonight.' He took Hadwisa's hand and pressed it firmly. 'I declare that having seen my bride ... in her home ... I cannot wait.'

So they prepared her and her mother came to her and she asked that they might be alone together.

'Come,' said her mother, when the attendants had gone, 'all is well. Every bride is nervous on her wedding day.'

'This is so quick.'

'My child you have been betrothed to the Prince for years.'

'But I never thought...'

'You are of a marriageable age now and so is he.'

'Mother, it is not meet that we should marry. We are third cousins.'

'It is because you have royal blood in your veins that you are a worthy bride for the King's brother.'

'But we are third cousins.'

'It is a slender link.'

'King Henry I was my great-grandfather. He was also John's.'

'Do not fret over such things.'

'I believe the Church might not sanction our marriage. There should be a special dispensation.'

'My dear child, do you realize that the King has given his consent to the marriage?'

'The King is not the Church.'

'What would you have us do?'

'Wait,' cried Hadwisa. 'Wait!'

'Can you imagine the wrath of your bridegroom if we suggested such a thing! What do you think he would do?'

Ah, there was the crux of the matter! What would he do? Would he burn down the castle? Would he cut off her father's head? Would he hang him on the nearest tree?

She was silent, thinking of what she had seen in her bridegroom's eyes.

*　　*　　*

The ceremony was over; they had feasted, the minstrels had sung, and Hadwisa and her bridegroom were conducted to the bridal chamber.

She was afraid of him.

Her fear amused him. A virgin! He had had his fill of such and they were interesting only for such a short while. When he had pillaged towns with his followers they had taken the best of the women; that had been good sport. The fear of others always excited him. It soothed him in some way. It made him feel important. He had the power at that moment to rule them absolutely. It made up for the fact that he was the youngest son.

Hadwisa was afraid of him and that pleased him. Not much else about her person did. But he had to remember the riches she brought him.

The richest heiress in the kingdom! That was worth a good deal.

'Why,' he said, 'you are reluctant. Do I not please you?'

'Why, yes, my lord ... but ...'

'But! What buts are these?'

'There is a strong blood relationship between us ...'

'Ah, indeed our great-grandfather scattered his seed far and wide. I'll swear that there is many a young girl in this kingdom who could be my cousin. So it is with princes. None dare say them nay.'

'I had thought we should have waited for a dispensation from the Church.'

' 'Tis too late ... the ceremony has taken place. I am your husband now.'

'But I meant to wait for ...'

'For?' He raised his eyebrows, taunting her. 'For what, my reluctant wife?'

'You know to what I refer.'

He caught her by the wrist and his grip was painful.

'You tell me,' he said. 'Come, let us hear it from those innocent lips.'

She lowered her eyes. 'The consummation ...'

He laughed aloud. Then he seized her and she knew that her fear had not been groundless.

*   *   *

For five days he stayed at the castle. He terrified her but she knew her ordeal would not last long. He was becoming weary of it already.

'It may well be,' he said, 'that I have already planted our son within you. Pray that it may be so for I know not when we may meet again. I shall go now to my brother's coronation and there may well be much to occupy me.'

As he was about to leave the castle a messenger arrived from Baldwin, Archbishop of Canterbury. He brought with him a letter for the Earl of Gloucester. When he read it the Earl grew pale.

'The Archbishop forbids the marriage on the grounds of consanguinity,' he said.

John burst into loud laughter. 'He is a little late, is he not?'

'My lord Prince, what can we do?'

'Burn the letter. Forget it. What's done is done. Your daughter is my wife. Who knows she may already be carrying a boy who could be heir to the throne. I'll not have the Church interfering in my affairs. Baldwin forbade the marriage when my father lived. My father cared nothing for Baldwin, nor should we.'

The Earl said: 'You are right, my lord. There is nothing we can do now.'

He rode away. Hadwisa had never known relief such as she felt when she saw his party disappear into the distance.

*   *   *

John arrived in London to find his mother and brother installed in Westminster Palace. There was great excitement in London at the prospect of the coronation; and there seemed little doubt that the new King was popular. By abolishing many of the harsh forest laws Eleanor had paved the way for the King; and with a new reign the people were ever ready to believe that it would be better than the last. Henry II had been a man who had brought much good to the country; many had heard of the state of affairs during the reign of weak Stephen when robbers had roamed the land abducting unwary travellers, holding them to ransom, robbing them and if they had little worldly goods torturing them for sport. Henry with his stern just laws had put a stop to that. But he had retained the cruel forest laws and that was what the people remembered rather than the good he had done.

Now here was a new King—a man who was by no means

old and who looked like a god. His reputation as a warrior
was well known; he was good to his mother who had acted as
Regent until he came. He had a younger brother who was
willing to serve him. It seemed to the people that everything
was set fair. And now a coronation. Revelry in the streets,
processions; and it was already whispered that this was going
to be the finest spectacle that had ever delighted the eyes of
the citizens of London. Naturally they were excited. Naturally they were all going out to cheer.

Richard greeted his brother warmly.

'How went it?' he asked. 'Don't tell me, I know. You are a
husband. Baldwin is fulminating. He says it is a sin for you to
live with Hadwisa of Gloucester.'

'That adds a spice to what would otherwise be a somewhat
dull matter,' replied John.

'Oh, 'twas so? Well, you have her lands and that is something to be pleased about. But what of Baldwin?'

'I shall ignore him. Shall you, brother?'

'It is not good for a king to be on ill terms with his archbishop.'

''Tis a by no means uncommon state of affairs. He is
officiating at the coronation, I doubt not.'

'He is,' said Richard.

'Will he denounce me from the altar think you?'

''Twould be most unseemly were he to do so at a coronation and would cost him his post.'

'Then perchance he will leave me in peace for a while.'

'Methinks you were pleased with your bride, John.'

'Pleased with her lands,' answered John.

'Well, you will be a very rich man now.'

'It is a comfort to contemplate how rich.'

Eleanor embraced her youngest son and asked how the
wedding had pleased him.

She commiserated. 'Alas, it is sometimes the richest heiresses who are the least desirable. It's a rare thing to find a
woman who is both.'

'You were I believe, Mother.'

She laughed. 'I have been loved for myself and for Aquitaine. I have never been quite sure which was the more
attractive. Well now, John is safely married...'

'I am not so sure,' said Richard. 'Baldwin is raising
objections.'

'The old fool!' retorted Eleanor. 'In any case it's too late. Why do you smile, John?'

'I was thinking that the old fellow could give me a chance of not seeing my wife if I didn't want to.' He put his hand on his heart and raised his eyes to the ceiling. 'Oh, I suffer sorely. My soul is in torment. I wish to be with my wife but in doing so do I sin against Heaven. She is my third cousin and that is very close. Her great-grandmother was my great-grandfather's whore and we share his blood ... though mine is pure and hers is tainted. If 'twere not for her nice fat lands I would willingly annul the marriage...'

'Be silent, John,' said Eleanor sharply. She could see that Richard did not like his brother's raillery on such a subject.

'I am concerned,' said Richard, 'as to the Jews. I do not want them practising their magical arts at the coronation. That could bring disaster to us all. I shall forbid them to attend the ceremony.'

'It would never do for them to be seen there,' commented the Queen. 'The people would think you are going to show leniency towards them and that would not be popular.'

'They are too rich,' said John. 'That is what's wrong with them.'

'They are industrious and know how to prosper,' declared the Queen. 'Such qualities arouse envy, and being envious of their wealth those who have been less industrious or lack the money-spinning gift seek to lay faults at their door. My son, you must issue a command that there be no Jews at your coronation.'

'It shall be done,' said Richard.

*　　*　　*

The morning of that third day of September of the year 1189 dawned bright and sunny. Yet there were many who remembered that it was a day of ill omen. Egyptian astrologers had named it as one of the *Dies Aegyptiaci* with the implication that on it only the reckless would undertake any important business; and what could be more important to a king than his coronation?

Scarlet cloth had been laid from the King's bedchamber in the palace to the altar of the abbey and crowds had gathered in the streets for the last day and night to make sure of getting a view of the spectacle.

In his bedchamber surrounded by the chief nobles of the realm, including his brother John, the King waited the coming of the Archbishops, the Bishops, the Abbots and heads of the monastic orders. They came bearing censers and vessels containing holy water led by one of their number carrying the great cross.

First in the processions from the bedchamber to the altar came the clergy, chanting as they walked, swinging incense and holding high lighted tapers; the priors and abbots followed and after them the barons. William Mareschal carried the sceptre surmounted by the golden cross and William Earl of Salisbury the golden rod.

Immediately behind them was Prince John, his eyes lowered, imagining himself not walking as he did but in the place of honour today occupied by his brother. How unfair was life, he thought, to make a man the youngest of his family! Yet in some ways fate had been kind in carrying off the others. That left Richard ten years his senior but still young. In the prime of his manhood some said. By God's Eyes, thought John, he could live another twenty years! But if he went to the Holy Land a Saracen arrow might pierce his heart. It was the only hope.

He must be encouraged to go on his crusade. He was not fit to be King. How could a man newly come to a throne, plot how soon he could leave it? Only if he were a fool, for if that man had an ambitious brother he could soon place his kingdom in jeopardy!

To the spectators who thronged about the abbey and crowded inside, it seemed that there could never have been a more handsome sovereign than King Richard. William Mandeville, the Earl of Albemarle, walked before him carrying, on a cushion, the golden crown beautifully ornamented with glittering jewels. Then came Richard himself, tall and stately, under the royal canopy which was poised on lances and held over his head by four barons.

Into the abbey he walked, through the nave to the high altar, where Baldwin was waiting for him.

They looked into each other's eyes—the King arrogant, reminding the Archbishop that he was the master. The Archbishop like all of his kind, as Richard thought, striving to place the Church over the State. He should remember what happened to Thomas Becket. An uneasy thought, for his father had not come too gracefully out of that affair; but it was Becket who had lost his life, though he had become a saint in doing it. Baldwin was certainly incensed because of John's marriage, but he would have to keep quiet about that today.

On the altar most of the abbey relics had been laid—the holy bones of saints, the phials containing what purported to be their blood; and on these Richard swore that he would honour God and the Holy Church, and that he would be just to his people and that he would abolish all evil laws.

His attendants stepped forward to strip him of all his garments except his shirt and hose. He was then anointed with the consecrated oil on his head, arms and breast while Baldwin told him of the significance of this and that the application of the oil to these parts of his body implied that he was being endowed with glory, knowledge and fortitude. His tunic and dalmatic were then put on him by the waiting barons and the sword of justice handed to him. Golden spurs were tied to his heels and the royal mantle placed about his shoulders.

Baldwin then asked him if he were indeed prepared to honour the oath he had just taken and, on Richard's assuring him that he was, the barons took the crown from the altar and gave it to the Archbishop who placed it on Richard's head; the sceptre was put in the King's right hand and the rod in the left.

After High Mass the procession back to the palace began and there the King was divested of his cumbersome crown which was replaced by a lighter one and in the great hall the feasting began.

In order not to offend the citizens of Winchester the dignitaries of that town had the honour of acting as cooks, while, so that the citizens of London need not feel they had been slighted, their leading citizens were the butlers. The hall was filled with tables at the chief of which sat the King, and the guests were placed according to their rank at the top table.

It was a merry and happy occasion and then sudden tragedy changed it from a day of rejoicing to one of bitter tragedy.

Richard had forbidden any Jew to come to his coronation, not because he wished to persecute them, but because he believed that as they were not Christians their presence might not be acceptable to God. It may have been that this edict had not been sufficiently widely circulated or perhaps some, so eager to be present, decided to ignore it, but while the feast was in progress several Jews decided to call at the palace with rich gifts for the new King. No ruler could object to being given costly objects, for even if he was indifferent to them, as an expression of loyalty he must be impressed by their value.

Among the richest Jews in the country who presented themselves at the palace was a man of particularly great wealth known as Benedict of York. They were immediately identified and protests were raised.

The cry went up: 'Jews! We'll not have them here. The King has forbidden them. They have disobeyed his laws.'

Benedict of York, who had brought with him a very valuable gift for the King, protested.

'All I wish,' he cried, 'is to let the King know of our loyalty to him. I wish to give him this golden ornament.'

It was no use.

For so long the Jews had been hated. There were many people in the throng who had lived close to them and who had seen them prosper. They were hated because they worked hard and because no matter how humbly they started they always seemed to succeed.

This was an opportunity.

'The King has ordered that we drive them from our towns,' went up the cry. 'He has forbidden them to come to his coronation.'

It did not take long to arouse the mob. Throughout London the cry went up. 'We are robbing the Jews. We are burning their houses. Their goods are to be our goods. It is the King's coronation gift to us.' Soon the streets were filled with shouting, screaming people. They had thought the day might bring dancing and feasting and perhaps free wine. They had not counted on anything so exciting as riots.

Outside the palace the mob set upon the Jews and the gifts they had brought were snatched from them.

Benedict of York lay on the ground convinced that his last moments had come. He saw fanatical faces peering down at him. Hands were at his throat. He cried out: 'You are killing me.'

'Aye, Jew. 'Tis the King's orders to kill all Jews.'

Benedict cried desperately: 'But I want to become a Christian. If you kill me you will have killed a Christian.'

The men who had been bending over him fell back a little. Benedict went on shouting: 'I am a Christian. I am going to become a Christian.'

The law was fierce. What happened to men who took life? The King's father had been determined to set down violence. Was the new King the same? Mutilation had often been the punishment for murder. Men had lost their ears, their noses, and their tongues; they had been blinded with hot irons because of it. It was necessary to be cautious and here was this man calling out that he wanted to become a Christian. What if any one of them was named as the murderer of a Christian!

'Let him be baptized without delay,' cried a voice. 'Then he will truly be a Christian.'

This appealed to the mob.

They carried Benedict to the nearest church where he was immediately baptized.

Meanwhile no time had been lost in circulating the news throughout the country. In every city there were riots against the Jews. The mob was not going to lose an opportunity for violence and robbery; and because the Jews were notoriously rich they were a desirable target.

The only city which did not take part in these riots was Winchester. The people there expressed the view that they thought it was not according to Christian doctrine to attack those who lived among them simply because they did not share their beliefs.

As for Richard he was angry because a day which he had meant to be one of universal rejoicing should have turned out to be one of tragedy for so many of his subjects. Moreover it was an indication that the horrors of the reign of Stephen when men had felt themselves free to let loose their natural instincts could easily break out again. He would need stern laws to suppress these instincts and he was determined to keep order.

When he heard of what had happened to Benedict of York he sent for the man and when Benedict arrived he found

Richard surrounded by his prelates. Benedict had had time to ponder on what he had done and he was ashamed that in a moment of panic when a particularly cruel death had stared him in the face, he had abjured the faith in which he had been brought up and to which he would in secret cling throughout his life.

As soon as he entered the hall his eyes went at once to the King. Richard from his chair of state commanded Benedict to come and stand before him. They took each other's measure and there was a bond between them. Richard thought: This man denied his faith when faced with death. It was not a noble thing to do yet how can any of us judge him?

'Benedict of York,' he said, 'yesterday you declared your intention of becoming a Christian.'

'I did, my lord.'

'That was when certain of my subjects were on the point of killing you. I gave no orders for these riots. I deplore them. Although I excluded members of your race and creed from my coronation I did not command my people to destroy you. You have been baptized. Are you a true Christian, Benedict of York, and will you continue in the faith in which you have so recently been baptized?'

The clear cool eyes of the King which proclaimed his courage to the world inspired Benedict.

He said: 'My gracious Lord and King I cannot lie to you. Yesterday I was on the point of death and suffered ignoble fear. To save my life I protested that I wished to become a Christian and I underwent baptism. I am a Jew. I can never be a true Christian. The faith of my fathers must be mine and now that I am calm and have had time to think, I will tell you the truth even though I die for it.'

'So you are more ready to die today than you were yesterday.'

'I have overcome my fear, my lord.'

'Then what happened yesterday was not in vain. I respect your honesty. Go from me now. Forget your baptism. Continue in the faith of your fathers and live in peace ... if you can.'

Benedict fell on his knees and thanked the King.

*　　　*　　　*

Richard sent for Ranulf de Glanville.

'Go through the country,' he commanded. 'Protect the Jews. Put an end to these riots. Let it be known that these disturbances were no wish of mine.'

And Ranulf de Glanville having quelled the violence in London rode out to the provinces but it was some days before peace was brought to the country.

Richard was indignant. 'This matter has spoilt my coronation,' he complained. 'A fine beginning to my reign!'

'You have conducted yourself with dignity,' his mother told him. 'The people will see that they have a strong king who is determined to govern them.'

The King remained uneasy. His thoughts carried him far away from England.

Alice and Berengaria

HE had come home; he had been crowned King; now he would set in motion that plan which he had always intended to carry out. Eleanor was distressed; she tried to remonstrate with him.

'I know you have taken an oath to go to the Holy Land,' she said. 'That was before you were King, but now you have a kingdom to govern.'

He snapped his fingers and his eyes shone with a fanatical light. 'I have one desire, Mother, and that is to fight the Infidel.'

'There is so much for you to do here.'

He shook his head. 'I tell you this: I would sell London if I could find a purchaser. I need money ... money ... money to take me to the Holy Land.'

'You are rich in worldly goods, Richard.'

'I need so much more. Much of my riches is such that cannot be realized.'

'I see you are determined to go,' said Eleanor.

He seized her hands. 'While I am away you will guard this realm for me.'

'I will with all my heart, but I am an old woman. What of John?'

'You mean make him King during my absence?'

'Indeed I do not. Once you did that he would never relinquish the power you gave him. Your father made one of the biggest mistakes of his life when he crowned your brother Henry King. Never make that mistake, Richard.'

'Have no fear of it. I had no intention of giving John that power. He has his estates to look after. He has plenty to do, and I trust you to guard my realm. I have good servants.'

'They are scarcely tried yet.'

He turned to her. 'Make no mistake of this, Mother. Nothing will turn me from my purpose.'

'I know well your nature. I realize this urge in you. What of your marriage? That will be expected of you.'

'I shall marry in due course. Forget not that I must free myself from Alice first.'

'And claim Berengaria.'

'You will do that for me, Mother. You will go to Navarre and take Berengaria from her father. Readily he will give her to you, and when I am free from my bond with Alice I will marry her.'

'And your crusade to the Holy Land?' asked the Queen.

'I can marry her there as well as anywhere else.'

'The people will expect...'

He laid his hand over hers. 'This is my desire,' he said quietly; and she knew that he was telling her that he was the King.

*   *   *

He was now thinking almost entirely of his crusade. His great desire was to raise money. He began by selling crown lands, which was legitimate enough, but when large sums of money were paid into the royal coffers for some post which should have gone to a more worthy applicant the practice was far from admirable. He began to think up wild schemes to raise money. It was not difficult to find men who were eager to accompany him; money was the great concern. But there were some who could not go; he would command them to join his party and then allow them to avoid the obligation by the payment of a huge fine. Nothing was too devious if it added to the funds; and the King who was honest enough in other matters grew more and more unscrupulous in his mad passion to raise enough money that there might be no more delay.

John was delighted to see Richard's determination and did his best to foster it. With Richard out of the way he would be a very important figure. He was the heir to the throne, although people had begun to talk of Arthur of Brittany, and some said that Arthur as the son of an elder brother had more claim than John who was only a younger son of the late King. But he did not think of Arthur as a serious threat. He was only a child and was far away in Brittany. If Richard were killed in his Holy War, John was the one the people would look to.

So Richard must be persuaded to go on his crusade. Not that he needed persuading. John laughed at the thought.

His mother was uneasy and well she might be.

She talked to Richard about his marriage. At thirty-two and a crowned king he could delay no more. 'You say,' she said, 'that you have a great fancy for Berengaria.'

'All in good time,' he said.

She sighed. She did not think he would ever have a great fancy for any woman. He was more excited at the prospect of joining up with the King of France than his marriage.

'Richard, you must marry soon.'

'As soon as I am free from Alice.'

'But what are you doing about freeing yourself from Alice? You have no need to consider her. She is dishonoured. No one could blame you for breaking your betrothal to her.'

'Remember she is Philip's sister.'

'As if I could forget that! But Philip's sister or not she has been your father's mistress and kept from you for years that he might enjoy her. It's a preposterous situation and one at which none would blame you for snapping your fingers.'

'You speak truth, Mother. I have long loved Berengaria, that elegant girl. Go to Navarre and let her be put in your care. I shall start off on my crusade and as soon as I have rid myself of Alice I will send for Berengaria.'

The prospect of making such a journey lifted Eleanor's spirits. Although she was now an old woman the thought of the crusade excited her. She longed to be young again so that she could accompany her son into the Holy Land as she had once accompanied her husband Louis of France. What a time that had been! Her senses still tingled at the memory.

She could not make such a journey again, but she would enjoy the visit to Navarre. It would be a mission for her; and once Berengaria was in her care Richard would be obliged to marry her. He had every excuse for declining Alice's hand and Philip must be made to accept this.

Well then, Richard would set out on his campaign; she, Eleanor, would go to Navarre; and Alice must be returned to her brother's court, soiled—no longer marriageable to royalty. Perhaps Philip would find some nobleman ready to take her off his hands for the privilege of marrying the King's sister.

As for John, she believed he was not actively ambitious. He would like to be King no doubt, but he would not want to fight for a crown. He really preferred drinking, gaming and the company of women. He could occupy himself in Ireland and with his vast estates. John would have enough to keep him busy.

So with the thought of a mission of her own Eleanor was less opposed to Richard's departure.

Meanwhile Richard chafed against delay. The sale of posts throughout the country had naturally displeased some people; but not many were ready to raise their voices against a campaign to the Holy Land. Superstition was rife and there was a fear that to attempt to oppose the King's desire to free Christendom from the Infidel might offend God.

People began to see or imagine they saw indications of Divine approval. At Dunstable it was said that a white banner appeared in the sky; someone else saw a crucifix there. Perhaps all that was needed was imagination and a certain cloud formation but people began assembling in market squares and announcing their intention to accompany the King on his crusade.

This was gratifying to Richard but there were delays. He chafed against them but he was a king and there was his mother to remind him of this. First the harvest had been disappointing, so much so that in some areas there was a threat of famine. Baldwin was critical of the King and did not hesitate to say so. Richard's half-brother Geoffrey joined Baldwin against him, much to the fury of Eleanor who could never forget that Geoffrey was her husband's illegitimate son.

Already there had arisen the recurring conflict between Church and State.

'Sometimes,' cried Richard, 'I think they are determined to do all they can to stop my leaving. They never will.'

But in spite of his determination it was necessary to remain and give time and thought to this trouble in the Church.

The outcome was that he and Geoffrey patched up their

quarrel and Geoffrey paid him three thousand pounds from his revenues to help finance the crusade, so it was not entirely wasted after all from Richard's point of view.

By December he was able to leave for Normandy on his way to see the King of France to make their final preparations.

* * *

It was January before the two Kings met at Gué St Rémi. It was an emotional meeting. Once there had been great amity between them. That had been at the time when Richard was at odds with his father and had been so angry and wounded because Henry had wanted to set him aside for the sake of John. Philip had been there to comfort him. He had sworn allegiance to Philip; he had been his constant companion; hunted with him, talked with him and shared his bed. There could be no greater intimacy and everyone had marvelled at the friendship between the King of France and the son of the King of England, none more than Henry the King of England who had been considerably discountenanced by it.

They had been happy days when they had been together, the more exciting perhaps because each had known they could not go on and were a little uncertain how deep their feelings for each other went.

Philip must ask himself: How much of this friendship is love for me, how much hatred of his father? How much the desire for my company, how much the knowledge that I more than anyone can help him make a stand against his father?

And Richard: This love for me, how much friendship is there in it, how much the need to flout my father, to mock him by keeping his son at his court?

How eager was the King of France to outwit the King of England? How could they be sure of each other? Yet it was there, the love which had flared up between them.

As King of England Richard could now meet Philip as an equal on one ground, but he still owed him allegiance as the Duke of Normandy.

Philip embraced Richard. 'Welcome, my brother. It does my heart good to see you.'

Richard was less fulsome but the coldness had left his eyes and they glowed with an unusual warmth.

'So you are now King of England. Our fears were ground-less.'

All noted how the King of France would have no ceremony with the King of England. He slipped his arm through his and they walked together. It was said: They will live in amity as they did before. This augurs well for the crusade.

Philip took Richard into his camp that they might talk intimately together. Philip had aged a little. He was ten years younger than Richard but often appeared to be the more mature. He was more of a realist, completely lacking Richard's idealism.

How like the old days it was! Philip lying back on his bunk, his head supported on his folded arms and Richard seated before him.

'You are as handsome as you ever were,' said Philip. 'Though a little drawn. Are you in good health, my friend?'

'I have had attacks of the quartan fever.'

'So you still suffer from that malady? How do you think you will fare in the hot climate?'

'That I shall discover.'

'Richard, do you think your health will permit you to go?'

Richard laughed aloud. 'Nothing will prevent me.'

'Ah indeed, it seems strange to talk of weakness to you. You were ever the one who rode the fastest, played the most skilful game. You should have taken greater care of your health, for it is sheer carelessness which has made you a victim of this fever.'

'A soldier cannot always sleep in a warm dry bed, brother.'

'Nay, alas. Ah, but you are as strong as ever, I doubt not. You will overcome this fever ... Do you realize that a dream of our youth is about to come true? Remember, Richard, how we would lie in my bed and plan our journey to the Holy Land ... together. It had to be together. Otherwise it would have lost its pleasure for us both.'

'I remember it well. I was always determined that it should come about.'

'And now you have a kingdom to govern!'

'You also.'

'Two Kings who will leave their kingdoms for a dream! Together we must go, for if we did not...' Philip laughed slyly ... 'How could the King of England go if the King of France did not go also?'

'Indeed! How could the King of France leave his kingdom if the King of England did not also leave his?'

' 'Tis a fact, Richard, that these two so fear the other that they could not know what one would be about during the other's absence. What a chance for the warlike fellow to take certain French castles he covets.'

'And it has always been a whim of the kings of France to take Normandy from the Normans.'

'Some of my ancestors believe it should never have been given to your ancestor Old Rollo. What a marauding pirate he was! He was not content with his lands of the North, he had to take a part of France as well. And you, my friend, are descended from those pirates. What of that?'

'I am proud to remember it.'

'As proud as I am doubtless of Charlemagne. I'll tell you this, Richard, that one day when I sat gnawing a little green twig one of my barons told another that he would give him his best horse if he could know what the King was thinking. One over bold asked me and I answered him "I am thinking of whether God will grant unto me or one of my heirs grace to exalt France to the height which she was in the time of Charlemagne." '

'It is not possible,' said Richard.

'If I were to admit that I would be sounding the death knell to my hopes. Nothing was ever achieved by deciding it cannot be done.'

'So you will begin by snatching the Holy City from Saladin.'

' 'Twill be a beginning.'

'I long to be there,' said Richard. 'It is inconceivable that the Holy Land can remain in the hands of the Infidel.'

'You long for military glory,' said Philip. 'You want your name to resound throughout the world. The greatest of our warriors! It is for this reason you go to the Holy Land?'

Philip had often been an uncomfortable companion. They were too intimate for hypocrisy. Richard's was the simpler mind; he was direct, he saw good and bad distinctly. Philip was analytical, intellectual, subtle, seeing many aspects of one question. Their characters were opposing and yet they were a complement to each other.

Talking to Philip Richard realized that he did indeed seek military glory. He wanted to recover the Holy Land for

Christianity but he yearned most to go into battle and win great honours there.

Philip watched him slyly. There were plans to be made; they had a great deal to talk of.

They rode out together; they hunted as they had done when Richard was at Philip's court, a beloved hostage.

They swore friendship. They would defend each other's realms and share any gains that came their way during their crusade. They would be as brothers.

'This pleases me,' said Philip. 'How I have missed you!'

They made plans to meet at Messina. But there was work to be done first. Richard must travel through Normandy to inspire more men to follow him and support him with their worldly goods; but they lingered awhile, neither anxious to cut short this interlude. Richard was less sure of his feelings towards Philip than Philip was towards him. In Philip's eyes Richard was physically perfect. He greatly admired the long Norman limbs, the grace of movement, the blonde good looks, the vitality which was not impaired even by the recurrent attacks of fever. He loved this man and yet at times he hated him. They were friends but theirs was too passionate a relationship to be peaceful. By the very nature of their positions they must be enemies. It was inconceivable that a king of England who was also a duke of Normandy could be regarded with anything but suspicion by a king of France. Normandy was a thorn in the side of all kings of France. It was the secret dream of every king who loved France to bring back Normandy to the crown. How could it be otherwise? The land had been filched from them by the pirate Norsemen and, although that had happened many years before, Normandy to the French would never be anything but theirs. And since William the Conqueror had brought the crown of England to add to the dukedom of Normandy there had seemed less hope of bringing the latter back to France.

Philip, the realist, was well aware that whatever his personal feelings for Richard he must always work against him. When Henry Plantagenet was alive he had had to reconcile himself to the knowledge that there would never be a conquest of Normandy. It was different now that Richard was king.

Richard—beloved friend—would be no match for him. He knew it well. Richard should never have agreed to go off and leave his kingdom so soon after acquiring it. Did he not see mean little John straining to get at it? Richard might be the greatest warrior of his age, but what sort of statesman was he? True he would leave his mother to govern for him and she was still a force to be reckoned with.

How different we are, thought Philip. There he is, my friend and enemy Richard, the strong, the brave and the foolish. He longs to be known as the greatest soldier in Christendom; he may well be that. But a king must be more than a great soldier. He is too simple-hearted, too direct. Oh, Richard Oui et Non, rulers have to prevaricate, to dissemble. It is necessary in this life, my dear friend.

He himself was subtle and ambitious . . . oh very ambitious. They had not understood him when he was a boy. They had thought him weak and peevish. Perhaps he had been before there had come to him that revelation of what it meant to be a ruler and a ruler of France. From then on he had developed a calm, a subtlety; he refrained from giving voice to his thoughts. He was discreet and sedate. Richard had often been impatient with him, little understanding that when he appeared to be indifferent his mind was working fast and he was seeing into the future perhaps years ahead.

As they played chess together, Philip deliberately brought up the subject of Alice.

'I doubt not your marriage to my sister will take place ere long.'

'There is much to be done before I can think of marriage,' replied Richard.

'You are no longer a young man.'

'I am young enough.'

'My sister is not young either.'

'Your sister is no longer a virgin.'

'Thanks to your father.'

Richard was relieved. He hated subterfuge. He believed that now Philip knew the position he would understand why there could not be a marriage.

'Two are involved in such games,' he said.

'Children are sometimes lured into them and can scarcely be blamed.'

'The fact remains that she is no longer fit to be my bride.'

'The sister of the King of France not fit for the King of England!'

'Not when she has been whoring with his father.'

'You talk like a peasant, Richard. This is a matter of royal birth not of morals.'

'With me it is a moral issue.'

'Oh, come, have you always led so blameless a life? We will forget Alice's indiscretions and those of your father. The marriage will take place before we set out.'

Richard had grown pale. 'I cannot marry Alice.'

'Oh, you will honour your bonds,' said Philip. 'Forget not that you are betrothed.'

'You will release me from the betrothal. I know you will.'

'Do you know me, Richard? How well do you know me? Everyone is not so straightforward as you. Let us shelve this unfortunate matter of your marriage. See, I have put you in check.'

And so they talked together, often fiercely, often banteringly; and to both of them the coming crusade was enticing and exciting because the other would share it.

They parted, Richard to make his journey through Normandy, Philip to make further preparation for departure. They would meet at Messina and from there begin together their journey to the Holy Land.

*   *   *

Eleanor felt young again since she had stepped into freedom. All those years a prisoner! How dared Henry treat her so! But she could laugh at him now, and hers was the last laugh. He was dead, mouldering in his tomb—a king who had once made men tremble—now nothing but dust and ashes while she, nearly twelve years his senior, as he had been fond of reminding her, was preparing to embark on a journey to bring her son's bride to him.

She could not resist going to see Alice before she left. She was irritated to notice that meek adaptability which had made Alice such a desirable mistress in Henry's eyes had now helped her to adjust herself to her new conditions. Surely she must rail against the fact that she, who was once the pampered darling of an indulgent lover, was now the prisoner of his wife. But no, Alice went her placid way, choosing her silken skeins and plying her needle.

'How fares it?' asked Eleanor.

'I am well, my lady,' answered Alice.

'So I see. I have come to say farewell to you. I am about to set out on a journey. I am bringing King Richard's bride to him.'

'How can that be?' asked Alice mildly.

'In the simplest manner. I am going to Navarre. He has long loved the elegant and beautiful Berengaria.'

'He cannot marry her,' said Alice.

'So you have become our ruler to tell the King what he may or may not do?'

'It is not I who tell him. It is the law. He is betrothed to me.'

'And you, missing a lover, can scarcely wait to put another in his place?'

'None could be in his place,' said Alice simply.

'Why not? Richard is a king also.'

'It was not of his rank that I was thinking.'

'Oh? Henry was incomparable was he? He was coarse and lusty, yes. Remember we shared him. So I know him as well as you do.'

'Sometimes I think,' said Alice, 'that none knew him as I did.'

Eleanor was impatient. She had come here to discomfit Alice, not to listen to praise of the dead.

'Your position is unenviable, Alice,' she said. 'I think you should prepare yourself. Life will not go on as it is now. The vital question will not be whether you are to use pink or blue silk but how you will explain your conduct to your brother, and discover what will be said to the world when it is known that King Richard will have none of you and has chosen to marry elsewhere.'

'That is for Richard to say. He is the one who will have to answer to my brother.'

'Think you so? Well, mayhap I should leave you in your ignorance. Your conduct with my late husband will no longer be a secret. All the world will know of your games. They will laugh in secret at you, and your brother will be hard put to it to find a husband for you.'

'I seek no husband,' said Alice.

'Have you then had your fill of men after knowing Henry so well?'

'I know that there will never be another like him.'

'Then I will leave you with your dreams of the past for those of the future must be nightmares.'

She came away angrily. Oddly enough the triumph seemed Alice's.

*   *   *

It was good to ride through the countryside to the sea. The crossing was smooth. A good augury. She began her progress down to Navarre. She was fêted at the castles at which she stopped as the beloved mother of the King of England who was on good terms with the King of France.

She had forgotten how exciting it was to be setting out on an adventure, to be treated with great honour, and above all to be free.

Oh, how dared you, Henry, she thought; and she was sorry that he was dead, for how could one be revenged on the dead? Just a little savour had gone out of her life with his passing. How often she had raged against him, made plans for his downfall. How she had exulted when she heard that his sons were marching against him. It was her hatred of Henry which had made her prison tolerable. Now he was gone. She missed him.

At last she came to the Court of Navarre.

The King, known as the Wise—and he certainly believed now that he had been wise in keeping his daughter Berengaria for this great marriage—received her with great honours. When Richard had first come to his court and shown a preference for Berengaria he had been but the son of a great king with an elder brother who had appeared to be strong and healthy and whom no one would have suspected would die young. Moreover Richard and his father had not been on good terms. Yet Sancho was not known as the Wise for nothing. He had resisted offers for the hand of his elder daughter and how right he had been, for at last King Richard's mother had come to claim her. It was true the waiting had been long. Berengaria was past twenty-six and it might have been wondered whether she would ever find a husband. But now those doubts were over. Or were they? There still remained the shadowy figure of Princess Alice of France.

Eleanor was delighted with the appearance of Berengaria.

She was indeed beautiful and the manner in which she wore her clothes could only be described as elegant.

Eleanor embraced the girl and told her that Richard was eagerly awaiting her coming. 'He would trust no one but me to bring you to him,' said Eleanor. 'I know how he will rejoice when he sees you.'

I hope he will, thought Eleanor. It seems he has little interest in women, but surely such a pleasant bride as Berengaria will captivate him.

There was feasting in the great hall to celebrate the arrival of the Dowager Queen of England; and she was able to delight them all with playing on the lute and her singing.

How good it was to be among Provençals, for although Sancho was descended from the Spanish the language spoken here and the manners were of Provence. This delight in music, this enchanting custom of honouring the poets and musicians filled her with nostalgia and she longed to be in her beloved Aquitaine.

She was delighted to meet Berengaria's brother, known as Sancho the Strong, of whom one of the musicians had sung telling of his victory over the Moors. He had defeated the Miramolin and with his battle-axe had severed the chains which guarded the Infidel's camp. Ever after he had been known as The Strong for it was the custom in Navarre to attach a descriptive adjective to the names of the rulers. Berengaria might well have been Berengaria the Elegant, thought Eleanor.

She warmed to the girl. They had much in common, such as their love of fine clothes and the ability to wear them to advantage as well as a passionate interest in music and poetry. Perhaps there the similarity ended for Berengaria was by no means forceful. She would be a loving and uncomplaining wife, thought Eleanor, and doubtless she would need to be, for Richard would not be a very attentive husband.

It was pleasant to walk in the gardens with her daughter-in-law-to-be and to talk with her and hear how she had first seen Richard years ago.

'So it will not be like going to a husband whom I have never met,' she said, 'though it was more than ten years ago when my brother brought him here. I have never forgotten the occasion. My father had staged a tournament in Richard's honour. I can see it now—the pennants stirred by the breeze and the trumpets sounding as he rode out. There was no mistaking him. No one was as tall, as noble-looking as Richard. I had never seen anyone like him.'

'And you loved him from that day,' added Eleanor.

'I have never ceased to think of him. As you know the custom is for a knight to ride for his lady and wear something of hers and to my joy I saw that in his helm he had placed a small glove of mine which I recognized at once by its jewelled border. He was riding for me that day.'

'Charming,' commented Eleanor.

'I shall never forget how he rode to the dais where I sat with my parents and my brother and sister Blanche. He bowed to me and I threw a rose to him. He kissed it and held it against his heart. It is a day which will live for ever in my memory.'

'You must have thought he would never come for you.'

'I did not think he could while his father lived. I knew too that he was betrothed to the Princess Alice.'

'That marriage will never take place.'

'It gave my father much cause for concern. I know that there have been times when he has been on the point of arranging another marriage for me. It seemed that I would never have a husband.'

'And now you are to have the most glorious of them all.'

'There is still Alice.'

'Alice is of no account.'

'Can that be said of the sister of the King of France?'

'My dear daughter, when you know your husband better you will understand that he can say anything of anyone and make it come to pass.'

'That must be so, for my father will allow me to leave with you, which he would never do if there were any doubts.'

'There are no doubts,' said Eleanor firmly. 'You will leave with me for Sicily. There we will await the arrival of the King's fleet and there I doubt not the marriage ceremony will take place. My daughter Joanna who is the Queen of Sicily will welcome us and I am delighted at the prospect of seeing my child again. Poor Joanna is now a widow, for her husband the King died last November. I doubt not she will be in need of comfort and will wish to discuss her future with Richard.'

The years of captivity had by no means diminished Eleanor's powerful personality and she could still give an impression that her will would be law. Thus she completely dispersed any qualms Berengaria or her father felt over the anomalous situation concerning Alice.

In due course Eleanor with Berengaria and her attendants left Navarre and made the difficult journey across Italy to Naples. The ships which Eleanor had commissioned were waiting there to take them to Sicily, but before they had time to put to sea a messenger arrived with disquieting news.

There was trouble in Sicily. Queen Joanna had been dethroned. They would be unwise to attempt the journey there and King Richard wished them to sojourn in Brindisi until he came to them.

Chafing against delay, asking herself whether there was indeed trouble in Sicily or whether Richard was finding it difficult to break his contract with Alice, Eleanor could do nothing but accept the delay and wait until it could be resolved.

Joanna

In the castle at Palermo, Queen Joanna of Sicily was asking herself what would become of her. In the last few months her future had become threatening and she could not know what would happen to her from one day to another. She, the honoured Queen, daughter of Henry Plantagenet and Eleanor of Aquitaine, once beloved of a doting husband now found herself virtually a prisoner.

Who would have believed while William lived that his cousin Tancred could have behaved in such a villainous manner? She had always known Tancred was ambitious—what man was not? And Tancred was a bastard and they always seemed to have an even greater love of power than their legitimate relations. He had seemed loyal but, as soon as William was dead, his true character had emerged and because she had opposed him, here she was a prisoner.

She was not a woman to accept such treatment lightly. She was after all a descendant of the great Conqueror himself; if her father had been alive Tancred would never have dared behave as he did; but in July her father had died and in November of the same year her husband had followed him to the grave. So she had lost two powerful protectors within a few months.

She was twenty-five years of age and comely. She had lived fully those twenty-five years. She had learned to stand on her own feet as members of the royal family must. She scarcely knew her family. She had caught glimpses of her brothers now and then, and it had been comforting to know of their existence. Her father had been a power throughout Europe. Now she felt bereft and lonely.

What could she do in her apartments which were in fact a prison, for she was not allowed to leave them without an escort? She could only think over the past and wonder what the future held.

As a young daughter of the family—only John was younger —she had not seemed of any great account until her marriage. Born in Angers she had been brought up in Fontevraud but there had been a time when she had been in England. She could remember the Princess Alice's being in the nurseries with her and her brother John. Alice had seemed a good deal older than she and John were but it could only have been a few years. What scandal there had been later concerning Alice! She could remember her father's visiting the nursery and how she and John had been a little jealous of the attention he gave to Alice. And what now he was dead? Would Richard marry her? It seemed hardly likely. Alice's situation, she reflected, was no more pleasant than her own.

What are we, the princesses of royal houses? she thought bitterly. Nothing but counters in a game. If it suits the country's politics we are married—wherever the most advantage is to be found, no matter what bridegroom we must take.

She herself had been fairly fortunate with her husband although the marriage almost did not take place. William had been a good husband, ten years her senior, but that was not such a bad thing as she had been only eleven years old when his emissaries had come to take her to Sicily.

The betrothal had previously been set aside as William who had been at this time seventeen did not want to wait for a child of seven and he had hoped to marry a daughter of the eastern emperor, Manuel Comnenus. This scheme did not come to fruition and in due course William had sent his ambassadors to England to inspect the little Princess Joanna.

This was the time when she had been brought to Winchester and shared a schoolroom with her brother John and Princess Alice, Richard's betrothed. She would never forget her father's coming to the schoolroom and there telling her that some very important noblemen had arrived from Sicily with the express purpose of seeing her. He had told her that she must conduct herself with decorum, for what these gentlemen thought of her could have a great effect not only on her future but on his.

She had stood before them and answered their questions and she knew that she had done well, for her father had laid his hand on her shoulder and pressed it affectionately and she had heard one of the men exclaim: 'But her beauty is out-standing. The King of Sicily will be pleased exceedingly.' Back in the nursery she had told a curious John and Alice what had taken place.

'Oh,' had said the knowledgeable Alice, 'it is a betrothal.'

She had told them that the King of Sicily would be exceed-ingly pleased.

'It is because you are pretty,' Alice had explained.

'Richard must have been exceedingly pleased with you,' Joanna had said.

'Like our father is,' John had added, at which beautiful Alice had blushed deeply.

'She's prettier than ever pink,' John had commented.

And now Joanna knew what the blush had implied.

We are surrounded by intrigue from our cradles, she thought.

And so she had come to Sicily when she was a girl of eleven. When she had landed in Normandy she had been met by her eldest brother, Henry. King Henry he had called himself be-cause he was so proud of the fact that their father had allowed him to be crowned. He was so handsome and charming that she loved him and was proud to have such a brother. He was also kind, gentle and full of fun. He wanted her to remember the time she spent with him. When they stopped at various castles on the way he would organize entertainments for her, and there had been tournaments where she could see him joust. He used to say: I'm going into this for you. You are my lady—my little sister Joanna.' Oh yes, Henry had had great charm. He was quite different from his namesake their father. Yet she knew now that he had been weak, that the charm had been superficial; that he had lied to his father and grieved him sorely. But to the young Joanna he had seemed perfect. How sad it was that childhood illusions must be shattered! She had wept bitterly when he had died and had prayed con-stantly for his soul. She feared it might be in torment for his going had been violent. He had betrayed his father; he had desecrated monasteries and robbed them of their treasures in order to pay his soldiers for his wars against his father. It was a sorry story and how far she had been from guessing its climax during those golden days when he had entertained her on the journey across Normandy and had done his best to make her forget she was going to a stranger husband in a strange new land!

He had conducted her to the borders of Aquitaine where another brother was waiting for her. She had thought that never could a princess have had two such wonderful brothers. If Henry had been the most handsome man she had ever seen, Richard was the most distinguished. She had thought this must be how the gods looked when they came down from Olympus. He too was tall, his hair fair and shining, and he looked noble and invincible.

He was not as warm and friendly as Henry had been, but he gave her a greater sense of comfort. He implied that while he was with her it was quite impossible for any harm to befall her.

Down to the coast she had ridden with this godlike brother beside her and at St Gilles her bridegroom's Sicilian fleet had been waiting for her.

She had taken a tender farewell of Richard but she did not weep. She felt that Richard would have despised tears. It would have been different with Henry. They would have wept together; she had wondered when she would see her brothers again and was very sad until rocked on that angry sea she was too sick to think of anything but her own misery and the desirability of death. So ill was she that the captain of her vessel had decided that they could not continue the journey and they had come ashore at Naples. By then it was Christmas time. Her attendants and the sailors had been entertained there and they did their best to make it a merry time and afterwards they had travelled by land across Calabria so that the only sea she must traverse was the strait of Messina.

This had been a good sign, showing as it did that her new husband was eager for her comfort and she was already grateful to him before she saw him.

And when he saw *her* he smiled with pleasure. He had heard reports of her good looks, but it was said that all princesses were good looking when they were marriageable—

at least so those who were eager to promote the union always averred. Occasionally they were true and so afforded a very pleasant surprise to their bridegrooms. This was what had happened in her case and William had been delighted with his bride. So were the Sicilians.

She would never forget coming ashore. Mercifully she had not been ill and was fresh and beautiful on that first meeting. William could not stop himself looking at her. He stroked her hair and kissed her hands. She was enchanting, he said.

She was young—twelve years old—but that was not too young for marriage and he had been eager for the ceremony to take place without delay. Her father would expect it, he told her.

She was given attendants who combed her long hair and petted her; and each day there were costly gifts from her bridegroom. She had felt cherished from the moment she set foot on Sicilian soil and some two weeks after her arrival, the Archbishop of Palermo officiating at the ceremony, she and William were married.

It was pleasant to look back on those days. He had been kind and tender and she knew now that it could so easily have been otherwise. It was true that she had brought with her a fine dowry which included a golden table twelve feet long which was very valuable, a silken tent and a hundred very fine galleys, enough corn that would need sixty thousand mules to carry it and the same quantity of barley and wine. There had also been twenty gold cups and twenty-four plates of the same precious metal. It was advantageous for a King of Sicily to be linked by marriage with the King of England, but even so William might not have been such a tender doting husband, and she had been fortunate.

So she had learned to love Sicily and had thought herself the most fortunate of queens when she gave birth to her son whom she called Bohemond. Alas, Bohemond had delighted her life only briefly and to the sorrow of his parents and the whole of Sicily he died soon after his birth. But perhaps not to the sorrow of all. There was Tancred.

Tancred! He was the source of her troubles. But for Tancred she would not now be kept in restraint. Tancred had appeared at court when William was alive. He had constantly sought to distinguish himself, being clearly piqued by the fact that he was a bastard. William, easy going and a little sorry for him, had always made him welcome but Joanna had believed that his ambition was dangerous.

As William was but in his thirties and appeared to be healthy Tancred's ambitions must have been dormant for some years, and the fact that little Bohemond had died did not mean that Joanna and William would not have more heirs. Joanna had proved that she could have sons and the fact that the first one had not survived was no indication that there would not be others. But when the baby died it was a fact that the only male heir to the Sicilian throne was Tancred, bastard though he was.

William's sister Constancia was married to Henry of Germany, eldest son of the Emperor Frederic known as Barbarossa, and should William die without male heirs it was logical to suppose that Constancia would inherit Sicily. When William had known he was dying he had asked Joanna to come to his bedside that he might talk with her. He was deeply concerned for her. Before he had known that death was close he had made provision that in the event of his death, and Joanna's being left a childless widow, her dowry was to be returned to her father that it might be used again to provide her with another husband. William, like most of the noblemen of his age had had dreams of joining a crusade, such an undertaking promising not only exciting adventures and rich spoil but at the same time remission of past sins, and he had been amassing treasure which would provide the means of financing such an expedition. He had decreed that if he should be unable to go these funds were to be given to the King of England to be used for his crusade.

King Henry had died in July, and it was August before the news reached Sicily. By that time William was sick.

He was comforted by the presence of Joanna whom he had loved dearly, but he was even more anxious for her welfare now that her father was dead.

'I thank God that you have a strong brother who will protect you,' he said. 'If our son had lived it would have been your duty to stay here and bring him up as King. But alas our little Bohemond was not destined for such a role. The true heir is my sister Constancia. Sicily will be well governed through her and her husband and one of her sons will in due course be King of Sicily. That is taken care of. But it is your future which concerns me.'

She bade him cease to fret. 'My father is dead, but my brother Richard is now King of England,' she reminded him. 'I know that he will care for me. I shall never forget how he looked after me when I arrived in Aquitaine on my way here. There is something invincible about him. I beg of you do not think of me. Prepare yourself. You have been a good husband to me, William.'

He could not bear her to leave his side and she was with him at the end. Then she went to her apartments to brood on her loss.

She had been amazed when Tancred came to her. Scarcely before William was cold, he had taken his place. Sicily needed a strong man he declared, and he was that man. He was of royal blood. It was inconceivable that the crown should go to the wife of the German Emperor when he, Tancred, was here on the spot.

She had protested indignantly. 'It was not William's wish that it should go to you,' she cried.

'William's wishes, he being dead, are no longer of moment.'

'That's where you are wrong,' cried Joanna.

'Nay,' said Tancred. 'You will see that I am right.'

'Do you think the Emperor Henry will allow you to snatch the crown from Constancia?' she demanded.

'Henry is far away. I am on the spot. You are to go back to England and it is in truth no concern of yours.'

'William's wishes are my concern.'

'What mean you?'

'That I cannot stand by and see you usurp the throne.'

His face was dull red. He was furiously angry with her. This was another slur on his birth. If he had been legitimate would there have been this question about his inheritance? Of course there would not. He was going to show them that bastard or not, he was a king. The finest example of a bastard's greatness was William the First of England who was known as the Conqueror.

'What will you do to prevent me, Madam?' he had asked.

'Anything in my power.'

Angrily he had left her, asking himself what she could do. She was powerless. She was merely William's widow who had failed to give him a son. Yet, she would have the people's sympathy as the grieving widow determined to carry out her husband's wishes. He did not want her rousing the people against him.

Soon after he had left her the guards appeared to tell her she had been put under arrest. And thus she had remained through the winter. From the windows of her prison she had watched the spring and summer come to Palermo.

'How long will it last?' she had constantly asked.

It was one day in late summer when one of her attendants came to her in a state of great excitement.

'Good news,' she said. 'I had it from one of the serving men who had it from a messenger who had come from afar. The King of England is setting out on a crusade to the Holy Land. The King of France is to accompany him. They are bringing their fleets to Messina and will sail from there to Acre.'

'My brother coming to Sicily!'

'Think not, my lady, that Richard King of England will allow you to remain Tancred's prisoner.'

'Nay,' she cried. 'He never will.'

'Great events are afoot, my lady.'

Joanna nodded slowly. Yes indeed, she was certain of it. Great events were afoot.

*   *   *

Richard's journey was taking longer than he had planned it should. He must make sure that his lands were well guarded against attack while he was away. He refused to listen to those advisers who suggested that having inherited the throne but a few months before it was a little soon to leave it. There were not many who put forward this view. They were afraid to. Giving voice to such an opinion could offend two mighty powers—Richard and Heaven—and both were believed capable of dire revenge.

There were some who raised their voices in criticism though. Fulke of Neuilly, although in favour of the crusade, doubted whether Richard was the man to lead it. That he was a great general, the finest soldier known to Europe, was accepted. But, preached Fulke, this was a holy war. How holy was Richard? There were certain ugly rumours about his private life. His passionate friendship with the King of France was remembered. And these two were the leaders of their crusades! True enough it was meet and fitting that such enterprises should be led by kings, but should not those kings mend their ways before they set themselves up as Heaven's generals?

Richard was present when Fulke was preaching and Fulke fearlessly ended his fiery sermon by crying out: 'Thou hast three dangerous daughters, oh Prince. They are leading you to the brink of a precipice.'

'You are a mistaken hypocrite,' responded Richard. 'I have no daughters.'

'Indeed you have,' retorted Fulke. 'They are Pride, Avarice and Lasciviousness.'

The King threw up his arms and cried to the assembly of peers who were present. 'Is it so then? I will give my Pride to the Templars and Hospitallers, my avarice to the Cistercian monks and my lasciviousness to the prelates of the Church.'

There was a murmuring among the congregation and it was of approval for the King, for although he might be proud was he more so than the Templars? The Cistercians were noted for their greed; and immorality was rife in the clergy. The titter of amusement, the applause of his friends and the discomfiture of the preacher made of that occasion a victory for Richard.

The proposed crusade was very popular. On his progress throughout Normandy people came out to wish him well and many to join his ranks. It was unthinkable that the Holy City should remain in the hands of the Infidel. Those who delivered it would be for ever blessed.

There was an uncomfortable incident at Tours where the Archbishop, when blessing the proposed crusade, presented Richard with the pilgrim's staff and wallet. Richard unfortunately leaned on the staff and as he did so it broke under his weight.

There was a cry of dismay from the watching crowd, who took it as a sign that no good would come of the crusade.

Richard wondered what his great ancestor would have done. He remembered then that when William the Conqueror had landed in England he had slipped and fallen, and with great presence of mind had seized a handful of the sand and declared that the land was already his.

Now he laughed aside the broken staff. It was a sign of his great strength, he said. It was a signal that nothing was strong

enough to stand against him and everything would be broken
by the weight of his strength.

This crusade must succeed, thought Richard. Nothing
must be allowed to go wrong with it. He had a great
adversary he knew in the form of the Sultan Saladin. Saladin
it was who had taken Jerusalem and had held it now for
several years. He was a great warrior it was said. Well,
Richard swore, there should be a greater, and that should
be himself, and he longed to come face to face with Saladin.

But there must be no hurrying over preparations. Many an
expedition had failed for just that. There was often a lack of
discipline in such enterprises, and Richard was determined
that his crusade should not fail for that reason. So many men
joined the company not for religious reasons but for love of
gain. They looked for rich spoils; they wanted to fight
because fighting could unleash their natural cruelty; the
greatest sport in their minds was the pillaging of towns and
the raping of terrified women and children; but perhaps
above all they wanted the rich ornaments, the fortune that
could come to them through war. To be able to enjoy all this
under the guise of religion was a heaven-sent opportunity.
The Infidel on the other hand was the defender of what he
believed was his by right and this gave him the advantage.
Many of them were protecting their homes and their religious motives were as strong as those of the Christians. Richard
knew full well that they would never be easily conquered.
But he was determined that his armies should be as efficient
as he could make them, and he saw that this could only be
achieved by a fierce discipline. He had discussed this with
Philip. Philip was too lenient with his armies he said. Philip's
answer was that men should not follow their leader through
fear. They should do so through affection.

Richard would not have conflict within his own ranks. He
had made new laws for his crusading armies and he was
determined that they should be enforced. If two men fought
together and one killed the other, he should die in the following manner: if they were on board ship, the survivor should
be bound to the dead man and the two of them thrown overboard; if the fight was on land, they should be bound together in the same way and buried together. Any man who
drew a knife against another or struck another and drew
blood was to have his hand cut off. If no blood was drawn the

miscreant was to be thrown into the sea and if he could save himself he should be thrown in again twice more. If he managed to survive after three immersions he would be considered to have paid for his crime. The penalty for uttering foul language was a fine of an ounce of silver. A thief should be shaved, tarred and feathered, boiling pitch poured over his head and a feathered pillow be shaken over him and he should be set ashore on the first land the ship touched.

Each man knew that these punishments would be carried out if he offended, for Richard was not a king to show mercy. Therefore there was little trouble in the ranks of his followers by the time he had reached Marseilles.

It was a great disappointment to discover that the fleet he had expected to find waiting for him had not yet arrived. He waited in great impatience for a week, after which he could endure the delay no longer. It seemed almost certain that Philip, in taking a more overland route, had been wiser. It was all very well for the English to sneer at the French and murmur that they were afraid of the sea. At least Philip had had the good sense not to expose his men to that uncertain element. What had become of his navy? wondered Richard and he was frustrated and anxious. In desperation he engaged twenty galleys and ten busses which could transport him with a proportion of his army, and set out, leaving the rest to wait for the navy and follow with it.

When he arrived at Genoa it was to learn that Philip was there. He was resting in one of the palaces which had been put at his disposal for he was recovering from a fever.

Richard at once went to see him, and found the French King looking pale and ill, but his face lit up with pleasure when he saw Richard.

'I had thought you would be at Messina by now,' said Richard.

'Nay,' replied Philip. 'You see me laid low with this accursed fever.'

'And I have been held up in Marseilles awaiting my fleet.'

'It came to no ill, I trust.' There was something in the French King's eyes which betrayed his thoughts. He was hoping Richard's fleet had met with some ill fortune—that he might come to his rescue. He would have been gratified to take him along with him in an inferior position and longed for their relationship to be as it had when Richard was a hostage in his camp and he had loved him dearly. He loved him still in a way. It was a strange relationship to exist between two rival kings.

Richard said firmly: 'I doubt not it is now on its way to Messina. And your army, brother? I trust your men are not dispirited to see their leader in such sickness.'

'They know I shall recover. I am not an old man. Ten years younger than you, remember.'

'I remember it well,' said Richard with a faint scowl.

'Why when we first met I thought you were quite an old man. Thus do the young think of those who are ten years their senior.'

'Age is a matter of health. If a man feels young then so he is.'

' 'Tis true and at this time I am the feeble one, you the strong. I remember when you had fits of fever. Pray tell me, Richard, have you had any bouts lately?'

'Nay, nay. I know no discomfort save that of delay.'

'You are too impatient, my dear friend.'

'Are you not?'

Philip hesitated and Richard went on: 'I fancy you have lost your passion for the fight.'

'That's not true.'

'Yet you seem less eager.'

'My affairs have changed. You know what care I took to leave my realm in good hands. I trusted my Queen, Richard. I knew she would look after my affairs as none other could. There is Louis my little son. He is but a child. He needs paternal care. The Queen's death has made me sad and sober. I think perpetually of France.'

'But you have set up a Regency, have you not?'

'Yes. My mother will serve me well as will my uncle the Cardinal of Champagne. But I could have wished that Isabella was there to care for our son.'

'It is because you are weak that you fret. Wait until you are well, then you will forget these trifling matters. I do not fret for my kingdom. If I could win back the Holy City to Christianity I would ask nothing more in life. I would give everything I possess to do that.'

'You,' said Philip, 'are a fanatic. I am merely a king.'

'Which of us think you will be in Messina first?' asked Richard.

'You have the advantage now.'

'What matters it? There we will meet. There we will make our further plans. We will sail together for Acre.'

Philip looked at Richard's face and said simply: 'It pleases me to see you. You have done me more good than all the doctors. You have aroused in me the determination to reach Messina before you.'

They kissed tenderly when Richard took his leave. Rivals, passionate friends and enemies.

* * *

Arrived at Naples the King disembarked and rested a while. He was expecting to hear news of the arrival of the fleet at Marseilles where he had left orders that when they came they were to go direct to Messina. It was important that he should not arrive before them with only the ships he had been able to muster.

It was while he was in this neighbourhood that he came near to losing his life through his own reckless folly. While he was out walking with but one attendant they passed through a hamlet and there he saw a peasant standing at the door of his cottage with a magnificent hawk. Passionate hunter that he was, Richard was immediately interested in anything concerning it and the hawk having caught his fancy he longed to possess it. Had he been with a party he would have commanded that the hawk be taken and the man given more than it was worth in money or goods. As he had but one attendant he went to the man and took the hawk meaning to bargain with him.

'What a fine creature,' he said to his attendant. 'I shall enjoy testing it.'

The peasant, not realizing who he was, began to shout to his neighbours that he had been robbed and in a very short while Richard and his attendant were surrounded by a vicious mob.

Richard drew his sword. The peasants armed with sticks sought to beat off the pair. Then one of the peasants drew a knife which he attempted to plunge into Richard's heart.

Skilled in combat as he was, the King could have slain them all, but this he had no wish to do. He wanted to tell them that he would reward the owner of the hawk, but he

saw at once that words were no use. Calling to his attendant
not to kill any of them but to use the flat side of his sword, as
he would, he began to fight his way through the mob.

With the flat side of his own sword he broke the knife in
two and the peasants realized that this was clearly a knight
practised in any form of warfare. Even so Richard needed all
his skill to save them from the righteous wrath of the
peasants.

Finally, hawkless, they managed to escape.

'The fools,' said Richard. 'I would have given them two or
three times what the bird was worth.'

'They would never have believed that, my lord,' said his
attendant.

'And now I shall never be able to test it.'

'I am grateful, Sire, for your skill in bringing us safely out
of that.'

'Ah, you were afraid, my man. If they had harmed you I
would have slain them all.'

And as they walked to their ships which lay at anchor he
was thinking of what Philip would have said had he been
there. He would have taunted him with making strict rules
for his men which he himself flouted. Philip could never
resist making a long discussion over such a point. There was
little Philip liked better than an argument and the reason
was that he always emerged the victor.

'Twas not robbery, Richard reminded himself. I would
have paid the fellow. No one can accuse me of a lack of
generosity.

'It is not the point...' He could almost hear Philip's voice.

He must stop thinking of Philip. He should be preoccupied with thoughts of his bride, for by now his mother
would be waiting with Berengaria for him to have extricated
himself from the engagement with Alice so that he might, to
the satisfaction of the world, take to be his bride the
daughter of the King of Navarre.

The Sicilian Adventure

The English fleet had arrived from Marseilles and lay off the Sicilian capital. There were a hundred galleys and fourteen large busses in which were soldiers, provisions, arms and horses. Pennants and banners fluttered in the wind and from the shore the Sicilians marvelled.

Tancred was seized by a great fear. This mighty fleet belonged to the brother of Joanna who was now his prisoner. What would Richard do when he arrived? Fortunately for Tancred Richard was not yet there. He had left Marseilles before the fleet and had come via a different route, but Tancred had to face the fact that he could reach Messina at any time now.

The Sicilians, who had heard stories of Richard's might, and knowing that their King had imprisoned his sister believed that the King of England had come in anger, trembled to contemplate what might happen next.

Meanwhile the French fleet limped into Messina. It had been beset by severe storms and it was said that only a miracle had saved it from disaster. As it was horses and provisions had had to be thrown overboard to lighten the ships and save men's lives.

It was with some relief that Tancred received Philip and his men. They were in a sorry state and needed shelter and the time to repair the damage to their ships; but at least this was the King of France and the storm's havoc could only be a temporary setback. It seemed to Tancred that if he fêted

Philip he could find an ally in him but when he looked at the
magnificent ships of the King of England and compared them
with the shattered ones of the King of France, he was uneasy.
All the same he felt he might be in urgent need of help, and
Philip was at least King of France.

Tancred entertained Philip in his own palace and told him
how much he admired his resolve to go and fight the Infidel.

'How I wish I could go with you,' he told him. 'It would be
the desire of my life fulfilled.'

'Why not join us?' asked Philip slyly.

'I have just taken over this kingdom.'

'Ah yes, and your presence is needed here I see. You fear
that Henry of Germany might take action on behalf of his
wife if you were not here to protect your newly acquired possession.'

Tancred shifted uneasily.

'When one has possessions,' he said, 'one has to be constantly prepared for enemies.'

'In particular when others feel they have a prior claim to
them,' added the King of France.

Tancred was unsure whether the King of France would be
with him or against him. He had heard that there was a
friendship between the Kings of France and England but he
did not altogether believe that those two monarchs could be
anything but rivals and therefore enemies.

He said: 'As you know the sister of the King of England is
in Palermo.'

'Your prisoner,' added Philip.

'Scarcely that. She is . . .'

'Under restraint?' Philip suggested.

'She had to be prevented from communicating with my
enemies.'

Philip shrugged his shoulders.

'Your losses must be great,' said Tancred. 'I hear the storm
was terrible.'

'It was nearly the end of us.'

'You must at this time be in need of money.'

'There is rarely a time in a king's life when he is not in
need of money.'

Tancred leaned forward a little. 'I am rich,' he said.

'Ah yes, you . . . er . . . inherited great wealth recently, I
know.'

'If I could be of use to you...'

Philip looked at him shrewdly. 'You would bargain with me?' he asked.

'I would wish to help you, my lord. Would you call that bargaining?'

'You are new to our profession,' said the King of France. 'It is customary when one King helps another that he requires to be paid for it.'

'I would be amply paid by your friendship.'

'The friendship of the King of France would have to go at a somewhat high price. Come, my friend. You see out there the galleys of the King of England and because you hold his sister captive you fear he comes in wrath. You perceive that you may need powerful friends and lo, here is one sent to your shores as if by Heaven.'

'I am ready to pay dearly,' said Tancred.

'You greatly fear the King of England, Tancred, I perceive.'

'They say he is a mighty warrior but not more so than the King of France.'

'Then they lie. There is not a better general in the world than King Richard. There is not a more courageous fighter. On the battlefield he has the strength of ten men and is worth twenty. Perhaps I can vie with him in strategy. Perhaps I can outwit him with words. If you could choose your ally you should choose Richard, but since you cannot, for he is the enemy, you are perforce obliged to try for me.'

Tancred was bemused. He did not understand the King of France. He fancied he mocked him, but he was in too desperate a position not to seize any chance that came his way.

'I can offer you a fortune in money,' he said. 'If you will allow your son Louis to be betrothed to one of my daughters.'

Philip shook his head sadly. 'The King of England and I have sworn an oath. We are going together to the Holy Land.'

Tancred knew then that he could not expect Philip to help him stand against Richard.

*   *   *

The Sicilian people were crowding on to the beaches for on the horizon appeared a wonderful array. The rest of

the English fleet was approaching and with it came King
Richard.

Those who had already arrived mingled with the French
and told each other that this would be a day of rejoicing.

Near to land came the ships. The sea was frothy with the
motion of the oars and on the decks stood the men, the sun
shining on their polished armour; banderols fluttered with
the pennants and banners. Never before had the Sicilians
seen such a glorious array. Trumpets rang out; those on the
shore who had been awaiting the arrival of their leader began
to cheer. The French as well as the English expressed their
delight that King Richard had arrived safely at Messina.

Philip, hearing the tumult and seeing the magnificent
array of ships off the coast, smiled wryly to compare them
with his own fleet. A fair escort, he thought, for the most
handsome of kings; and because he longed to see Richard, to
take his hands and look up into those ice-blue eyes which
could warm on occasions, he went down to the shore to be
among those who first greeted him.

There was a hush among the people as Richard came
ashore. He certainly had the bearing of a god. None was as
tall as he, none stood so straight, none had those clean cut
beautifully modelled features, that brilliantly fair colouring.

Philip forgot all enmity, all rivalries as he went forward to
greet him.

They embraced not as rival kings but as the dearest friends
they were at such moments.

'I feared for you,' said Philip.

'Did you doubt then that I would come?'

'I knew only major disaster could prevent you. But alas
such disasters there can be. See how my own fleet suffered.'

' 'Twill not delay you?'

'Nay. I hope to leave at once for Acre ... now you are
come.'

Richard nodded and arm in arm the Kings of France and
England left the beach.

*   *   *

Philip accompanied him to the house set among vineyards
which belonged to a certain Reginald de Muschet who had
felt himself honoured to place it at the King's disposal.

'So you got there first,' said Richard. 'Who would have believed it when I saw you on your sick bed in Genoa!'

'My illness passed as soon as I had seen you, and I set out.'

'Determined to be here first.'

'That I might be here to greet you,' said Philip with a
smile. 'You look ... magnificent.'

'It has been a long journey. Acre is only fifteen days away.
How soon shall we set out?'

'You know what is happening here. You know Tancred is
now the King.'

'I had heard he had taken the crown on William's death.
That is an affair for the King of Germany.'

'He has imprisoned your sister.'

Richard's face turned pale. 'For what reason?'

'She has opposed Tancred. He is a usurper, she declares.'

'If he will give me her dowry back, which is what I have
come to claim, I should have no quarrel with him. But if
he has imprisoned my sister by God he shall free her.'

'I thought that was what you would say, and I trust this
matter will not delay your stay in Messina.'

'I shall certainly see that my sister receives her dues,' said
Richard. 'I will send a message at once to Tancred demanding her release and the return of her dowry. By God's eyes, if
the man does not free her and return her dowry I will take
the whole of Sicily from him.'

'Send to him then without delay. I have no doubt that he,
trembling, awaits your commands.'

*   *   *

In her apartments in the Palermo palace Joanna knew that
great events were on the way. Tancred had come with all
speed to Palermo and her guards had suddenly become more
respectful.

From one of the women who were in attendance she heard
that the English fleet had arrived at Messina and that the
King of France was there with his, which had been considerably battered by the storm. When it seemed that
Richard's arrival was imminent, Tancred had apparently
thought it wise to leave Messina for Palermo.

And Richard would soon be here—the handsome invincible brother. She exulted at the thought. She spent long

periods watching from the window expecting to see him riding into Palermo any day.

It was not long before she received news.

Early one morning the guards told her that she was to prepare at once for a journey. She was going to Messina and she was free.

'So it would seem that King Richard has arrived,' she said.

'That is so, my lady,' was the answer. 'He is now at Messina and wants you to join him there.'

With what joy did she ride across the country to Messina. Foolish Tancred, to think he could flout the sister of a man like Richard, of whose power the whole world must be aware.

Messina lay before her; she sent riders ahead to tell her brother that she would soon be there. She wanted their greeting to be public so that all might recognize his power. The people would know that Tancred had imprisoned her but that Richard only had to appear and she was set free.

It was as she had planned. There he was riding out to greet her, more magnificent than ever. He embraced her while the people looked on; and then they rode side by side to the villa of the Knights of St John where she would stay until a residence worthy of her rank was made ready for her.

'It is an act of God,' she said soberly, 'that you have come at this time. If you had not who knows how long I might have remained Tancred's prisoner.'

'I should have come to your rescue when I heard.'

'But you might have been in the Holy Land and I a prisoner for a year of more while awaiting your arrival. Suffice it that you have come and I am free and I thank God for my good brother.'

'I have a further score to settle with Tancred. You arrived in Sicily with a good dowry. I want to know what happened to that golden table, the silk tent, the galleys and the golden plate.'

'Tancred has taken them as he has everything that was mine and William's.'

'My first task was to free you, sister,' said Richard. 'My second will be to regain the treasure. Your husband left a legacy to our father and as he is dead I shall claim that. I need all the money and treasure I can lay my hands on for the Holy War.'

'I shall pray for you, Richard.'

'Doubtless we shall need your prayers.'

'The King of France is your ally in this venture?'

'Aye, he is my ally ... I think.'

'You are not sure?'

'There must necessarily it seems be rivalry between kings.'

'I have heard that a great friendship exists between you two.'

'It has its uncertainties,' he said shortly, and Joanna sensed that he did not wish to speak of it.

'You will ere long see our mother, I doubt not. She is at this moment in Brindisi with Berengaria, the Princess of Navarre.'

There were tears in Joanna's eyes. 'Forgive my emotion. But a short time ago I was a prisoner and now this is too much joy too suddenly. I have often thought of our mother when she, like myself, was a prisoner. I can sympathize with her more readily now.'

'Her imprisonment is over as yours is.'

'And all thanks to you, Richard. How grateful she must be, as I am.'

'Think not that I should allow my mother and my sister to be ill-treated if there was aught I could do to prevent it.'

'Thank you, Richard. A thousand thanks.'

'Come, let us talk of other things. I will tell you of my adventures.' He described to her how he had arrived at Marseilles and found his ships not yet there and in great impatience he had gone on without them. Hence the fleet's arrival at Messina before him. He told her of how he had tried to take the poor man's hawk and nearly lost his life.

'If you had what would have become of us?' she cried.

'Oh, I am not so easily disposed of. We have heaven's blessing on our crusade. I have evidence of this. My sailors have told me that when a great storm blew up off the coast of Spain, they prayed to God and there appeared on the seething waters a vision of St Thomas à Becket of Canterbury. "Have no fear," he told them, "for God has appointed me guardian of this fleet and if you repent of your past sins and commit no more, you will have a prosperous voyage." And the men took heart and soon the storm abated and they came safely to Marseilles.'

'God is on your side, Richard.'

'So must He be when we are engaged in his holy war.'

They had arrived at the house and servants came out to welcome her.

Having made sure that everything was there for her comfort Richard left for the Villa de Muschet.

*   *   *

The next day Richard called to see his sister and with him he brought the King of France. Philip was clearly impressed by her beauty and charm and they talked long and earnestly together.

Philip wanted to know where she would go when he and Richard left for Acre. She was not at all sure, she told him, but she was hoping to join her mother.

This raised a certain awkwardness because Philip would know that Queen Eleanor was with Berengaria and he would wonder how there could be a marriage between Richard and the Princess of Navarre when she was betrothed to his sister Alice.

Philip knew this but he was determined to be courteous and the unfortunate subject of Alice was allowed to lapse. Joanna would be naturally curious to learn how the matter was to be resolved but she could see that she could not raise it when Philip was present.

As for Richard he knew that Philip was waiting for the opportune moment to bring up the matter of his betrothal; and then he could be sure that it would be the King who was bargaining and he, Richard, could not hope to escape lightly, nor would Philip allow him to if he could help it—great friends though they were.

Richard said hastily that he had no intention of leaving Messina until he had settled the matter of Joanna's dowry.

'Which could delay you for some time,' Philip pointed out.

'Then delay there must be for I'll not allow this avaricious fellow to take what is mine.'

'I believe,' said Philip to Joanna, 'that your brother cares not if I take Acre without him.'

'You will need my help,' said Richard, 'as I shall need yours. We may be assured that the place will be well fortified.'

'If we delay too long the winter will be upon us.'

'Still, I shall not allow Tancred to flout me.'

Philip shrugged his shoulders. He devoted himself to Joanna and told her about his little son Louis whose welfare gave him so much concern and how his heart was torn between the desire to lead a campaign into the Holy Land and to be at home to govern his kingdom.

'You see,' he explained, 'when I planned this crusade my Queen was alive. She was there to care for our son. She was to be my Regent, and now I have lost her.'

There was a rapport between them. Joanna had so recently lost a beloved husband. She shared his sense of bereavement which was increased as it often was in the case of people in their position by a loss of security.

They talked together and when the Kings took their leave the attendants were whispering together that the King of France seemed mightily taken with the Queen of Sicily and since he was recently a widower and she a widow, could there be a happy outcome of their meeting?

*   *   *

Settling into his quarters, awaiting the return of the dowry, Richard had discovered that his men were causing a certain amount of discord in Messina. Among the population of Sicily were some of mixed European and Saracen origin; they were a hot-blooded people quickly aroused and ready to fight on the least provocation and they did not like having foreigners on their soil.

Before he had arrived there had been quarrels between the crusaders and the Sicilian natives. Dissension arose for the most trivial reasons. And when the Sicilians realized that King Richard was making arrogant demands to their King, they became more resentful. In such a situation Richard realized that it would be very easy for the men to get out of control. He was determined that this should not be so.

He conferred with Philip. He wanted rigorous discipline. The men must fear their leaders but Philip insisted that as the men were away from their homes and the conditions in which they lived must necessarily be trying there should be a certain amount of leniency.

Richard said that was nonsense and erected a gallows opposite his house.

'Let all men beware how they conduct themselves,' he

decreed. 'I shall have no mercy on those who offend my laws.'

People trembled before him. Sicilian babies were frightened by the warning: 'King Richard will have you if you are not a good child.' He was called The Lion, and in contrast the French King was given the nickname of The Lamb.

In spite of Richard's severity trouble continued to break out. The Sicilians complained that the crusaders seduced their wives and daughters and swaggered about the town as though they owned it.

Philip thought they should not linger and that while they did so the men would be restive but Richard refused to think of leaving until he had satisfaction from Tancred. He wanted the dowry or its equivalent in money and treasure and he was going to have it or go to war.

Philip watching the situation shrewdly knew that Eleanor was waiting for the command to come to her son bringing with her Berengaria of Navarre. It was amusing to contemplate how little enthusiasm Richard appeared to have for the marriage. He was far more interested in getting even with Tancred. Of course there was Alice. How was Richard going to break free of the bonds which bound him to Philip's sister? Philip was well aware that Richard would refuse to marry Alice and he knew why. Who would wish to marry a woman who had been his father's mistress and borne him a child? But he was affianced to her.

The amusing angle was that although Richard did not want to marry Alice he did not seem eager to marry Berengaria either.

The fact was that Richard did not want to marry.

He would be quite happy to sail away to Acre without Berengaria and ... with Philip.

*   *   *

When Richard received Tancred's reply to his demand for the return of his sister's dowry he was filled with rage, for Tancred quite clearly had no intention of returning the treasures.

'He must be taught a lesson,' cried Richard.

Philip who had been with him when Tancred's reply was delivered urged him not to be rash; but Richard was not one to pause when his anger was aroused. Tancred had defied him and was trying to cheat him out of what he considered was his by right. Tancred therefore must be made to understand that he could not flout the King of England.

Ignoring Philip's advice, Richard gathered his forces together and took possession of a fort and a monastery. The latter he intended to use as a storehouse; but the operation was to bring home to Tancred and the Sicilians that when Richard of England was not treated with the respect to which he was due that was the time to beware.

Tension was rising. Richard's crusaders now believed that they were like a conquering army. They swaggered through the market places; there were stories of their forcing their attentions on unwilling women, robbing the Sicilians of their goods and behaving in a manner which was sooner or later going to destroy the peace. They assumed that as they were crusaders on their way to a holy war whatever misdemeanours they were guilty of would be forgiven in the eyes of Heaven because of their cause.

The Sicilians were not, of a nature to accept this conduct uncomplainingly and it was not long before violence broke out. This began with a trivial incident. A party of crusaders walking through the market place saw a woman selling bread. One of them took one of the loaves and when the woman demanded payment refused it. She tried to snatch the bread from him and several of the stall-holders came to her rescue. In a very short time there was a riot. The citizens gathered together against the intruders and armed with sticks and stones began to fight. The crusaders retaliated and soldiers began marching on the city although they had had no orders to do so.

When he saw what was happening Richard tried to call a halt to his army, but they were now determined on conquest and even Richard riding among his men found it difficult to call them to order.

Finally this was achieved but the incensed populace was determined to be revenged and large numbers of them prepared to attack the English camp. Richard placed himself at the head of his troops and drove the people back to the town; but this was not enough for him. These people had dared attempt to menace his soldiers. They must be taught a lesson. He marched into Messina.

The fighting was fierce and during it five of Richard's knights and twenty men-at-arms were killed. The sight of their men lying dead infuriated the crusaders and they gave vent to their fury. That night they forgot their holy mission entirely; they were soldiers, far from home, determined to satisfy their lustful desires. They stormed the town pillaging, robbing and setting fire to the boats in the port.

When dawn came it was seen that they had set up the English standard on the walls of the city.

*   *   *

When he arose that morning Philip saw the flag and he was angry. Richard went too far. How could the French who had their quarters in the town allow the English to fly their flag in such a manner? It was an admission of their superiority over their allies.

He sent a messenger at once to the Villa Muschet and asked that Richard come to him. It was some time before Richard appeared. Philip marvelled when he saw him. He was fresh and alert; none would have guessed that he had been fighting far into the night. Battle stimulated Richard; there was no doubt of it. It was inactivity which he found hard to endure.

'This is a sorry state of affairs,' said Philip.

'You think so?'

'I do indeed.' He slipped his arm through Richard's and drew him to the window. He pointed to the English standard flying on the city wall. 'That will not do.'

'Methinks it does very well. It is an indication to these people that they must not insult me or my people.'

'It would appear that your soldiers insulted them in the first place.'

'They were over-sensitive.'

'We are engaged n a Holy War. We cannot waste lives and money on petty battles such as this.'

'We need to rest here. We need to refit our ships which have been damaged in the storm. We are engaged in a holy cause and Christians on the way must succour us in friendship. If they do not it is war.'

'You are always so quick to take offence. Sometimes I think you live for your battles.'

'I am a soldier, Philip.'

'It seems sometimes you forget you are a king. That is something I never do. That is why I tell you that standard must come down.'

'It stays where it is.'

'Nay, Richard, it comes down.'

'Tancred has to be shown that I mean what I say. If he does not pay me my dues I will take them. I will subdue the entire island. I shall not allow him to treat me and mine with impunity.'

'This is no quarrel with Tancred. It is a dispute between your soldiers and the people. They resent them here and I am not surprised at that. Would you care for foreign soldiery on your lands, swaggering through the market places taking what they wished, insulting the women...?'

'These people attempted to march on my camp.'

'Because your men were making life intolerable for them. No matter, take that standard down.'

'Is that a command?'

'It is.'

'And who is the King of France to command the King of England?'

'I do not command the King of England, but the Duke of Normandy, who has sworn fealty to me as his liege lord.'

'You are unjust.'

'Nay, within my rights. Richard, we are together in an enterprise which needs all our skill and courage. Do not try our friendship too far. French troops are stationed here. How can they be content to rest under the English standard?'

'Because the English placed it there in battle.'

'A battle which should never have been fought. You are too impetuous, Richard. Have I not always told you so ... even in the old days?'

Richard turned on his heel. His anger was great and he did not care to be reminded of the days when he had been content to ride with the King of France, to talk with him, to sleep in his bed.

Several of his most trusted counsellors were waiting for him when he returned to the villa. They knew of his visit to the King of France and what must have been its purpose.

'One thing which would be fatal at this juncture,' they told him, 'would be conflict between our men and the French.

This there will assuredly be while the English standard floats over the town.'

'Let there be,' cried Richard in a passion. 'I placed that standard there and there it shall remain. Tancred is going to understand that if he does not meet my demands I will take the whole of his island.'

'All very well, my lord, if it were not for the French. What if Tancred should ask their help and they give it...?'

'Philip would never fight against me.'

'He has ordered you to remove the standard, commanding you as King of France to his vassal of Normandy. If you left it there he might be forced to take action to save his face. You have come here not to fight against the French but to stand with them against the Infidel. It was for this cause that the treasure was gathered together.'

Richard was a little sobered and when one of his friends suggested he go to the King of France and see what might be worked out, he agreed.

Philip anxious not to alienate Richard, was ready to be reasonable. He was longing to leave with him for Acre and to get away from Sicily where everything seemed to be going wrong.

He understood how embarrassing it would be for Richard to remove the standard, so he would not ask him to do that. He would suggest that the Golden Lilies of France be placed side by side with it and the two flags together float over the town. As for the keys of the city which were now in Richard's hands, these should be put in the custody of the impartial Knights of the Temple and every effort should be made to persuade Tancred to return Queen Joanna's dowry.

This was a reasonable solution, and the shrewdness of the King of France had saved the situation created through the impetuosity of the King of England.

*   *   *

Tancred, realizing that he could no longer evade Richard's demands, suggested that he and Richard meet to discuss this troublesome matter of Joanna's dowry. The outcome of this meeting was that Tancred admitted to Richard's right and offered to pay him twenty thousand ounces of gold to compensate him for the goods his sister had brought with her as a bride. This he pointed out would be far more useful to the crusading King than a golden table. Richard agreed to this and the matter was concluded. There was also to be considered the legacy which William had left to the last King Henry and which Richard, as his son and heir, was claiming.

He had a daughter, Tancred said, whom he was anxious to see married well. If Richard could offer her a suitable bridegroom he would add her dowry to the legacy and that would make a considerable amount. In fact for a good husband he was willing to make the legacy up to another twenty thousand ounces of gold.

Forty thousand ounces! Richard's eyes sparkled at the prospect. He must have those forty thousand ounces!

'If I should die childless I intend to make my nephew Arthur of Brittany my heir,' said Richard. 'He is the next in succession for he is the son of my brother Geoffrey who was older than my brother John; though John was falsely led by my father to believe that he had a right to the throne that is not so while Arthur lives. Arthur—in the event of my dying childless—is my heir and I shall proclaim this. I am agreeable that your daughter shall be affianced to my nephew Arthur.'

Tancred was delighted. He had come well out of his troubles. True he had had to compensate Richard but that was preferable to losing his island. But in doing so he had gained the prospect of a very brilliant marriage for his daughter. She would be Queen of England after Richard's death if Richard had no children, and he had heard rumours that Richard was not over fond of women. Of course he would doubtless do his duty and marry and then attempt to produce a son. Tancred like everyone else had heard the rumours about Princess Alice of France who was betrothed to him and he knew too that Queen Eleanor was waiting with the Princess Berengaria of Navarre for Richard to summon them.

It was a strange affair. Richard and Philip such dear friends and all the time Richard trying to escape from his betrothal to Philip's sister and seeming in no hurry to enter into marriage with Berengaria.

There were rumours about Richard's private life. Tancred hoped they were true, for his great hope now would be to see his daughter Queen of England which she could very well be if Richard died childless.

So the matter of the dowry was settled to Richard's satisfaction and Richard ordered that all the valuables which his men had taken when they sacked Messina should be returned to their rightful owners. This was done with reluctance by those who had taken possession of the treasures but Richard's word was law. Philip suggested that he and Richard should meet in public, and there embrace and swear to each other that they would be good friends, that they would not quarrel together nor allow their armies to do so.

This was done with great effect and the tension through Sicily was considerably relaxed, and with the matter of the dowry settled there was only one thing to keep them in Sicily: the weather.

'We have tarried too long,' Philip complained. 'We dare not face the seas now that winter is coming on. We shall have to wait for the spring.'

This was good sense and Richard had to agree with it. There was still no mention of Berengaria who was waiting now at Naples with Eleanor for Richard to send for her. Yet how could he until Philip had agreed to release him from his betrothal to Alice?

*   *   *

As they had delayed so long that they must pass the winter in Sicily, Richard built a fort-like palace of wood which was called Mate Griffon. This meant Kill Greek, a rather unfortunate name as there were several Greeks in Sicily. Here in this wooden palace he lived in great style and it was his pleasure to entertain the King of France there. They gave entertainments for each other and there were only occasional disturbances between the French and English. All knew that by fighting together they displeased their Kings who had become the dearest of friends once more.

The Lion and The Lamb were lying down together, it was said.

There would always be the uncertainty between them though. Richard often thought of Alice and asked himself how he could broach the matter to Philip. Philip too thought of his sister and wondered when Richard would raise the subject of her future. He wanted to discuss his sister with Richard but he knew Richard would ask him to release him from his promise to marry Alice, and although Philip did not wish to refuse Richard any request at the same time he could not allow his sister to be cast aside. It was true she had been the mistress of Richard's father and possibly borne her lover a child, and no man could be expected to marry her in such circumstances. Yet she was a Princess of France.

And Berengaria? Philip laughed slyly to think of her waiting and waiting, each day looking for the messenger who did not come, wondering what was happening to her laggard lover who was so slow to claim her as his wife.

'He is sporting with the King of France, my lady,' murmured Philip.

It was a situation which amused him. He had contemplated suggesting a marriage with Richard's sister Joanna, but let that wait. She was a charming woman, but like Richard, he did not want to think of marriage now.

So they vied with each other to give the better entertainments and there was much to occupy them during the waiting months.

Sometimes Philip was overwhelmed by Richard's brilliance. There has never been such a general, he thought. Any army he commanded would come to victory simply because he was there. But Richard had his weaknesses and while these saddened Philip as a friend, as a rival King he must be grateful for them. Richard's impetuosity over the Tancred affair could have caused a great deal of trouble and if Richard had not been such a brilliant commander it might have ended in disaster for the English, even disaster to this crusade. Yes in certain ways he was a weak man and never did he show this weakness more clearly than over the affair of the canes.

On a sparkling February day Richard and some of his knights rode out with the French to engage in a mock battle in the meadows outside Messina. This they did with great verve and Richard as usual showed his skill to such advantage that all agreed he was the greatest warrior of the day.

Riding back to Mate Griffon they passed through the town and there they encountered a peasant leading a donkey which was laden with canes.

Richard stopped him and offered to buy the canes and as the peasant dared not refuse he handed them over.

'Come,' he cried. 'Instead of lances we will use canes.'

His opponent was the French knight, William des Barres, noted for his prowess and a worthy adversary for Richard.

They had soon broken their canes on each other but in doing so William des Barres had torn Richard's cappa which was a kind of riding hood. Richard had inherited the notorious Plantagenet temper and the thought that this Frenchman had dared to tear his garment infuriated him. Angrily he went into the attack and unseated des Barres but in doing so was thrown from his own horse. One of his men immediately brought forward another horse for him but his fury affected his judgement and it seemed that des Barres would have to be declared the victor. To be beaten by a Frenchman who had had the temerity to tear his cappa was too much for Richard. He lay about him furiously at the same time shouting abuse at the Frenchman. Had des Barres been one of his own knights doubtless he would have considered it expedient to allow himself to be beaten. Not so the Frenchman. He continued to fight with all his skill and vigour and for once Richard was in danger of defeat. One of his men came hurrying to his rescue which only angered him the more.

'Let be, let be!' he cried. 'Do you think I am incapable of settling this Frenchman? I will kill him ere I have finished with him.'

What had begun as play was becoming serious. French and English knights looked on in dismay. Richard was hot with rage, des Barres cool with the determination not to give way simply because he had offended the dignity of the King of England.

It was obvious that Richard was not going to succeed in overthrowing des Barres. His cane was broken and he threw it away from him.

'Get from my sight,' he shouted. 'I never want to see you again. I see you are an enemy of mine and as such I shall regard you.'

Alarmed, des Barres went to Philip and told him what had happened.

'I believe, my lord,' he said, 'that Richard has it in his heart to kill me.'

' 'Tis that hot temper,' replied Philip. 'His father had it. With him it was worse than with Richard. He would lie on the floor and gnaw the rushes and often came near to doing himself an injury when these rages were on him. I have seen the King of England possessed with this wild anger on one or two occasions. Though fortunately for him these spells of rage are less frequent than they were with his father. Leave this matter to me, I will speak with him. Have no fear; it will pass.'

When they were next together Philip mentioned the matter to Richard.

'I hear you are angry with one of my knights.'

'William des Barres insulted me.'

'He meant it not. It was an accident. You sported with him and your garment was torn.'

'He did it on purpose. It was my cappa that was torn. He was going for my face with the cane. He hoped to put out my eyes.'

'So that was what you thought.'

'Indeed it was so. I will show you the cappa. He was clearly aiming for my eyes.'

'He is contrite.'

'So well he may be. He will regret this.'

'Richard, it was an accident and it happened in sport. Take it as such.'

'Nothing will induce me to receive that man. He had better keep from my sight.'

'You whipped up your anger against him. You know you do this now and then. It's not good, Richard.'

'Oh, and who are you to criticize me?'

'Your sovereign lord, my lord Duke of Normandy.'

'You are fond of reminding me of that.'

'I find it necessary from time to time.'

'One of these days...'

'Yes, Richard, one of these days you will try to take France from me so that you do not have to acknowledge me as your sovereign lord.'

'How could that be? Moreover I prefer to think of myself as the King of England.'

'King of England, the King of France, who loves you, warns you to guard your temper. You inherited it from your father. He was a great King but he would have been a greater one without that temper. Forget this trouble with des Barres.'

'I shall never forget it. Let the man keep out of my path.'

'I will see that he does that until you are yourself again. We want no more trouble. Methinks we have been too long in this place. We should have left earlier and so should we but for your quarrel with Tancred.'

'We shall start for Acre as soon as the spring comes.'

'Do you plan to take Tancred with you?'

'Tancred! What gives you such ideas?'

'I thought you had become very friendly with him.'

'We have made an agreement.'

'To marry your nephew to his daughter. I thought your attitude towards him had undergone an abrupt change.'

'He's a reasonable enough fellow.'

'When he knows himself beaten, yes.'

'Philip, are you jealous of Tancred?'

'Perhaps ... a little.'

Richard laughed loudly. His good spirits were considerably restored and he seemed to have forgotten the ire which the des Barres incident had aroused in him.

*　　*　　*

Tancred was indeed determined to court Richard's good will. His position was dangerous. King Henry of Germany, husband of Constancia, was naturally incensed at the truce between Tancred and Richard, and, as Henry was shortly to be crowned Emperor, he would be more powerful than he was before. Richard's sister Joanna had supported Constancia's claim and had been imprisoned for it. Her brother had understandably rescued her from that indignity but it had not been expected that Richard would call a truce with Tancred. Henry now regarded Richard as his enemy. Philip was aware of this and that was why he had shrewdly kept out of the quarrel. He knew that when one embarked on a crusade one needed all the friends one could muster. It could never be certain what an army might encounter on its journey, and it was foolish to make enemies.

Richard did not consider such matters. Tancred had paid him well and the quarrel with Henry of Germany was not his affair, but a matter between Tancred and Henry.

Tancred, however, fully aware of Richard's prowess as all must be who had seen him in action, was eager to have him as his ally and because of this he invited Richard to pay a state visit to him at the Sicilian court which was now at Catania.

It was on the first day of March when Richard set out. He was certain that it would not be long before he would leave for Acre and was debating with himself what was to be done about Berengaria. When he approached the town Tancred rode out to meet him and he had arranged that everything should be done to make him aware of how welcome he was. Tancred embraced him, tears of emotion in his eyes, and they went side by side into the palace, where a lavish entertainment was carried out for his pleasure and the banquet was sumptuous. Richard was delighted.

The following day Tancred took him to the shrine of St Agatha for which Catania was noted and they both prayed for the success of the crusade. Tancred told Richard how at all times of the year pilgrims came to the shrine and there was very good evidence that their prayers were answered.

Richard's visit lasted three days and on the last of these Tancred displayed rich treasure which he said he wished to present to him. There were gold and silver ornaments set with sparkling gems, but Richard said: 'My friend, I cannot take these rich gifts from you.' He selected a simple ring which he put on his finger. 'This only will I take as a token of the love between us.'

All the company professed to be profoundly moved and Richard then said that he would give to Tancred one of his most prized possessions. This was the famous sword known as Caliburne, which was said to have belonged to King Arthur and to have magical qualities. Richard knew this was not the case. The sword was a fine one but the magic was lacking; if it had been he would not have been so foolish as to give it away when he was on an expedition to destroy the Saracens. But the legend attached to it gave it great value and Tancred kissed it and told Richard that he could not accept it unless he was allowed to give something to the King of England of more value than the ring he had chosen.

Richard could not help thinking that had Philip been present he would have laughed wryly to see the two Kings who had such a short time ago been wrangling over Joanna's dowry now bestowing valuable gifts on each other.

The outcome was that Richard received from Tancred four large ships and fifteen galleys which would be of great value to him in his campaign.

When Richard prepared to leave Catania for Messina, Tancred said that he could not bear the meeting to be so brief and he was going to ride some of the way with Richard in order to have the extended pleasure of his company.

As they rode side by side Tancred urged Richard to ride ahead of the cavalcade with him for he had something very secret to say to him.

'I shall tell you this in great confidence,' he said. 'It has caused me much heart searching but since we have sworn such friendship I feel I must speak to you of it.'

'Please tell me what this is,' begged Richard.

'It concerns the King of France.'

'In what way?' demanded Richard.

'I know that there exists great friendship between you, but how deep does that friendship go?'

'What are you trying to tell me?'

'To beware of the King of France.'

'You are thinking that naturally we must be enemies. It is not so.'

'I believe it to be so,' said Tancred. 'At least Philip is your enemy.'

'That cannot be.'

'I know that it is.'

'Philip and I have been friends in the past. We have sworn to support each other during this crusade.'

'You, who are of a direct and honest nature, cannot understand the devious ways of others. Philip seeks always his own advantage; he wants to see France supreme. Every French King since the Normans arrived in France has sought to drive them out and bring Normandy back to the French crown. Is that not so?'

'It is indeed.'

'Do you think Philip—one of the slyest of them all—is any exception?'

'I know that he is determined to defend his country as any good king should be.'

'And in doing so he will attempt to destroy all those who, he thinks, are its enemies. You, my lord King, are one of those.'

'I understand your meaning. We are rivals and must be by nature of our position, but on this crusade we are as one. Our interests are the same; we have one motive: to drive the Infidel from the Holy Land.'

'I can see there is only one way to convince you. Philip has tried to assure me that you are my enemy. He says that you will not keep the peace, that you are waiting for the moment when you can conveniently attack me and take the whole of Sicily.'

'This is nonsense,' cried Richard. 'I am engaged on a crusade. I have no time for conquests on the way.'

'This is what he has told me and he has assured me that if I will give the order for my troops to attack the English in the night, the French will come to our aid.'

'This is perfidy.'

'And you are my friend, that is why I warn you.'

'I cannot believe this of Philip.'

'He is clever and has managed to deceive you.'

'He could not so far deceive me.'

'Then I see you want proof. I can give you this. I have with me a letter which he has written to me. If you will read it you will see that I have not lied to you.'

'Show me this letter.'

'When we rest for the night I will have it brought to you.'

As soon as they came to the castle where they were staying for the night, Tancred produced the letter. Richard read and the blood rushed to his face. It appeared to be in Philip's handwriting and it was as Tancred had said. A wild rage possessed him. He wanted to go to Philip and challenge him to combat. Philip would have little chance against him. He would kill Philip . . . if he had indeed written this letter.

If! What did he mean? That was Philip's handwriting. He had seen it often enough. But how could Philip, who had been such a tender friend, write of him so?

His rage was halted. There was the unmistakable shadow of a doubt.

He *must* see Philip. He would know no rest until he did.

He took his leave of Tancred. 'I am no traitor,' he assured him. 'The peace I have concluded I will not transgress. I confess to you it is not easy for me to believe this letter true, for the friendship between the King of France and myself has been of long standing.'

Tancred said: 'I have shown you the evidence. I can do no more.'

Richard rode with all speed to Messina. He immediately sent one of his knights to the French camp asking for audience with Philip.

The messenger returned with the news that Philip had left for Catania there to join Richard and Tancred.

Richard bit his lips in frustration. So Philip was in Catania. They must have passed on the way. Either he was concerned because he feared what Tancred might have told Richard or it could have been that he was simply jealous of their relationship and wished to prevent its becoming too warm.

It was not long before Philip returned to Messina.

* * *

They faced each other. Richard was never one to prevaricate.

'So,' he began, 'you would plot with Tancred against me.'

Philip looked bewildered. 'What's this?' he asked.

'It is useless to feign ignorance. I know what has been happening. I have evidence. You have incited Tancred to rise against me in the night when I am unprepared and have offered him your help.'

'Where have you heard such nonsense?'

'From Tancred himself.'

'He has been lying.'

'He has been telling what appears to be the truth.'

'And you would take his word against mine? This new friend of yours is believed before those who have stood by you in the past and have proved their love and loyalty?'

'I have been deceived.'

'Yes, by Tancred.'

'I would prefer it to be so.'

'Yet this man only has to whisper a few calumnies . . .'

'That is not all. He has shown me a letter. I have it. It is in your own hand. You have told him that if he rises against my army by stealth you will be behind him. The object being to destroy me.'

'You can believe such nonsense! Why should I destroy my ally in this crusade? Why should I wish to go on to Acre without you?'

'You want all the glory. Confess it. You want Normandy.'

'If I defeated you here in Sicily would that give me Normandy?'

'Who would defend it? My brother John. He has shown little prowess on the battle field. My three year old heir

Arthur? Nay, you are sly, you are devious. You scheme and dissemble.'

'Show me this letter.'

'I will. It offers irrefutable proof of your perfidy.'

Richard thrust the letter into Philip's hands. The King of France studied it and his eyes opened wide with incredulity. Richard thought: If he is acting, he does it very well.

'But this is monstrous. This is incredible. I ... write such a letter! I never did. Richard, how can you believe for one instant that I could do such?'

'I could believe it,' said Richard. 'When that letter was put into my hands surely I could believe the evidence of my eyes.'

'I am deeply wounded that you could do so.'

'Philip, is that not your hand writing?'

'It is a fair enough copy to deceive even me. But I know I never wrote it.'

'You would swear to it?'

'On God's holy word.'

Richard narrowed his eyes. He sometimes suspected Philip's piety. He would never really know his friend. It might be that therein lay the fascination. He could never understand Philip and Philip understood him too well.

Philip was either suddenly angry or feigned to be so.

'By God, Richard,' he said, 'you doubt me. Do you? Do you?'

'It would seem to me that you wrote that letter.'

'It is a forgery. You must see that.'

'The handwriting is exact in every detail.'

'I will admit that it is a good imitation. What hurts me is that you should doubt me.'

'With such evidence?'

'But I have told you it is false and you still doubt.' Philip went to the window and looked out for a few seconds, then he swung round. 'You are seeking to pick a quarrel with me, Richard, and you are using this letter. You know full well I am incapable of writing it. You attack me to cover your own fault.'

Richard knit his brows and stared at Philip.

'Oh yes,' went on Philip. 'It's Alice, is it not? My sister Alice to whom you are betrothed. You do not want to marry Alice. You have another Princess in mind. At this moment she is nearby waiting to be summoned. You have not told me this but I know it, of course. All know it. You do not say to me: "I intend to break my contract with your sister." You pick a quarrel instead.'

'You know I could never marry your sister.'

'Why not? You are betrothed to her.'

'My father's whore.'

'Take care, Richard. You speak of your sovereign lord's sister.'

'I speak of her for what she is. I'll not marry her.'

'You will insult the House of France.'

'I will not marry your sister, Philip.'

'Well, let us say she provides a good excuse. You'll not marry her and while you are betrothed to her you can marry no one else.' Philip laughed aloud. 'Poor Alice she served your father well. You too methinks.'

He saw the signs of Richard's rising temper. He came to him and laid his hand on his shoulder.

'Nay, Richard, I must help you out of this impasse. What hurts me is that you should think I would betray you. You should know that Tancred is not to be trusted. Let us not quarrel for that grieves me sorely and I fancy it does not make you happy. I will free you from your contract with Alice. Marry Berengaria. Get her with child and you and I will go off to Acre together.'

'You mean you will truly free me from that contract?'

'I will indeed. Alice shall come back to my court. Some nobleman will be glad to take my sister. And you will be free, Richard, to marry where you will. This Berengaria, is she very beautiful?'

'She is an elegant Princess.'

Philip nodded.

'Then all is well. We will conclude a treaty that all the world will know there is amity between us.'

They drank together and made plans for the future and a few days later the treaty was drawn up.

Richard was to be free to marry where he pleased, in spite of the bond entered into with the Princess Alice. He must however pay the King of France three thousand marks to round off the bargain and there were other clauses concerning territories on French soil which were to be exchanged.

Richard signed the contract without demur. He was grow-

ing a little anxious, for Queen Eleanor had sent urgent messages to him. England had long been without a ruler—in
fact ever since the King had set out and she had not been
there to represent him. Richard must not forget that ambitious men in his realm might well be ready to exploit the situation for their advantage. It was time she returned to England
to keep an eye on affairs; she did not see how she could do
that while she had the Princess Berengaria in her charge.

It was imperative, she said, that the marriage take place
without delay. Then Berengaria could accompany him and
she, Eleanor, could return to England.

As for Joanna, she could not remain in Sicily, for could
Tancred be trusted to treat her with respect when Richard
was not there to enforce this?

Eleanor thought that as she herself must return to England
it would be a good idea for Joanna to accompany Berengaria
and Richard. Joanna would be a companion for the young
Queen and as Richard would be engaged in battle it would
be good for the two young women to be together.

Richard saw this as sound common sense.

He wrote to his mother to bring Berengaria to Sicily.

The Wedding is Postponed

THE water sparkled in the Bay which was dominated by the great peak of Vesuvius, and every morning when Berengaria awoke she looked at it and asked herself whether that day the message would come.

All through the winter she had waited and she knew that her future mother-in-law was also growing restive. Queen Eleanor hated inactivity. She would have liked to sail to Sicily without waiting for Richard's commands but even she realized that could not be done.

Berengaria would sit for hours with her embroidery while Eleanor read aloud or played her lute and sang; but, although Berengaria was noted for her skill with the needle and Eleanor was a poet and musician, neither of these occupations could satisfy them.

Berengaria was filled with longing to be with her bridegroom elect; Eleanor yearned for activity—anything rather than nothing. She had had her freedom too recently not to wish to exploit it to the full and here she was confined in this house lent to them by a member of the nobility until such a time as Richard would send for them.

March had come. 'It can't be long now,' said Berengaria as they sat together at the open window looking out over the Bay. 'One day his ship will come and with it orders to take us from this place.'

'I cannot think what is happening,' grumbled Eleanor.

'We can rest assured that as soon as it is possible he will send for us,' said Berengaria.

Eleanor brooded in silence. What was happening at Messina? She had heard of course that Tancred had imprisoned Joanna and that Richard had quickly brought about her freedom. But why should the Kings of England and France dally there all through the winter? Of course they had to consider the weather and it would have been folly to set out in December. But surely they had known this and should have left earlier. What could it mean? There were whispers about the friendship of the Kings. How significant was this? Louis' son Philip and her son Richard!

Oh God, she thought, how You have interwoven our lives!

She looked at the charming profile of the girl who was to be Richard's wife. How innocent she was! She would have no idea of the dark passions which beset human beings. How different she, Eleanor, had been at her age. She laughed at the thought. But then she had been born worldly. Poor Berengaria! But should one say poor? Perhaps it was an enviable state of mind which enabled one to go through the world seeing good and evil clearly defined.

To Berengaria Richard was a noble hero. All he did was right; she saw him as a man dedicated to a holy cause rather than a soldier seeking personal glory. She thought he slaughtered for the sake of a cause not to satisfy some cruel aspect of his nature which gloated on the sufferings of others.

I must not disillusion her, she thought. She will be a better wife to Richard if she continues to believe he is some sort of god. She will need patience, poor child. She will need to keep her beliefs.

'It may be that he cannot get his release from Alice,' said Berengaria fearfully.

'He is determined not to marry her. He is betrothed to you now. Have no fear he will send for us as soon as he is free to do so.'

'The King of France is with him. Could they not settle the matter together?'

'My child, powerful kings are not like ordinary men. They seek to take advantage of every situation and you can be assured that Philip is no exception.'

'What will become of Alice? I feel sorry for her.'

'Do not waste your feelings on her. She has had her day.'

'It could never have been a happy day, could it? The King visiting her in secret ... and the shame of it.'

'Such as she is revel in shame. You do not know what my
husband was like. There was something overpowering about
him.'

'Then I daresay she found it hard to resist him.'

Eleanor laughed bitterly. 'Well, she must pay for her
pleasures. Philip will have to take her back and leave Richard
free to marry you.' Eleanor rose and went to the window and
stood there watching. 'Now that the weather is becoming
more clement they will want to sail for Acre,' she said.

'Do you think I shall be married in Sicily?'

'It seems likely that you will. I trust so because I wish to see
you married and I must return soon to England.'

'How I wish that we could all go there!'

Eleanor laughed. 'Do not let Richard hear you say that. He
is set on this crusade. It has long been a dream of his that he
will be the one to drive the Infidel from the Holy Land and
he believes God has chosen him to do this.'

Berengaria let her needlework fall into her lap and gazed
to the ceiling. 'What a noble ideal!' she murmured.

'He would not wish anything or anyone to stand in his way.'

'Nor must they.'

Eleanor turned round. 'Nay my child. We must both
remember that. How *I* should love to go with him to the
Holy Land. I did go once, you know, with my first husband,
the King of France. You may have heard something of my
adventures there. They were much talked of at the time.'

'Yes,' said Berengaria quietly, 'I have heard.'

'I was young and full of high spirits. There was much
scandal. But this passes. If you go with your husband you will
be very discreet, I know. That will be best ... for you. You
will be a good wife to Richard, Berengaria. Never question
his motives. Always remember that you cannot understand all
that goes on in his mind. Do not attempt to stop him when he
wants to follow a certain course. His father and I quarrelled.
We disagreed on everything. I could not bear his infidelities.'

'I do not think I shall suffer so with Richard.'

Eleanor looked with pity at the girl. She did not know.
Perhaps she did not understand these innuendoes about the
King of France. Let her go on in ignorance. It was better
so.

'And because we disagreed,' went on Eleanor, 'I spent years
in captivity and his sons went to war against him. We were

neither of us very happy in our family life. Strangely now, I
see how it might have been so different. But one must never
look back. That is one of the lessons I have learned from life.
You act in such a way because you want to. All very well but
don't whine when you are asked to pay the price such action
demands. It is a good maxim.'

'You are very wise,' said Berengaria.

'And old,' said Eleanor. 'Those who shared my youth are
now dead or nearly so. Yet I go on.'

'Long may you do so,' said Berengaria fervently.

'You are a good child and I wish you happiness. I hope our
paths will someday lie together.'

'Why should they not?'

'Because, my child, you have a roving husband and I fancy
that my duty lies in England. Indeed I fret about that land
now. It is without a ruler. It was a mistake to leave it so soon.
I shall have to return ere long. I have sent messages to
Richard telling him that I have had uneasy reports. I shall
have to go back soon.'

'You will not leave me?'

'Nay, child. But I must give you to your husband soon. I
long too to see my daughter. Joanna was always one of my
favourites. Such a pretty child she was. Her husband was
delighted with her when she went to him and it was a happy
marriage ... and then he died and she became Tancred's
prisoner.'

'That is over. Richard came and rescued her.'

'Let us hope he will soon rescue us from this uneventful
existence.'

Within a few days their wish was granted. A ship arrived to
take them to Messina where Richard was awaiting them.

*   *   *

Philip came to the Villa de Muschet among the vineyards
and Richard received him in his private chamber.

'To what do I owe this honour?' he asked.

'To the fact that I have come to say I shall be leaving Sicily
immediately.'

'Why the hurry?' demanded Richard.

'Because, my dear friend, I have tarried here too long.
Tomorrow I set sail for Acre.'

'So you would take the city that all the honour might be yours.'

'It is easy to prevent that by coming with me.'

'My bride and my mother are on the way here.'

'Divert them to Acre.'

'What! To an enemy stronghold?'

'We have dallied too long, Richard. I intend to go now. Come with me.'

'What of my bride?'

'What care you for your bride?'

'You are mad, Philip.'

'Is it mad to speak the truth? You and I have little time for women. Oh, we must get our heirs it is true and I was blessed in my consort. I would she were alive now. But I felt no yearning to be with her, even as it is with you and Berengaria. I wish you to accompany me, Richard. Have you forgotten our plans?'

'Nay, I have not forgotten, but I cannot leave Messina now. I must receive my bride and my mother.'

'Then perforce it is farewell.'

'We shall meet before the walls of Acre.'

'It may be that you will find the golden lilies flying over that town by the time you make your sluggard's entrance.'

'We shall see, Philip.'

'Then you will not come with me?'

'I see that you would force me to a folly that you might say: "See Richard of England cared more for the King of France than he did for his bride." '

'You wrong me. It is your company I crave, not what people should say of us.'

'And I must say Nay. If you go now, you go alone.'

'Then I shall see you at Acre.'

Richard nodded.

Philip came to him and embraced him. 'Richard, mayhap you will change your mind.'

Richard shook his head. Philip turned away and went from the room.

In the bay the French fleet was preparing to leave.

It sailed out of Messina just as the ship bearing Berengaria and Eleanor sailed in.

*   *   *

Richard was on the shore to greet his bride and his mother. Eleanor came first, her eyes alight with pleasure to see her noble-looking son. Every time she saw him after an absence she was amazed at his good looks. She glanced at Berengaria beside her. The girl was bemused. What bride would not be at the sight of such a magnificent bridegroom?

How graciously he received them; he took Berengaria's hands in his and gravely kissed her. Then he embraced his mother.

As they rode together to the lodging which he had pre-pared for them. Richard's spirits were lifted a little. Beren-garia was indeed elegant. She was exquisitely gowned, her hair was hanging loose and was covered by a mantilla-like veil; her long gown flowed about her slender figure and those who had come to watch her were enchanted by her grace.

At the house Joanna was waiting for them. When she saw her mother she forgot all ceremony. They ran to each other and Joanna was clasped in a loving embrace.

'My dear dear child,' cried Eleanor with emotion.

'It has been so long since I saw you,' replied Joanna. 'Oh, Mother, you are still beautiful ... in spite of everything. You always will be.'

'And you too, my dear. Oh, it has been such a time and what events have plagued us both and now we are together for but a short time.'

'Need it be so?'

'I fear it. There is much I have to say to your brother and I want you here, daughter, for I think we shall need you.'

'Everything I have is at your service and that of Richard.'

'He has been a good brother to you.'

'None could have been better,' said Joanna fervently.

Berengaria and Joanna appeared to have taken to each other. Berengaria was ready to be delighted by any member of her new family and Joanna wanted to show her gratitude to Richard by being charming to his bride.

Eleanor, watching them together, was delighted. That they should be good friends was part of her plan.

She was very eager to talk to Richard and she wished to do so out of earshot of the two young women. She suggested that Joanna conduct Berengaria to her apartment and leave her a while with her son.

When she and Richard were alone she said: 'Well, events

are moving at last. It is time. I am deeply concerned about affairs in England.'

Richard looked a little weary. A fact which disturbed her.

She spoke to him somewhat sharply. 'Never forget, Richard, that you are King of England.'

'Indeed I do not.'

'You have responsibilities there.'

'I have one great responsibility at this time, Mother. I have sworn on my solemn oath to free Jerusalem from the Infidel.'

'I know this well, but you have also been crowned in Westminster and sworn another oath. The English grow restive under Longchamp. Sometimes I think it was unwise to raise that man so high.'

'He is clever and Hugh Pusey of Durham is his co-justiciar.'

'They are quarrelling. Your father always said that Longchamp was a man to be wary of.'

'I found him hard-working and devoted.'

'He is unpopular. Appearances are important and he is far from prepossessing. Being deformed and lame is bad enough, but as his manners match his looks the people are against him. There is going to be trouble in England, Richard. Either you or I must be there without delay and if you will not go, then I must.'

'Will you do that?' asked Richard eagerly. 'Only you can.'

'I will, Richard, but you must know that each day could be important.'

'Do you wish to leave us as soon as you have come?'

'I must. As soon as the wedding is over I must go back to England.'

'The wedding...' murmured Richard. 'It cannot be hurried.'

'Hurried!' cried Eleanor. 'My dear son, we have been waiting weeks to get here.'

'We are in Lent.'

'Well?'

'You cannot suggest we should marry at such a time. It would be a bad augury. It might affect the outcome of the crusade.'

She looked at him in dismay. Oh, God, she thought, he is reluctant for this marriage. Why so? Where could he find a more attractive and docile princess?

But he had never complained about the delay in his marriage to Princess Alice. The answer was, of course, that Richard was not eager for any marriage. The controversy over Alice had not disturbed him in the least. In fact he had been glad of it.

She could see at once that it would be unwise to press for an early marriage.

She did say: 'The King of Navarre will expect his daughter to be married soon.'

'So shall she be when the time is ripe.'

'And I dare not tarry here, Richard. If you would hold England I must be there to see none try to snatch it from you.'

'You are surely not thinking of John?'

'I am thinking of any who might try to cheat you of your inheritance. I must be there, Richard. You know I am the only one you can be absolutely sure of.'

'I know it well.'

'Then I will leave for England.'

'When?'

'Within a day or so.'

'Oh surely not so soon, Mother!'

'It must be so. Berengaria needs a chaperon ... until you marry her. Of course if the ceremony took place now while I was here...'

'It is quite impossible. I have to think of the consequences of a Lenten wedding.'

She was silent. Then she said: 'You must marry her, Richard, as soon as Lent is over.'

'Indeed it is my wish to do so.'

'But I cannot stay for the end of that season. By good fortune Joanna is here.'

'Joanna yes. She shall be Berengaria's duenna.'

Eleanor sighed. There were deep misgivings in her heart. Possible trouble in England, and Richard, after all the anxieties and difficulties of extricating himself from marriage with Alice showing no great desire for marriage with Berengaria.

She would speak to Joanna. Her daughter was wise. Then she must make her preparations to depart. It was imperative that Richard should not lose the crown of England.

*　　　*　　　*

Eleanor was desolate, she told Joanna. She had so recently joined her family and now she must tear herself away from it. Alas, this was a common enough turn of events in royal families.

'My dearest daughter,' she said, 'how wonderful it is for us to be together and how sad that we soon must part. You have been more fortunate than most for, although you are a widow now, your husband was a good man.'

'He was very good to me, Mother.'

'Fortunate Joanna! How many of us can say that? Torn from our families as we are and given to men because they have a crown or some title, ours is a hard lot and when it turns out happily that means God and all his angels are with us. I am concerned for our young Berengaria.'

'She will be happy, Mother. Richard will be good to her.'

'He might be a little neglectful.'

Joanna looked startled, and Eleanor went on quickly: 'Richard is a warrior. His great obsession now is with this crusade. He would not want it jeopardized in any way even by marriage.'

'I have just met Berengaria but I am sure that she is gentle and kind and will be a good wife and that only Richard's well-being will matter to her.'

'I think this, too, but it is not of Berengaria that we speak, daughter. It is of Richard. I want you to stay with Berengaria. Be a good friend to her. I know you will be to your brother. She will have to accompany him to Acre. For some that might be an exciting adventure, but I fancy Berengaria would prefer a less eventful beginning to her married life. Go with Berengaria, Joanna. Be a good friend to her.'

'It is what I wish with all my heart.'

'You give me great comfort. Berengaria will help you and you will help her and I can return to England with an easier mind.'

'You will surely stay to see them married, Mother?'

'I had believed the wedding would take place immediately.'

'Why should it not? There is no obstacle now.'

'Alice is swept out of the way but it seems there is Lent.'

'It could be a quiet ceremony. We could celebrate afterwards.'

'Your brother thinks otherwise. He wishes to postpone the wedding until after Lent.'

'Then stay with us until then.'

'I cannot, Joanna. I know it would be unwise. I do not wish your brother to lose his kingdom. I must leave immediately.'

'But you have only just come.'

'I know, my child, but there is a kingdom at stake. I must go back without delay.'

Joanna was appalled. The fact that it was Lent did not seem an adequate excuse for postponing the wedding in such circumstances. She was saddened by the thought that her mother was leaving them so soon but at the same time happy to think that she could be of use to her brother and a friend to his affianced bride for whom she was already beginning to feel affection.

In some apprehension Eleanor took leave of her family and set out for England. She had been only three days in Sicily.

As she stood on the deck watching the land fade from sight she wondered how long it would be before the wedding did take place and if at the end of Lent Richard would find some other reason for postponing it. He *must* marry Berengaria. There would be war with Navarre if he did not. He could not afford to lose friends. None could understand the call of adventure more than she did but it was adventure enough for a king that he had a kingdom to govern. It was also a duty to marry and get sons.

All would be well, she assured herself. It was merely a postponement. The marriage would take place; the children would come.

She deplored the fact that she was growing old. True, she retained her energy. Most people of her years would have retired to a nunnery. Perhaps she should think of expiating her sins but it seemed to her that a better way to do this might be to devote herself to her family rather than piously to prepare a way to Heaven for herself. There were not many who would agree with her and perhaps when Richard was safely back in England, the Holy City captured for Christianity, Berengaria the mother of several lusty sons ... perhaps that would be the time. And when would that be? She laughed knowing that the time if it ever came was years ahead.

When she reached Rome it was to find that Henry of

Germany was about to be crowned Emperor of the Holy Roman Empire. It seemed to her politic that she should be present at that ceremony.

She quickly became aware that her reception by the Emperor elect was a cold one. And no wonder since his wife was Constancia, sister of the late King of Sicily, who considered herself the heiress of that island on the death of her brother. Joanna had suffered imprisonment for supporting Constancia's claim but Richard had since made a pact with Tancred and had tactically accepted him as the new King of Sicily when he had offered his nephew Arthur as the husband of Tancred's daughter.

Richard had congratulated himself that he had come out of that affair well. He had forgotten that while he made his truce in Sicily he was making an enemy of the powerful Emperor.

Eleanor believed that Henry would have been a more useful ally.

She attended the ceremony at St Peter's Church and saw Henry and Constancia anointed and proclaimed Emperor and Empress. There was one moment during the ceremony when she was filled with secret mirth. The Pope, who was officiating, sat on the Papal chair, the imperial crown placed incongruously on the floor between his feet. The new Emperor, his head bowed in reverence towards this awesome figure, received the crown when the Pope sent it towards him with a movement of his foot and placed it on his head. To show that he could without preamble dispossess him if he wished the Pope then lifted his foot and kicked the crown off Henry's head.

Poor Henry looked extremely discomfited in spite of the fact that this undignified gesture was an accepted part of the procedure.

One of the Cardinals then picked up the crown and replaced it on the Emperor's head and the ceremony continued.

It was a thoughtful Eleanor who continued her journey back to England.

*　　*　　*

Berengaria was a little bewildered. She could not understand why her marriage should not take place. She knew that

Eleanor had been anxious about leaving her although she had impressed on her the fact that Joanna would be a substitute for herself. The Queen of Sicily would be Berengaria's companion and her chaperon, for although they were almost of an age—both being in their twenty-sixth year—Joanna because she had been a wife and was now a widow was more experienced of the world.

Berengaria could not help but be happy in the change, for although she had had the utmost respect for Eleanor she had been greatly in awe of her. It was comforting therefore to have as her constant companion a girl who was not in the least formidable.

The greatest similarity between Eleanor and Joanna was that they both admired Richard almost to idolatry and this was very comforting to the girl who was to be his bride.

Joanna now had excuses to offer for the delay. Richard was devout, she said, and he would feel it was wrong to indulge in all the celebrations which his marriage would entail. It was for this reason that he was postponing the wedding.

'It is only a delay of a few weeks,' soothed Joanna. 'You see, he has to be so careful for he must not offend Heaven by any act which could bring disaster to the crusade.'

Berengaria was only too ready to accept this explanation.

Joanna went on: 'I doubt not the wedding will take place on Easter Day. What a lovely day for a wedding! It is almost certain that this is what Richard has in mind. Then we shall be sisters in very truth. I was so happy when I heard that I am to accompany you. Do you feel perhaps a little alarmed at the prospect of travelling with Richard to the Holy Land?'

'It is not quite what my father thought would happen when he told me I was affianced. I think he thought that Queen Eleanor would take me back to England.'

'Without Richard! That is no way for a bride to live ... apart from her husband! You would hate that. Do you not think he is the most handsome man you ever set eyes on?'

'I do indeed, Joanna.'

Joanna extolled his virtues, told of his brilliant feats in battle, his sense of poetry; she sang the songs he had written and made Berengaria sing them with her; they talked of him continually and each day they expected to be told that the wedding was to take place. But time was passing and Richard was occupied with preparing for the next lap of his journey. He saw little of Berengaria and only when others were present; then he was always gracious to her although a little aloof, Joanna thought.

It was Joanna who decided to ask Richard what his plans were and she chose a moment when she could be alone with him which was not easy to do.

But Joanna was determined.

'Richard,' she said, 'what of your marriage?'

He frowned slightly and looked her straight in the eyes.

'What mean you, sister?' he said. 'My marriage ... it will take place at the right time.'

'When will the right time be?'

'It cannot be here at Messina.'

'But Richard, it is what we are expecting.'

'Who is expecting this?'

'Berengaria ... Everyone.'

'My dear sister, I am engaged on a holy crusade.'

'But your marriage is important too, Richard. Berengaria has travelled far and has at last reached you.'

'I know. We shall be married, but I could not allow the ceremonies to take place in holy week. You see that.'

'I do, brother. I see that clearly but it will soon be Easter. We thought perhaps you had decided on Easter Day. We should like to know, for there are certain preparations we must make.'

'Easter Day would be good indeed, but alas I must depart before that.'

'Before Easter Day! But that is but a week away!'

'I know it well. I must be sailing for Acre before that. The King of France is already on his way there and I have given my word that I will not delay longer. I waited here only for Berengaria's arrival. I cannot remain until Easter Day.'

'Then brother, should not the ceremony take place *before* you sail?'

'Nay, I must have a public wedding and I cannot have it during Lent, and as I must leave Sicily before Lent is over I clearly cannot marry here.'

'Could you not tarry a few more days?'

'Nay, sister, I have already tarried too long.'

'Then there will be no wedding here! Poor Berengaria, she will be so disappointed.'

'Berengaria will understand that I am engaged on a crusade.'

'Perhaps a quiet ceremony...'

Richard's eyes had grown a little cold. Joanna had begun to notice that this was what happened when he was displeased and she had learned it was a warning to stop pressing the matter under discussion.

'Well,' she said, 'we must needs wait. It means that you and Berengaria will not be able to travel in the same vessel since you will not be married.'

'I shall know what custom demands, sister. You may safely leave such matters to me.'

She was disturbed. Richard was certainly no eager bridegroom. She remembered that her mother had told of his coronation which had taken place on the third of September which everyone knew was a date to avoid, yet he had not been superstitious then. It was not as though he did not know at that time that he was going on a crusade. Why should he be so concerned about marrying in Lent when surely a quiet wedding, in such unusual circumstances, could not have offended Heaven?

Joanna had begun to think that there could only be one reason.

Richard was so eager to postpone his wedding that he sought any excuse for doing so.

*   *   *

In the middle of holy week they set sail.

Crowds had gathered to watch the ships depart, for it was a magnificent sight as the two hundred vessels left the harbour and started their journey eastwards.

The three ships which were in the lead, equipped for battle, their towers being raised above the decks so that they could with ease fire on enemy ships, were known as Dromones. In one of these ships the King's treasure was carried; in another were Berengaria and Joanna. The third, like the others, carried armaments and was prepared to go to the defence of any of the fleet should the occasion arise when it would be needed. These three were followed by thirteen troopships—the busses, two-masted vessels with strong firm sails. Richard brought up the rear with his war galleys—long slim ships equipped with rows of oars.

Berengaria and Joanna side by side on the deck could not help but be thrilled by the spectacle. The crowds on the shore were relieved to see the departure of an army which had brought trouble with it.

Berengaria, suffering from disappointment because their wedding had not taken place, was thinking how much happier she would have been had she been travelling in Richard's ship; Joanna had comforted her but it was bewildering after all this time to be still unmarried. It was true that it might have been wrong to have married during Lent, but why did they have to leave on the Wednesday before Easter Day? Surely they could have waited four more days since Richard had been so long in Sicily? If it were not for the fact that she knew Richard was such an honourable man she would have had very uneasy doubts.

However Joanna was beside her and a very warm friendship was growing up between them.

'Are you not thrilled, Berengaria,' she asked now, 'to be sailing with Richard's fleet?'

'Oh yes, but I wish we were in his ship.'

'My dear sister, and you not married to him! That would be most improper and quite out of the question.'

'We *could* have been married...'

Joanna put her arm through Berengaria's. 'It seems so to us, but how can we know all that is in Richard's mind? It was so with my husband. He was a ruler and sometimes he acted in a manner which was strange to me. When we are married to men who hold high office we must be patient, for things are not always what they seem.'

Berengaria nodded gravely. 'You are right, of course. How beautiful the island looks from the sea!'

'And let us thank God for calm seas. We shall be in Acre very soon.'

They were both silent thinking of the Holy Land and the desperate battles that were going on and had been for so many years. Berengaria and Joanna were both convinced that Richard would be the one to save that land for Christianity.

* * *

Good Friday dawned. A strong wind had arisen and was sending the louring clouds scudding across the sky. Richard following his fleet in his galleys spoke on the enormous trumpet which carried his voice to the leading vessels.

'A storm will break at any moment. Keep within hailing distance.'

They would do their best, but with the firmest of wills how could that be achieved in such a storm? Rarely had Richard encountered such violence. The sails were useless against the mighty wind and Richard's voice, shouting through the trumpet, could not carry beyond his own deck. He realized that his fleet would be scattered. Briefly he wondered what was happening to Berengaria and Joanna. If their ship was wrecked they would drown, but an even worse fate might befall them if they were washed up on an alien shore.

Peering through the rain, battling against the wind, calling encouragement to his men he endeavoured to raise the spirits of the crusaders who had come to the conclusion that there must be some among them who had incurred God's displeasure to such an extent that He wasn't pacified even by their vow to undertake a crusade.

'We are lost,' said one of his men.

' 'Tis not so,' cried Richard. 'We will weather the storm.'

'The rest of the fleet, Sire ... they are lost!'

'They will battle their way to Acre never fear ... or perhaps they will await us in Cyprus. We shall come safely through this storm, I promise you. All we must do is wait for the wind to drop.'

'God is against us,' was the despairing cry.

'Nay,' replied Richard. 'He but seeks to test us. If we are to have His help in taking the Holy Land we must show ourselves worthy. This storm is sent to test us. We shall come through. The Grey Monks will be praying for us now. They promised me they would do this in our need and God *must* answer their prayers.'

His words had a sobering effect, or it might have been that quality in him that made all men feel that he was unconquerable, for a calmness settled on the men. The fleet was scattered; their ship was being buffeted by the wind; the oars were useless and it seemed that at any moment the waves would engulf them; but their leader was Richard, and he was certain that they would come through. He had a mission and was convinced that he would not die until he had achieved it.

Such was the power of his personality that he could make

men believe this even as he did himself, so that they overcame their fears and went about their work calmly with the certainty that they would survive.

When in the night the wind dropped, a great shout went up from the decks of the King's ship: 'The storm is over.'

Richard shouted through his trumpet: 'All follow me. I shall light the way we are to go.'

He had a large lantern placed on the ship and ordered that by night this should always be lighted so that the other ships could see where he was.

In a few hours the wind had become light, and billowing the sails favourably, and the ship went on without further mishap into Crete, there to discover what havoc the storm had wrought and how many of the ships were lost. It was now the Wednesday following Easter day so he had been a week at sea.

To Richard's horror he discovered that the vessel which contained his royal treasure and that in which Berengaria and Joanna were travelling were not among those which had come through the storm to Crete.

He could not delay long. He must discover what had become of his gold and treasure and of course of his sister and his bride.

* * *

How frightening was the storm at sea!

Joanna and Berengaria had been advised to go below where they might not see the mighty waves pounding against the side of the ship.

They both felt ill but Joanna roused herself to comfort Berengaria.

'These Mediterranean storms arise quickly and as quickly fade away,' she told her. 'Richard will bring us safely through.'

'Alas,' said Berengaria, 'we are not sailing with him.'

'But under his command,' Joanna reminded her. 'Lie down, Berengaria, and I will lie with you. 'Tis better so.'

They lay side by side holding each other's hands for comfort.

Joanna talked of Richard and what success he had had in war.

'There is always war,' said Berengaria. 'How I wish there could be peace!'

Joanna was silent. There were some who wanted peace—her husband had been one. But what would men such as Richard do if there were no wars? They were made to be warriors. War was the main force in their lives.

She was fearful thinking of his ship now and wondering whether it was following them. In storms fleets were often scattered. What a hazardous undertaking it was to travel by sea and it was amazing how often it was undertaken. If they had been on Richard's ship she would have been much happier. This brought her back to the strange fact that Richard had not been in any hurry to marry. Joanna had thought a great deal about that. Why was it? she wondered. Berengaria was beautiful—not outstandingly so perhaps but still beautiful. She was eager for the marriage, ready to accept Richard as his mother and sister had presented him as the most handsome hero in the world. It was Richard who procrastinated.

He was not young. He should be getting sons.

And as the wind buffeted them Joanna could not help wondering whether the sea would claim Berengaria for its bride since Richard was reluctant to take her. Or how could they know what would await them on some foreign shore? Joanna had been a prisoner of Tancred and although she had not been ill treated, to be a prisoner was not a happy state. One could never be sure when one's jailer might decide it would be better to remove the prisoner altogether.

As she lay side by side with Berengaria and thought how innocent she was, she feared what might happen to them both if they were thrown upon some unfriendly shore.

They should have sailed in Richard's ship for the hazards of the sea were known to be great. How could a lover contemplate allowing his bride to face, not in his care, the unpredictable elements when one short ceremony could have made it possible for them to travel together?

The same thought which had worried her mother kept recurring to Joanna: Was Richard regretting his promise to marry Berengaria?

None of this did she convey to Berengaria. And as they rocked in their bunk, clinging to the sides of it, now and then involuntary exclamations of dismay breaking from them, suddenly it seemed that the storm was abating.

Joanna said: 'I believe we have come through.'

And during the fifteen minutes which followed it became obvious that this was so. They slept fitfully and as soon as the dawn came they went on deck and by the morning light were dismayed to discover that they and the other two dromones which had left Messina together were alone.

'Where is the rest of the fleet?' cried Berengaria. 'Where is the King?'

That was something which could not be answered. They could only wait and see what the day brought forth.

Battered and in sad need of repair they drifted on and at the end of the day they came in sight of land.

They had reached the island of Cyprus.

*   *   *

They dropped anchor.

What peace to be at rest! How wonderful not to feel the sickening roll of the ship under their feet! But they could not enjoy this peace so great was their anxiety, for Richard's ship was nowhere to be seen. The Captain of their vessel came to them and told them that he intended to land at Cyprus. There it seemed certain that Isaac Comnenus, who was known as the Emperor, would offer them hospitality. They could rest there until they had some news of what had happened to the rest of the fleet.

Feeling very uneasy and visualizing the many disasters which could so easily have befallen Richard, they prepared to go ashore, but before an hour had elapsed the Captain came to them to tell them that a small boat had come alongside with a message from Isaac Comnenus to the effect that he would not receive them. Such inhospitality was astounding, especially as he must know that Richard would be incensed at this treatment extended to his sister and his bride-to-be. It could only mean that Isaac believed Richard would never arrive at Cyprus.

A dreadful foreboding had settled on everyone aboard. They were at the mercy of the sea; their ships were in need of repair; the Emperor of Cyprus was refusing his help and the rest of the fleet with the King among it, had disappeared.

There was worse to follow.

During their first night off Cyprus a small boat rowed out to the ship and in it were several English sailors.

They had an alarming story to tell.

A few days earlier they had arrived at Cyprus in a very sorry condition. They had been helped ashore by seemingly friendly Cypriots who had assisted them in salvaging what they could from their vessel; and then, as soon as they and their goods were on land, had promptly taken the goods and cast the sailors into prison. By great good luck a few of them had endeavoured to escape and so had returned to the ship with the news.

This was very disconcerting, especially as the wind had risen again and was buffeting the ship as it lay at anchor. On one side were the unpredictable elements of the ocean, on the other the unfriendly Emperor.

The next day there was a turn in events. Berengaria watching for a sight of Richard's ship noticed a small boat coming out to their ship.

She ran to Joanna and, with her, watched the boat come alongside and two men board the ship.

In a short time the Captain appeared.

'There are messengers from the Emperor Isaac Comnenus who would speak with you.'

Joanna said: 'Please bring them to us.'

The Captain came with the two men who bowed low and showed great deference to the ladies.

'Our Imperial Lord sends his greetings,' he said. 'He fears there has been a misunderstanding. He now knows that the ships which were wrecked on his coast belong to King Richard of England. He has heard that you ladies have arrived and he wishes to offer you the hospitality of his country. If you will come ashore with us you will be received with all honours and the Emperor has had apartments made ready for your comfort.'

Joanna looked at the Captain whose expression was grave.

Berengaria was about to speak when Joanna pressed her hand.

Joanna said: 'I beg you convey our thanks to the Emperor. We need a little time to consider his invitation.'

'Time, my lady? You must be weary of the sea. The Emperor has a luxurious apartment waiting for you. All he wishes is that you will both be comfortable in the one he has prepared for you.'

'May we send you a message when we are ready?'

'If it is your wish, but the Emperor is waiting to greet you now.'

'We could not come at such short notice,' said Joanna. 'I beg you to convey our thanks to the Emperor and give us time to consider his kindness.'

The two messengers were persuasive. They enlarged on the delights of the island. The most luscious fruit grew there and the Emperor was very eager for the ladies to enjoy the delights it could offer.

Joanna however was adamant. Time, she reiterated. They must have time.

Finally the messengers rather ruefully retired. It was a relief for them all to see their little boat being rowed back to the shore.

'I was afraid,' said the Captain, 'that you would agree to go ashore. That is something you must not do ... as yet. I don't trust the Emperor.'

'I remembered that some of our men had been lured ashore, robbed and put in prison,' said Joanna. 'What think you they would do with the Princess Berengaria and myself if we fell into their hands?'

'Like as not keep you as hostages,' was the answer.

'So I thought,' said Joanna. 'We must hold out against his invitations.'

That they were right was borne out by further events of that day.

Some of the sailors who had been shipwrecked were seen fighting their way to the coast. The captain of the ships which lay at anchor immediately sent out boats to rescue the sailors on the shore and when they were brought on board the story they had to tell was alarming.

Two of the busses had been driven ashore and immediately seized on by the rapacious Cypriots. They had been helped salvage what they could from the ships and then imprisoned in the fort of Limassol, and left there without food or drink, the obvious intention being to starve them to death. Fortunately some of them had smuggled in their bows and arrows and were able to fight their way out in the sheer desperation born of the knowledge that certain death would be their fate

if they did not do so. Their joy was great when they saw some
of their own ships at anchor and their cries for help brought
immediate succour.

'How right we were not to go,' said Berengaria. 'What do
you think would have happened to us if we had?'

'The Captain thinks that we should have been held as
hostages,' replied Joanna. 'Richard would have had to pay
dearly for our release. It would have been disastrous for him.'

'He will be pleased with what we did,' added Berengaria.

'Yes, he will, when he comes '

When he came, yes. But where was Richard?

*   *   *

For several days they waited. The weather was bad and
they were in an exposed condition. Both Joanna and Berengaria were ill: and there was still no sign of Richard.

Joanna staggered on to the deck. On the island she could
see that troops were massing and apprehensively wondered
for what purpose.

Each day a small boat came out bringing the messengers
who had approached them before. They were always courteous and so patient. The ladies should trust the Emperor, they
advised. He was very angry with the first discourteous message they had received. It had been none of his doing to send
such a message. He wanted them to give him a chance of
showing how delighted he would be if they would but consent to become his guests.

Joanna replied that she and the Princess Berengaria
thanked the Emperor but they were not sure of King Richard's wishes and if the Emperor would but be patient with
them, they were sure the King's ship would soon appear and
then doubtless he could share in this kindly offered hospitality.

The messengers went away once more defeated and Joanna
went back to Berengaria, who looked pale and ill.

'Oh Joanna,' she said, 'how much longer do you think we
must stay here?'

'It can't be for long. Something will have to happen soon.
They are massing troops on the shore. I think it may mean
that they are planning to take the ships.'

'Oh, where is Richard?'

'If we but knew!' said Joanna. 'Oh, if only...'

But what was the use of bringing that forward again! Richard had been in no hurry to marry and because of this they were on different ships.

Two or three days passed. Joanna and Berengaria talked of their predicament.

'What if Richard is lost,' said Berengaria fearfully.

'I can't believe it,' answered Joanna fervently.

'But surely he would have come by now.'

'It is not so long. We came here on Wednesday. It is now Saturday. Only three days.'

Three days of being buffeted by fierce winds, three days of uncertainty!

'It seems like months,' said Berengaria.

On Sunday morning Joanna had made up her mind. She talked it over with Berengaria. 'We can't go on like this,' she said. 'We are getting short of stores and you are ill.'

'I shall be all right as soon as I am on dry land.'

'That is what I feel. We cannot stay here.'

'Then what shall we do?'

'We shall have to go ashore.'

'Trust the Emperor!'

'It seems the only way. He has troops on the shore and we are getting short of provisions. Perhaps he really did repent of the inhospitality.'

'And what of our men? Some of them are still held prisoner.'

'He surely could not hold us prisoner. My mother would bring a force against him and so would your father. Besides ... when Richard comes...'

'Yes,' put in Berengaria quickly, 'when Richard comes there would indeed be trouble if he did aught to harm us.'

'Then,' said Joanna, 'when the messengers come this afternoon, which it seems likely they will, we will go ashore with them.'

'Anything,' said Berengaria, 'would be preferable to staying at sea.'

Not anything, thought Joanna, but during that morning they made their preparations.

It was about midday when the ships hove into sight.

Joanna shouted joyously to Berengaria and the two young women stood on the deck shading their eyes against the glare of the sun. There was the King's fleet with his long lean ship to the fore. Their joy was complete when they heard his voice coming to them from the trumpet.

Richard had come. They had held out against the Emperor's blandishments. Now Richard would decide what had to be done.

The Fruits of Cyprus

WHEN Richard heard that his men had been imprisoned and their goods stolen, he was enraged. He did not however, as might have been expected, let loose the notorious Plantagenet temper.

He was seriously studying the position. He had suffered considerable delay in Sicily and did not want the same thing to happen in Cyprus if he could help it.

He knew that Isaac Comnenus was no friend to the crusaders. Indeed it was said that he was in league with the Mohammedan Princes and that the favourable position of the island on the route to the Holy Land, the perpetual violence of the storms which blew up suddenly in the area and his unscrupulous nature had brought riches to him and disaster to many a pilgrim or crusader. It was even said that if the opportunity arose his people would lure ships to disaster that they might rob them; and that any survivors were hastily thrown back into the sea so that they could tell no tales.

This might have happened to other fleets but it was not going to happen to Richard's.

His first act was to send a message to Isaac Comnenus demanding the return of all his seamen and reparation for the goods that had been stolen.

Contemplating the state the fleet must be in after battering its way through storms, realizing that Richard's men must be weary and many suffering from seasickness, Isaac was truculent.

He would not free his prisoners, he said. He would not return what he had taken. Anything that was washed up on his shore, he considered was his, and Richard should take care, for it seemed likely that he might soon join his friends in their prison and his treasure ship become the property of the Emperor.

No reply could have angered Richard more.

He spoke through his trumpet. He knew his men were suffering from fatigue but they would want to fight this arrogant Emperor, a friend of the Saracens who had been responsible for the death and imprisonment of many of their comrades.

'We are a little weary after all that has befallen us,' said Richard. 'You are tired and so am I. But by God's eyes, when I think of what this wicked man has done to those who trusted me and you, I am ready to go in and do battle as I never did before. I shall not rest until every living man who sailed with me is free and all that for which we have worked has been restored to us. You will follow me, I know, for God's honour and your own.'

A shout of approval went up. Yes, they were tired, they wanted nothing but to feel the dry land beneath their feet, they wanted to sleep off their weariness, rid themselves of their sickness, but when Richard commanded them, they would always follow.

The battle had begun. It was brief, for the Cypriots were useless against the practised skill of Richard's men. They quickly realized their inferiority and as they had little heart for the fight they dropped their weapons—which were only stakes of wood and knives—and ran.

Richard stepped ashore and, seeing a peasant with a horse, a sack, its saddle and stirrups of rope, he seized it and rode along the shore shouting to his men to follow him, for he saw at the head of a band of horsemen an impressive figure which he knew at once was the Emperor.

He shouted: ''Tis you then, Isaac Comnenus? Come then! You who have so boldly imprisoned my men and robbed them of their goods, come and we will joust. Fight me single-handed.'

Because Richard was to tall and because he had a bearing

which none other could rival, because his fame had travelled before him, Isaac began to tremble with terror. Confronted by this man who was a legend he saw death staring him in the face for he knew that Richard would have no mercy on his enemy, particularly one who had insulted and ill-treated crusaders.

Richard exulted when Isaac turned his horse and fled. He would have liked to give chase but on such a horse he saw that was useless.

Soon his horses would be brought ashore and then he would tackle the Cypriots in earnest. It was however dark before fifty of the horses could be brought on land.

'Enough,' he said. 'We will charge them with this small band.'

'Sire,' said a timid voice at his elbow, 'they are a large force and we shall be but fifty.' The voice belonged to a certain Hugo de Mara who was a clerk and had joined the crusade rather as a pilgrim than a fighter.

Richard turned on him angrily. 'You are fit only for clerking,' he said. 'Go back to your scriptures and leave matters of chivalry to me.' He turned and cried: 'Who is ready to follow me?'

Cries of: 'I am!' came from fifty throats.

Exultantly, perhaps a little delighted that his force was so small, for theirs would be the greater victory, they rode to the top of the hill. Below them in the valley were Isaac and his men. Shouting his rallying cry Richard galloped downhill and with great uplifting of his spirits, a feeling which was always with him on such occasions—and there had been many—he had the satisfaction of seeing his enemies scatter in all directions and the Emperor himself take to his horse, with the one desire to put as far between himself and Richard as possible.

Richard did not follow them. He contented himself with capturing Isaac's banner—a beautiful object wrought in gold. Nor was that all. The Emperor had left his treasures behind him, eager only to save his life. There were armaments and rich garments, food and wine. Taking these and several prisoners, Richard went in triumph back to the fort of Limassol.

There he made a proclamation to the people. He had not come in war. He had merely come to take back what had been taken from him. He had no quarrel with the people. Only with their Emperor. All citizens might go about their business in peace. If any of his followers subjected them to insult or ill-treatment, those of his men should be punished. He came in peace on his way to fight a Holy War. If the people of Cyprus showed friendship to him they had nothing to fear.

There was rejoicing among the people. They were not very happy under their Emperor who could be tyrannical. Many of them now came to the camp Richard had set up to present him with gifts. Cyprus was noted for its delicious wine so this was brought for the King and crusaders. There was also corn and oil, plump poultry and meat.

The men who came with these gifts assured Richard that the fact that he had put the Emperor to flight was a delight to them and they offered to help him in his conflict with Isaac Comnenus.

Richard accepted the food with appreciation and the offers of help with caution. But it was a good beginning. His hungry men could feast as they had not done since leaving Messina; he had kept his image clear for them—in fact perhaps he had added an extra lustre to it.

He was not displeased with the day's work.

He looked out to sea and saw the ships lying there. His next task must be to bring Berengaria and Joanna ashore.

*   *   *

Richard stood on the shore and looked out at the ships. There on the most elaborate of the dromones were Joanna and Berengaria. They must be conducted ashore immediately and he would himself go out to their vessel and bring them in. There had been a time when he had thought they might be lost and if they were would there be some recrimination from Berengaria's father because he had delayed his marriage and he and she had been obliged to sail on different ships. He realized that there could be no more prevarication and the wedding must take place before they left Cyprus.

He climbed on to the deck where they were standing waiting to receive him. Joanna gave Berengaria a little push forward. Berengaria would have knelt but he raised her up and kissed her warmly on both cheeks.

'My Queen,' he said.

Berengaria was enraptured. This was so much like an incident from her dreams. He had come and he was a godlike hero; he was all that she had dreamed he would be. She forgot his reluctance which had forced her to face the perils of the sea without his support; she forgot that he had somewhat churlishly postponed their marriage; she only knew that at last they were together, that the wedding was imminent and he was the greatest hero she had ever known.

How handsome he looked! The coldness had gone from his blue eyes and they were shining with pleasure. It could have been because of his recent triumph over Isaac Comnenus but Berengaria believed it was for her.

'And my dearest sister.'

They embraced.

'It will always be wonderful to see you, Richard,' said Joanna. 'But never could it be more so than at this time.'

'My poor dear ladies! It has been a trying time for you. But you never doubted, did you, that I would come for you?'

'Never,' said Berengaria fervently.

'Now we will leave this ship and go ashore. I have had a lodging made ready for you.'

'And the Emperor?' asked Joanna.

'He is cooling his anger some miles away. He dare not come too near. His people do not greatly love him. I have had very little difficulty in making friends with them.'

'Did we do right not to go ashore?' asked Berengaria.

'Indeed you did. He would have made you hostages. I should soon have rescued you, there is no doubt of that; but by staying on board you have saved me that trouble.'

'I am so glad we did,' said Berengaria.

Richard watched her stealthily. He thought: She will be docile. If I must marry, Berengaria is as good as any wife could be.

'Now,' he said, 'I wish you to be luxuriously housed. I have ordered that a banquet be prepared for you. This is a fruitful island and the people live well here. I want to compensate you for all you have endured at sea for my sake.'

'We are amply repaid by having you here with us,' replied Berengaria.

Joanna asked when the wedding was to take place.

'It will be here in Cyprus,' said Richard. 'I cannot risk

having you two sailing in any ship but my own from hence-
forth.' He turned to his sister. 'How happy I am that you are
with Berengaria. It was a thought which gave me great comfort. It was sadness which brought you with us, of course, for
had you been a wife instead of a widow you must have remained in Sicily. But then had your husband not died we
should not have lingered in Sicily. We should be at Acre by
now. But what is the use of saying if this and if that. So it is
and so we must accept it. But, sister, you give me comfort.'

'My dearest brother, then I am as happy as it is possible for
me to be in these circumstances. I am a widow but I have my
uses, and your bride and I love each other already as good
sisters.'

He slipped an arm about both of them and they made their
way to the waiting boat.

They were quickly rowed ashore.

One of the noblemen of the island had put a house at
Richard's disposal and in this he installed the ladies. It was
luxurious.

Berengaria and Joanna shared a room, for they agreed they
would feel uneasy if they were separated.

'But, my dear sister,' said Joanna, 'you have Richard to
protect you from now on.'

*   *   *

Richard slept that night in the magnificent tent which he
had captured from Isaac Comnenus. Made of silk, it was the
finest he had ever seen.

He did not, however, pass a restful night. Sleeping on
foreign soil he must be constantly alert. It was hardly likely
that Isaac would allow things to remain as they were and there
would most certainly be a counter attack, and when it came he
must be ready. He was not unduly disturbed on this score.
Battle was his life; it thrilled him, stimulated him, made life
exciting as nothing else could, and he had little doubt that
when the time came to do battle the Emperor would be
vanquished.

There was another matter which gave him great uneasiness.
His marriage! There would be no avoiding it now. He had
gained a brief respite but there could be no more procrasti-
nation. Already people were asking why he had not married

Berengaria in Messina. Why had he not? Even he did not quite know the answer. He had intended to marry her. He must marry her. He was thirty-four years of age and he must get a son. It was expected of him.

Oddly enough the thought of a son did not excite him very much. Most men—and perhaps in particular kings—passionately desired sons, in fact considered them necessary for they were eager to see the direct line of succession carried on. Yet he felt indifferent.

What if he died without sons? There was Arthur, his brother Geoffrey's son, whom he had made his heir. The English would not care for him though, because he would not seem English to them. He had a foreign mother, Constance of Brittany, whom Geoffrey had married for the sake of her estates, and the boy would have lived most of the time far from England. But besides Arthur there was his brother John.

Ah, that was the darker side of the picture. John was in England and doubtless casting covetous eyes on the throne. John was not meant to be a king. He was sure of that. There was a cruel streak in John; there was a selfishness, a ruthlessness, an indifference to public opinion ... all characteristics which would not make a good ruler.

Perhaps he should order Constance to take Arthur to England so that the boy could be brought up in the court there.

What thoughts were these for a youngish man to have on the eve of his wedding! He was strong and lusty, and Berengaria was a healthy young woman. Why should he be considering his brother's son, even if the boy concerned was the true heir to the throne?

He knew the answer which was that he did not want to marry. He did not care for women and he did not particularly want children. Was he thinking of his own family ... that brood of sons, of which he was one, who had fought against their father and made his life an unhappy one? No, it was not that. He was a man who loved to go into battle. The feel of a horse beneath him, the sight of the enemy in full flight, conquest—and best of all a Holy Enterprise. This was what he wanted ... this and this only.

He seemed to see Philip smiling at him slyly.

This only, Richard?

He must face the truth. He had been guilty of lewd pleasure. There were times when he indulged without restraint in orgies which later filled him with shame. He would repent and for a while he would care for nothing but his battles. He was a great soldier—none could deny that—the greatest of his day. It was what he wanted to be; and more than anything in the world he wished to be known as the man who drove the Saracens from the Holy Land and brought it back to Christianity.

'And certain friendships are good to have.' He could almost hear Philip speaking.

Why had he allowed Philip to go on to Acre without him? What when they met there? He could picture the sly smiling eyes of the King of France.

'And your marriage, Richard, how was it?'

And all the time Philip would know full well that there had rarely been a more reluctant bridegroom than the King of England.

He slept at last. Day had broken when he awoke. There were noises outside his tent, the sound of excited chattering voices.

He dressed hastily and went out to see what was the cause of the excitement.

No sooner had he appeared than several of his knights came hurrying to him.

'Three galleys have just come into sight, Sire. Look. You can see them ... out there on the horizon.'

Richard could see them.

'By God's eyes,' he cried, 'whose can they be?'

For the moment he had felt a wild excitement, for he had thought that they might well be Philip's. The storms which had beset him would have worried the French fleet and the French were not as good sailors as the English. They lacked that passion for the sea which most Englishmen felt, and preferred to travel by land when possible.

But it was clear that they were not French ships.

'I myself will go out and see who comes into Cyprus,' said Richard.

His friends began to dissuade him but he waved them aside. He wanted to know who the visitors were and was too impatient to wait on shore while someone else was sent out to discover.

He was rowed out to the galleys, taking his trumpet with him.

When he approached the first of the galleys, he shouted through the trumpet: 'Who is this who comes to the Island of Cyprus?'

Someone was standing on the deck shouting back.

'This galley belongs to the King of Jerusalem.'

The King of Jerusalem! thought Richard. Alas, it was now an empty title. But he guessed that this was Guy de Lusignan who had been deposed when the Saracen armies had captured Jerusalem. Saladin now reigned in the place which had once been Guy's.

'And what do you here?'

'I come seeking the King of England.'

'Then your search is ended,' replied Richard. 'The King of England is here before you.'

'Praise be to God. Will you come aboard?'

'Aye, I will,' said Richard.

When he stood on the deck, Guy de Lusignan knelt and kissed his hand.

'The Lord is with me at last,' he said. 'I knew that you were on your way to Acre and I hoped to intercept you.'

'You have come from Acre?' said Richard.

'I have. The French King is already there.'

'Has he made many conquests?' asked Richard jealously.

'Nay, he is no great soldier. But he is a great schemer as I know to my cost.'

'How is that?' asked Richard.

'He works against me.'

'How can that be? His aim is to take the crown from Saladin and restore it to a Christian king.'

'A Christian king, my lord, but he has chosen his own man, whom he will support. If we regain the Holy City ... *when* we regain the Holy City he will nominate Conrad de Montferrat as King in my place.'

'Why so?'

'Because Montferrat would be his man.'

'Philip is a statesman. He thinks always of the advantage to France.'

'He has shown himself to be my enemy. I have come to you. I wish to put my services at your command. If you will support my claim I would snap my fingers at the King of France.'

Richard said slowly: 'My friend, we must talk of these matters.'

*   *   *

He did, but his main preoccupation now must be his wedding, never forgetting of course that Isaac had been driven back only a few miles and could at any time muster his forces for an attack. Nevertheless the people of the island were clearly friendly and the prospect of a royal wedding delighted them. Such was Richard's personality that although he had come to their island a short while before and was now installed as a conqueror they were ready to accept him and share in his wedding celebrations.

His own chaplain Nicholas was to perform the ceremony and Richard smiled grimly to think how chagrined the Archbishop of Canterbury was going to be because it was a prerogative of that Archbishop to officiate at the weddings of England's Kings. It was certainly going to be an unconventional wedding.

Still, the circumstances were such as made that necessary, and although Richard would have been prepared to postpone the wedding until his return to England he realized that was quite out of the question.

In their apartments Joanna helped prepare Berengaria for her wedding. She was a beautiful bride. Her long hair was parted in the centre and fell on either side of her face; a transparent veil covered the hair and this veil was held in place by a jewelled diadem. She looked serene and happy and even more than usually elegant in her long clinging white gown.

Joanna studied her with pleasure. What a relief that the marriage was at last going to take place! Surely nothing could happen to prevent it now. Would Isaac Comnenus decide to attack while the ceremony was in progress? No, he was in no position to attack. He had been driven away and Richard was so confident that he had been beaten that he was considering having himself crowned King of Cyprus. He had the people with him and now Guy de Lusignan had come with his three galleys full of men to support him. No, Isaac would not be so foolish and the marriage must go through without a hitch.

'You are happy, Berengaria?' said Joanna.

There was no need for Berengaria to answer that. 'Richard is so wonderful,' she said. 'I never cease to marvel that I should be his chosen bride. From the moment I first saw him when he came to my father's court I loved him. I had never seen such a handsome, such a chivalrous knight. And then...'

'You waited,' said Joanna. 'You waited a long time for him, Berengaria.'

'But the waiting is over now.'

'May you be very happy,' said Joanna fervently.

'I shall. I know I shall.'

'Amen,' whispered Joanna.

'Joanna, I wonder what Alice is doing now. I wonder what she will think when she hears...'

'She will be going back to her brother's court now I doubt not.'

'Poor Alice!'

'Do not pity her too much, Berengaria. Perhaps she was happy while the King lived.'

'But the shame of it!'

'Perhaps she did not feel the shame.'

'How could she not when it was there?'

'It may not have seemed so to her.'

'Oh, but it must have, Joanna.'

Joanna thought: How innocent she is! May all go well with her.

She wondered whether she had heard the whisperings about Richard and whether she would have understood them if she had.

*   *   *

When Richard rode out to his wedding the people stared in astonishment at this splendid figure.

This was to be a double celebration. First the wedding and then the coronation for he had decided to have himself crowned King of Cyprus. The island was rich; its people were dissatisfied with Isaac Comnenus and he, Richard, was in a position to defeat Isaac utterly. What treasure would be his! He could install a deputy of his own choosing to hold the island for him when he went on his way to the Holy War. He had done very well in Sicily but he would do even better in Cyprus.

Because this was his intention he had exploited to the full that which he knew to be one of his major assets—his dazzling appearance. He appeared as a god and was accepted as such; his height and fair good looks gave all that was necessary to add to the illusion. So he rode out in a rose-coloured tunic, belted about the waist. His mantle was dazzling, being of silver tissue patterned with stripes and decorated with half moons of silver brocade. His head-dress was scarlet decorated in gold. He shone; he glittered; he was indeed like a being from another world.

He did not ride but walked to the church, his Spanish horse being led before him by one of his knights also splendidly garbed though of course in a fashion not to be compared with that of the King. The horse's saddle was decorated with precious stones and gold, and never before had the Cypriots seen such glory.

And in the church he was married to Berengaria. She felt exultant, for this was like a dream coming true—a dream that had haunted her since she had seen this perfect knight ride into the joust with her favour in his helmet.

Not only was she Richard's wife, she was also Queen of England and Cyprus, and the heavy crown that was placed on her head when the diadem was removed was a double crown.

How the people cheered them—not only the crusaders but the islanders.

With Richard she sat at the table and the feasting began. There was merrymaking, songs and dancing; and Richard himself played his lute and sang a song of his own composing.

This, thought Berengaria, is the happiest day of my life.

When night fell he conducted her to their bedchamber. He was not an ardent lover but she did not know this. To her he was the most perfect being the world had ever known and she was in a state of bliss because fate had made her his bride.

*   *   *

The day after the wedding, messengers came from Isaac. He craved a meeting with the King of England and their meeting place should be in a field near Limassol. He wanted to treat for peace.

Richard was eager for the meeting too and it was arranged.

Donning his wedding finery Richard rode out to the field and when he reached it he saw that on the far side Isaac waited with a company of men.

Richard dismounted and his magnificent Spanish steed was led before him as it had been when he was on his way to the church for his wedding. He had never looked so glitteringly godlike and formidable. At his side hung his tempered steel sword and he carried a truncheon. He came as the conqueror and Isaac quailed before him.

Isaac knelt and Richard inclined his head.

'You sue for peace,' said Richard. 'That is well but I shall expect recompense for what you have taken from my men.'

'I shall be happy to give it, my lord,' said Isaac humbly.

'My men have been shipwrecked and their goods taken from them. Many have suffered imprisonment.'

' 'Tis true, I fear, my lord.'

'These wanton acts deserve punishment.'

Isaac studied the King. There was an innate honesty in those blue eyes. The King of England it was said was very different from the King of France. Richard was direct—Yea and Nay, they called him, and that meant that when he said something he meant just that. There was no subterfuge about him. In a king this could be naïve, and Isaac was far from naïve. He was in a difficult position. He had made a great mistake when he had allowed his people to plunder Richard's ships. He should have welcomed them, curried favour with Richard; but how was he to have known that Richard would arrive in Cyprus? He might so easily have been drowned. He should have waited though and made sure.

Now here was Richard, the legend, the unconquered hero. One only had to look at him to see that he was a dangerous man to cross.

Thus it seemed to Isaac that there was only one course open to him. He must be humble, never forgetting that the weakness in Richard's armour was his inability to dissemble; his knowledge of warfare was great but his understanding of people non-existent. He made the great mistake, characteristic of his kind, in thinking everyone reacted and behaved as he did.

'Alas, my lord,' he said, 'my people have sinned against you and I must take responsibility for their acts.'

'You yourself have shown me no friendship.'

'For that I am at fault.'

'Then we are of one mind. As I said I shall need reparations.'

'That is to be expected. I will pay you twenty thousand marks in gold as recompense for the goods which were taken from the shipwrecks.'

'That is well but not all,' said Richard.

'I have thought a great deal about your mission to the Holy Land. I shall pray for your success.'

'I need more than your prayers, Isaac. This is a costly enterprise.'

'The twenty thousand marks will doubtless be of use to you.'

'They will, but I need men. You must come with me. I doubt not your sins are heavy and you are rich ... or you were until you fought against me and my holy project. This will be a lesson to you, Isaac. Not only did you work against me but against God. You must ask forgiveness for your sins and the only manner in which you can do this is by joining my army.'

'My lord, I have my island...'

'Nay, Isaac. You no longer have an island. I have been crowned King of Cyprus and your people were very willing that it should be so. You will join my company and bring with you one hundred knights, four hundred cavalry and five hundred armed footmen.'

'I have not these men.'

'You can find them. You *will* find them. For these services I will appoint you the Lord of Cyprus, my vassal ruler. You will rule Cyprus in my name. If you do not agree to these terms you have lost Cyprus for ever.'

'But if I am to rule in your place how can I do this if I am fighting in the Holy Land?'

'You will name a deputy. He will rule under you who in your turn rule under me. I have had to appoint deputies to rule for me in England.'

'I see that it must be so,' said Isaac. Then realizing that it was no use pleading with Richard and that the King believed that if he had made a promise he meant to keep it he began to talk enthusiastically of what he would take with him on his journey to the Holy Land.

Richard said: 'You have a daughter.'

'My only child,' answered Isaac. 'She is very young.'

'And your heiress.'

'I fear to leave her,' began Isaac.

'She must be placed in my care,' said Richard. 'I will see that no harm comes to her and when the time is ripe arrange a good marriage for her.'

Isaac bowed his head. 'I know that I can trust my child with you,' he said.

'I think we have settled everything,' answered Richard.

Even he, however, was not entirely sure of Isaac. He told him he would have him lodged within the English lines and make sure that he was treated according to his rank.

Isaac thanked him for his consideration.

'It makes me happy,' he said fervently, 'that you and I are no longer enemies.'

*   *   *

Richard lay beside Berengaria in the silken tent which was part of the spoils he had taken from Isaac. He looked at her innocent face and felt suddenly tender towards her. He could be fond of her for she was gentle and undemanding. He supposed that, since he must have a wife, he could not have a better one.

He thought of Philip and his Isabella. Philip had his son, young Louis, and was proud of the boy. Perhaps *he* would be proud of a boy, if there was one.

There was nothing now to keep him in Cyprus and he could think of leaving very soon. Now that Isaac had made his terms and was ready to accompany him, he could be pleased with the manner in which everything was going. It was mid May—a long time since he had left England, but his mother might well be there by now and he need have no qualms for his realm. She would keep him informed of what was happening. And soon he would be at Acre. He would be with Philip. Together they would storm the place as they had always planned to. He would arrive richer than he had set out for he had treasure from Sicily and more from Cyprus.

He had added another crown to that of England. It had been worth the delay.

Berengaria stirred and his attention was drawn back to her. He had forgotten her in his contemplation of the battle to come.

She would always be there in his life to come; he would have to think of her occasionally. It had been less onerous than he had feared it would. He could accept Berengaria. She need not take up too much of his time and he would do his duty now and then; they would have sons and his mother and the people would be satisfied.

He rose and left his tent. It was early morning yet but he liked to be astir soon after dawn. He wanted to get on with his plans for departure for the weather was favourable and there was now no longer any reason why he should delay.

He would go to Isaac's tent and awaken him. He wanted to talk to him about an early departure. He felt sure that Isaac had little knowledge of what equipment he would need.

He noticed that there was a deserted air about that part of the camp in which Isaac and his followers had been lodged so he went into Isaac's tent. It was empty.

While he stood looking around he saw that Isaac had left a message for him.

Isaac had gone, the note told him. Surely Richard did not imagine that he could agree to the harsh terms that had been imposed. He had in any case changed his mind and was determined that he would keep no peace nor enter into any agreement with the English King.

Richard's fury was great. He had been deceived. Isaac was no doubt laughing at him now, but he would not laugh for long.

There was no time now for wedding celebrations.

*　　　*　　　*

Richard marched across the island towards the capital Nicosia. He found the Greek style of fighting strange and it was not easy at first to adjust himself to it. They did not face him and fight; they sniped at the flanks of the army, and having shot their arrows fled. As he had led his army he could not at first see the enemy so he immediately placed himself at the rear where he could more easily detect the marauding bands and whenever he caught sight of them prepared to charge.

It was unsatisfactory but in a way exhilarating as any new techniques in fighting must be to him.

At one time he caught sight of Isaac. A small party of Greeks had come up from behind and suddenly becoming aware of them Richard had turned to see Isaac himself but a short distance away. Before he could act Isaac had shot two arrows at him. They missed by inches ... poisoned arrows which would most certainly have killed him. Exhilarated to be so near his enemy Richard immediately gave chase, but Isaac's steed was especially fleet and he got away.

A horse made for running away, commented Richard, but he was a little shaken that the enemy had been able to creep up on him in such a manner.

He hurried on to Nicosia, the inhabitants of which surrendered immediately.

This was victory. When his capital fell to Richard, Isaac must realize he was defeated. In fact only a fool would have attempted to hold out against such a superior foe.

There was one thing which was troubling Richard. When he had started his advance he had felt the first signs of fever. It may well have been due to this that Isaac had almost succeeded in killing him with his poisoned arrows, for had he been as alert as he usually was, he would have been more prepared.

He trusted that he was not going to have one of the old bouts of fever, but as the days passed it became more and more certain that this was exactly what was going to happen.

To be ill at such a time could be disastrous.

He asked Guy de Lusignan to come to his camp. There was something about the young man that he liked. His nature seemed to be as frank and open as that of Richard himself, and the King felt that they were two of a kind.

Guy looked at him with real concern.

'Why, Sire, what ails you?' he asked.

'I fear it is a return of an old complaint.'

'You are often ill like this then?'

Richard laughed grimly. 'I know it seems incredible, but this fever has dogged me for years. It started through sleeping on damp earth when I was quite young. You know how it is.

One is careless. One fancies one is above the common ailments of the body. Alas, it is not so.'

'Will it soon pass?'

'I doubt not it will be worse before it is better. That is why I have asked you to come to me. In a day I may not be able to leave my bed. The fever will run its course. I want you to take over command of the army.'

Guy was astounded. He could not believe that the man on the bed, his face pallid, cold sweat on his brow was the great and glorious warrior who such a short time ago had been married to the Princess Berengaria.

Guy said: 'Should not the Queen be told? She will wish to look after you.'

'Neither Queen must be told—my wife nor my sister. I do not wish them to pamper me as though I am a woman. I know this fever well. It comes and it goes. I must keep to my bed until it passes; but we cannot wait for that to subdue this island. So, my friend, I wish you to take over. The time has come to conquer the entire island. We must not be satisfied with Nicosia. We must show Isaac that he has lost everything.'

'I will do exactly as you wish,' answered Guy.

'Then having taken possession of Nicosia we shall be lenient with those who thought they could stand out against us. There is only one order I give: All the men must shave off their beards. This I demand for it will show their humility. If any man defies me then he must lose not only his beard but his head with it. Make that clear. And once an order is given it must be obeyed. There must be no leniency. That is the secret of good rule. All must know that when the King speaks he means what he says.'

Guy listened attentively. He would let the King's command be known throughout Nicosia and then he would set out to subdue the rest of the island.'

Richard trusted him. He liked the man. Guy would serve him well not only because he was an honest man but because he needed Richard's support against Conrad de Montferrat, the candidate for the crown of Jerusalem whom the King of France was supporting.

*　　*　　*

He lay on his bed, tossing this way and that, the fever taking possession of him. He was a little delirious. He thought that his father came to him and told him that he was a traitor.

'That I never was,' he murmured. 'I spoke out truly and honestly. I fought against you because you tried to deprive me of my rights ... but I never deceived you with fair words...'

And as the waves of fear swept over him he asked himself why his father had always been against him. He seemed to hear the whispered name: 'Alice ... it was Alice...'

Alice! He thought he was married to Alice; she had become merged in his delirious imaginings with Berengaria. Alice, the child; Alice, seduced by his father in the schoolroom. An echoing voice seemed to fill the tent. 'The devil's brood. It comes from your Angevin ancestors. One was a witch. She went back to her master the devil but not before she had given Anjou several sons. From these you sprang. You ... your brothers Henry, Geoffrey, John ... all of them. There was no peace between them nor in the family.'

It was as though Philip were speaking to him, mocking him.

This accursed fever! Philip had said: 'How will you be in the hot climates? Shall you be able to withstand the sun?'

'As well as you will,' he had answered.

Philip had said: 'I believe you have had bouts of this fever for years. It's the life you have led.'

But if he remained in his bed the violent sweating fits would pass and with them his delirium. His brain would be clear again. It was only a matter of time.

There was good news from Guy. He had taken the castles of St Hilarion and Buffavento with very little trouble and in that of Kyrenia he had found Isaac's young daughter. He was awaiting Richard's instructions as to what should be done with her. Clearly she must not be allowed to go free, for she was Isaac's heiress.

All was well. He had been right to trust Guy. The fever was beginning to pass but he knew from experience that it would be folly to rise too soon from his bed.

He had given instructions that the news of his sickness was not to be bruited abroad. He did not want his enemies to set in motion a rumour that he was a sick man which they would be only too happy to do.

Soon he would rise from his bed; and if by that time Cyprus was completely subdued he would be able to set out on his journey to Acre.

When one of his knights came in to tell him that Isaac Comnenus was without and begging to be received, he got up and sat in a chair.

'Bring him in,' commanded Richard.

He remained seated so that Isaac should not see how weak he was.

Isaac threw himself at Richard's feet where he remained kneeling in abject humility.

'Well, what brings you here?' asked Richard.

'I come to crave mercy and forgiveness.'

'Dost think you deserve it?'

'Nay, Sire. I know I do not. I have acted in great error.'

'And bad faith,' added Richard.

'I come to offer my services. I would go with you to the Holy Land.'

'I do not take with me servants whom I cannot trust,' answered Richard tersely.

'I swear...'

'You swear? You swore once before. Your swearing had little meaning.'

'If you will forgive me...'

'The time for forgiving is past. I should be a fool to forget how you swore to recompense me for your misdeeds and then tried to kill me with poisoned arrows. I would never trust you again, Isaac Comnenus.'

Isaac was terrified. If he had hoped to deceive Richard as he had before, he had misjudged the King. Having cheated once he would never be trusted again.

All his bravado disappeared. 'I entreat you to remember my rank.'

'Ah, an emperor—self styled! I call to mind how you felt yourself superior to a mere king.'

'None could be superior to the King of England.'

'You are a little late in learning that lesson.'

'I beg of you, do not humiliate me by putting me in irons. Anything ... anything but that. Kill me now ... if you must, but do not treat me like a common felon.'

'I will remember the high rank you once held.'

'I thank you, my lord. All Cyprus is yours now. You know

how to be merciful. Have I your word that you will not put me in irons?'

'You have my word.'

'And all know that the word of the English King is to be trusted.'

'You shall not be put in irons,' affirmed Richard. He called to his knights. 'Take this man away. I have had enough of him.'

When he had gone he sat their musing and, remembering how he had been deceived by Isaac, he laughed aloud.

He called in two knights.

He said: 'I want Isaac Comnenus to be kept a prisoner until the end of his days. He can never be trusted while he is free. I have promised him that he shall not be put in irons. Nor shall he be. But he shall be chained nevertheless. See that he is made secure and that he is in chains. But the chains shall be of silver. Thus I shall keep my word to him. Chained not in irons but in silver.'

Richard was amused and suddenly pictured himself telling the story of Isaac Comnenus to Philip of France.

*   *   *

No word from Richard. Where could he be? Why did he not send a message to them? Surely he knew how anxious they had been.

Joanna tried to soothe Berengaria. He was engaged on a dangerous enterprise, she explained. It would need all his skill to subdue Cyprus. He knew they were safe and they must not expect him to be sending messages to them describing every twist and turn of the battle.

They sat together in the gardens of the house where he had lodged them.

'Here we are,' said Joanna, 'in this comfortable house. We can enjoy these lovely gardens. We should consider ourselves fortunate that he is so concerned for our well being.'

'I know,' said Berengaria, 'but I think of him constantly. I wonder if he thinks of me.'

Joanna did not say that she believed that when Richard was engaged in battle, he thought of nothing but that battle. She had always guessed he would be a neglectful husband, but it was sad that Berengaria must discover this so soon.

How could this girl so newly a wife be satisfied with anything but the undivided attention of the husband she adored?

Joanna watched a green lizard dart across the grey stone wall and disappear within it. What peace there should be in this garden where there were bushes of brightly coloured flowers and the pomegranates grew in abundance among the ever present palms. So quiet it was and yet not far away there was bitter fighting. Isaac would not give in easily even though he must know that he could not stand out against Richard.

'I heard a rumour last evening,' said Berengaria.

'What was this?'

'That Isaac has a daughter who is the most beautiful girl on the Island. She is very young and she has been held as a hostage.'

'It is inevitable that she should be.'

'She will be ... with Richard?'

Joanna looked astonished. Berengaria could not be jealous of Isaac's daughter!

'I doubt not that she will be well guarded.'

'We have not heard from him for so long.'

'Come, tell me what you have heard about Richard and Isaac's daughter.'

'That she enchants him. Joanna, can it be for this reason that we have heard nothing of him?'

Joanna laughed. 'My dear sister, do you imagine Richard sporting with this girl while the enemy is at the door?'

'There must be some lulls in the fighting.'

'You have much to learn,' Joanna smiled. 'Listen to me, Berengaria. Isaac's daughter may be the most enchanting creature in the world, but I'll swear Richard would hardly be aware of this.'

'Surely any man would be.'

'Not Richard.'

'You seek to comfort me.'

'So that is what has been ailing you. You have been jealous. You have listened to malicious gossip. I'd be ready to swear that Richard is aware only of Isaac's daughter as a hostage.'

'I wish I could believe that. But we have not heard for so long.'

'Berengaria, now that you are married to Richard you will have to understand that there may be long periods when you hear nothing from him and have no idea where he is. He is a soldier ... the greatest living soldier ... and he will always be engaged in some conflict. Now it is the conquest of Cyprus. Later it will be an even greater enterprise. You will need much patience and loving understanding. You must realize that.'

'I do. I do. But we have not heard and there is this girl. She is with him. People are talking.'

'People will always talk. Heed them not. Love Richard, and most of all never question him. He would not like that. He must be free. If you would lose his regard the quickest way to do so is to make yourself a burden to him. He has put you ... indeed both of us ... in a safe place. That was his great concern. Be grateful that he is so anxious for our welfare. It is the measure of his affection for us. I would be ready to wager a great deal that there is nothing in this gossip. I know Richard...'

She stopped and looked at Berengaria rather sadly. What if she told Berengaria the real reason? What if she said: Richard is not like some men who think that women are part of a conquest. Richard is not very interested in women.

No, she could not tell her that. All she could do was comfort her.

'There is always gossip about royal people,' she said. 'We look at a man or a woman and people immediately decide to bed us. Remember this, Berengaria. Stop fretting. Richard is engaged in a bitter struggle. You will hear from him as soon as he is free to think of us.'

'I had hoped he would be thinking of me constantly ... as I am thinking of him.'

'My dear sister, he has a mighty war to fight. You have but to sit here with your embroidery. You must see the difference.'

'Oh, I do,' cried Berengaria. 'I'm afraid I am foolish.'

'You are inexperienced of the ways of the world and of men,' said Joanna.

'How grateful I am that you are with me. You teach me so much.'

'I have been a wife and a widow, remember. These experiences tell.'

And while they sat in the garden they heard the arrival of horsemen.

Berengaria started up, her eyes alight with excitement.

'It is messages from Richard at last.'

They went out into the courtyard and there seated on a horse was a very young girl, a child merely. Her dark hair, thick and luxuriant, fell about her shoulders; her deep set eyes were dark, black-lashed and at that moment apprehensive.

On either side of her rode two knights and one of them had a message from Richard.

He wanted his wife and his sister to take this girl into their household. She was a Cypriot Princess, daughter of Isaac Comnenus. They were to treat her well for it was no fault of hers that her father had deceived the King.

Berengaria laughed with pleasure. The newcomer was an innocent child.

'Let the Princess dismount,' she cried.

Joanna said: 'We will ourselves look after her and see that she is treated in accordance with her rank.'

The girl stood before them and they were both filled with compassion for this poor child whose home was now in the possession of a conqueror. They determined to look after her. Indeed that was what Richard had ordered, but they would give her that especial care to make her feel she had nothing to fear.

Together they took her into the house. A room should be prepared for her near theirs. She should be their companion. They would tell her about their homes and she should tell them about hers.

The girl seemed comforted.

As for Berengaria, one sight of this child, so young and helpless, had dispelled the jealousy which had tormented her since she had heard that the beautiful daughter of Isaac Comnenus was in Richard's hands.

She asked her: 'Did you see King Richard?'

'But briefly. I was taken before him. My father was there and he held me in his arms and begged the King not to harm me. Then King Richard ordered that I be sent to you.'

Berengaria said gently: 'Have no fear. We will look after you and see no harm befalls you.'

'There is my father...' said the little girl, her eyes filling with tears.

'Try not to fret. He had defied the King but you are not to blame. I am glad that my husband has sent you to us.'

Indeed she was, for the coming of the child had made Berengaria realize how false were the rumours. Later that day, Joanna heard her singing softly to herself, and the song she sang was one which Richard himself had composed.

*   *   *

The fever was passing, but it had left Richard emaciated and he was careful not to mingle too freely with his men. The image of superhuman being must not be tarnished. Of course that he could be assailed by illness and emerge as strong as ever was in itself worthy of him, but he would wait until he was full of the old vitality before he would let his humbler followers see him.

He was grateful to Guy de Lusignan. But for him events might have turned out differently. It was well to have near him someone whom he could trust and he fancied that it was not only because of the support he could give his claim to the crown of Jerusalem which had inspired Guy. Guy was a great warrior.

He must rest awhile. He must suppress the almost irrepressible desire to be up. He had suffered so many bouts of this fever that he knew the course it would take and that he must be careful that there was not a relapse.

And as he lay there messengers came from the King of France. Richard received them eagerly. News of Philip always excited him and he had been wondering what was happening in the French camp. Fervently he hoped that Philip had not succeeded without him; on the other hand he felt apprehensive as to his rival's safety. Philip had declared to him when they parted that he would not take Acre until Richard joined him. It was to be a joint venture. This he had sworn, but Richard was wondering how far he could trust him. If the opportunity arose surely the desire to take the city and glean the accompanying glory would be too much for Philip to resist.

But apparently the opportunity had not occurred.

'How fares the King of France? Is he in good health?' he asked the envoys.

'The King of France is in good health,' was the reply.

'And what military success has been his?'

'There have been many skirmishes and he has made useful progress,' was the guarded answer. Ah, thought Richard exultantly. He has not progressed far. He needs me beside him.

'Our lord frets at your dalliance and commands the Duke of Normandy to come to him without delay.'

Richard's temper flared. It was always so when Philip reminded him that he was his vassal for Normandy.

'Pray tell the King of France,' he replied haughtily, 'that the King of England will leave when it pleases him.'

'The King of France was emphatic that the Duke of Normandy should come at once. His presence is needed at Acre. The King of France thinks that the Duke of Normandy forgets the purpose of this enterprise which is not to indulge in facile conquests on the way but to restore the Holy Land to Christianity.'

Richard rose; he tottered slightly. It was as much with rage as with weakness.

'The King of France must learn that one of the reasons for the fall of Jerusalem is the hostile treatment crusaders receive on their way to the Holy Land. I have subdued Isaac Comnenus who was no friend to the Christians though he ought to have been. It is my belief he accepted bribes from the Saracens to delay us all he could. Tell the King of France that he robbed my sailors, stole my stores and imprisoned my men. Does the King of France expect me to allow that to pass? Perhaps the King of France would. Perhaps that is why the Christians were short of provisions and weapons and the Saracens had the opportunity to take the Holy City.'

The messengers were taken aback and did not know what to say, but they felt that they had Philip's authority to remind Richard that as Duke of Normandy, he must bow to the wishes of his suzerain.

'We but repeat the orders of the King of France,' they muttered.

'Then return to him and tell him that the King of England does not receive orders from the King of France and that he will stay in Cyprus until that time when he feels the island to be completely subdued. Thus it will be a port of call for crusaders in days to come. Here they will rest in safety and comfort. They will be provided with the rich fruit of this island and we shall not have men arriving in Palestine emaci-

ated and sick from a long sea voyage. Nor shall we lose them
to the greed and villainy of rapacious islanders. Go now and
tell this to the King of France. Tell him I shall join him in
my own good time.'

When they had gone he lay on his bed exhausted.

He smiled slowly, contemplating Philip. Philip wanted
him there. He knew he could not take Acre without him. If
he had been able to he would have done so. Philip wanted
the glory of victory. The man who restored the Holy City to
Christianity would be received with acclaim everywhere in
the Christian world—not excluding Heaven itself.

It was an honour all crusaders sought.

But it was more than that. Philip wanted to see him.

*   *   *

And he wanted to stand with Philip before the wall of
Acre. Together they would take it, just as they had planned a
long time ago, when he had been a hostage in Philip's
hands during the lifetime of his father—and they had gone
everywhere together, riding, walking, playing, dreaming and
lying in bed together talking of the glorious deeds they
would perform when they went on their crusade.

Times had changed—they were no longer king and hostage; they were two kings of countries where rivalry was inevitable. Was it possible for the King of England to be
friendly with the King of France? Normandy stood between
them. Philip could never forget it. He would, like all the
kings of France, for ever remember how the Norseman Rollo
had ridden along by the Seine and taken possession of that
strip of land which became known as Normandy. Richard was
of Norman stock. This stood between them now and it always
would.

They were natural enemies and yet they were beloved
friends. They yearned to be together but they must constantly seek ways of scoring over each other.

It was an exciting relationship.

And now Philip was commanding him to leave Cyprus,
and for that reason he would stay longer than he had intended.

He talked the matter over with Guy who had become his
constant companion. Philip would be jealous of Guy. The

thought amused Richard. Philip had already set himself against Guy by offering his support to another candidate for the crown of Jerusalem when that city should be brought back to Christianity: Conrad de Montferrat. Why was Philip supporting him? Because he thought it would be to the advantage of France to do so. Always Philip thought of the good of France. Richard thought very little of the good of England. He was pleased to leave the governing of that country in his mother's capable hands.

'Guy,' he said, 'this island is now in our hands. Isaac is in his silver chains. His daughter is with the two Queens; the people like to live in peace and get on with their daily lives. We shall have no trouble here while Isaac is in captivity. It is merely a matter of appointing regents to hold the island in my absence.'

'That's so, Sire,' replied Guy. 'Have you any in mind for this task?'

'There are two Englishmen whose conscientious work has singled them out to me. I would trust them. They are Robert of Turnham and Richard de Camville.'

'I have noticed these men. I think they would serve you well.'

'Then you endorse my choice.'

'I do, my lord.'

'Go and bring them to me that I may put the matter to them. I will explain their duties and that I trust them to be good servants. They will administer the island and make sure that crusaders can always be sure of fresh meat, fruit and wheat when they arrive here on their journey.'

'You have already served the cause well, my lord. If you did nothing more crusaders would be grateful to you for ever.'

'The King of France does not share your opinion. He thinks I dally here and am more interested in making conquests than sailing on to Palestine.'

'The King of France is doubtless envious of your fame.'

'That may be. But I will not take orders from him although he continually reminds me that he is my suzerain through Normandy.'

'I doubt not that my lord reminds him that the King of England enjoys as great a name throughout the world as that of the King of France. Aye, and becoming greater every month.'

'I intend it to be so, Guy. Well then, we shall appoint our regents and then set sail. The ships should be well stocked with the good things of this island. What a fruitful place it is! A paradise! I confess I could linger here awhile. But on the other hand I feel the urge to go forward. I long to be storming the walls of Acre.'

'I doubt not, my lord, that you will soon have brought the siege to an end.'

'That shall be my endeavour.'

In the next few days Richard had fully recovered his health.

He immediately gave a banquet to celebrate his possession of Cyprus. The people came out of their houses to cheer him as he rode by. They liked the look of him; he was stern but just; and they were heartily tired of Isaac.

Richard had seen little of Berengaria. He sent a message to her and to Joanna to tell them that he was very much engaged with preparations for departure, but would come to them when it was possible.

When he did arrive he embraced them both rather absent-mindedly and told them to make their preparations to leave.

Berengaria looking up at him adoringly said that she always looked for his own ship, *Trenc-the-mere*, when she was near the sea and she was delighted because now that she was his wife she would sail with him in it.

'You cannot guess, Richard, the anxieties we suffered,' she told him. 'Not knowing where you were ... whether you were dead or alive.'

Richard was thoughtful. 'I have been thinking,' he said, 'that after all it would be most unwise for you to travel on *Trenc-the-mere*.'

'Oh but that is where I want to be. I want to be with *you*, Richard.'

'That is a good wife,' he said indulgently. 'But as a good husband I am concerned for your safety.'

'My great concern is yours.'

'Nay,' he said firmly, 'you cannot sail with me. What if already you are carrying our child, the future King of England!'

'We have been so little together,' she said mournfully.

'Oh, it is enough. I have hopes.'

'Could we not...?'

His lips smiled but his eyes were cold. 'I am a king, Berengaria. I have my duties. I am not even in my own country. Responsibilities are heavy on my shoulders. I have just conquered Cyprus, which is going to make a great difference to crusaders. Think of them hungry, racked by storm, all those days at sea and then coming to the haven of Cyprus where there will be fresh meat and fruits for them. They will bless King Richard.'

'There are already many who have reason to do that,' she said.

'It may be. But my orders must be obeyed. I cannot have you or Joanna exposed to the dangers which could befall my ship. As we progress our journey becomes more hazardous. There is one whom these people will seek first to destroy. I am that one.'

'Oh, Richard, let us come with you. The dangers will be nothing compared with our anxieties.'

'Nay, the dangers will be great. You will obey my orders, Berengaria. I say that you shall sail in another ship. Do not look so disconsolate. Joanna will be with you ... Joanna and the little Princess from Cyprus.'

He doesn't want me, she thought sadly. Why? What is wrong with me?

The King and the Sultan

THE June sun blazed down on the fleet of ships—one hundred and fifty of them. They were on their way to Acre and leading them was *Trenc-the-mere*. Shouting orders through his trumpet, commanding that none was to attempt to pass him, sailing close to the arid land, Richard's spirits soared. He would soon be in Acre. Before he had left Cyprus he had heard that Philip had broken the siege and filled with dismay he had hastened his preparations to depart. It had been a great relief to learn that the news was false.

And now on to Acre, to Philip, to make their plans together, to bring about the realization of a dream.

As they had sailed from Cyprus, Richard heard that one of his galley men wished to speak to him. This man told him that he had been in Beyrout and there seen a wonderful ship—the largest he had ever seen.

'It was a Saracen, Sire,' he said. 'Her sides were hung with green and yellow tarpaulins. I asked what this was for and was told that the Byzantine navy frequently use the deadly Greek Fire in their fighting and these tarpaulins are protection for the hull. Sire, this ship was being loaded with men and food. It was said that there were eight hundred Turks and seven Emirs to command them and they were on their way to Acre.'

'If this be true,' said Richard, 'it is small wonder that the siege goes on. They must be constantly supplied with food and troops.'

'And, Sire, that was not all. It was said that two hundred deadly snakes were being put on board the vessel and these were to be let loose in the Christian camp.'

'By God's eyes,' cried Richard, 'is this so then? I would to God I had the chance to meet such a ship.'

It seemed that his prayers were answered for between Beyrout and Sidon a ship was sighted on the horizon. Three-masted and flying the French flag, she was one of the biggest ships Richard had ever seen.

'I never knew Philip owned such a ship,' said Richard. 'If he had, surely I would have seen it. He would certainly have boasted of her.'

Richard suspected that she was not French and as they came nearer he saw the green and yellow tarpaulins on her sides and sent for the galley man who had told him of the ship he had seen in Beyrout.

He did not wait to be asked. 'That is the ship, Sire, the one I saw being loaded in Beyrout.'

Richard ordered one of the galleys to go forward and make contact with the ship.

The ship's answer was a shower of arrows, javelins and stones.

' 'Tis true,' cried Richard. 'She's an enemy. She must not be allowed to reach Acre.'

He gave the order to close in on her but the extreme height of the ship gave her the advantage and she was able to send down such a shower of arrows on to the galleys that the wise action seemed to be to retire.

Richard was furious. She was not going to escape. He could see that his men were losing heart for what they considered an unequal battle doomed to failure. But Richard never accepted failure. He was either going to capture or sink that vessel. She was not going to reach Acre with her reinforcements of men and food and her deadly serpents to wreak havoc in the Christian camp.

'Are you such cowards,' he cried to his men, 'that you shrink from action with the enemy? She is one and we are many. Shall you, soldiers of the Cross allow her to carry succour to the Saracen? If you allow these enemies of God to escape you deserve to be hanged, every one of you.'

As ever his magnetism mingled with his personal valour had its effect. Those men who, a few moments before, had grumbled to each other that to attack was folly, were now straining for the fight.

Some of them even attempted to board the ship, and as they did so their hands or heads were cut off and the air was filled with their piercing cries as they fell back into the sea. When several men leaped into the water and tied a rope to the Saracen's helm so that her progress might be impeded, this was more successful.

Then to the Saracens' relief Richard gave the order to retire. It was but a respite. His mind was made up. He deeply regretted that he could not take the vessel, and the thought of all that treasure on board dismayed him. What he could do, what he must do was sink her; and that was what he was going to do.

The prows of the galleys were iron which made of these ships excellent battering rams. They could drive themselves into the sides of the Saracen with such force that they broke her up. This they did until the sea was darkened by the bodies of drowning men and the ship's cargo. Richard tried to salvage some of the latter but without much success.

But the victory was Richard's. The Saracen would not sail into Acre. The besieged who would be eagerly awaiting succour would be disappointed.

Surely, thought Richard, this action must have brought the fall of Acre nearer.

*   *   *

After such an engagement the fleet must put in at Tyre. At last he had reached the Holy Land. How enthralled Richard was at the prospect of setting foot on that soil. For so long he had dreamed of this; now fulfilment was at hand. He felt sure that ere long he would have captured the Holy City itself.

Flushed with victory he landed, but if he had expected a warm welcome, he was disappointed for the Governor came riding down to the shore. He bowed coldly and said: 'My lord, I have orders from the Marquis Conrad de Montferrat that you are not to enter the town.'

'What means this?' cried Richard dismayed.

'My orders, Sire.'

'So I am to be governed by Conrad de Montferrat?'

'He has the backing, Sire, of the King of France.'

'Is this the Holy Land?' cried Richard.

'It is indeed, Sire.'

'Know you what I have but a few days ago sunk a great Saracen who was taking supplies and men to Acre? My men are weary. They seek rest, lodging, food, relaxation.'

'They may camp outside the city.'

'I shall remember this,' said Richard.

'Not against me, my lord, I beg you,' answered the Governor. 'I but obey orders.'

'Then I shall remember it against Montferrat and the King of France.'

'If there is aught I can do for you, sire, *outside* the town...'

'Nay,' snapped Richard. 'There is naught. We shall not stay long on your inhospitable shores. Have you heard what happened to one who was similarly churlish? He lost his island and now lies in chains.'

The Governor began to tremble and Richard thought: It is no use blaming him. He is not the enemy.

He shrugged his shoulders and turned away.

'Set up the tents,' he said. 'We rest outside the city.' And he thought: If this were not a Christian stronghold Tyre would go the same way as Cyprus.

But the men were weary and he was eager to get to Acre. There must be no more delay. And why had Montferrat backed by Philip behaved so to him? He supposed it was because he had sponsored Guy de Lusignan for the crown of Jerusalem when it was won. Well, Guy was worth a little friction. He did not regret favouring him one jot.

And now to rest.

The Queens came ashore—Berengaria with Joanna and the pretty little Cypriot maid.

'We watched the fight,' said Berengaria. 'Oh, Richard, I was terrified. But I knew of course that you would win. You will always win.'

Joanna embraced him. 'I was afraid for you,' she murmured.

'I am grieved,' he answered, 'that you were in a position to watch it. How glad I was that you were not in my galley!'

'Richard is so wise,' said Berengaria, but she spoke a little wistfully.

And the little Cypriot looked on with wondering eyes.

'There is much to be done,' said Richard. 'I have ordered that you shall be comfortably lodged. I must now leave you. There is much to be done.'

Was that all? wondered Berengaria as Richard turned away.

*   *   *

It was an auspicious moment. There before him lay the walled city of Acre, its towers and minarets set against a blue and cloudless sky. To the south of the city stretched ten miles of golden sands with palm trees dotted here and there; and on these sands were camped the armies from all over the Christian world.

Richard gazed in wonder. At last after so many irksome months he had arrived. He turned his gaze to the thick walls of the city—strong, formidable. Behind them lurked the Saracen enemy, as determined never to be driven out of this stronghold as Richard was to take it, for since the fall of Jerusalem it had become the capital of the Holy Land. For two years those Christian armies had sought to break the siege and take the city which was the gateway to Jerusalem.

Why was it so difficult to capture the city? How could the men and women of Acre hold out so long? Surely God was on the side of the Christians! And when Richard considered the ship he had sunk and all the men and provisions which had been lost in the sea he was not surprised at the endurance of those people. If such stores were being brought to them regularly, they had nothing to fear from a siege.

But he was here at last . . . yearning for the battle and when the fleet came into sight there were shouts from the shore and as he came nearer Richard saw the people gathered there to meet him.

There was an august figure there on horseback surrounded by a company of men. Philip! He was looking eagerly towards the ships. Richard knew for whom he was searching.

When Berengaria was ready to go ashore Philip waded out to the galley and, so that she should not get her feet wet, himself carried her to the beach. This was a significant gesture indeed, for Alice's fate was still undecided. It was characteristic of Philip to show the world that he felt no ill will towards Berengaria because she was now Queen of England in place of his sister.

But, wondered those who saw this gallant gesture, how true was his apparent acceptance of this state of affairs? With Philip no one could be sure.

Richard was the last to go ashore and there in view of all, he and Philip embraced affectionately.

'At last you are here!' said Philip. 'What delays there have been!'

'Necessary delays,' replied Richard.

'It seems years since Messina.'

'What a goodly array,' cried Richard. 'Men from all over the Christian world! How can we fail with such a company?'

'Come,' said Philip, 'I wish us to be alone together. There is much to be discussed.'

'First,' said Richard, 'I would inspect the troops. I want to know what we have here. What a motley!'

It is true. There were French, and English of course, Germans, Italians, Spanish, in fact as Richard had said every Christian nation appeared to be represented.

As Richard rode round the camps, cheers went up. There could be no doubt that his presence was a signal for rejoicing. His fame had gone before him. He was the unconquered and unconquerable hero of the Christian world. There could be no failure with him to lead them. They had long awaited his coming and now here he was, and this must mean that ere long Acre would fall.

He was glad to see that besides the troops from the Christian countries there was a goodly number of the company of Hospitallers—necessary to any army. These people lived up to their name and tended the sick and wounded and were very skilled in their work. They knew the value of foods and which were good in the treatment of certain ailments; they had linen for bandages and wine in which to soak them because this appeared to have healing qualities. When it was necessary to amputate a limb, which was often, they could brew a concoction of opium and mandragora with which to numb the patient's senses. They were an essential part of an army.

Richard's spirits rose. He could not see how these armies could fail—with God's help, and surely God would not deny that to men occupied in such a cause!

It was with great optimism that he came at length to Philip's camp.

Philip dismissed all his men that he might be alone with Richard.

'You should never have delayed as you did,' he chided. 'I've watched and waited and the days passed with still no sign of you.'

'I dallied with good results. I got treasure from Tancred and the island of Cyprus is now mine.'

'You did not come for personal conquests, Richard.'

'Cyprus is now a haven for crusaders. They may refurbish their stores and rest there. The men can have a few days' respite in delightful surroundings—fig trees, palm trees, beautiful flowers. It is an enchanting place. You will see how this will help us in our war against the Saracen.'

'Well, suffice it that you are here. That gives me great satisfaction.'

'Tell me, Philip, what has been happening in the last six weeks? I heard that you had taken Acre.'

'No. As if I would without you! Wasn't that a pact we made?'

'Pacts are not always remembered.'

'They should be between us two. Nay, we have had ill luck. These Saracens are fighters, Richard. Mistake that not. The climate here is terrible. We have been tormented by the hot wind from the south which they call the *khamsin*. It is horrible. There is sand everywhere. In one's clothes, in one's food ... there is no escaping it. It is a case of sand and flies everywhere. I hate this place, Richard. I want nothing so much as to be out of it.'

'How can that be? When Acre is taken we have to march on to Jerusalem.'

'Do not imagine it is going to be an easy victory. There is one man whose reputation matches your own. It is said that he is undefeatable. He is the great Moslem hero; even as you are the hero of the Christians. His name is Saleh-ed-Din. He is known throughout the camp as Saladin. He is a sort of legend. Yes, indeed, he is to them what you are to the Christians. I know not what will be the result when you two meet.'

'I shall be the victor, I assure you. I am going to take Acre within the next few days.'

'It is not as easy as you think.'

'It would not do to think it impossible to achieve.'

'Nay, but do not turn your back on the difficulties. I assure you they exist and they are many.'

'What happened while you were awaiting my arrival?'

'I was determined not to make a general assault until you came, so I contented myself with skirmishes. There is a tower known as the Accursed Tower because it is said to have been built with Judas's thirty pieces of silver. I thought this should be taken and we have battered it continuously but because we were using bores and battering rams our task was made impossible by the enemy's use of Greek Fire.'

Richard was acquainted with his deadly weapon used so frequently by the Saracens. It was a mixture of sulphur, wine, pitch, Persian gum and oil. When these substances were mixed together and set on fire they were almost inextinguishable. The only substances which could reduce their fury were vinegar and sand. The Byzantine Greeks had perfected this as a weapon and because of their many skirmishes with them the Saracens had adopted it to good effect. From a great height they would squirt this fire down on an enemy thus destroying all the contraptions which were put into action.

'Then,' said Richard, 'if they are using Greek Fire with such effect we must attack them from afar.'

He went on to tell Philip of the weapons he proposed to use. There was the tower which he had built in the Sicilian campaign, Mate Griffon. This he had brought with him and it should be set up again. It should be put on wheels and when the moment was ripe should be run up against the walls of the city and his men from its tower could step over the walls.

'You will see that my dallying as you call it has not been wasted. Valuable experience came my way because of it.'

'It was your presence I missed,' said the King of France. 'All has changed now you are come. The soldiers know it. And what is more important so does Saladin. Imagine him ... encamped on the hills beyond the city ready to come in if we should take it, ready to attack us when we are most exhausted. I should like to know how he is feeling this day with the knowledge that Richard the Lion is here.'

'To be more greatly feared than Philip the Lamb.'

'Do not underestimate me, Richard.'

'Nay, I should not be so foolish. If I did you would be reminding me of my Dukedom in Normandy.'

'You know that the friendship between us is greater than any rivalry. You know that we are friends before King and vassal.'

'Or King and King.'

'Aye, my Lord of England. And how I rejoice that at last you have come.'

He was not the only one. Bonfires were lighted that night. They sprang up everywhere in the Christian camp. The crusaders sang of his exploits. They had begun to call him the Lion-hearted.

In his camp Saladin heard the sounds of rejoicing and he knew that the name of Richard the Lion-Heart struck terror into the hearts of his men.

He wanted very much to come face to face with this hero whose fame had spread through Christendom and into his own ranks.

*   *   *

In the tent the two Queens waited for Richard to come to them. To Berengaria it seemed strange that she was never alone with her husband. She knew, of course, that he had a Holy War to fight; the sight of the camps and military activity before the city filled her with apprehension and the thought of what those people within its walls must be suffering made her very sad.

'I know they are not Christians,' she told Joanna, 'but they are people. I have heard that they are starving.'

'If that is so,' said Joanna, 'they will not hold out much longer and then it will all be over.'

'It will not be the end,' said Berengaria sadly. 'When they have taken Acre, what next? There will be more fighting, more camps like this. I thought we were all going to die during that terrible battle with the Saracen ship.'

'Nay, we'll not die. Richard will take too much care of us for that.'

Did she really believe it? wondered Berengaria. She herself had changed a little. She was beginning to realize that

Richard was not over anxious for her company. If he were surely there would be some time when they could be together?

The little Cypriot Princess who was constantly in attendance listened to their conversation and wondered what would become of her and whether she would ever be allowed to go home to her father.

Richard seemed to have forgotten their existence, though they heard that he often rode out with the King of France.

'He spends a great deal of time with Philip,' Berengaria commented, 'although he has little to spare for us.'

'It is good for the men to see them together,' Joanna excused him. 'It gives them confidence in their leaders.'

One day Richard did come to their tent, and with him was the King of France. Richard was kind and enquired after his wife's health but it was not the occasion for intimate conversation. As for Philip he was very courteous, particularly to Joanna, but as Joanna said afterwards to Berengaria, it did not mean anything.

'Would you like to be Queen of France?' asked Berengaria.

'No. If I married again I would wish to marry for love.'

'Perhaps you could love Philip.'

'I do not think I could and I would not want to marry merely because it would be a link for our two countries if I did. I believe that a Princess may be in duty bound to marry in the first place for state reasons, but when that marriage is over she should have a free choice.'

'Yet if Philip offered for you?'

'I could refuse.'

'Even if Richard wanted it?'

'Let us not consider that. At the moment neither of them has time for women. They have their battles to think of.'

'I believe some of the men have time for their women.'

'They are not kings,' said Joanna shortly. She turned to the little Cypriot and said: 'You listen. Perhaps you are wondering when a husband will be found for you?'

'Do you think there ever will be?'

'I am sure of it. Richard will find a husband for you when he is no longer preoccupied with his battles.'

And when would that be, wondered Joanna. She could not imagine Richard without a war to fight.

*   *   *

Richard was preoccupied with the coming assault on the walls of Acre. He had brought with him several contraptions which it was necessary for him to assemble. There was, of course, his tower, the Mate Griffon, on which men were working so that when the time came it could be wheeled into position. There was another machine known as the Belfry; this like the Mate Griffon was intended to be placed close to the walls of the city when the time was ripe for entry. Because of the Saracen's frequent use of Greek Fire, Richard had ordered that it should be covered with tanned hides as a protection against the fire. Another of his machines was a war engine which was used for throwing stones high in the air and at great speed so that they fell into the city. This mangonel had been called the Bad Neighbour and when the Saracens invented a similar machine to throw stones back among the Christians this was nicknamed the Bad Kinsman.

All through the days that followed Richard's arrival work went on to make these war machines ready for use. The spirits of all the Christians had been so lifted by the arrival of Richard that they forgot all they had suffered through the abortive attempts to take the city, even the discomforts of the *khamsin* and the devastating effect the terrific heat had on them. When he rode round the camps he was cheered by all nationalities and they all felt comforted by his presence. He was so certain of victory that he communicated his confidence to them. This uplifting of spirits was obvious even to the Saracens encamped beyond the city on the hill of Ayyadieh.

Saladin himself talked of it with his brother, Malek-Adel. 'What manner of man can this Richard be? They call him the Lion-hearted. They say he is brave and never knows defeat. There is a change in their ranks since he has come.'

Malek-Adel replied that they would soon prove to the Christians that their hero was but human after all. He promised Saladin that he himself would bring him Richard's head and that without his body.

Saladin shook his head. He was not given to such boasts nor did he care to hear his brother talk in such a fashion. He believed that Allah did not love the boastful; and he knew from experience that it was never wise to underrate an enemy.

His men looked to him and expected miracles from him and because they believed so fervently that these would come, they sometimes found their miracles. So must it be with this King Richard.

We are of a kind, he thought. It is a pity that we should fight against each other. But they were two men each with his fixed idea—Saladin's to hold Jerusalem and Richard's to take it.

*   *   *

In the midst of the activity Richard fell ill. The recurrent fever took possession of him and though he attempted to fight it off with all his strength, he failed to do so.

How maddening it was to be laid low where he could hear the noise from the anvils as the great war machines were perfected. The action would have to be delayed and this would give the Mussulmans time to prepare. They must have seen the swelling of the Christian ranks. Their spies would have taken back reports of the great war machines. And now the fever had come to torment him!

Berengaria came with Joanna to his tent. They were horrified at the sight of him.

'I am not so ill as I look,' said Richard. 'I know this accursed fever by now. It will pass. It infuriates me, though, that it should come at this time.'

'At least,' said Berengaria, 'now we can look after you.'

And they did. Through the haze of his fever Richard was aware of soft and gentle hands that smoothed the hair back from his face, and put cooling drinks to his lips.

When she could forget her anxieties for his health, Berengaria was happier than she had been since the first days of her marriage.

As the fever grew less virulent, he would ask anxious questions about what was happening outside his tent. She would soothe him and say: 'All is well.'

How could it be, when he was on a sick bed? he demanded irritably. Who was going to break the siege?

'The siege can wait,' said Berengaria; and he sighed in exasperation at her feminine ignorance.

How could he talk with Berengaria? Joanna would have understood more readily. Joanna was there but she kept in the background knowing what pleasure it gave Berengaria to attend to her husband. He was also aware of a third figure—a very young girl of great beauty who seemed like Berengaria's shadow.

Once he said: 'Who is the girl?'

'Isaac's daughter.'

He was immediately alarmed. 'What does she here?'

'She is with us all the time. You gave her into our charge remember.'

'Her father is my prisoner. She could be looking for revenge.'

'Nay. We have taught her that you are the noblest king that ever lived.'

He was uneasy. But Berengaria soothed him. The little Cypriot Princess was innocent. She was with her and Joanna all the time. She was like a little sister. She would never harm any whom Berengaria loved. Moreover Berengaria herself prepared his food. She would trust no other to do so.

He watched the girl; it seemed Berengaria was right. None could imagine evil in such a dainty child. Berengaria became a little jealous.

'You find her beautiful?'

'The Cypriot women have a certain charm.' He was suddenly remorseful for his neglect of Berengaria. 'Not to be compared with those of Navarre,' he added.

That contented her. It was easy to please her and he felt happy in his marriage for the first time. When he was well he would pay more attention to Berengaria. She was a good woman and by no means ill-favoured; he liked her natural elegance, and it was comforting to feel her there when the fever took possession of him.

Philip came to see him. He stood by the bed looking down on him.

'So the fever can do what no human enemy can. My dear Richard, you look very ill.'

'It will pass.'

'This accursed climate! How do the natives endure it?'

'They are accustomed to it, I doubt not. Their robes protect them from the sun and so they remain cool.'

'How I hate it!' cried Philip vehemently. 'Flies and sand in everything ... in one's clothes, in one's hair, in one's food. The mosquitoes are a pest. Some of my men have died of their bites. The terrible spiders are a danger. Their sting is death. They come out when it is quiet and the men are asleep. Several men have been killed by these tarantulas. We have found that they dislike noise and it drives them away, and the men clash symbols before they lie down but they cannot continue this throughout the night and as soon as quiet falls the danger returns. Sometimes I think of home, of my fair land of France where it is never too hot, where there is no sand to plague me ... no dust, no poisonous spiders ... And now you are sick, Richard. In God's name let us take this town and then go home.'

'When we take this town that is but a beginning,' protested Richard. 'After that we have to march on to Jerusalem.'

Philip clenched his fists and was about to speak but he changed his mind.

After a pause he said: 'And it grieves me to see you thus. You too need the temperate winds of home.'

'We took an oath, Philip. We are soldiers of the Cross. Do not forget that.'

'I forget it not. That is why we are going ahead with the assault on Acre.'

'I am in no condition, I fear, and shall not be for a week or so. I know these bouts. The truth is, Philip, if I tried to stand on my feet I should fall.'

'Then you must rest. In the meantime I shall begin the assault.'

'But, Philip...'

'I know we were to do it together. But Saladin is arming. He knows the assault is coming. We cannot delay further. You were so long in getting here. We *dare* not delay longer.'

Richard looked up at that sly clever face which he knew so well.

Perhaps somewhere in Philip's mind was the thought that if he took Acre without Richard, to him would be the glory.

There was love between them, yes, but there was something else; this irrepressible rivalry. The desire to score over the other would always be there. They excited each other more than any other person could. There was a love relationship between them but sometimes there was something near to hate.

Richard who always said exactly what was in his mind burst out: 'You want the honour for yourself. You do not want to share it.'

'My dearest friend, get well. Join me. Nothing would

please me more. But delay I cannot. Even for your sake I cannot run the risk of defeat.'

'I forbid you to start without me. Oh I know what you will say. The Duke of Normandy forbids his suzerain!'

'And you will say the King of England is perfectly entitled to challenge the King of France. Forget our ranks, Richard. Know this: I am going into battle. You are too ill to join the fight. Your men may. You will not hold them back. For I am going to take Acre and that within the next few days.'

Richard was silent. He knew he could not prevail upon Philip to wait.

*   *   *

The battle had begun. Richard could not stay in his tent while this was going on. He tried to stand but he was too weak from fever. He could not go out there and join in the fight.

He called to his servants and commanded them to bring him a litter. This was done and when he lay on it he asked for his cross-bow.

'Now,' he said, 'carry me out.'

They hesitated and he shouted at them: 'Obey my orders, you oafs. Do not dare defy me.'

They were afraid and did his bidding and he insisted that they carry him to a spot near the walls of the city. There under cover of raw hides he watched what was going on and when he saw any of the enemy appear on the battlements he took a shot at them with his cross-bow, and as he was the finest shot in the army he rarely missed his mark.

But this was Philip's assault. Richard could not be in command from his litter and this gave the French King his opportunity. He was determined to succeed ... without Richard. He longed to be the master. Again and again he thought of those happy days when they were younger and Richard was not yet a king, his inheritance in jeopardy because of his father's hatred of him and determination to put John in his place. The King and the beloved hostage. That was the way he wanted it.

And now this rivalry had been formed to corrupt their relationship. Both of them perhaps were kings before they could be lovers.

If he could take Acre while Richard was actually on the spot, this would indeed be glory. Some might even say that Richard had feigned illness because he knew he could not compare with the King of France. A ridiculous statement of course, and Philip would be the first to admit that Richard was his superior on the battlefield, but there was no end to the foolish things people said, and desperately Philip needed the glory Acre could give him.

He was going to take the Accursed Tower. That was important. The Tower which had been built with the thirty pieces of silver given to Judas and had before withstood his attack. He would undermine that Tower; it should crumble; the bricks should be taken away so that in time it tottered to the ground.

Over the walls of the city flew the deadly stones discharged by the giant mangonels; but down from the walls came the deadly Greek Fire.

One of Philip's greatest delights was a movable screen of mantelets which had been given the name of The Cat. This protected his soldiers from arrows and stones. He had ordered that it be wheeled close to the walls and he himself was there to watch its protective effects. To his great dismay the Greek Fire sent down upon the attackers from the walls of the city caught it alight. Philip groaned in despair as he watched it burn.

Everything seemed to go wrong after that. Philip shouted abuse at his men and at God. It was so rare for him to lose his temper that they were aghast. The French King must be deeply disturbed so to lose his calmness in this way; the English King was suffering from a fever, and the Saracen armies seemed unconquerable. The Christian foot soldiers in their heavy armour over long padded coats, suffered cruelly from the heat. The only asset of these accoutrements was that often arrows could not penetrate them. Some were seen walking about with arrows lodged in their mail and which would have killed them but for it. But the discomfort was hard to bear.

Philip longed for France; he cursed the day he had sworn to set out on a crusade. How different the reality was from the dream! It had seemed so desirable. Marching along at the head of his men, making easy conquests, scoring over Richard —which did not seem too much to hope for since what he lacked in military skill he made up for in subtle diplomacy—winning glory, and a remission of his sins. And the reality—dust, the ever-present sand, the flies, the mosquitoes, the tarantulas and the incessant heat.

I want to go home, thought Philip. Oh God I would give anything to go home.

The Accursed Tower would not fall. Even when they made a breach in it it was not enough to break through. Seeing his dismay one of his finest soldiers, his Marshal of France and dearest friend Alberic Clement, cried out to him: 'Despair not, Sire. I swear that this day I will either enter Acre or die.'

Alberic fixed one of the scaling ladders and sword in hand started to climb with some of his men following him.

God was not with them that day, mourned Philip. The ladder broke and the men fell to the ground with the exception of Alberic who was left alone hanging there exposed to the full fury of the enemy's fire.

To see this dear friend die deeply wounded Philip.

He turned away from the arrows and the Greek Fire and went back to his camp.

He had begun to shiver. He was suffering from the same symptoms as those which had beset Richard.

*   *   *

So the siege of Acre had not been broken and the two kings were sick. The crusaders were despondent. They cursed God. They had come all this way to fight for His Holy Land and He had deserted them.

The fighting had slowed down. Richard was still carried out and beneath his protection of raw hides took shots at any enemy who came within his range. He was thus able to kill the Saracen who appeared on the wall of Acre wearing the arms of Alberic Clement. This gave him great satisfaction for he had heard of that brave attempt to scale the wall. But the fact that the King of France was indisposed and that he himself was ill had made the soldiers apprehensive. They feared they were to be left without leaders.

Richard began to think a great deal about the enemy and the man who led them, the great Sultan Saladin. The stories he had heard fascinated him. He had not before thought of a Mohammedan as human but it appeared that this man Saladin was humane, a man of sensitivity and culture. The fanatical manner in which his armies fought had long been a source of wonder and it seemed that these men were fighting for a cause even as the Christians were.

Saladin's name was mentioned with an unmistakable awe.

As he lay on his litter cursing the evil fate which had smitten him down at this time, he wondered if it would be possible for them to meet.

*   *   *

Saladin himself was thinking a great deal about Richard. He had been aware of what was happening in the Christian camp. The spies who slipped into enemy terrain kept him well informed of what was going on. From the heights of Ayyadieh he had seen the arrival of Richard's fleet; he had heard of his conquests in Sicily and Cyprus, and he felt a great desire to see this man, whose fame had spread throughout the Moslem Empire.

He talked of him to his brother Malek Adel, who was delighting in the news which had been brought in of Richard's sickness.

'We see in this the hand of fate,' said Malek Adel. 'As we feared our people in Acre could not endure the siege much longer, and lo, the great Richard has fallen sick. Allah has answered our prayers.'

'Let us not be too sure that he will not rise from his sick bed. It may be that he has already done so.'

'The people in Acre will be rejoicing,' said Daher, Saladin's son. 'It is said that the great King is unable to walk, is carried out on his litter and lies there with his cross-bow. If we could find him thus we could capture him or kill him. Where would they be without their leader?'

Saladin shook his head. 'I would not wish it. I do not care to take advantage of a great King thus.'

'My lord,' cried Daher, 'he is our enemy.'

''Tis true, my son, but one must respect one's enemy. I want to overcome him in fair battle, not to slip in and take him while he lies unprotected.'

'Is this the way to win a war?' asked Malek Adel.

'It is the honourable way to conduct a war,' retorted Saladin.

While they talked one of the soldiers begged for an audience. His news was that a magic stone thrown from one of the enemy's war machines had landed in the centre of Acre and had killed twelve people.

'One stone to kill twelve!' cried Daher. 'I do not believe it.'

'It is so, my lord,' replied the soldier. 'I saw it with my own eyes. I narrowly escaped being one of its victims. It was large but there have been others as large. It landed in the town square and killed the twelve.'

'It's unbelievable that one stone could do this,' said Saladin.

'If it did, it was magic,' replied Malek Adel.

Saladin said that he would see this stone and he ordered that it should be brought to him.

This was done. It was set down and they examined it. There was nothing extraordinary about it as far as the eyes could see, but when the number of deaths from this one stone had been confirmed there was no doubt in the minds of the Mohammedans that the stone had been given some special properties.

Malek Adel wanted to try it against the enemy, but Saladin did not want to lose the stone. It was to be preserved and studied. A stone which could kill twelve people at one throw must have magic properties.

Into Saldin's camp came a messenger. He was a daring man to brave coming into Saracen lines, but Saladin was not one to allow such a man to be ill-treated. He had given orders that this was not to be so, for such messengers came on the orders of their leaders and unless they behaved with insolence and arrogance they were to be well received.

'I come from King Richard,' said the messenger.

Saladin asked all to retire except his brother Malek Adel.

'Pray state your business,' he said.

'King Richard wishes you to know that he believes there could be much good in a meeting between you and himself.'

Saladin was excited at the prospect. He looked at Malek Adel about whose lips a cynical smile was curving. Saladin was too astute to allow a personal desire to influence him and much as he desired to see Richard and talk with him he must view this approach with the utmost care.

Malek Adel said: 'So the King of England is sick. He despairs of taking Acre. Therefore he would like to talk peace.'

This could be so, thought Saladin, but it was true that the besieged town of Acre was in a pitiful state. When he had heard of the lost ship, which Richard had sunk, he had cried out in despair, 'Allah has deserted us. We have lost Acre.' And it was a fact that the loss of all that ship was bringing to the beleagured city could have a decisive effect on its survival. It was true that Acre was not yet taken but it could fall at any moment. Another assault could bring the citizens to their knees. There had been an arrangement that if they were in dire distress within the town they should indicate to the army on the heights that this was so by the beating of kettle drums. During the recent assault those kettle drums had been heard.

It was typical of Malek Adel to display this blind confidence in their armies. Saladin applauded it up to a point. Confidence was essential, but this must be tempered with sound good sense.

'Your King lies sick,' he said to the messenger.

'It is an intermittent fever,' was the reply. 'He has had it before. He will rise from his bed in due course as strong as he ever was.'

'*'Tis not what I heard,' growled Malek Adel.

The messenger said: 'My King offers to meet you, my lord.'

Saladin said slowly: 'There is much to be settled first. After eating and drinking familiarly we could not fight afterwards. That would be offensive to our beliefs. The time is not yet ripe for a meeting.'

'My King wishes to show his good will by sending you gifts,' said the messenger.

'I could not accept gifts from him unless he took them from me in return.'

'My King says: "It does not become kings to slight each other's gifts even though they are at war. This is one of the lessons our fathers taught us."'

'It is is true,' replied Saladin. 'If the King will accept gifts from me I will take gifts from him.'

'My lord, we have eagles and hawks which my King would send you. But these birds have suffered from the long sea journey and a lack of rightful food. If you would give us some fowls, and young pigeons with which to feed them, my King would then present them to you.'

'Ah,' said Malik Adel, 'you see what this means, my brother. The King of England is sick, so he longs for doves and in due course he will send hawks to us.'

'I will deal with this matter as my heart dictates,' said Saladin. 'None in the world could have aught but respect for King Richard. Let this messenger be clothed in fine robes and give him safe conduct back to his King with young pigeons and fowls and turtle doves.'

Malek Adel was astonished but even he dared not criticize too strongly the Sultan's action.

The messenger went back to Richard with an account of what had happened.

*　　　*　　　*

The fever had returned. Doubtless due to the inclement air it was not as easy to throw off as it had been on other occasions. He was a little delirious. Once more he fancied he was with his father and he felt a terrible remorse because of the ill feeling between them. It was only when he was ill that he felt this. When he was strong he was convinced that his sons' enmity was entirely their father's fault.

Philip haunted his mind. He had at first believed that Philip was feigning illness because he wanted an excuse to go home. But this had proved to be untrue. He had heard that Philip's hair was falling out and his nails flaking off and that he was in a very poor condition. 'It's this climate,' he wailed continuously. 'This accursed climate ... this dust ... these insects ... they are killing me.'

It was said that his longing for France was an illness in itself.

Are we both going to die? wondered Richard.

If so, they would die with their sins forgiven for how could a man die in more sanctified state than in a campaign to bring the Holy Land back to Christianity?

There was Saladin. A great man, a good man. Who could believe that a man who was not a Christian could be good? Yet it seemed so. He had noticed how Saracen prisoners spoke and thought of their leader. If my men think thus of me I am happy, thought Richard. How could a man who was not great and just inspire such respect?

They did not believe in Christ, these Saracens. But they believed in Mahomet. He it seemed was a holy man. He had laid down a set of rules even as Moses had, and it seemed they were good rules.

And yet how could a man who was not a Christian be a good man? Yet were all Christians good? Richard found himself laughing in a hollow way.

Then he thought: I am dying. This accursed fever has caught up with me at last. I should never have camped in the swamping ground all those years ago. How the insects plagued me! Those maddening mosquitoes. And here they are again ... worse than ever!

And if I die what will become of England, of Normandy? Philip will take Normandy. He is waiting for the chance. What of John? Will John try to take England? And what of young Arthur whom I have named as my heir?

As the waves of fever swept over him he started up, for it seemed to him that someone had slipped into his tent. It was one of the guards.

'My lord, there is one who says he must speak with you. He is unarmed. Will you see him?'

I am too ill, thought Richard. But he said: 'Bring him in.'

The man knelt by the bed and laid a hand on his brow. It seemed cool and soothing. There was a certain magic in its touch.

'Who are you?' asked Richard.

'One who comes in friendship.'

'You are not an Englishman.'

'Nay. I would speak with you alone.'

'Leave us,' cried Richard to the guard. The man hesitated but Richard cried: 'Begone.'

When they were alone Richard said: 'What brings you?'

'You are near to death and I come in friendship.'

'Tell me who you are.'

'Perhaps you know.'

'It cannot be.'

'Do you feel this bond between us? I have heard much of you. I craved to see you. You are in a high fever.'

'I am seeing visions,' said Richard.

'It could be so.'

'Saladin ... why are you here?'

'I felt the need to come. I have a magic talisman. If I touch you with this and God wills it, the fever will pass.'

'You are my enemy.'

'Your enemy and your friend.'

'Is it possible to be both?'

'Lo, we have shown it to be.'

Richard felt something cool pass over his brow. 'I have touched you with my talisman. The fever may now pass. There are foods you need now to strengthen you—fruit and chicken, such things as you do not possess in the camp. These will be sent to you. You will recover.'

'Why do you come to me with succour?'

'I understand not my feeling except that I must. We shall fight together and one of us will be victorious. It may be that we shall die in battle. Yet this night we are friends. We could love each other but for barriers between us. Your God and my God have decreed that we shall be enemies, and so must it be. But for this night we are friends.'

'I feel comforted by your presence,' said Richard.

'I know it.'

'If you are he whom I believed you to be, I am filled with wonder. While you are near me the fever slips from me. But I have suffered such delirium that I tell myself I am in delirium now.'

The cool hand once more touched his brow.

'This is no delirium.'

'Then if you are who I think you are ... why did you come here ... right into our midst?'

'Allah protected me.'

'I shall add my protection to his when you go back. You shall not be harmed by any man of mine while on such a mission.'

'We shall meet again,' was the answer.

Richard said: 'Call the guard who brought you to me.'

The guard came in. 'Go with this man until he dismisses you,' he said. 'Let any who harm him know that he does so on pain of cruel death. That is my order.'

Richard was alone.

Almost immediately he fell into a soothing sleep and when he awoke from it the fever had left him. He told himself, I had a strange hallucination but the next day grapes and dates arrived with young chickens. They were gifts from the Sultan Saladin.

There were many who feared the gifts might be poisoned but when they were tried they were found to be good and wholesome.

In a short time Richard had recovered.

On the Walls of Acre

THE King of France was well again; and there was no reason why the assault on Acre should not be renewed.

The citizens were in desperate straits after two years of siege; the failure to receive the promised stores which had been on the ship which Richard had sunk had been a vital blow; their walls were already badly breached and they could not hold out any longer. The combined Christian forces were formidable; the coming of Richard had put such heart into them; it was true that many had believed he must die but now that he had recovered they were of the opinion that he must be immortal and they were convinced that victory would soon be theirs.

In such a mood did they storm Acre.

The fighting was fierce; the losses were great; thirty thousand Christians died in the battle for Acre; but at last came victory. The town had surrendered and Saladin's army was in retreat.

Both Richard and Philip agreed that such a valiant people must be treated with some respect and they ordered that the usual pillage which was generally the result of such a situation should not take place. Prisoners should be taken that these might be bartered for Christian captives. This was wise for later it was arranged that two thousand Christian captives should be returned with a ransom of two hundred thousand pieces of gold in exchange for the release of the prisoners of Acre.

Now there was victory. Over the town should fly the Christian flag. Philip set up residence in the Palace of the Templars and the royal palace was given to Richard. Here he immediately installed Berengaria, Joanna and with them the Cypriot Princess.

It was greatly comforting for the women to be in such surroundings after living in tents with the army, but they were delighted more with the victory than by the luxurious way of life.

'We must make the most of it,' Joanna told Berengaria, 'for you can be sure it will not last long.'

'I wish they would be content with taking Acre,' sighed Berengaria.

'They will never be content until they have taken Jerusalem,' replied Joanna.

*　　*　　*

Richard, riding round the walls of the captured city, saw a flag he did not immediately recognize flying high.

He shouted: 'Whose flag is this?'

'It belongs to the Duke of Austria, my lord,' he was told.

'Will you bring the Duke of Austria to me here,' he ordered.

Leopold of Austria, a proud man, did not like the peremptory summons but he knew that he must obey it. He came reluctantly to where Richard stood beneath his flag.

'Who ordered that this flag should be placed here?' asked Richard.

'I did,' answered Leopold.

'Why so?'

'It is my flag and I and my men have just taken part in the capture of this city.'

'If every man who has brought a few men to fight for the Cross begins waving his flag we shall be ridiculous. Leave flags to your betters.'

With that Richard seized the flag and ground his heel on it.

Leopold of Austria was purple with rage. Those watching were astounded. Richard was in bad mood. He had heard very disturbing rumours about the King of France and he could not help believing that they had sound foundations. He was fighting his own battle with the Plantagenet temper and it had won a round when he saw Leopold's flag. He was uneasy not only concerning the King of France, but he could not forget the strange visitation which had occurred during his fever, and although he must rejoice in the victory at Acre he could not help pondering morosely on Saladin's defeat.

The arrogance of this petty Duke had angered him and given him a reason for giving vent to his feelings, and he had let his rage grow out of all proportion to the offence.

Saladin, he was thinking, you came to me and laid your magic talisman upon my brow. This happened ... I know it did. It was not a fancy. And we are at war.

Saladin was his enemy and in a strange way he loved this man.

'In other circumstances...'

Was that not what Philip had once said? 'If I were not the King of France and you the King of England...' And Saladin: 'If I were not the Sultan, ruler of the Saracens and you were not a Christian king...'

It was a complex situation and Richard loved that which was simple and straightforward: and because he was baffled he was angry, so he had let his fury loose on the Duke of Austria.

He turned abruptly away. He knew that he had acted foolishly. What harm was the Austrian flag doing there? In that moment of rage when he had torn it down and trampled on it, he had insulted Leopold and Leopold was a vindictive man. Moreover some of the Germans had seen what he had done and the rest would soon hear of it.

'I will never forget this insult,' muttered Leopold.

Richard had indeed made a bitter enemy.

Philip's Farewell

THE disturbing rumours which Richard had heard concerning the King of France were that he was weary of the campaign and was making secret plans to return to France.

Richard went to the Palace of the Templars and asked for an audience.

Philip received him there with affection. The French King had certainly changed; he was pale and emaciated from his recent fever; his hair had become thin and his nails had not yet begun to grow normally.

He took Richard's hands in his and kissed his cheek.

'I have heard whispers which I know cannot be true,' said Richard.

'It is always wise never to trust rumour,' said Philip. 'What have you heard?'

'That you are planning to return to France.'

Philip was silent for a few moments. Then he said: 'It is unwise for kings to leave their countries for a long period of time.'

'Even when they have an important mission, when they have taken a holy oath?'

'God would not have given us our kingdoms if He did not believe we have a duty to defend them.'

'Kings have regents.'

'Nay, a kingdom needs a king. When he is away there will be trouble.'

'So it is true that you intend to desert us?'

'I intend to do my duty to my country.'

'And break your oath?'

'I have expended wealth and health in this cause. I have done enough.'

'Your name will resound with dishonour throughout the world.'

'But not with such effect as it would if I lost my kingdom.'

'I see you have made up your mind to go. Does your oath mean nothing to you, your vow to God, your vow to me!'

'Aye, these are great matters. But I am a king. I have a little son; he is but four years old. He is ailing. He needs me there. If I stay in this land another year my son will have no father. France will have lost her King. I cannot live in this vile climate. The heat is unendurable. The dust chokes me; the flies nauseate me. The mosquitoes and the tarantulas are killing my men. I tell you this, Richard: I have not come to this decision lightly but I see that if I remain here, I shall die.'

'I am ashamed,' said Richard.

Philip smiled sardonically. 'As long as you are not ashamed of yourself that is all that matters. Let those who incur shame suffer it. I have cleared myself with my conscience and with God. I love my country more than this hopeless task.'

'Hopeless! You can say that! It is the duty of every Christian to restore the Holy Land to Christianity.'

'I have seen these Mohammedans in action and so have you. Have you ever seen braver men? They have defeated us often, Richard, because while we have a cause they have one too. They have a God. Allah. He seems to work as well for them—perhaps better—than ours for us.'

'You blaspheme.'

'It may be so. But I must state what I see. These are not the barbarians we were led to believe they were. They are noble fighters. They say their leader Saladin is a man of great wisdom and goodness.'

'I believe that,' said Richard.

'A noble enemy! Does that not disagree with what we have always believed?'

'The Mohammedans have taken the Holy City. They have desecrated our churches. They have insulted God, Christ and the Holy Ghost. Is that not sufficient reason for us to fight against them?'

'I would like to meet this man, to talk with him. I would like to hear what he has to say.'

Richard was silent. Had it really happened or had it been part of his imagination? One dreamed strange dreams in fever.

He was on the point of telling Philip but he refrained. His mind was now occupied with what Philip's departure would mean.

'You cannot break your oath,' he said vehemently.

'Would you condemn me to death, for die I surely shall if I stay in this place. You know how ill I have been. See how scanty my hair has become. Look at my hands. I am in a sorry state still. I shall die, Richard, if I stay longer in this poisonous place.'

'How could a man die better than in the service of God?'

'I believe I can serve Him better by saving my life. He has shown me clearly that death awaits me here. I must go home.'

'I too have been ill—more so than you.'

'You have had fevers all your life, Richard. With me, it was my first. I know I came very close to death and I know too that I have my duty to my son and my country.'

'And I see that you are determined to go home. What effect do you think this will have on the enemy?'

'When I go,' said Philip, 'I will leave you five hundred of my knights and a thousand foot soldiers. Moreover I shall pay for their support. My soldiers will continue to fight for the cause, only I shall not be here.'

Richard narrowed his eyes. He thought: And what peace of mind shall I have knowing that you are in France casting your covetous eyes on Normandy?

'You *must* not go, Philip.'

'I *am* going, Richard.'

'So in spite of our protestations of friendship you will desert me?'

'Of what comfort would a corpse be to you? I go because I must, Richard. The choice is simple. Life or death. As a dead man I should be an embarrassment to you. While I live I can command my men to fight with you. If I were dead what would they do? Desert! Nay, I have pondered this matter and the way is clear to me. I must leave this land. It has defeated me, you may say. That is true. The insects and this terrible heat have done to me what a human enemy could not. But I have been warned. Yes, very clearly have I been warned. If I stay here I shall die and I must live.'

It was no use talking to him. He was determined on departure.

This was indeed so. When the Bishop of Beauvais and the Duke of Burgundy presented themselves before Richard to tell him formally what Philip had already stated in private they were in tears.

'Weep not,' said Richard. 'I know what you come to tell me. Your lord, the King of France, desires to go home and you come in his name to ask on my behalf my counsel and leave for him to be gone.'

' 'Tis true, Sire,' said the Duke. 'Our King says that if he does not leave this land speedily he will die.'

'It will be for him and the Kingdom of France eternal shame,' said Richard. 'I could not advise him to do this. I would prefer death to such shame. But if he must die or return home let him do what he thinks best.'

'My lord King,' said the Duke of Burgundy, 'our King says he will leave knights and foot soldiers under my command to serve you and obey you.'

Richard bowed his head. 'Return to the King of France and tell him that I have nothing more to say on this grievous matter.'

When Richard took his farewell of Philip, the King of France said to him: 'You are misguided. This siege of Acre has taught me much and you, too, I doubt not. These enemies are fierce fighters. They are a match for your best. I believe that we are not in position to succeed against them.'

'How so? Have we not taken Acre?'

' 'Tis so. But we have seen what resistance these men show. They are fighting for what they believe to be theirs. They are as firm in their beliefs as we are in ours. They are a formidable enemy. Our men are emaciated from fever, and these Mohammedans can withstand the heat better than our people. It is natural to them. It is my firm conviction that we are not in a fit state to take Jerusalem. We need new troops, fresh supplies. It is enough that this crusade ends with the taking of Acre. If we were wise we would leave Acre well fortified. We have Cyprus as a stronghold. This is a good result of our crusade. Now we should return home and other men—and perhaps we should join with them—could prepare for the next crusade.'

'You seek to comfort yourself,' said Richard scornfully. 'I tell you I shall not return until the Christian flag flies over the Holy City.'

'Do not boast of that to any who do not love you as I do,' said Philip.

'You love me! Yet you leave me!'

'Forget not that I have entreated you to come with me.'

'I have let you see that I do not want you to go.'

'Is it for myself you wish me to stay or because you fear that my departure may please the enemy? Or do you fear that I shall be in France while you are in Palestine?'

'Before you go you must give me your solemn word that you will do nothing to harass my dominions while I am away.'

'I will give you that word.'

'You must keep it, Philip. You must remember our friendship, the oaths we have sworn to each other.'

'Did you always remain true to yours, Richard?'

'What mean you?'

'I have heard that you have made friends with strange people, that gifts have passed between you.'

Richard flushed slightly. 'You refer to the Sultan Saladin.'

'Our enemy I thought ... but perhaps your friend.'

'He sent gifts as you know. It is an Arab custom.'

'To sustain an enemy?'

'It seems so.'

'Can it possibly be that you have become his friend?'

'How could that be so?'

'I remember Tancred. You were very friendly with him, were you not?'

'I made terms with him.'

'As you now make them with the Sultan Saladin?'

'I have made only the terms which we made regarding the ransom to be paid to us.'

'Richard, is that all?'

'I have made no other terms. You are of a jealous nature, Philip.'

'You and I were once good friends.'

'Let us vow always to be so.'

'That would be a comfort to you would it not?'

'Of great comfort.'

'Only because you fear for the dominions you have deserted.'

'I like not the term but I will say that in view of our vows to love each other which we once made I would be happier that these vows were kept rather than broken. Friendship is a good thing particularly so between those whom the world would call natural enemies.'

They embraced.

'It grieves me deeply to leave you, Richard,' said Philip.

'Then stay.'

'I have my duty to my son and my country. I cannot afford to die yet. My son is not ready. I must remember my duty to France.'

Richard could see that Philip had made up his mind. There was one matter which must be settled and this was who, when Jerusalem was captured, should reign there as King. This had been a matter of dissension between the two kings, Richard supporting Guy de Lusignan's claim and Philip that of Conrad de Montferrat.

Philip was so eager to be gone that he was ready to give way and it was finally agreed that Guy should be King in his lifetime and then the crown should pass to Montferrat.

On the last day of July Philip sailed away from Acre.

Joanna and Malek Adel

RICHARD missed Philip. His temper was more easily aroused. He was still feeling the after effects of his illness and he suffered from the climate as Philip had. He chafed against the delay which kept him in Acre. Until the ransom was paid he could not leave. He worried a great deal about Philip and wondered what his action would be when he returned to France. He believed that when Philip was with him he cared for him; but when he was away from him he might well forget his affection and see only what was to be gained by Richard's absence. Always kings of France had taken advantage of the difficulties of dukes of Normandy. Ever since they had lost that stretch of land it had been the unspoken law that no king should fail to take an opportunity to regain it.

He must move on. As soon as the ransom was paid and the prisoners exchanged he would do so.

Saladin's army was drawn up on the heights not far from the city in which the Christians were now living in comfort. It was not good for them to remain thus. Many of the soldiers, starved for so long from what they considered to be the good things of life, had decided to make the most of them while they could. There was drunkenness and sexual orgies— neither of which was good for an army—yet Richard knew that to stop this could result in revolt against him. He was a strong ruler and he was stern and quick to punish those who broke his laws; but he understood soldiers. He himself at one

time had indulged in such activities as were now taking place
within the city of Acre. To expect men to endure heat,
hunger and sickness and give them no rewards was unwise.
Let them feel now that war was worthwhile and they would
fight the better for it later. At this time they had forgotten
that they were supposed to be engaged in a holy war. They
were ordinary soldiers with the lust of conquest upon them.
Very soon must begin the march to Jaffa and Richard knew
that this was going to tax their strength, endurance and
fidelity to the cause to the utmost of their strength. Therefore
give them this relaxation now. Let them satisfy their lusts
and dream of the next conquest as they marched.

But not for long . . . only until that ransom was paid.

The day arrived when it should have been paid. Richard
waited eagerly for the coming of Saladin's emissaries, but all
through that day and all through that night he looked in
vain.

Where were they? It had been their solemn agreement that
the ransom should be paid. But where was it? Through the
next day he waited.

At last came Saladin's messengers. They brought gifts—
more grapes, dates and young chickens.

Richard said: 'We thank the Sultan for these gifts but we
need the ransom.'

'It will come,' was the answer.

Then the messengers came again with more gifts but still
no ransom.

'What means this?' cried Richard. 'It seems that Saladin
would deceive me.'

The messengers assured him that this was not so. The
Sultan was merely asking for more time to raise the ransom.

And so it went on. Three weeks passed. The Sultan is
deceiving me, thought Richard. And he remembered that
night when Saladin had come to his tent—if it had not been a
dream—and touched him with his magic talisman. He had
believed it was Saladin and that there was a special bond
between them. Was Saladin laughing at him now? Was he
mocking him? Was he saying to his friends: See how easily
the King of England can be deceived? This is the great
leader! He so believed in my magic talisman that he rose
from his sick bed. Now when I promise him to fulfil the
terms of our agreement he believes me.

That Saladin should play him false, wounded him deeply
—his pride and something more. He could not bear to think
that he had been mistaken; and because he was uncertain his
temper flared against the Sultan and all his Saracens.

He cried out in his wrath: 'I will wait no longer.'

He was glad that Philip had gone. Philip would have tried
to restrain him. But he was not going to be restrained. He
was going to show Sultan Saladin what it meant to attempt to
delude Richard of England.

It was the morning of the 20th August—three weeks after
the departure of Philip. Through the gates of the city of Acre
Richard rode on his favourite horse Fauvel which he had
taken from Isaac Comnenus. He looked magnificent with the
sun glinting on his armour. Behind came the army of
crusaders. Richard led the way to the top of a hill, his men
following him to the summit. He was immediately opposite
Ayyadieh where the armies of Saladin were stationed. At the
sight of the Christian army the Mohammedans were watchful.

Immediately behind the King came the cavalry followed
by the infantry with their bows and arrows. They divided
and placing themselves so that the watching enemy could
have a good view, they remained still while the two thousand
five hundred Moslem prisoners were brought out. Their
hands were tied behind their backs and cords held them all
together.

There they stood in wretched knowledge of their fate.

The Mohammedans watched in incredulous horror while
the cavalry advanced on the prisoners and drawing their
swords, decapitated every one of them.

Saladin called to his troops. This hideous spectacle enraged
them; he gave the order to advance on the enemy, but before
they could collect themselves for the advance every one of the
Moslem prisoners was dead. Richard then shouted to his men
to prepare for the battle.

Saladin's army and Richard's armies met, but the attack
was indecisive. Saladin was horrified by the result of his
delaying tactics; Richard was remorseful. In a moment of
fury he had commanded his men to do this bloody deed and
he felt that it would live with him for ever. He must ask himself what Saladin would think of the man whom previously
he had so much admired.

The skirmish was over and the two armies retired to their camps.

As was to be expected before long there was news that Saladin had slaughtered Christian prisoners as a reprisal.

*   *   *

Richard's great desire was to leave Acre. Sometimes he believed he would never forget that place. He would never be able to get out of his nostrils the smell of decaying bodies; he would never be free from haunting memories of brave men who stared death in the face unflinchingly. Philip had perhaps been wise to leave.

The men were sullen; they had not wished to leave Acre, where they had lived in comfort within a city. They had food, wine and women, and no doubt believed that all they had suffered was worth while for this spell of luxurious living. But it was not what they had come crusading for.

They must march on. They had eighty miles to cover between Acre and Jaffa. It was not really a great distance, but when it was considered that Saladin's army would harass them all the way, and they would be equally tormented by the heat and pests, it was a formidable undertaking.

When Richard told Berengaria that his stay in Acre was coming to an end, she said: 'I shall be glad to leave this place.'

And he knew that she too was thinking of the slaughtered Moslems.

'You will have to stay here,' Richard told her. 'It is unthinkable that you should undertake the march.'

'Oh, no, Richard,' she cried, 'I want to be with you. You may need me.'

'My dear wife, if you were with me, I should suffer such anxieties as would take my mind off my armies.'

She was pleased at the implication, but sad because she was aware that he had made up his mind not to take her.

'Nay,' he said, 'you will stay here in the palace. You will be well guarded. Joanna and the little Cypriot Princess will be with you.'

'Oh, Richard...' she began sadly.

But he waved his hand to imply that the subject was closed. He must move on with his armies. She must remain in safety.

They had been together so little since their marriage. She knew of course that he had to devote himself to his armies; but could he not have spared a little time to be with her? She thought of the soldiers carousing with their women in the town. They had time for pleasure, why not Richard?

Alone in his apartment he thought of Berengaria and wished that he could have felt more tender towards her. But soon he dismissed her from his mind and was thinking of the march to Jaffa. He must set out soon, for to delay was dangerous. He thought of Saladin's armies which would be waiting for him. What had Saladin thought when he saw his fellow countrymen slaughtered? But he had promised the ransom; the date for its delivery had passed. He would have learned by now that Richard was a man of his word. And he had retaliated by slaughtering the Christian prisoners in his camp. How many lives had been lost in this dispute?

Richard did not want to think of that. All the Christians who had died would now be in Heaven. And what of the Moslems? Had he sent them to Hell? Well, they would have gone there in any case.

He wondered what Philip's verdict would have been. He had to stop thinking of Philip, and what would happen when he reached France. But he knew he could not trust him.

What was happening in England? A king should govern his own land, said Philip. But what if he had made a vow to restore the Holy Land to Christianity?

He was perplexed and ill at ease. Then he heard the strumming of a lute and a high treble voice singing a song— one of his, Richard's, own compositions.

What a pleasant voice—so fresh, so young! On such lips the song sounded better than before.

He rose and went to the anteroom. There on a stool sat a fair youth gracefully playing his lute as he sang the words.

Suddenly he was aware of Richard. He started to his feet, flushing with embarrassment.

'My lord, I fear my song disturbed you.'

'Nay,' said Richard, 'it pleased me.'

' 'Tis a beautiful song, Sire.'

'My own,' answered the King. 'I never heard it sung better.'

The boy lowered his eyes; there was delight in the gesture. It was as though he feared to gaze at such a dazzling figure.

'Come,' said the King, 'let us sing it together. You take the first verse and I will answer you in the next.'

The boy lost his nervousness when singing, and together they harmonized.

Richard patted the boy's flaxen curls.

'Tell me your name,' he said, 'that I may ask for you to come and sing to me when I wish it.'

'I am Blondel de Nesle, Sire,' answered the boy.

*   *   *

None who had taken part in the march from Acre to Jaffa would ever forget it. The heat was intense, being one hundred degrees Fahrenheit in the shade; armour became so heated by the sun that it burned the skin and gave additional torture to that suffered by the bites and stings of insects. The men's dress was most unsuitable. The gambeson, a quilted garment made of linen, and sometimes leather, was padded with wool; over this was worn a hauberk with long sleeves and made of chain mail, attached to which was a hood which could be pulled up to cover the head. Beneath the hood a skull cap of iron was worn for protection and over this was a cone-shaped headpiece covering the wearer's face with only a slit through which he could see. Beneath the armour was a long linen tunic, and in addition to these garments, the knight had his weapons to contend with. The sword, with its broad blade and square hilt, which was strapped to his side, was heavy; and very often in addition to his sword he would carry an iron hammer.

To march so accoutred added to the soldiers' discomfort, and the watching Saracens were delighted to see the enemy so burdened that their speedy elimination seemed inevitable. In their own loose flowing robes, and accustomed to the weather as they were, they believed they were much better equipped for victory.

Richard, however, was not known as the greatest living general for nothing. He assessed the situation. His men would be protected in some measure by their heavy clothing and armour and if they marched but two miles a day and rested frequently they could endure the strain. He sent orders to the galleys containing food and other stores to sail along the coast keeping pace with the army. Thus what was needed would always be available during the journey.

No sooner had the march begun than the Saracens started their harassing tactics. To endure the terrific heat, the persistent thirst, the torment imposed on them by the insects would have been unbearable but for the courage of their leader who was always there to spur them on; and his knights seeking to emulate him were of great value to the King.

The Saracens tried to break the line but they could not do so. The fact that the army progressed so slowly enabled them to keep close together; and the constant stream of Saracen arrows, although they found their targets, could not penetrate the mail and many a footsoldier marched along with arrows protruding from him at all angles, giving him the look of a porcupine. These men then became reconciled to their heavy equipment because they realized its life-saving qualities.

By night they camped close to the sea where the galleys carrying food and ammunition were in sight to comfort them.

Richard, knowing that many of them would be thinking of the recent riotous living in Acre and perhaps losing heart because of it, arranged for the heralds to go through the camp shouting 'Help us, O Holy Sepulchre!' to remind them that they were on a holy crusade. When they heard the heralds call every man would stand to his feet and raise his hands together and cry to God to help him.

Each day the rising of the sun would remind the men that another day of discomfort and danger lay ahead before that blazing tormenter set again. But with the appeals to God ringing in their ears and the example of Richard and the knights and the belief that what they were doing would win Heaven's approval, they were ready to march on. It might be, thought Richard, that their recent carousal in Acre would add zest to their days because they were in urgent need of a remission of their sins after the orgies in which they had indulged, so it could be said that the life they had led in Acre was a good thing after all.

There was one knight who won Richard's special approval. Where the fighting was the fiercest that knight could always be seen; when the enemy circled about Richard he was there beside him and when the affray was beaten off Richard sent for him.

'I want to thank you for your good work,' said Richard. 'I

have seen you in action and that has given me comfort. You are an example to the men.'

The knight lifted his headpiece and when Richard recognized that face there was a moment of embarrassment as he recalled that incident of the canes when this man had torn his clothes and he had been unable to beat him.

'So it is William des Barres,' said Richard.

'I fear so, Sire.'

'Fear nothing,' cried Richard. 'But no need to tell you that. I know you fear nothing . . . not even the wrath of kings.'

'I have always kept out of your way, Sire.'

'Until today. You were close to me then.'

'I was there as an unknown knight. I did not think you would discover me.'

'You fight well,' said Richard, 'whether it be with sword or canes. Let me see more of your skill.'

Then he laughed aloud. He was pleased. The affair of the canes had always made him feel ashamed when he recalled it.

'Let us bury our quarrel by becoming the best of friends,' said Richard.

*   *   *

At Arsouf a battle took place. The crusaders were greatly outnumbered, there being but one hundred thousand of them to three times that number of Saracens. The fighting was fierce and at first it seemed that the victory would go to Saladin; but the crusaders stood so firm that it was not possible for the Saracens to break their ranks. The lightly clad Saracens were very vulnerable to the crusaders' arrows whereas the heavy crusader armour continued to save Christian lives.

Saladin in the thick of the fight was amazed at the skill of the crusaders, while at the same time Richard could not help but marvel at the bravery of the Moslems.

Richard thought: We should not be fighting against each other, and wondered if that same thought might be in Saladin's mind.

He hoped that Saladin was understanding why he had had the prisoners slaughtered. A promise had been broken and this must be avenged. He believed now that had he waited

Saladin would have sent the ransom and he had encountered nothing but a little oriental prevarication. His impatience had cost so many lives that he was horrified to consider this.

But Saladin must understand that when a great king gave his word that he would do something, he must do it.

The fact was that however much respect the leaders had for each other this was war.

By sunset Saladin conceded victory to Richard and he retired leaving the town of Arsouf in Richard's possession. It was a Saturday and Richard said they should spend the whole of Sunday resting there.

There was mourning in the Saracen camps when their losses were counted. Some seven thousand Saracens had fallen in the battle while the Christian losses were comparatively slight.

Saladin, retiring to the woods, went about his camps to comfort his soldiers. The humble ones had fought well and valiantly; it was the Emirs, the leaders, who had been no match for the Christians.

Saladin sent for his brother and his son and asked why they had failed.

'It is Richard,' answered Malek Adel. 'There is something unnatural about him. He is there in the thick of the battle one moment, and then, where there is a weakness and we are about to break through, he suddenly appears. His men who are on the point of surrender fight like lions when he is seen to be there. He shouts to them abuse and encouragement and it is as though he gives them special powers. If he had gone home instead of the King of France we should have driven them into the sea by now. No one can stand against him.'

Saladin nodded understandingly. 'I know this to be so,' he said. 'I wonder what we can do against such a man. He has the valour to subdue all lands. What can we do against such a mighty foe? I would that he were our friend. But if I had to lose my land, then I would rather lose it to this King than any other.'

He could not eat. He sat brooding on his slaughtered ranks; and in his heart he was torn by his admiration for Richard now known as Coeur de Lion and his desire to drive him from the land.

He roused himself both from his melancholy and his preoccupation with the near divinity of his enemy.

'Richard is but a man after all,' he said to Malek Adel. 'For the love of Allah do not let us see him as a god or we are indeed lost. We know him for the most formidable enemy who has ever come here. Very well, we must be shrewd. If he has bettered us on the battle field perhaps there are other ways in which we can beat him. He will now march on to Jerusalem. Instead of harrying him on the way as we have been doing without great success let the main army ride on ahead of him. Raze to the ground the walls of the towns through which he must pass. Make sure that he cannot get supplies there. You may depend upon it he will make for Ascalon and attempt to cut off our supplies from Egypt. Let us be one step ahead of him.'

This seemed a good idea. No army could carry on without food and supplies. Saladin went on ahead to carry out the plan and thus Richard and his army reached Jaffa with comparative ease.

Although the walls had in places been razed to the ground, what comfort there was in Jaffa among the orange groves and the almond trees! Fruit, which they had sorely missed, abounded, Figs, grapes and pomegranates were theirs for the taking. To slake their thirst in such a pleasant manner seemed the height of bliss after the long hot marches.

But many of the company were sick of the adventure. They thought of the wily King of France who was on his way home. He was the wise one. They thought of weary journeys to come, and the chances of meeting death on the way. That they would go straight to Heaven had suddenly become a small compensation. The fleet was plying back and forth between Jaffa and Acre and under cover of darkness many of them slipped out of camp and stowed away in one of the galleys and so sailed back to Acre.

It was not long before it came to Richard's ears that the Saracens were destroying the walls of the cities on the road to Jerusalem so that the Christian armies would find no shelter in the towns. Realizing that this was the reason for the recent easy progress, Richard sent one of the galleys to Ascalon to discover whether this was true; when the galley returned with the news that it was, he decided that they should leave Jaffa and march immediately to Ascalon there to prevent the complete demolition of the city.

He knew that the men were restive. They had suffered

more than soldiers should be asked to. There came a time when they were near breaking point, and having been among soldiers all his life Richard was well aware of this. He called a council consisting of the Dukes of Austria and Burgundy, Guy de Lusignan, and knights in whom he had great confidence such as William de Preaux and William des Barres.

He put to them the theory that they should march on in spite of the fact that the winter was almost upon them—and the winter could be as hard to bear as the heat of the summer. They should make for Jerusalem with all speed, he said, and once that city was in their hands they could fortify it and return home, the object of the crusade successfully achieved.

The Dukes were against it. The men were in need of a rest, they said. They were revelling in the fruits of Jaffa. They must have this respite. To march now after such a brief respite would mean that many would desert to Acre. The Duke of Austria who had never forgiven Richard for tearing down his flag from the walls of Acre hinted that he for one might do so and if he went, with him would go the German contingent. The ranks were depleted enough and Richard was aware that several of the men had slipped away.

He knew that he was right. He was supported by Guy de Lusignan but he recognized the signs of rebellion in the eyes of the Dukes and some of the knights and he said he would shelve the decision.

How restive was Richard at Jaffa! He longed to press on. He would get young Blondel to come and sing with him. He liked the boy to sit at his feet and he would caress his yellow curls as he sang. Blondel was quite a musician; he could compose both music and words. They wrote a ballad of a king and a minstrel and Richard said: 'Sing this song to none other. Let us make it the song for us two.'

Blondel adored him and it seemed to Richard that there was a magic in those young fingers which could strum a lute to such perfection as to bring peace into the troubled days.

'I want to march on to Jerusalem,' he told Blondel. 'The greatest moment of my life will be when I enter that city.'

But still he stayed at Jaffa.

Once he rode out on a hawking expedition. Like music the hunt brought him comfort; and as he rode along on his beloved Fauvel, he saw a party of Saracens and set chase. Fauvel could outpace all other horses and in a short time he had followed the Saracens into a wood. No sooner had he entered than he knew this was an ambush. They had deliberately set out to lead him here.

They might have taken him had not William des Preaux ridden up and shouted to him: 'What do you here, knave? How dare you leave me! Because I allow you to ride my horse you do not take my crown as well.'

The Saracens many of whom could understand the language of the Franks which was spoken by most of the crusaders immediately believed that they had lured the wrong man into the woods and that William des Preaux was the King.

They started to chase him, thus giving Richard the opportunity to escape. William des Preaux also managed to elude them.

Afterwards Richard and William des Preaux laughed over the adventure which was such as the King loved; and he spent much time in the company of William des Preaux and William des Barres playing chess and mock jousting with them, riding out to hunt, but taking greater care in this than before, for daring as he was Richard saw that had he been captured that would have been a most ignoble end to the crusade.

During that stay in Jaffa he realized how many had deserted and that he had to contend with weary men and arrogant leaders such as the Duke of Austria. They were enjoying a period of peace but it was uneasy and could end at any moment. It must be that Saladin's army was suffering in a similar fashion and it occurred to Richard that, since Saladin had once before shown himself amenable, this might be an opportune moment to come to some agreement, that they might have a temporary truce to give them both a little respite.

The idea of negotiating with Saladin excited him. He sent out feelers and discovered that the Sultan was as eager to make terms as he was.

*　　*　　*

Richard's terms for peace were that Jerusalem with the territory between the River Jordan and the sea should be given to the Christians.

When Saladin heard this he raised his eyebrows. It was a

big demand. Richard could not seriously believe it would be granted, but nevertheless Saladin would not reject it immediately. Both sides were weary of fighting. They needed a rest; discussions of terms of peace would be one way of getting it.

Saladin could not openly visit Richard. If they discussed terms they must eat and drink, and to sit down at a table together meant more to all Arabs than appeasing hunger and thirst. It was a symbol of friendship. No, they could not accept the fact that their great leader—as godlike to them as Richard was to crusaders—should sit down and eat with a Christian.

Saladin sent for his brother Malek Adel. 'Go to Richard,' he said, 'discuss these terms with him. I do not believe for one moment that he wants peace. He wants to drive us out of Jerusalem that it may be restored to the Christians. It is a matter of religion with him. But what he needs and what we need is a respite from fighting. Go then and hear what he has to say.'

Malek Adel was eager to undertake the mission. He wanted to know more of this myth-like figure who had the power to strike terror into the hearts of Saracen warriors merely by appearing.

He went to Richard bearing rich gifts, among them seven valuable camels and an elaborate tent. They sat together and food was served to them and they treated each other with the utmost respect as they discussed the possibilities of making a truce.

Each was impressed by the other. Malek Adel had a grace and charm only second to that of his brother; he was witty, astute and, Richard knew, courageous. Richard marvelled that these people whom he had in the past been led to believe were little better than savages could so please him with their company.

With adroitness Malek Adel skirted the subject. It never occurred to Richard, such was his forthright nature, that Malek Adel could be anything but in deadly earnest. He was led to believe that there was the greatest possibility of a peace treaty being signed.

They talked of music and Richard sent for his favourite minstrel, Blondel de Nesle, who sang for the delight of Malek Adel; then Malek Adel sent for Syrian dancers and musicians who performed for Richard's pleasure.

It was a congenial meeting.

Malek Adel went back to report to Saladin who had now received overtures from Conrad de Montferrat hinting that he would be ready to negotiate with Saladin separately.

'This man is a traitor,' said Saladin. 'Let us hear what he has to say. He hates Richard because Richard gave his support to Guy de Lusignan in the conflict between Guy and Montferrat. And see he promises me that he will take up arms against Richard if I guarantee him possession of Sidon and Beyrout.'

'And will you?'

'I would not trust him as I trust Richard. But we must see him, and, brother, let Richard know that Montferrat is negotiating with us. It will serve two purposes. It will make him anxious to come to peace with us and it will let him know that Montferrat is a traitor.'

*   *   *

Thus it soon reached Richard's ears that Montferrat was visiting Saladin. This could only be for one reason. If he was conferring with the enemy he was no longer Richard's friend. He never had been, of course, but at least he had recognized Richard as the leader of the crusade now that the King of France had gone home.

It was clear how Montferrat's mind was working. He was furious because Richard had got Philip to agree to make Guy King of Jerusalem until his death. That could mean that it would be years before it came into Montferrat's possession and perhaps it never would.

Was Saladin likely to make terms if he knew that there was dissension in the Christian ranks? It was hardly possible. The winter lay before them. Richard desperately needed respite and it occurred to him that there was nothing like a marriage to cement the bonds between rulers. What of Joanna? She was a widow and he should find her a husband sometime. He would have done so by now had he not been so exclusively engaged in the crusade.

He had rarely met a man of such charms as Malek Adel. He was cultured; he had graceful manners. Surely any woman would be attracted by him. He remembered that his own mother had once been in love with a Saracen. His name had been Saladin and he had been related to the present

Sultan. There had been talk of a marriage. If her mother had been ready to marry a Saracen of high rank why should not Joanna?

The idea persisted.

There was another matter which concerned him. Many crusaders had been slipping away to Acre. They had forgotten their vows in the terrible march across the desert. He would go to Acre. He could travel there easily on one of the galleys and the journey undertaken that way would be quick and easy to make. He would harangue the deserters and at the same time have a word with Joanna.

Within a few days he arrived in Acre. There was great rejoicing in the palace. Berengaria and Joanna greeted him with great joy. They prepared a feast and Berengaria arranged a concert of all the best musicians to delight him.

It was easy to see that he was preoccupied.

'I cannot stay long,' he told them, 'and when I return I wish you to accompany me.'

Berengaria was delighted.

'You have missed me perhaps?' she asked wistfully.

'There have been many times during the march when I have rejoiced that you were not with me. We suffered torments. I could not have permitted you to endure that. Moreover it would have been an additional anxiety to know that you were there and God knows we had enough.'

Joanna said fondly: 'Richard always thinks of our comfort.'

He assessed her afresh. She had always been devoted to him. He did not think he would have much difficulty in persuading her to accept Malek Adel once she knew he desired it.

But it occurred to him that he would not mention the matter until they were in Jaffa. While he was here he would devote himself to commanding or shaming the deserters into rejoining the army.

This he did. He went through the city declaiming his disgust of those who took vows and then did not honour them. Such men would be ashamed to face their Maker when they died. They would go to Him heavy with guilt and the burden of their sins still upon them.

So eloquently did he speak, so impressive was his personality—many of them had forgotten how dynamic he could be—that in a short time he had persuaded every man of them that his only hope of peace in this life and salvation in the next was to return with him to Jaffa.

When they arrived in that town, the army was increased considerably by the return of those who had previously slunk away and Richard decided to put his plan before Joanna.

Berengaria was with her when he began and the Cypriot Princess who never seemed to leave them was sitting quietly stitching in a corner of the room.

'I have something to say to you, Joanna,' he began. 'You have been on my mind a good deal. You have lost your husband. Would you like another?'

Joanna looked startled.

'Why ... so much would depend ... If he were suitable ... if I were fond of him...'

'I know,' said Richard, 'you have been married once and happily. You would naturally look with favour on another husband. Particularly if he were handsome and of high rank.'

'You cannot have chosen someone for me ... here.'

Richard nodded. He went to Joanna, pulled her to her feet and kissed her brow. 'My dear sister, it is exactly what I have done.'

'Who could it possibly be?' cried Joanna.

'It is Malek Adel, the brother of Saladin.'

Joanna stared at him incredulously, and Richard hurried on: 'He is a man of high rank and great charm. He is handsome; he is...'

Joanna cried: 'He is a Mohammedan! A Saracen. You cannot seriously suggest that I should marry such a man!'

'You have the familiar belief that these people are barbarians. Let me tell you that is far from the case. They are charming people; they are brave, cultured ... everything that a woman could wish.'

'Not this woman!' cried Joanna firmly.

'You need time to grow accustomed to the idea.'

'I need no time. I know immediately and without consideration that I would never marry a Saracen.'

'You are being unreasonable. You have been listening to ignorant people. I know these Saracens. I have eaten with this man. Together we have listened to music. He is clever ... He is charming ... a man any woman would be proud to marry.'

'A Saracen woman perhaps but not a Christian, not the daughter of King Henry of England and Queen Eleanor.'

Joanna had changed suddenly. All the docility had dropped from her. There was no doubt in those moments whose daughter she was. She had no need to remind her brother. There was all the fierceness, the arrogance, the self-will of both her parents.

'How many wives has this Saracen already?' she demanded.

'I doubt not he has a few but that is no problem.'

'No problem! Not to you nor to me either, for I refuse to consider this matter for one moment.'

'I must ask you to be reasonable. This is a matter of great importance. It could help to decide the issue of this crusade.'

'Then the issue of this crusade must remain undecided.'

'Men's lives are involved.'

'And so is mine.'

'You are unreasonable.'

'And you are arrogant. Would you take a Saracen woman to wife?'

'If it were necessary.'

'For you it would be easy. You could marry a wife and proceed to neglect her. You could indulge in your wars to such an extent that you would find excuse enough never to see her.'

Berengaria gave a little cry and Joanna flushed a little, knowing how she had hurt her sister-in-law.

'Richard,' said Joanna, 'I will not do it. You can tell your Saracens that I would rather jump from the towers of this town than marry a man who is not a Christian.'

Richard said: 'Perhaps we could persuade him to become a Christian.'

Joanna burst into wild laughter. 'Perhaps they would want me to become a Mohammedan.'

'Nay,' said Richard seriously, 'I would not ask that!'

'How kind,' cried Joanna sarcastically. 'How good you are to me! You would marry me to a savage, a man who doubtless has a harem of wives. You would send me to join them, but because you are so good and kind you would say, "Please will you become a Christian." I can imagine how the man you have chosen for me would laugh at that.'

'You are in an unreasonable mood.'

'Aye,' cried Joanna, 'and shall remain there as long as you ask me to marry so. Let me tell you this, Richard, it is something I will never do.'

Richard walked hastily away.

Berengaria and Joanna looked at each other. They took a step forward and flew into each other's arms.

Joanna was half laughing, half crying. Berengaria was pale and sad.

'Joanna,' whispered Berengaria, 'could he insist?'

'Never,' replied Joanna. 'He knows I mean what I say.'

'You would not ... kill yourself.'

'Rather than marry such a man ... yes.'

'Oh, Joanna. It is a terrible thing to be a Princess who is sent where others wish her to be. I used to think I was fortunate.'

'And are you not, Berengaria?'

'What is the use, Joanna? Why should we pretend? He does not care for me. He makes excuses to be away from me.'

'Take comfort that he is not with other women.'

Berengaria's lips tightened. She stared straight ahead and said: 'Perhaps there are others of whom I should be jealous.'

Alas, thought Joanna, she has grown up and she finds the world is not what she thought.

All pretence between them had disappeared. From now on if they remained together, there would be no necessity to placate Berengaria with excuses for all Richard had to do. Berengaria knew that he did not want her; that any relationship she would have with him would be because of a sense of duty to the crown.

They were two unhappy women—Berengaria more so than Joanna, for Joanna had declared that she would never marry the Saracen and she meant it.

The Cypriot Princess watching them sat so quietly that they forgot she was there.

Yes, it was true, it was sad to be a Princess. She wondered what her own fate would be. Her father was in chains—silver ones—and Cyprus belonged to Richard. She had no home. Would she ever see her father or her old home again? Would a husband be found for her? Perhaps not, for homeless and with a father in chains, she was not important any more.

*   *   *

Richard realized that Joanna would never marry Malek Adel; he had a niece, however, who could take Joanna's place and marry the Saracen leader. He sent a message to Saladin and Malek Adel telling them that before a marriage could be arranged with his sister Queen Joanna it would be necessary to get a dispensation from the Pope which would cause delays and difficulties. He therefore proposed that Malek Adel should take his niece.

When Saladin heard this he laughed aloud. He had never expected for one moment that Richard's sister would marry his brother. It had all been part of the bargaining, which was not to be taken seriously.

He sent a message to say that Malek Adel could not consider anyone of lesser rank than the King's sister; and Richard had to accept the fact that that idea could not be pursued.

Saladin was not displeased with what had happened. The terms could never of course be considered seriously but at least the peace talks had delayed action and both sides were resting. The autumn was passing into winter and that was scarcely the season to wage a successful campaign.

Leaving Berengaria and Joanna in Jaffa Richard with the army moved on to the town of Ramleh, which Saladin had evacuated when he decided that he would move back to Jerusalem and prepare for an assault on that town should it come.

There was a conflict of opinion in the Christian camp. The fact that Saladin had gone to Jerusalem could only mean that he was building up defences there and as the peace talks had come to nothing it was clear that he was determined to defend Jerusalem with all his strength.

Some of the crusaders wished to press on to Jerusalem and subject it to a siege. Richard knew very well that they were not equipped to do this and Saladin would be in a much stronger position than they were. They would be utterly defeated and they must remember that such defeat to them would be disastrous whereas the Saracens on their own territory could after a while get men and supplies for further attacks.

The failure of the peace talks and the inability of Richard to arrange a match between his sister and Malek Adel had slightly tarnished his aura of invincibility, and there were some who questioned his judgements. As the majority of the crusaders wanted to press on to Jerusalem Richard gave way.

He too wanted to see the Holy City; he wanted to crown the crusade with the ultimate glory. If he could set the Christian flag flying over that city he would die contented.

It was the twenty-second of December when Richard left Ramleh on the march to Jerusalem. The crusaders had never seen such rain; it poured in torrents; the hailstones were the size of pigeons' eggs and they felt that one of the plagues of Egypt was being visited upon them. From the mountains the swollen streams became rivers and the paths were so muddy that men sank up to their knees.

After days of disaster it became clear that no progress could be made. The army was miserable and dispirited. The only thing to do was to return to Ramleh.

This they did, disgruntled and weary, blaming each other for the disaster. Richard did not know then that in the town of Jerusalem, Saladin, his army depleted, his stores scarce was fearful that Richard would continue the march to Jerusalem and that had he done so at that time he might have had a good chance of success.

At Ramleh Richard discussed the position with the dukes and the knights. Those who knew something of the Palestine winter were certain that they must wait for the spring. An army could not progress through such rain as was customary in this land and the cold would be intense, also. Richard decided that they would spend the winter repairing the walls of cities which Saladin's army had destroyed, while doing so making ready for the spring offensive.

It was depressing. He had reckoned on taking Jerusalem before Christmas and here he was in January still far from achieving that purpose.

They were in need of food and he believed that their ships would be lying off the coast of Ascalon so he ordered that they should leave at once for that town.

The journey was even worse than they had anticipated. The men were blinded by the rain; again and again their baggage sank in the mud; they cursed the climate and asked themselves which was worse, the heat of summer or this devastating rain, snow and cold which seeped into their bones.

Their spirits were not lifted when they arrived at Ascalon. The walls were in complete ruin, for Saladin, guessing they would wish to use this town, had done his best to make it uninhabitable. There was one hopeful sign. The supply ships had arrived but alas even in that they were thwarted, for it was impossible for the ships to land on account of the stormy weather.

So there they were, a dejected army—with food and other supplies in sight but unable to reach them.

Richard, always at his best in adversity, ordered them to occupy the town. They would take what was there, repair the walls and make the place habitable. The storms must subside at some time and then they would have their provisions.

They settled in and to inspire his men he himself joined them in the manual labour of repairing the walls.

Inspecting the men, taking a share in the work, he encouraged them to carry on and it was comforting to see a revival of spirits. He noticed however that Leopold, the Duke of Austria, was not working with the rest.

Coming face to face with the Duke who was strolling in a leisurely manner close to the wall where men were working, Richard said to him: 'I do not see you joining with us in this necessary work, my lord Duke.'

'You do not see me because I do not do it,' answered Leopold. 'My father was not a mason and I am not a carpenter.'

The Plantagenet temper boiled over. This was the kind of incident Richard was most anxious to avoid. The soldiers had suffered great hardship and he wanted them to know that this was understood and appreciated and shared by them all.

In a sudden rage he kicked the Duke of Austria on the shin so fiercely that he fell sprawling on the ground.

This affront to his dignity infuriated the Duke. He scrambled to his feet, scarlet with rage. Richard by now had stalked away.

'A curse on you!' shouted Leopold.

A few days later he and his men, which meant the German contingent, had left the crusade.

*   *   *

That was a dispiriting winter. The departure of Leopold of Austria in high dudgeon was followed by that of the Duke of Burgundy who, finding himself short of money, had asked

Richard to lend him some. He had believed, he explained, that he would have had his share of the ransom for the prisoners of Acre which he had been relying on. Now that it was lost, because in his wrath Richard had slain the prisoners of that city there was no money forthcoming from Saladin, and Burgundy, like many others, was finding himself in difficulties.

Richard who had lent him money at Acre and not been repaid refused to help him. So infuriated was the Duke that he went off taking the French contingent with him and declaring his intention to join Monteferrat.

His plans going wrong, victory seeming far away, Richard longed for an end of inactivity.

With the coming of the spring he would go forward to Jerusalem; surely this year would see victory.

Letters came from Queen Eleanor. The news they contained was very disturbing. She expressed her fears with vehemence. There was trouble in England. The people deplored the long absence of their King. Philip of France was being over friendly with Richard's brother John; and there was no doubt that John had his eyes on the throne and had a good chance of getting it if Richard did not come home to prevent him.

'You cannot wish to lose your crown,' wrote his mother, 'and if you want to keep it you must come back to England without delay. There is no time to lose.'

When Richard read those letters he was thrown into a state of terrible indecision. At one moment he was almost on the point of returning home; at another he was telling himself it would be folly to go now that he was so near to Jerusalem.

While he was pondering on this Conrad de Montferrat asked for an audience and Richard immediately granted it.

What hatred Montferrat harboured against him! He could sense it. He felt weary. This man had made a split in the crusader's army.

'You came,' said Richard, 'not to fight for God but for yourself.'

'Who does not?' replied Montferrat. 'Some achieve great conquests like the Island of Cyprus. Others are content with less. And we do our duty to God at the same time as to ourselves.'

'You must know that before the King of France left we

made a treaty that Guy de Lusignan should be King of Jerusalem during his lifetime and then you and your heirs should
follow him.'

'I wish to be King of Jerusalem during my lifetime.'

'And if I do not agree?'

'Many of your men are already with me. I have the Dukes
of Austria and Burgundy with their followers to swell my
ranks. There are others.'

Yes, thought Richard sadly, there are others.

He curbed his temper and instead of shouting abuse at
Montferrat which he might have done a short time before, he
said: 'I will consider this matter.'

When Montferrat had left him he thought of trouble in
England and he knew that his mother was right when she said
he should come home.

What if he should reconquer Jerusalem and lose England?

I will not, he assured himself fiercely; but something
within him told him he could not have both ... not yet.

So later when he was urged by his counsellors to forget his
promise to Guy de Lusignan and bestow the crown of Jerusalem on Conrad de Montferrat he surprised himself by his
agreement.

He sent for Guy and wearily told him what he had agreed
to.

'But, my friend,' he said, 'do not despair. The crown of
Jerusalem has yet to be won and it would have been yours
but for a lifetime. I have a better proposition for you. Suppose you were King of Cyprus now, and your heirs followed
you to the throne. Would that please you as much as the
crown of Jerusalem?'

Guy replied that spiritually nothing could compare with
the crown of Jerusalem; but he believed he would please God
best by pleasing his King, for his duty was to serve him while
he was on earth. He would accept the crown of Cyprus and he
could see that by bestowing the as yet unattained crown of
Jerusalem on Montferrat Richard had taken from a treach-
erous enemy a reason for breaking away from the crusading
army.

Richard embraced Guy. He had always known that he
could rely on him.

The Old Man of the Mountains

RICHARD firmly believed that, when shortly after this Conrad de Montferrat was murdered, this was by the hand of God who had no wish to see him reign over the Holy City.

There was a strange company of men and women who lived in the Lebanese mountains. They had a religion of their own and over them ruled a despotic dictator whom none of them dared disobey. Any who did so was instantly killed; and this did not only apply to those of his own sect. Occasionally they came down from the mountains and took a part in affairs which were likely to affect them.

They were called the Hashashen; this implied that they took a certain drug which was reputed to give men twice their normal strength and to rob them of all fear.

It was unwise to offend them—a fact which Montferrat had chosen to ignore, for while he was in control of Tyre one of the ships belonging to the Head of the Hashashen, who was generally known as The Old Man of the Mountains, had been in trouble off the coast. Instead of going to its rescue Montferrat and his men had refused help to the ship and had, moreover, robbed it of its cargo and allowed its sailors to drown.

The 'Old Man' was a title which was handed down from one head of this Ismaelite tribe to another. It meant the supreme head, whose word was law. The tribe was notorious throughout the middle east, for it was one of the most power-ful sects in that area.

There were many legends about the tribe. They had existed it was said in the days of Christ and their way of life had remained unchanged through the centuries. Another legend—but this was said to be true—was that the Old Man had created a Garden which was a replica of the Moham-medan paradise. In the most exquisite setting were flowering trees and luscious fruit growing in abundance. Palaces of great beauty had been erected there. Among the trees wan-dered the most beautiful girls, to dance, to sing or to delight in any manner possible. Delicate perfumes wafted through the air. Everything that could enchant had been thought of.

It was ancient custom to seek through the world certain young men whose characters indicated that they would best serve the tribe. These would be brought to the Old Man to sup with him and during the meal the visitors would fall into a heavy sleep. They would wake up in the garden and there they would live for several weeks until one day they would once more go into a heavy sleep, awaking from which they would find themselves shut out of the Paradise Gardens.

After experiencing paradise there was no peace to be found outside.

'You can earn your way back,' said the Old Man, 'by fulfil-ling a task I shall set you.'

The task was invariably murder. Someone had offended the Old Man and must be removed. When the murder had been satisfactorily committed the murderer would be given another spell in the gardens before being sent out on a new task.

The result was that the Old Man had his assassins planted in all manner of places and none felt safe from him.

The kings and rulers of the neighbourhood paid tribute to the Old Man knowing full well that if they did not comply with his wishes disaster would fall upon them.

Thus the sect grew rich and powerful and more and more young men were carried to the garden so that any offence committed against the Old Man brought its swift retribu-tion.

Montferrat should have known better than to steal the cargo of the ship; had he gone to the succour of that sinking ship, had he done his best to salvage the goods, he would not have suffered an untimely death just as he was about to realize his ambition.

Montferrat had dined rather well with the Bishop of Beauvais and was going home to his palace with a few of his close friends who had been with him throughout the evening.

As he was about to enter the palace two shadowy shapes emerged from behind a pillar. They fell upon the Count and plunged their daggers into his body.

The palace guards quickly killed one of the assassins, but the other escaped—not with any hope of getting away, for he hid behind the altar in the nearby church and when the body of Montferrat was carried in he rushed from his hiding place and thrust his dagger again and again into the dead body.

The assassin was seized and submitted to horrible torture with rack, screw and fire but he refused to say a word nor did he utter a cry of protest.

There were many who believed that Richard had ordered the deed to be done, but the manner of the crime and the fact that the Old Man of the Mountains had a grudge against the Count made it almost certain that he was behind the attack.

With Montferrat dead Richard wondered whether it would be wise to bestow on Guy de Lusignan the as yet unconquered Jerusalem; but another claimant had come into the picture. This was Count Henry of Champagne who, since he was the nephew of both Richard and Philip of France, seemed the ideal successor. He was popular, too, and when it was suggested that he should marry Montferrat's widow this seemed a happy solution to the affair.

Richard was agreeable, for he knew that he could trust Henry of Champagne as he never could have trusted Montferrat and as Guy was satisfied with Cyprus, the assassination of Montferrat brought nothing but good to Richard—which was probably why the rumour started that he—not the Old Man of the Mountains—had been responsible for the murder.

Farewell Jerusalem

RICHARD was depressed. He had just conquered Darum, a walled city which had presented little difficulty. Some fury had suddenly possessed him as his stone-casters had gone into action; he had felt an intense anger against the Saracens who were beginning to make him feel that they were invincible. He had planned to take Jerusalem before Christmas and here they were hampered by the terrible winter and no nearer to their goal than they had been since the fall of Acre.

So few were to be trusted. He had quarrelled with many. The French had always been uneasy allies. It had not happened as he had believed it would when he had made his glorious plans and dreamed what now seemed an impossible dream.

And as his troops had stormed the city and the citizens had cried for mercy he had shown none. In lust for vengeance on a fate which had denied him the victory he had craved he had struck off heads right and left with no consideration for the age or sex of his victims. The wild Plantagenent temper had charge of him and had demanded blood.

His men, as always taking their cue from him, inflicted ruthless horror on that town. And now it lay in ruins and of what good to the cause had that senseless slaughter been?

What had come over him? he asked himself. Was this Christian behaviour? Would God ever deem him worthy to enter Jerusalem?

Would he for ever after have moments when he remembered the cries of old men, women and children, their hands tightly bound behind them, as they were marched off to be sold as slaves?

I am fighting a desperate war, he excused himself.

But his conscience would not accept that.

As though in retribution for what had happened at Darum, as he rode out to Gaza messengers from England met him, with letters from his mother.

Apprehensively he read them.

'You must return at once. Your kingdom is in acute danger. John is conspiring with the King of France. If you do not come back you will lose England and Normandy.'

*   *   *

The news spread through the camp. 'Richard is leaving us. The news from England is so bad that he plans to go back.' The King of France had long gone. The governing of his country being more important than the capture of Jerusalem. Now it was the turn of the King of England.

Richard paced up and down. Again and again he cried out: 'Guide me, oh God; give me a sign. Tell me what I must do. Why did You not let me take Jerusalem before Christmas? Then I could have returned with a good heart.'

God remained silent under these reproaches mingled with pleas for guidance; and Richard's terrible dilemma continued.

So near to the capture of Jerusalem and yet so far.

He re-read Eleanor's letters. There was no mistaking their urgency. Philip, who said he had loved him! John, his own brother! Whom could one trust?

In deep melancholy he remembered his father who had complained so bitterly when his sons had fought against him. He understood something of his feelings now.

I did not deserve this though, thought Richard; and he seemed to hear his father's voice echoing from the tomb: 'Did you not, my son? There is something you have to learn. You cannot hold a kingdom by going off to do your pleasure.'

'My pleasure! This was a holy crusade.'

'Your pleasure, my son. A king's duty is to his kingdom.'

'But I am so near,' he murmured.

His army knew of his quandary. There had been other letters from home. Most people had known that John would seize the first opportunity to play the traitor. Why hadn't Richard? Philip and he had been strange friends; love such as theirs turned to hate. Philip would never forget that he was the King of France whose rival was the King of England and Duke of Normandy and when Richard was not there to remind him that he was also his beloved friend, the King of France would forget that.

'I must go home,' thought Richard. 'But how can I when Jerusalem is within my grasp?'

*   *   *

He had made his decision. He would stay and make his assault on the town. He would put from his mind the warnings. He would capture Jerusalem and then go back to England and deal with John. If he was the one to set the Christian flag flying once more from the walls of the Holy City men would revere him throughout Christendom; they would flock to his banner, seeing in him the saviour of the Christian world. He would quickly regain anything that Philip or John had taken from him.

June had come and with it a return of the heat. As the rain and snow had hindered, so now did the heat. The pests returned—the sand storms, the flies, the mosquitoes, the tarantulas. Another had appeared—poisonous snakes whose sting was death.

But we are close now to Jerusalem, thought Richard, and he thrilled at the prospect of the coming conflict with Saladin who was himself in Jerusalem, as determined to hold it as Richard was to take it.

Reports came in of the supplies which were reaching the city. Saladin's army was waiting to attack hidden away somewhere in the neighbourhood. There were great numbers of Saracens.

Richard sent for Henry of Champagne, a man whom he believed he could trust not only because he was his nephew but also because he had put nothing in the way of his becoming King of Jerusalem. His desire to regain the city must be as great as Richard's own.

'I need all the men I can muster,' said Richard. 'This attack must not fail. We have to face Saladin's might and we known by now that he is one of the greatest generals.'

'No match for yourself, Sire,' said Henry dutifully.

'Let us not underestimate him,' replied Richard. 'I have great respect for him. Many of our men deserted as you know and went back to Acre. I want you to go and tell them that we are on the point of attacking, make them see that they will regret it to the end of their days if they are not with us.'

'I will go, with all speed,' said Henry.

'Do not delay. The sooner we make the attack the better.'

So Henry left for Acre and Richard continued to make his preparations.

Each day he watched for the return of Henry with the reluctant crusaders. The time was passing. One, two, three weeks. What was happening in England? All these weeks Saladin would be making Jerusalem stronger.

Henry of Champagne was not finding his task an easy one. Living was good in Acre. How different from the discomforts of the march, harassed by Saracens and perhaps even worse by the plagues of the land, and men found it hard to choose between the combined displeasure of Richard and Heaven and all the easy comfort of Acre.

The waiting was irksome, and all the time Richard was tortured by the thought of what was happening in England.

There were forays with the enemy; Richard now and then led a raid against the Saracens. They were bringing supplies into Jerusalem by various routes and when news of them was brought to Richard he would take some of his men and make a raid. This kept the men in fair spirits and Richard knew well enough that there was nothing so dangerous as boredom.

On such an occasion he went to the stronghold of Emmaus which he very successfully raided, killing twenty Saracens and taking possession of their camels and horses as well as supplies. The rest of the garrison, who had been deluded into thinking that Richard's entire army was with him, fled in disorder.

As they paused to view the spoils one of Richard's knights rode to him and said: 'Sire, if you will ride to the top of yonder hill I will show you Jerusalem.'

Richard rode to the top of the hill but when he reached the summit he pulled his surcoat across his eyes.

'Nay,' he said, 'I will not look ... yet. Fair Lord God,' he went on, 'I pray Thee that thou suffer me not to behold Thy

Holy City if so be that I may not deliver it out of the hands of Thy enemies.'

And he refused to look on the city.

*   *   *

They were long delayed at Beit Nuba. By this time Henry of Champagne had arrived with those crusaders who had finally been persuaded to return with him. Richard looked at them with contempt. Such men could scarcely be expected to fight as he knew they would have to.

All the time there hung over him the shadow of events in England. He was unhappy knowing that Philip had broken his word. That John was a traitor was not surprising. He had been spoiled by their father and led to believe he would one day inherit the throne.

When an opportunity came to intercept a caravan which was travelling from Egypt to Jerusalem with supplies for the Saracens, Richard seized it joyfully. It would give the men the excitement they so badly needed and help to keep up their spirits. Saladin's spies were everywhere and it soon reached his ears that Richard intended to waylay the caravan. He sent men out to protect it and when Richard's force came to that spot in the Hebron Hills known as the Round Fountain, because of the spring where the horses were brought to drink, he found the Saracens there.

A great battle took place in which many on both sides were killed; but the Christians were victorious and the spoils were great. There were almost five thousand camels as well as mules, horses, gold, silver and rich materials, besides foodstuffs such as flour and barley and skins for carrying water.

In Jerusalem Saladin mourned the loss of the caravan and fervently prayed that Richard should never know how weakly the city was defended. That he did not know was obvious as he was delaying the attack. Saladin did everything possible to let everyone believe that he was confident in his strong defence, but this was not the case and he knew very well that Richard's greatest mistake was in delay.

He sent his spies into Richard's camp with rumours that he, Saladin, had poisoned the wells outside Jerusalem; and Richard decided that without water they must retire from Beit Nuba and fall back on Jaffa.

Great was the jubilation in Jerusalem.

'Praise be to Allah,' cried Saladin, 'He has saved Jerusalem for me.'

*   *   *

There was another enemy which raised its head against Richard: the ever-recurring fever.

He knew now that it had laid him low that he must return to England. He was tortured by nightmare dreams of what was happening at home. Not in this crusade was he to have the glory of winning back the Holy City.

Saladin was too mighty a foe. They were too much alike. They were the two greatest warriors of the age pitted against each other, and it seemed that neither could conclusively defeat the other. They respected each other. Richard thought: I can never take Jerusalem while Saladin lives. And Saladin thought: I can never drive the Christians out of Palestine while Richard the Lion-hearted leads them. We two should have been friends. We have too much respect for each other to be enemies. There is love of a strange kind between us.

There were times when Richard thought he was dying of the fever, but in his more lucid moments he realized that if he recovered there was nothing to be done but leave for home, his task incomplete. This, which was to have been the most glorious crusade, was to end in failure. He must go back, make his kingdom and his dukedom safe and come again with more men and more supplies. At least he had gained experience. Somewhere in his mind was the thought that Saladin could not live for ever and that he must wait for his death before he could conquer the Saracens.

There was ill news of the Duke of Burgundy, who had returned to serve under Richard after the death of Montferrat. He had an attack of fever and it seemed unlikely that he would recover. This gave the French the excuse they wanted to retire. Richard knew that all these men who had come out with such high hopes were now weary of the battle; they all longed to go home. They missed their families and their native land; they had dreamed of glory and found overpowering heat, devastating cold and poisonous insects.

'It is time to go,' Richard told himself. 'I will come again and next time I shall succeed.'

Saladin was an honourable man. Perhaps he could make a truce with him. He would tell him the truth, for if he did not, Saladin would discover it. He was sick; there was trouble in his realm; while he fought in this land half his thoughts were of his home.

He called messengers to him and sent them to Saladin. Would Saladin consider a truce?

There was in fact nothing Saladin wanted more. His men, too, were weary of the fight. They, too, longed for their homes. They had suffered terrible losses and they greatly feared Richard the Lion-Heart.

Most willingly would he come to terms.

It was decided that the truce should last three years, three months, three weeks and three days starting from the following Easter. Part of the coast was to remain in Christian hands; and during the time of the truce Christians might have free passage and safe conduct to Jerusalem and be allowed to worship at the Holy Sepulchre. But they must come in peace and in small parties.

Richard knew that Saladin would keep his word.

'Is it not strange,' he said, 'that I should know this and trust a heathen, when he who declared himself my good friend and ally, the Christian King of France, should conspire with my own brother against me?'

And he thought often of Saladin as Saladin thought of him; each was aware of the almost mystic bond between them.

*   *   *

In the palace at Acre the two Queens heard of his illness and that preparations were to be made for them to leave.

Joanna, watchful of her sister-in-law, noticed that she did not express the usual anxiety for Richard's health. She was sorry. She had to admit that Richard had neglected Berengaria shamefully. True he was engaged on a mighty venture, but he made no effort to be with her and there surely must have been occasions when it was possible.

Berengaria had changed a little; her lips had tightened. Perhaps she was no longer in love with the romantic warrior.

Joanna was sad. She had to admit that Richard was ruthless. Had he not tried to marry her off to a Saracen? Yet he had made no effort to force her. She would have done anything rather than agree to such a marriage and he knew that. Poor Berengaria! She was learning with bitterness that there were often disadvantages in being born a princess.

The little Cypriot in her role of watcher asked herself whether there was not after all something to be said for being a dispossessed princess. No one would try to force her into marriage; and if marriage was not for her how could she have a neglectful husband to make her unhappy?

Berengaria said to Joanna, 'When Richard comes I would speak to him alone.'

'But of course you will be alone with him. You are his wife.'

A hard smile curved Berengaria's lips. 'None would believe it,' she said. 'Sometimes I find it difficult to do so myself.'

Joanna did not pursue the subject. She wanted to turn away from it. Perhaps some day Berengaria would confide in her when the wounds were less fresh.

Richard arrived, looking pale and somewhat hollow-eyed but considering the malignancy of the fever far better than might have been expected.

He asked the two queens to come to him and was surprised when Berengaria came alone. She thought how magnificent he looked. Illness could not destroy the appearance of great strength and virility.

'So,' she said, 'we are to leave here.'

'The news has come in advance of me?'

'It is customary, my lord, to hear news of you not from your lips but those of others.'

He shrugged his shoulders. 'There is so much to occupy me.'

'That I know well and the company of others is preferable to that of your wife.'

He looked astonished. 'Why say you so?' he asked.

'Indeed why, since it is truly unnecessary to voice such an obvious fact,' she replied. Then she burst out passionately: 'How think you I endure the pity of those around me?'

'Pity, Madam?' he said in surprise. 'Should you be pitied ... here in this comfortable palace? I and my soldiers should be the ones who are given that ... marching in the heat or the mud, tormented by noisome insects...'

'And your friend Blondel de Nesle?' she asked. 'Does he suffer so?'

'The minstrels accompany the army. They have their work as do the others.'

'I trust this Blondel is happy with his work.'

'He would seem so.'

'So much enjoying the favour of his master.'

He pretended not to understand. He said: 'Music is an essential part of our army. A minstrel's songs can lighten the spirit and put heart into weary men.'

She shrugged her shoulders impatiently.

'I am no wife to you,' she said.

'Is that your wish?' he asked, almost eagerly.

'If it be yours,' she answered.

'This seems to me a fruitless conversation,' he said. 'You are the Queen. I am the King. We are married whether we call it so or not. I am much pressed for time. I wished to see you and my sister that I might arrange for our departure.'

'We shall not, of course, travel with you?' She could not look at him. She fixed her eyes on the glittering belt he wore about his waist. She had seen it before for it was a favourite of his. It was an object of startling beauty, set with unusual gems.

'It is wiser not,' he said.

She laughed bitterly. 'For our comfort or yours?'

He looked surprised, wilfully misunderstanding her. 'For yours of a certainty.' He looked at her coldly. 'I think you are unaware of what is happening in my kingdom. My mother writes to me that traitors plot against me. I must go back by a quicker route and that may be a dangerous one. You and my sister will travel with the fleet to protect you. I am putting you in charge of my faithful knight Stephen of Turnham whom I would trust with my life.'

'It is good of you,' she said, 'to take such care of me.'

He bowed his head and answered: 'I would speak with my sister. There are many plans to be made.'

She went to her chamber and there lay on her bed.

The Cypriot Princess crept silently into her room and knelt by her bed. She took her hand and held it.

The little Princess saw that the tears were on Berengaria's cheeks.

*   *   *

On the first day of October the fleet with the two queens and the Cypriot princess set sail. Richard remained for nine more days. He said he must wait for those days to regain fully his strength for the journey.

He stood on the prow of the small ship which was carrying him and a few of his attendants away from Jerusalem.

A great sadness possessed him. He had failed to achieve that which he had come so near to winning.

Leaning on the rail he cried: 'Oh Holy Land, I commend thee to God. May He, of his mercy grant me such space of life that I may one day bring thee aid. For it is my hope and determination, by God's good will, to return.'

Only with the belief that one day he would come back and win Jerusalem could he be at peace with himself.

The land faded from sight. The crusade was over. He would not brood on the number of lives which had been lost, the amount of blood that had been shed, the torture and agonies which had been inflicted on myriads.

He must think now of what was happening at home; he must make plans for defeating the traitors. But first of all there was the hazardous journey ahead of him.

The Royal Fugitive

THE journey to Corfu was uneventful. During it Richard fully regained his health and had time to assess his situation.

The crusade had failed in its purpose. He might have left with Philip for he had gained very little by staying. Had he gone back to England then, he could have prevented whatever trouble was brewing with John, and he could have planned a greater crusade in the light of what he had learned from the last one.

He had emerged with but little gain: merely the three years truce during which time Christians could visit Jerusalem. But his reputation as a soldier had grown to spectacular magnitude. Richard the Lion-hearted was known throughout the Christian world; minstrels sang of his prowess and his courage in battle. He was the greatest soldier of his age and yet he had not been able to vanquish Saladin. Perhaps in his heart he had not wanted to, and he believed that Saladin had not wished to destroy him. Saladin would have preferred to make him his hostage. He knew that, because there had been several attempts to take him when he was in a vulnerable position, perhaps in some lonely spot with but a few of his knights. He could visualize such a situation. The courteous treatment, the honours, the conversation, the growing friendship. It would have been as it had in those long ago days when he had been a hostage of Philip of France. He would not have believed it possible then that Philip who had loved him so dearly in those days should now be plotting against him.

He had many enemies. This journey of his could be full of dangers. If he were to be washed up on some alien coast defenceless, many willing hands would seize him, and not in order to honour him. The French hated him. They had never agreed during their sojourn in the Holy Land. How often they had shown their enmity. And the Germans disliked him. Henry the Emperor would not forgive him for making an ally of Tancred and Leopold had a personal grudge against him.

He must get back quickly, and to do so he must go as far as possible by land, for who could tell when the sea was going to make progress impossible. At any time ships could be driven on to a coast if they were lucky and kept there for months waiting for favourable winds.

Time was important. His mother had made it clear that urgency was needed; and even after receiving her warning he had delayed.

He would make the journey by land and as it was going to be a dangerous one it would be folly to let it be known that the traveller was Richard of England. He must disguise himself; it was not easy for a king. He could wear the clothes of a beggar but somehow the arrogance, the dignity, the kingly air would seep through and betray him.

Such were his thoughts as he sailed away from the Holy Land and a month after leaving he reached the Island of Corfu.

*   *   *

Two days out from Corfu Richard sighted two vessels on the horizon.

He shouted to his friends to come and see.

'By God's eyes,' he cried, 'I know not to which country they belong. They would seem to be pirates.'

'Better pirates, Sire,' said one of his friends, 'than French or German.'

'Be ready,' cried Richard. 'We may have to fight them.'

One of the ships came alongside. It was well armed and Richard regretted that his fleet was not with him. He would have made short work of the impudent fellows if it had been there.

The sailors were ready with arrows and stones but Richard

did not give the order to attack. He said that first he would try to parley with the pirates.

Using his trumpet he did this. It was not easy. They spoke a variation of Turkish and Arabic; but the stay in Palestine had helped him to understand something of this language and it was just possible to make himself understood.

The vessels were indeed pirates, looking for booty.

Richard had an idea. He cried: 'If you attempt to board my ship I will have the blood of every man of you. But there is a way in which you could gain a great deal of money without fighting for it.'

The pirate leader was interested and Richard said that he would board the larger of their vessels to parley with him, accompanied by only two of his knights.

The pirate leader was astonished that he could so trust them, and said so.

'Why, fellow,' said Richard, 'if you attempted treachery we would sink your two ships and your men with them. Have no doubt of that. But you have given me your word and I have given you mine. Wise men know that it is never good policy to betray a trust. If you wish to fight and take the spoils of my ship, then I will return to it and we shall battle together. But you are not so foolish.'

'You are a great lord,' said the pirate. 'What is your will?'

'I wish you to take me on board and convey me and a few of my followers to a spot I shall choose on the Adriatic coast. If you will do this you will be amply paid. If you fail you will surely die with all your sins on you—and a pirate could scarcely pursue his trade without indulging in a goodly number.'

'You are a brave man,' said the pirate.

'It has been said of me.'

'There is about you a manner different from that of other men. I would say that only great lords and kings have such manners.'

'Then perhaps you are a discerning man.'

'There is news around,' said the pirate, 'that a great king is on his way back to England.'

'You hear news then.'

'We pick it up here and there. It is said that many great lords are looking for the King of England.'

'For what purpose think you?'

'That which would brook no good to him, I trow,' said the pirate with a laugh.

'And if they were to find him, I trow that would brook no good to them.'

'He is a mighty man. One 'twould be good not to cross.'

Richard nodded and the pirate smiled slyly.

'We will do your bidding, my lord,' he said. 'We will take you and some of your friends to the spot you choose and if you wish to reward poor men for the trouble they have had, they will be grateful.'

'You shall be rewarded,' said Richard. He looked down at the clothes he had adopted soon after leaving Corfu. They were those of a Templar. 'You see me thus garbed.'

'My lord, it does not become you as other garbs might.'

'Then mayhap I should change it. I shall come to your ship as a palmer. Would that fit me better?'

The pirate shook his head. 'Mayhap 'twill pass but I see you in shining armour, my lord, with a red cross on your breast.'

'And I see you are a man of insight,' said Richard, 'which if it is tempered with discretion should serve you well.'

Thus Richard, in the garb of a humble pilgrim, and a few of his most trusted men boarded the pirate ship. His own he sent off to join his fleet if possible; if not to return to England.

*   *   *

The pirates treated him with a respect which grew during his voyage with them. That he was a man of great courage was obvious to them, that he was Richard the Lion-heart was almost equally so. They knew they could trust him to reward them if they landed him safely for his honesty was as renowned as his courage. He was a guileless man in many ways; he gave a straight answer and he had so often been deluded because he had trusted others to be as frank as himself. Richard Yea and Nay was a man whose word was his bond.

When one of the ships ran into trouble and was forced on to the island of Lacroma he worked with the men during the violent storm in the hope of saving the ship. As this was impossible he with the other members of the crew transferred to the remaining ship and he travelled in that to Ragusa.

There he took his leave of the pirates after paying them as he had promised and still dressed as a pilgrim, accompanied by a band of followers and with rich garments, jewels and money on pack mules, he began his journey across the land.

It was ill luck which had brought him to Ragusa, for the governor of that land was related to Conrad de Montferrat who had been murdered by the Old Man of the Mountains just as he had been declared King of Jerusalem.

When he landed Richard found a lodging which was not very grand, explaining that he was a merchant who was returning from pilgrimage. There he called his followers together and decided what must be done.

'First, my friends, we must conceal our identity. Our party must consist of Sir Baldwin de Bethune and his retinue. I shall not be of that retinue for it seems to me that if I attempted to ape a servant I should fail in some way. For myself I shall take the role of a wealthy merchant from Damascus who had joined your party for company. My name shall be Hugo . . . Hugo of Damascus.'

'Where shall we go from here, my lord?' asked Baldwin.

'We must make our way to the coast, avoiding French territory, for I should not care to fall into the hands of the King of France.'

'Nor those of Leopold of Austria, my lord,' said Baldwin.

'I liked him not,' said Richard. 'An arrogant fellow who came to the crusade in no humble spirit. He sought only gain. Do you remember how he flew his flag on the walls of Acre and refused to help us rebuild the walls of the cities?'

'Aye, Sire, I remember it well,' answered Baldwin, 'and doubtless he does.'

Their host chatted with them as they sat at his table. He had been told he would not regret his hospitality.

Richard asked if they had many pilgrims passing through the land.

'Nay,' was the answer, 'they do not often come this way.'

'Any Christian country would allow pilgrims to pass through unmolested, I believe,' said Richard.

'Nay, Master Hugo, that is not so. Those who wish us ill could so easily hide their identity behind the pilgrim's robe and palm.'

' 'Tis true enough,' said Richard, 'and it may be that the most honest of merchants would be suspected.'

It was so difficult for him to deceive. He was not meant to play any role but that of a king. His manners would have betrayed him again and again to any who was suspicious.

'We are watchful,' said their host. 'I shall be obliged to let it be known that a party of pilgrims has passed this way. Did you know that King Richard has left Palestine?'

'Is that so?' said Baldwin before Richard could speak.

'He has to return to his kingdom where his brother is causing trouble and it seems that he made many enemies when he was in Palestine.'

'It is difficult not to,' began Richard.

Baldwin interrupted: 'There will always be rumours. It is well not to believe them all.' Even as he spoke he threw an apologetic look at Richard for interrupting him. It was not only impossible for Richard to disguise himself; it was almost equally so for his men.

'I have heard it said often that the king of France and the Emperor of Germany are against him, as well as Duke Leopold of Austria. My own Governor had reason to hate him.'

'What reasons are these?' demanded Richard hotly.

'My Governor is Count Meinhard of Goritz, nephew of the Marquis Conrad de Montferrat, who was murdered on the orders of Richard of England.'

'That is not true,' cried Richard indignantly.

Again Baldwin had the temerity to interrupt. 'Who says this?' he asked mildly.

'All say it. The Marquis was to be King of Jerusalem. Richard of England did not wish this, wanting the crown to go to his own man, Guy de Lusignan; but it was Conrad who had the right. The King of England finally relented and gave his consent to the appointment. It is said that he did this because he was planning to despatch the Count.'

'It was not the King of England who murdered him,' said Richard. 'I swear it, on my pilgrim's palm.'

'Ah, my dear merchant, what can we know of these matters? Very soon after Conrad's election he was returning home after dining with a friend when he was set upon by assassins and stabbed to death.'

'These assassins were in the employ of the Old Man of the Mountains.'

'Rumours have come from the mountains that it was Richard of England who ordered the murder of the Count.'

'Then the Old Man lies.'

Their host looked furtive. Then he said: 'I must beg of you not to speak ill of the Old Man at my table.'

'So you fear him,' cried Richard.

'All wise men fear the Old Man, sir. It is said that he never forgets a slight. I would not care to be set upon by one of his men. Nay, I speak well of the Old Man. I but wish to warn you that as pilgrims it will be necessary for you to have safe conduct from the Governor.'

'This Count...' began Richard.

'Count Meinhard of Goritz, nephew of the Count Conrad de Montferrat.'

'Very well,' said Richard. 'We will ask his permission to pass safely through his land.'

* * *

In the room assigned to them they talked in whispers.

'Think you he knew who I was?' asked Richard.

'It is certain, Sire, that he knew you were no ordinary merchant.'

'Do not call me Sire. People listen. Call me Hugo. Now, Baldwin, we shall have to ask permission to cross the country. Do you think this fellow is suspicious of us?'

'It might well be so, Sire ... Hugo.'

'I will send the Count a gift—a ring I have. I will tell the messenger that I bought it from a Pisan merchant at a bargain price. I would wish him to have it to show our gratitude for giving us free passage through his land.'

'My lord ... Hugo,' said Baldwin, 'that ring is a very fine one.'

'Nay,' said Richard, 'but a bauble. Let us send it without delay, for I am eager to proceed with the journey. Now we must get a night's sleep and in the morning be ready to continue our journey.'

He lay down on the pallet his host had provided. One of the men lay across the door, while the others placed themselves in strategic positions.

He lay brooding, thinking of the wasted months, of what was happening in his kingdom, of the treachery of John and Philip—an ill assorted pair—of the nobility of Saladin.

* * *

When the ring was brought to Meinhard of Goritz he looked at it intently.

'A merchant gave it?' he said. 'A merchant Hugo who is with a band of pilgrims?'

He sent for his jeweller.

'It is a very fine ring,' said the jeweller.

'Scarcely one that a merchant would bestow for a free passage,' said Meinhard.

He dismissed the jeweller and discussed the matter with his ministers.

'There is something unusual about these pilgrims,' he said. 'I hear that one has a bearing of great dignity. He is said to be a merchant but the other members of the party seem very respectful towards him while attempting not to be.'

His chief minister smiled slowly. 'My lord Count,' he said, 'we know that Richard of England has left Palestine. He will be wishing to reach England by the shortest route. This might well be by land.'

Meinhard nodded. 'And you imply that our merchant Hugo could be the King of England?'

'Who but a king would bestow such a ring as though it is a trifle. What is of great value to most men is a bagatelle to a king.'

'If this is indeed King Richard, the murderer of my uncle, then what shall we do?'

'We will take him prisoner. The Emperor will not easily forgive us if we allow him to slip through our fingers.'

'I will send for the messengers whom we have been holding and give them back the ring. Then we will take him captive.'

'There are many who would not forgive us if we did not make it known that he had arrived.'

Meinhard of Goritz sent for the messenger.

'Take this ring back to your master,' he said. 'It does not belong to Hugo the Merchant. It belongs to King Richard of England. I have given my word to seize and question all pilgrims who pass through my territory and not to take gifts from them in return for a safe conduct. But this is a different matter. This is the King of England whose fame has travelled ahead of him. It is Coeur de Lion himself. Therefore take the ring and tell him that I have given my word not to accept gifts but because of his greatness and his generosity in offering it to me, I will give him free leave to go.'

When the messenger rode back with the ring and the message there was consternation among Richard's friends.

'I like not those words,' said Baldwin. 'There is a threat beneath them.'

'I think so too,' answered Richard. 'We will not leave by sea. They will be watching the coast, and if I travel with a large party I shall be recognized immediately. I will go from here with a few of you and some of my possessions and I will start at once. I feel that to delay would be dangerous.'

They parted company and Richard set out. He had not been gone more than an hour when troops arrived at the lodging. Those who remained of Richard's followers were arrested and taken to Meinhard of Goritz.

When they were brought before him he said: 'Where is the merchant Hugo?'

Baldwin said: 'I know not. He left us to pursue his journey alone.'

Meinhard was furious. He saw that he had acted in a manner to arouse suspicion. He should have sent the troops back with the ring. He had presumed that Richard would have accepted his promise for safe conduct and have landed right into his net.

There was no help for it. He had lost the King ... but temporarily, he promised himself.

There was no time for reproaches. He sent messengers at once to his brother Frederick of Betsau, for the host of the previous night when questioned had revealed in which direction Richard had gone, which indicated that he must pass through Frederick's lands.

Frederick was to look out for the King of England. Every house likely to be used by pilgrims must be watched.

When he received the message, Frederick sent for his cousin Roger of Argenton.

'A mission for you, Roger,' he said. 'The King of England is nearby. He has slipped through my hands but I don't intend to allow him to continue to do so. I want to capture him. This would mightily please the Emperor. And if he escapes I shall doubtless be reprimanded for allowing him to. He murdered Conrad de Montferrat.'

'I believed that to have been the Old Man of the Mountains,' said Roger.

'Nay, it was Richard who was his enemy. The Old Man's followers swear that it was Richard who had him killed.'

'Murderers often like to shift their crimes on to the shoulders of others.'

'No matter who murdered Conrad, I need Richard here. Go, Roger, and bring him to me. Do not spare yourself or anyone, but bring me Richard.'

*   *   *

Riding across the country Roger of Argenton encountered a company of pilgrims. There was one among them, tall, fair and of such dignified carriage that Roger's suspicions were immediately aroused.

He asked permission to ride with them. This was granted for Richard liked the look of the young man. He asked him to ride beside him.

'Tell me,' said Roger, 'what is your destination?'

'We are on our way to England,' said Richard. 'Do you know of a nearer route than the one we are taking?'

'You should head northwards,' Roger told him, 'and to the west. You would in due course come to France and from there cross to England.'

'We have a long journey ahead of us,' said Richard. 'Tell me, my friend, have you travelled much?'

'I have been in Normandy.'

'Normandy. Ah, a fair land.'

'As a Norman I agree with you.'

'By God's eyes, you are a Norman. I knew it.'

'How so?'

'Your bearing, your height. You have the look of a Norman.'

'That is a compliment.'

'None greater. Let us talk of Normandy.'

They talked of that land for which it was clear they both had a great affection.

'Tell me,' said Richard, 'did you ever meet its Duke?'

'To my regret I never did. But he is King of England now and on a crusade to the Holy Land.'

'Kings mayhap should stay in their own kingdoms, think you?'

' 'Tis a noble thing to fight for the Cross, but it is said that duty lies first to the homeland.'

'It may well be that you are right,' answered Richard quietly.

Roger suggested that they should stay a night at one of his castles. There he would be happy to entertain a party whose company he had so much enjoyed.

As they entered the castle Richard could see that his friends were uneasy.

'My lord,' whispered one of them, 'can we trust this man?'

'I trust him,' said Richard.

Alas! thought his men. Was Richard perhaps a little too trusting?

The pilgrims were given a large room in which they could spend the night and they were invited to eat in the great hall with Roger's family.

Afterwards Richard sang for them and they brought a lute for him to play. Then Roger asked that Richard play a game of chess with him.

They removed to a quiet corner of the hall and sat there, the board between them.

Richard noticed the fine handsome face, the noble bearing, the fair colouring, the long Norman legs, and liked well what he saw.

'I could find it in my heart to linger here,' he said.

Roger flushed slightly and said: 'Naught would delight me more, my lord.'

Richard saw that the hand on the piece Roger held trembled a little. He had not noticed he had called him my lord.

Their eyes met and there was understanding between them.

Here is a man whom I could love, thought Richard.

He looked at the rafters above the hall, at their companions still at the table, at the serving men and women passing back and forth.

'It has been a day I shall remember,' said Richard. 'I shall never forget you, Roger of Argenton.'

'Nor I you, my lord.'

'What do you know of me, Roger?'

'That you are no humble pilgrim.'

'Pilgrims are not always men of humble standing.'

'Nay, but there is that about you that proclaims you to be of the highest rank.'

'Do you know who I am?'

'I know who I believe you to be.'

'And who is that?'

'I dare not say, my lord, but if you would tell me it would make me happy.'

'Can you keep a secret, Roger?'

'I would let them pull out my tongue, my lord, rather than betray one you told me.'

'Then here is one: I am Richard of England. Nay, do not rise. It is our secret, remember.'

'You know they are seeking you?'

'I know I am surrounded by enemies.'

'They seek to trap you.'

'Let them try.'

'There is an order in this land that you are to be sought and when found taken to the Lord Frederick.'

'Fret not, Roger. I will elude them. Think not that Coeur de Lion will be disturbed by some petty ruler like this Frederick.'

'But if you fell into his hands ... as you are ...'

'He would be the one who would have to fear. Come, I have put you in check.'

They returned to the game which Richard won and then he said that it was time for retiring.

He lay on his pallet but he could not sleep. He was thinking of Philip who had betrayed him and then he thought of the gentle eyes and the Norman bearing of Roger of Argenton.

Would he would follow me, he thought.

He was awakened by one of his attendants.

'What now,' cried Richard. 'Is it morning then?'

'Nay, my lord, just past midnight. Roger of Argenton is without. He says he must speak to you. It is of the greatest importance.'

Richard rose from his bed.

'Have a care, my lord.'

'Fear not. I trust this man.'

One of his knights put a robe about his shoulders and he stepped out of the room.

Roger immediately knelt at his feet.

'Pardon, my King,' he murmured. 'Pardon.'

'What is your sin?' asked Richard, 'that you get me from my bed to ask forgiveness for it.'

Roger was on his feet, his eyes wide. 'My lord, you must fly from here without delay. I have had a horse made ready. Do not delay.'

'Why so? You were hospitable enough last evening and now would be rid of us.'

'I must confess. I knew who you were. I was sent by Lord Frederick to intercept you, to bring you here, to trap you. I want you to go before they come for you. I would rather die than be the one who betrayed you.'

'So you set out to do that then, Roger?'

'I was ordered by my lord. But I cannot do it, Sire. That is why I warn you. You must go at once. The horse is ready. I shall tell them that I was mistaken. That you are not in this area.'

'Thank you, Roger.'

'I could not betray you, for I love you.'

'I love you, too,' said Richard. 'Nor shall I forget this night.'

'Then prepare and be gone. It has been the greatest honour of my life to receive you here, but I shall not rest until you have gone.'

Richard drew Roger to him and kissed him.

Then he turned and went back into the room.

'Dress!' he cried. 'Prepare. We are leaving here without delay. Roger of Argenton was meant to betray us and he has saved us instead.'

*　　　*　　　*

When Roger reported to Frederick that the pilgrims were in fact a certain Baldwin de Bethune and his companions, Frederick was bitterly disappointed. So much so that he said he would like to examine the pilgrims himself and he sent out orders for their arrest.

Roger was ahead of him. He knew in which direction they had gone and he reached them before they were discovered.

'The pilgrims will be arrested,' he told Richard. 'They are to be taken before Frederick. You, my liege lord, must not be with the party when it is taken. Leave it now. Your horse will carry you a long way from here. Take with you but one servant. Go northwards as fast as you can. Do not seek rich lodgings. Be careful that you are not noticed.'

So once again Roger had saved him, for a day after Richard had parted with his knights they were discovered, arrested and thrown into prison.

* * *

There he was, the King of England, accustomed to being surrounded by a retinue of followers, alone in a strange land, save for one page. When he had left his friends he and his page had galloped northwards for some hours until his horse was exhausted; when they had come to a forest, the page tethered the horses to a tree, spread out a cloak upon the grass and they slept.

It was dawn when Richard awoke. He looked about for his friends and seeing only the sleeping page realized with dismay what had happened.

He faced the situation. Richard of England was wandering across Europe, with no knowledge of geography, realizing that he was surrounded by enemies, with no servants except the page and only the treasure they could carry to pay for his journey.

It was an incongruous situation. The man who had but a short time ago commanded men in their thousands was now a fugitive.

He was not entirely dismayed. This was adventure, although of a different kind from those that usually came his way, but he was ready for any sort of adventure.

He shouted to his page, who hearing his voice sprang up in confusion.

'Come, page,' he said, 'we must be on our way. We have to reach the coast somehow and take ship for England. There are just the two of us which is not a bad thing, for none would suspect a king would travel with just one servant. I doubt not you are as hungry as I am. We will ride on and perhaps find food somewhere.'

The page brought his master's horse and they started off.

For three days they travelled, living as they could. Richard would wait outside a town in a thicket, if that were possible, while the page went and bought food. They rode through the day and slept from exhaustion in fields and woods and on the third day they came to a city.

Richard did not realize that this city was Vienna and that he was in the heart of that territory which belonged to his bitterest enemy, Leopold of Austria.

'Now,' he said, 'we must find a humble lodging and there we shall rest for a while before pursuing our journey. While we stay we will find out where we are and what direction we should take. But first we must rest and eat to sustain ourselves after these days of hardship.'

The page had grown closer to his master than he had ever been and was filled with pride to think that fate had chosen him to be the one to accompany King Richard on this perilous journey.

They found a humble lodging on the outskirts of the town where no questions were asked when they explained they just needed a room. Richard told the woman of the house that he was a merchant and dealt in fine objects. This would allay her suspicions if she saw any of the treasures he had managed to bring with him. He told her that he and his servant would like to stay for a week or so for they were tired with travelling and still had far to go. When he asked her the name of the nearby city she told him it was Vienna.

'Ah,' said Richard, 'that would belong to Leopold of Austria.'

'He is our noble Duke,' said the woman.

Richard smiled inwardly recalling that occasion when he had kicked the fellow for refusing to help build a city's walls. What would he say if he knew the King of England was now travelling through his realm?

He was determined this time not to betray himself and prepared to learn the ways of humble folk. He found he enjoyed talking to the woman and her husband. He could speak their language tolerably well and he took an interest in their way of life. He would sit in the kitchen while the woman baked and would watch her and chat while she worked. She took to giving him little tasks and he was often set to turn the meat as it roasted.

He was recovering from the three days spent in riding fast and picking up food where it could be found. He was strong but he always had to remember that that virulent fever could overtake him at any time and he must always be prepared for it.

The page penetrated deeper into the town to find where he could find food. He would take some article which Richard gave him and sell it. One of these articles was the jewelled belt—a beautiful thing most delicately wrought and which had often been admired when Richard wore it, which was often. He was sorry to part with it; yet it was necessary to pay for food and lodging.

In the market place it was inevitable that the page should be noticed. The goldsmith to whom he sold the belt had rarely seen such a fine piece of workmanship. He talked of it and showed it to certain of his noble customers. It was bought by one who was most curious about it.

Who was this young man who came every day and spent so lavishly?

One of the traders said to him: 'You are clearly a gentleman of quality.'

'I serve a greater,' boasted the page.

'Who is this rich and noble gentleman?'

'He is a merchant.'

They talked of him when he was not there and watched for him.

The page greatly enjoyed the sensation he made. He was so proud to be serving the King. One day he took one of the King's gloves which was very richly embroidered and stuck it in his belt before he went into the market.

There was one man leaning against a stall who watched him. He swaggered up to him and said: 'That is a fine glove, my man.'

'Is it not?' answered the page.

'And not yours I'll swear. How come you to be wearing it?'

'It is my master's,' answered the page. 'I wear it because I am proud to be in his service.'

'Where is this master of yours?'

'He is making a journey and resting here but a while.'

'A rich merchant is he not?'

'Aye, 'tis so,' answered the page.

The man took the glove and studied it intently.

'A royal glove, I'd say,' he commented.

The page snatched it from him and sticking it in his belt

did not stop to buy what he had come for. He was terrified that he had betrayed his master.

Hurrying back to the lodging he found the King in the kitchen talking to the woman of the house. He signed that he must speak to him without delay and Richard went to the small room they shared.

'Sire, we must fly without delay. They know who you are.'

'How can they know that? You did not tell anyone?'

'Nay, Sire. I never would. But they watch me. They ask me questions about my master.'

'And you told them I am a merchant.'

'Yes, I told them that.'

'Well, since they are asking questions, we must be wary. We will make our plans to leave within a few days.'

'But, master...'

'You are trembling. Why should they guess who I am? They but think me a merchant. If we left too hurriedly they would be suspicious. Nay, since they are curious about you, do not go to the market today. Go tomorrow and buy what we need. Then we will be off and I will tell these people that I am ready to pursue my journey within the next few days.'

The page was terribly apprehensive. He dared not confess that he had worn the royal glove in his belt and that it had been seized and studied by a man who had asked if his master was royal.

*   *   *

When the page next went to the market he was aware of two men who followed him. He paused at a stall and they came up beside him.

'Who are you?' he stammered.

'You will discover. Come with us.'

'Nay, I cannot. I have to buy and return to my master.'

His arms were seized and he was dragged from the stall.

He was taken into a building where men sat at a board on trestles. Those who had seized him took him to this board and held him while one of the men with a hard cruel face smiled at him. It was a smile which made the page feel as though a snake was coiling itself about him.

'You come to the market to shop now and then,' said this man.

'Yes, I do,' answered the page.

'And you bring objects which you sell.'

' 'Tis true. I see no harm...'

'Who talks of harm? It may be that you have done much good. Who is your master?'

'He is a merchant...'

The smile again distorted that cruel face.

'It would be better to tell the truth. It could save us much time and you much pain.'

'I am answering your questions. What more can I do?'

'You can tell us the truth.' One of the men beside him twisted his arm. 'Come, fellow. The truth.'

'I tell you that he is a merchant...'

'Silence. His name. They are pretty eyes. I doubt not that they serve you well. Have you ever thought what it would be like to be deprived of them?'

The page began to tremble.

One of the men seized his head and forced him to open his mouth. He took his tongue in his hands and twisted it. The page gasped with pain and the man released it.

'See, it is still there. Have you thought what it would be like to lose it? Come, foolish fellow. We have strong suspicions who your master is. You have but to confirm it and you keep those pretty eyes, that useful tongue. But, by God and his Heavens, if you refuse us you will most certainly lose them.'

There were tears in the page's eyes. 'I will not betray my master.'

'Oh, so there is something to betray! Whose glove did you wear in your belt? What a fine glove. It was like a king's glove. Be sensible. Do you want to suffer in vain? We are asking very little of you. The name of your master—his true name which you know and which you are going to tell us. Give us his name. Lead us to his lodgings and you go free unharmed. Refuse us and you will be thrown into prison and dealt with as we have already explained.'

The page fell on his knees. 'Let me go, master.'

'Assuredly when you tell us what we want to know. Don't be a fool. We know already. We merely want you to confirm this. We shall not blame you. You are a servant. You must do as you are bid. Come, think of the hot irons and your precious eyes. Think. You would never be able to speak again. So look while you can and speak while you can—for you might as well be dead when we have done what we will do to you if you refuse to tell us.'

The page broke down. 'I will tell you. My master is Richard the King of England. I will take you to our lodging. He is trying to reach England and we lost our way...'

'Enough. He is a good and wise fellow after all and deserves to keep his eyes and tongue. Come, show us the way.'

*　　*　　*

The dwelling was surrounded by soldiers. The news had circulated that Richard Coeur de Lion was in the house.

The captain of the troop strode into the house and was met by the woman who came from her kitchen to discover what the noise was about.

'King Richard of England is in this dwelling,' said the captain.

'I have no king here,' was the reply. 'There is no one but a merchant who is a pilgrim.'

'We want that pilgrim,' said the captain.

'He is in the kitchen watching the chickens on the spits.'

They burst into the kitchen.

'There he is,' cried the captain.

Richard stood up to his full height. 'What means this?' he demanded.

'We know you to be the King of England,' said the captain. 'We have orders to take you.'

'Whose orders?'

'From a high place, Sire.'

'From your Duke no less. From Leopold. Go and tell Leopold that I will give my sword to no one less than himself.'

The captain was undecided what to do but at length he kept his guard on the house and sent a messenger to the Duke to tell him what had happened.

Later that day Leopold arrived.

They faced each other in the kitchen. Leopold was smiling smugly. 'It is a little different now from when we were on the walls of Acre,' he said.

'Is it?' retorted Richard. 'You were arrogant then and at no good business and so you are now.'

'You are mistaken. This is very good business. You are my prisoner and there are many who will rejoice to hear it.'

'Weak men such as yourself who are afraid of me?'

'I am not afraid of you now, Richard of England.'

Richard laughed aloud. 'You are backed by your soldiers and I stand alone. That makes a very brave man of you.'

'You are under arrest.'

Richard bowed his head. 'Allow me to present my sword to you. I do not keep it in the kitchen.'

He went to the room he had shared with the page and taking his sword handed it to Leopold.

'Now,' he said, 'you may tell your masters that you have captured the King of England.'

*   *   *

High on a hill, dominating the landscape, built as a mighty fortress against any invaders, its dungeons so strong that no man had ever escaped from them, the castle of Dürenstein was the ideal prison for the most important prisoner in the world. Built on the banks of the Danube where that river cuts through rocky gorges with the few houses which comprised the little town of Dürenstein clustered at its feet, it was remote and isolated, for few travellers came that way; and here in this fortress, Richard was placed in the custody of one of Leopold's most trusted officers, Hadamar von Kuenring.

The importance of his charge had been impressed on von Kuenring and he was determined to hold him against no matter what odds.

The two men quickly became friendly in spite of the fact that one was jailer, one prisoner. Richard liked to talk of battles he had won and von Kuenring listened eagerly; they played chess together and each looked forward to enjoying the company of the other. Through Kuenring Richard learned a little of what was happening outside. There was excitement throughout Europe, Kuenring told him, because it was being whispered that Coeur de Lion was the prisoner of his enemies.

'If they know where I am, I shall soon be rescued,' cried Richard.

'They do not know. The Duke is determined that your prison shall be kept a secret. I will tell you something.

Leopold has sent word to the Emperor that you are his prisoner.'

'He would not dare to do otherwise,' commented Richard and added ruefully, 'Much good will that do me. The Emperor is no friend of mine since I became the ally of Tancred.'

'My lord, you made many enemies.'

'For a man such as I am that is inevitable,' said Richard sadly. 'Even those who I thought were my friends turn against me. But never fear. It will not always be so. Think not that I shall spend my life in this prison.'

Von Kuenring looked wistful. He wished it were in his power to help his prisoner escape.

Richard understood his feelings and gripped his hands saying: 'You have your duty. Think not I would wish you to forget that.'

He was fortunate to have such a jailer.

When Philip of France heard the news he was filled with an excitement he could not fully understand. They could never be friends again. The old days had gone for ever, and Richard was his enemy. His feelings were difficult even for him to understand. How he wished that Richard were *his* prisoner! He visualized how he would have gone to him and treated him with tender respect as he had when they were younger. But now a fierce exultation seized him. Richard had been wrong to linger in Palestine. What good had he achieved? How much wiser, he, Philip, had been, to leave when he did.

And now Richard was a prisoner. Let him remain so. It was better for France that he did; and let sly, greedy John take the throne. There was nothing for France to fear from England with a king like John.

It was different with Richard.

And so those who had recently been his allies against the Saracens now gloated on his imprisonment. There in his fortress on the banks of the Danube Richard could look out on the ragged rocks on which it stood. His was a prison from which it would not be easy to escape.

The Jewelled Belt

BERENGARIA was sad as the galley carried them away from Acre.

She stood on deck with Joanna beside her watching until the land faded away.

'Come,' she said, 'let us go below. There is nothing more to see.'

'We will pray for Richard's safe journey,' said Joanna. 'I would we were with him.'

'Oh, he is happier with his friends,' answered Berengaria bitterly.

It was true, Joanna knew. Poor Berengaria! She, Joanna, had had a husband older than herself but at least he had been a husband to her.

Joanna said: 'He is concerned for our safety. Remember he has given us Stephen de Turnham to care for us. Think how such a noble knight could have served him.'

But Berengaria was impatient. 'I have done with pretence,' she said. 'It is true that in the beginning I was happy to deceive myself, but it is no longer so.'

She sighed and Joanna knew there was nothing more to be said on that subject.

They were fortunate in the journey. As though to make up for Berengaria's disappointment the sea remained calm and there was just the right amount of breeze to carry the ship on its way; the sky was clear; each day was perfect. In good time they arrived at Naples and there they alighted to make the journey to Rome.

*　　　*　　　*

Stephen of Turnham was a man who took his duty seriously and he was determined that no harm should befall the ladies if he could help it. On that long journey he guarded them well. He himself slept outside their door each night at the various houses in which they stayed; and if they must pitch their tents he was at the door of those also. No one should come to them, he said, except over his dead body.

It was a comforting gesture.

Berengaria often thought what a strange married life hers was. Most princesses were sent off to their husband's country when they were children and brought up there. Some had never known their husbands when they were betrothed. She had counted herself lucky because she had fallen in love with Richard long before and had cherished an ideal ever since. How false her dreams were proving to be. And was she to spend the whole of her life following him about the world?

But she must not complain. She had her good friend Joanna, who had lost a husband she had cared for; and there was the little Cypriot Princess who constantly prayed for her father's well-being knowing that he was Richard's prisoner.

'My lot is not worse than theirs,' she reminded herself.

And so they came to Rome. There it lay before them this city built on seven hills and round the silver stream of the Tiber.

'Here we shall stay,' said Sir Stephen, 'until we find out whether it is safe for us to proceed.'

A nobleman of Rome offered his mansion to the Queens of England and Sicily and here Stephen decided it would be wise to rest awhile until they could make arrangements to get across Italy and perhaps proceed by ship.

'If only we could have news of Richard's journey!' sighed Joanna.

It was Stephen who heard the news.

'In the markets,' he told them, 'it is said that King Richard has been shipwrecked in the Adriatic Sea.'

'Do you believe he is drowned?' asked Berengaria, her eyes large with horror.

She loves him after all, thought Joanna. It is all a pretence to say she does not. She is trying to show an indifference to the world which she does not feel.

'I cannot believe Richard is dead,' said Stephen. 'If he were shipwrecked, rest assured that he would save himself in some way.'

'If he were shipwrecked,' replied Berengaria, 'he must land somewhere. Where would he land and would we not have heard if he were pursuing his journey? How could Richard with all his company avoid being recognized?'

'We shall hear in due course,' said Joanna. 'In the meantime let us rest and try to be easy in our minds. We shall need strength to pursue our journey.'

The days began to pass. There was no news. Stephen thought that they should soon be continuing with their journey. If they could get to Pisa they could take ship to Marseilles and there they could rely on the good friendship of the King of Aragon.

But something seemed to warn him not to leave in haste and he decided to seek an audience with the Pope that he might solicit his help in getting a safe conduct for his party.

Meanwhile the Queens were a little restive. There was something in the city air which excited them.

It was Joanna who had the idea that if they disguised themselves they might slip out and visit the markets. There were good things to buy in Rome.

It relieved the tedium to study the dress of the women of the city, to acquire similar clothes, to dress themselves in the loose garments girded at the waist by leather belts. Over their long hair they wore wimples not of silk but of linen in the hope that they could mingle unnoticed with their ordinary women of the city.

It was a great adventure to visit the shops, slipping out of the house without the knowledge of Sir Stephen who would have been horrified at the thought of his precious charges roaming the streets.

But how it relieved the days! The three of them—for the Cypriot Princess was still their constant companion—would venture out in the quiet of the afternoon and walk along by the Tiber and savour freedom.

They loved best to visit the market and so carefully had they disguised themselves that they were not recognized and were thought to be ordinary travellers who were pausing on their journey to spend a short time in Rome as so many people did.

All three loved to visit the goldsmiths' and silversmiths'

shops, there to see the wonderfully wrought pieces of jewel-
lery at which the jewellers of Rome seemed to excel.

They had bought several trinkets and were known as good
customers so that when they were seen the traders would
bring out what they considered choice pieces.

One afternoon the three young women had dressed in their
simple gowns and wimples and gone out into the streets
making their way to the market and the goldsmith's shop.

Berengaria was interested in a ring and wanted to look at it
again. It was a glowing emerald set in gold.

She turned it over in her hand, tried it on her finger.

'The setting is exquisite,' she said, 'but there is a flaw in
the stone.'

'I see you have an eye for precious stones, my lady,' said the
jeweller.

Joanna said: ' 'Tis a pretty ring. But if you do not like the
emerald why do you not choose some other stone?'

'I have the very thing,' cried the jeweller. 'Some very fine
stones have just come into my possession. One moment
please.'

He disappeared into a room behind the shop and came
back holding a belt which was set with many dazzling gems.

'I have only just bought this...' he began.

Berengaria swayed a little and Joanna caught her arm.
'What ails you?' she asked.

'I feel unwell,' said Berengaria. 'But no matter ... May I
look at the belt?'

'Assuredly, my lady. These stones are very fine indeed. It is
rarely that such have come into my possession.'

Berengaria held out her hands and took the belt. She
turned it over and looked at it closely.

'You see, my lady, this emerald ... It is finer than anything
I have here. And I would not ask much. The one who sold
the belt knew not its value. I got a bargain so I am in a position to make you a very fair price.'

Berengaria handed him back the belt.

She turned to Joanna. 'I must go back,' she said. 'I feel
unwell.'

'Then let us go at once,' said Joanna. She turned to the
jeweller. 'We will come again when my sister is better.'

They came out into the street.

'Berengaria, what ails you?'

Berengaria said slowly, 'That jewelled belt ... I know it well. I have seen it before. Richard was wearing it the last time I saw him.'

'What does it mean?' murmured Joanna.

'I don't know. I am very uneasy.'

'It could be another belt.'

'There is only one such belt.'

'It might mean that he gave it to someone who sold it to this merchant.'

'I do not know,' said Berengaria, 'but I greatly fear that some harm has befallen him.'

*   *   *

Sir Stephen was horrified when they told him—not so much at first about the belt but the fact that they had been out in the streets without protection. It must never happen again, he said; if they must go out he would send two men to guard them.

'And let it be known who we are!' cried Joanna. 'The fun of the adventure is in our not being recognized.'

'I want no one to know your identity,' said Sir Stephen, 'until I have seen the Pope.'

'But what think you of this belt?' asked Joanna.

'If it is indeed the King's ...'

'It *is* the King's,' insisted Berengaria. 'I know it well. I noticed it the very last time I saw him wearing it.'

'I will go to this goldsmith,' said Stephen, 'and ask for fine jewels. I will ask him to show me the belt, and ask him how he acquired it.'

'And if it is Richard's ...' began Joanna.

'He may have given it away.'

'To whom would he give such a valuable piece?'

'We cannot say,' said Sir Stephen. 'It is something we must attempt to find out.'

Later that day he went to the goldsmith and came back with the news that he had seen the belt and agreed with Berengaria that it belonged to Richard. The goldsmith told him that he had bought it from a merchant who had come from Austria.

'That means Richard must be there,' said Joanna.

They were startled by the news. Richard should never have

set foot in Austria. They all knew how Leopold had disliked
him. He had never forgiven him for what he called the slight
on the walls of Acre, and that other incident when Richard
had actually kicked him before his followers.

They were all very uneasy.

Sir Stephen had told them not to return to the goldsmith.
He would be suspicious of too much interest in the jewelled
belt. They could not resist going out but they did follow Sir
Stephen's orders by taking two men servants with them.

There was a great deal of gossip in the streets. As they
mingled with the crowds they heard Richard's name mentioned.

They went into a shop to buy silk for which the city was
renowned, and there they heard more rumours.

The owner of the shop told them that he had heard that
the great Richard Coeur de Lion had been travelling near
Vienna with his page and that he had been captured.

'Captured!' cried Joanna indignantly. 'How could this be?
He would never allow himself to be captured.'

'I but tell what I hear, my lady,' said the shopkeeper. 'The
rumour is that the great King was shipwrecked and came to
the Austrian coast and that many of his friends were captured. He was the last to be taken but he had gone on with
only his page and the page was taken and confessed who his
master was.'

'Where is he?' asked Joanna.

'That no one knows,' was the answer. 'But it seems certain
that the hero of the crusades is now in the hands of his
enemies.'

They hurried back. There they found Stephen. He too had
heard the rumours.

'If it is true that Richard is indeed in the hands of the
Duke of Austria that means also the Emperor of Germany.
We must take especial care. Were we to venture out of Rome
it might well be that we too should be captured.'

'Of what use would that do Richard's enemies?' asked
Joanna.

'They would doubtless give a great deal to lay their hands
on the wife and sister of the King. Nay, we shall not now ask
the Pope for safe conduct to Pisa, but that we may rest here
for a while until we can learn whether there is any truth in
these rumours.'

There must be no more wandering in the streets. The situation was perilous. If the King were indeed the prisoner of his enemies, then he was in no position to protect his wife and sister. Any ill might befall them and there be none to avenge them, for there was another rumour which was to the effect that the King's brother John was in no mood to help his brother.

Stephen was relieved when he received the Pope's permission for the Queens and their party to remain in Rome.

*   *   *

How endless the days seemed now! There was no longer any doubt that Richard was a prisoner though none knew where he had been incarcerated. That he was in the hands of the Emperor Henry VI of Germany there seemed to be no doubt, and Henry would certainly not feel very friendly towards the man who had allied himself with Tancred, the usurper of his wife's crown of Sicily. The future looked black for Richard unless he could contrive to escape.

There was little news of England and that which came was disturbing. It seemed that Richard's brother John was determined to take advantage of Richard's absence and was seeking to take the throne itself.

The two Queens with their Cypriot friend, who never seemed to wish to leave them, passed their days in embroidering, playing chess and conversing with each other.

'It seems it would have been better if Richard had never left England,' said Joanna. 'What good has he achieved in Palestine? What lasting good I mean; and when you think of all the blood that has been shed and treasure that has been lost ... and now where is the King? And we are here in this foreign city depending on the good will of the Pope. What is the good of it all, Berengaria?'

'Life is sometimes hard,' said Berengaria. 'Sometimes I wonder whether I shall ever lead a natural life with Richard.'

'And you, little one,' said Joanna turning to the Cypriot, 'what do you wonder?'

'When I shall see my father again. Whether I shall ever have a husband.'

'Who can say what will befall any of us,' said Joanna.

So they talked again and again of their plight and constantly they speculated on what the future would bring.

'We cannot stay here for ever,' said Joanna to Sir Stephen. 'It is five months now since we came.'

Sir Stephen replied that if the Pope would give them safe conduct to Pisa and from thence to Genoa, they could now sail for Marseilles.

'I would he would do so,' said Joanna fervently. 'I am tired of remaining in one place.'

'We must remember though,' said Sir Stephen, 'with the King a prisoner if we were taken it might go hard with us.'

'I would take the risk,' declared Joanna.

The others agreed with her.

Finally the Pope sent word to them that he would instruct one of his Cardinals to give them safe conduct to Pisa. They were overjoyed when at last Cardinal Mellar came to them and told them that on the Pope's orders he would look after them.

The journey to Pisa was made without incident and from that town they were conducted to Genoa where a ship was found to take them to Marseilles.

It was a great pleasure for Berengaria on arriving at Marseilles to find that they were met by Alfonso of Aragon, a friend and a kinsman whom she was sure she could trust. He embraced her with great warmth and was gracious to Joanna and the Princess.

He welcomed them to Marseilles and he said how pleased he was that they had escaped mishap on their arduous journey.

'You are safe now,' he told them. 'I myself will conduct you from my Provençal lands and I shall make sure that I place you in the hands of one whom I can trust.'

Travelling with Alfonso was very different from travelling with the Pope's emissary. There was feasting and entertaining wherever they stopped and Berengaria could not help hoping that the journey would take a very long time. Her future seemed uncertain whether Richard remained a prisoner or came home. It was disconcerting to have a husband who was no husband.

Too soon it seemed they reached the borders of Provence where they rested, while awaiting the coming of the Count of Toulouse.

'The Count of Toulouse,' cried Berengaria. 'Did he not invade Guinne recently?'

'That was the father of this Raymond,' explained Alfonso. 'He is a strong man and a gallant one; he is eager to conduct you to Normandy and to give his life if need be in your defence.'

Berengaria was worried. Her brother Sancho had beaten the Count of Toulouse in battle and it seemed strange that an enemy should be their protector.

However when the Count arrived, she was charmed by him. He was very handsome and his manner charming. He immediately disarmed suspicions by declaring that he wanted to wipe out his father's indiscretion and if he could serve the ladies with his life he would be content.

Even Joanna, who was never impressed by flattery, was charmed by him.

And as they made their journey towards Poitou she became more and more so. She and the Count rode together, talked together, and could not it seemed have enough of each other's company.

'You will be sorry when we have to say good-bye to the Count of Toulouse,' said Berengaria.

Joanna admitted this would be so.

Longchamp and Prince John

WHILE Richard was on his way to Acre, Prince John was riding towards the west. His feelings were mingled whenever he went that way—pride was uppermost, pride in his great possessions; distaste was there, too, when he considered the woman he had had to take to wife to win such lands. She bored him, except when she had been frightened of him in the first days when they were together. It was not that she was less frightened later, but that her fear no longer amused him.

She was a plain little thing, Hadwisa. Fate was perverse in making women like that the heiresses to great fortunes. Hadwisa ought to have married some minor nobleman and lived quietly in the country all her life. That would have suited her. She was no wife for a man who would one day be King of England.

Oh yes, I shall be, he told himself savagely. I should be now, for that was my father's wish.

His friends told him it was necessary to bide his time but he was tired of biding his time. He hated waiting for anything. He wanted his desires immediately. It had always been so with him.

Still the stage was set. Richard was only just starting on his crusade and—who knew—some Saracen arrow might be the end of him—an arrow with a goodly serving of poison at the tip, and might it go right through his heart . . . or perhaps his eye. That would make him smart. Perhaps even proud brave

Richard would cry for God's mercy if that happened to him.

'And I should mount the throne,' murmured John.

Still, as those who wished him well kept reminding him, he must be patient. The unpopularity of Longchamp was rising and if he could drive him out of the country ... well, then it would not be so difficult.

He could see the turrets of the castle and he wondered whether Hadwisa was looking out for him. Once he had made her confess that she looked every day. He could picture her trembling with fear when she saw a party of horsemen approaching, asking herself, Is that my doting husband, John?

He saw her rarely, but when he did he liked to remind her that she was his wife. He wondered why she was barren. Not that he gave her many opportunities to bear his child, but she had had a chance to conceive. He was not sure whether he cared or not. He would have liked a son; on the other hand if the day came when he could rid himself of Hadwisa, which he would do if he became King, her infertility would be a good excuse to put beside that of consanguinity.

'Sound the trumpets,' he ordered; and he laughed inwardly. Let her hear them. Let her start to tremble.

Immediately the trumpets sounded. Every one of his servants was afraid of his temper. It was as violent as that of his father, only he could be more vicious. Henry II had always prided himself on being just but John did not care for justice if it interfered with his desires, and he enjoyed seeing men tremble before him.

They rode into the castle. As he had expected Hadwisa had heard the trumpets. She was down there with the stirrup cup.

'Ah, my love,' he cried. 'My heart beats faster to see you. And you show me clearly that you are as eager for a sight of me as I am for you.' He laughed at the irony of this. 'Good mulled wine,' he went on. 'Come, sweetheart, sip the loving cup with me.' Let her taste it first. Who knew, she might make up her mind to poison him one day. If so let her be the one to take her own poison.

She sipped.

'Again, my love,' he said. 'Again! Again!' and he jerked the goblet so that she must either drink or choke.

Then he put it to his lips.

He leaped from his horse and embraced her in a manner which brought a blush to her cheek.

'Come to our chamber,' he said. And turning to his attendants: 'You know how impatient I am. So first leave me with my wife.'

She was aware of the sly smiles. They knew that he was laughing at her, that last evening he had made sport with other women and that he had said of them, when complimenting them on their skill in that art in which he declared he excelled more than in any other, that they reminded him of his wife by the very difference in them.

Hadwisa trembling in his grip could do nothing but be taken to their chamber. There he ordered her to take off her gown and await him. His method was always different. On the journeys to the castle he would enjoy planning how he could best frighten her. There were times when he made fierce onslaughts which nauseated her; at others he would ignore her altogether. He enjoyed watching her terror and her sudden relief when she thought she was going to be ignored and then he would find the greatest pleasure in letting her see that she was deceived.

As for Hadwisa, who had been gently nurtured in a household where she had been witness to the tender affection of her parents and who had attended the weddings of her sisters, she truly believed that she had married a monster.

Her modesty which he called prudery sometimes amused him, sometimes angered him. It would depend on his mood.

On this day the torturing of Hadwisa was of secondary importance. His mind was on the unpopularity of Longchamp and how he could best take advantage of it.

He was not thinking of her lying there on her bed asking herself what form the torture would take on this occasion but he went over and looked down at her. She was by no means voluptuous. Yes, he would rid himself of her when the time came. Perhaps then it was better not to plant his seed in her. Children made difficulties. If she could read his thoughts she would be relieved so he would not tell her. Her family must not know yet that it was in his mind to cast her off. He had her lands safely enough, what did he want with her?

He sat down on the stool and looked at his boots.

He said: 'There are great events afoot, wife.'

She did not answer. He shouted: 'Heard you not my words?'

'Yes, I heard, John. There are great events afoot.'

'The people hate Longchamp.'

'I have heard that many murmur against him.'

'The son of a French serf who ran away and hid himself in a Norman village. Longchamp was the name of that village and they took that as their name. Doubtless they thought it had a noble ring. The man is a low-born knave.'

'He is very powerful,' said Hadwisa.

'Powerful! At this time maybe. It is not going to last though.'

'Is it not?'

'Indeed it is not, for I say so and you know don't you, wife, that when I command all obey me.'

She was silent and he shouted: 'Know you it, wife?'

'Yes ... yes ...' she answered.

'Then when I speak to you, pray do not remain silent. If you do I shall be angry and you would not like that, you know.'

'No, John.'

'Remember it. I tell you this: it will not be long before Longchamp is sent back to Normandy. You believe that, don't you?'

'If you say so, John.'

'Yes, I say so! I hate the fellow. Low-born upstart! Do you know I think he would take the crown if it were at all possible.'

'But that could never be,' she said.

'Nay. Though 'tis true it now rests with one who does not deserve it.'

'You speak of the King.'

'Who is at this moment in Palestine fighting the Saracen. Or is he there, do you think? Mayhap his ship foundered. Ships do that often. Mayhap he is at this moment lying dead with an arrow in his body. By God's holy eyes, if that be so then your husband, Hadwisa, is King of England. Would it were so. Oh God, I pray you send that arrow quick ... let it pierce his heart. He must lose that for which he shows little love for if he loved England how could he have deserted her to be a soldier of the cross?' Hadwisa trembled. He looked down at the bed and pushed her over on to her face. 'There!

I would not see your traitorous eyes, my lady. You have no spirit. You are frightened of God, of Richard! Fool that you are. There is one whom you should fear. The new King, your husband.'

She said: 'I do.'

'Then you have some sense. I tell you this, wife; that I am going to take this kingdom. Whether God sends that arrow or not. Richard is not here. Then he shall lose his kingdom. The people are restive. They will be with me.'

She raised herself and looked steadily at him. 'What of your mother?' she asked.

He narrowed his eyes. 'I am her son am I not?'

'She loves Richard.'

'Aye, and she loves me too. She is a wise woman, a woman of great experience. She will see that this must be. He deserts his kingdom. There must be a king.'

He looked at her without seeing her. He could see nothing but the crown on his own head. That vision was more exciting than anything he could conjure up. He was bored with her. He could not discuss his dreams with her. What was she? An ignorant little country girl! He would never have known her if she had not been the richest heiress in the land.

To her great relief he left her. She dressed hurriedly and said a prayer of thankfulness, adding a request that soon he would go away.

She began to think of what effect it would have on her life if he truly became King. She then would be the Queen.

It was not so much the thought of being Queen that terrified her but of being *his* Queen.

Down in the hall the venison was being served ... a very special occasion for the coming of the King's brother. John sat at the table, his wife beside him, but he had little to say to her. His thoughts were far away from this hall. He was seeing himself being crowned in Westminster. It was all he could do to restrain himself from talking of this matter but he was not so foolish as to do so in such varied company.

He glanced at Hubert de Burgh, a young man to whom he had taken a great fancy, and he wished they were alone together so that he could have talked to him.

It was while they were at dinner that messengers arrived for John. He had his spies everywhere and it was one of their duties to bring news to him wherever he might be.

So thus while they sat at dinner and the minstrels strummed their lutes and sang, there was a clatter of horses' hoofs in the courtyard which proved to be the arrival of one of John's messengers.

Hoping that he brought news of Richard's death he went out into the courtyard to meet the messenger. The man was mud-stained for he had travelled fast and far knowing his master would wish the news to be brought to him without delay.

'Come, man, what is it?'

'I have news of the King, my lord,' he said. 'He has left Sicily. He has made a pact with the usurper King Tancred.'

'So he still lives,' said John, his brow darkening.

'Aye, my lord,' said the messenger, 'and there is ill news.'

'Ill news!' he cried. 'What news?'

The messenger looked alarmed. It was not good to be the harbinger of news which did not please and he knew what he had to tell Prince John would send him into a passion. But he must tell it. It would be more than his life was worth to withhold anything.

He blurted out: 'The King has promised Prince Arthur of Brittany to Tancred's daughter. It is one of the terms of the pact.'

'Arthur!' screamed John.

''Tis so, my lord.'

'By God's teeth,' muttered John. 'He has offered Arthur as the heir of England!'

''Twould seem so, my lord, for Tancred has accepted the offer most joyfully.'

John's face was distorted with rage.

'By your leave, my lord,' said the messenger bowing and hastily taking a few steps backwards.

But John did not see him. He was thinking of what this would mean. Their nephew, Arthur, son of their brother Geoffrey, had been named by Richard as heir to the throne of England!

'No, no, no,' screamed John.

Then he smiled slowly. Of course Arthur would never be King. He was a baby. He had never been to England. The English would never accept him.

But, by God, how he hated his brother for attempting to cheat him!

Could some say that Arthur had the greater claim? Geoffrey was older than he, John. Geoffrey's son! No, it was nonsense. It could never be. He would see that it never was.

By God, he would take the throne now while Richard lived if need be. What had he to fear from a puling infant?

He was in no mood for Hadwisa. He had matters of greater moment to consider than her discomfort.

'We are leaving,' he shouted. 'There are matters of business to claim me. I can no longer rest here.'

Hadwisa stood at the turret watching his departure.

She blessed the messenger who had brought such a message to drive her from her husband's thoughts.

*   *   *

William of Longchamp was too clever a man not to have realized that his most dangerous enemy was Prince John, and that sooner or later the Prince's simmering hatred would boil over into dangerous action.

Longchamp believed that he could deal satisfactorily with the Prince, who for all his blustering and violent temper was a weak man. Had he not been the son of a King he would never have risen very far. Whereas he, Longchamp, had done so, although severely handicapped, his grandparents both being fugitive slaves who had come from France to the little village of Longchamp and lived out their lives in obscurity, their great ambition being never to be discovered.

He had been determined not to remain in obscurity. Nature had seen fit to bestow on him an unattractive body but a clever brain and all wise men knew that the second was more desirable than the first. When he had been younger he had longed to be tall but he soon realized that he never would be. In fact unkind people called him 'that ill-favoured dwarf'. That was not true but he was of very low stature so that his head seemed bigger than normal, as were his hands and his feet. It was as though nature had joked with him, giving him a chin that receded and a stomach that protruded; and as if that were not enough one leg was slightly shorter than the other which meant that he walked with a limp. But to compensate him for his physical disabilities he had been given not only a lively mind but the understanding that it could take him far if he nurtured it; so he learned where he could, observing constantly and making himself agreeable to those who could be useful to him.

It was great good fortune which had brought him to the notice of Richard when he was in Aquitaine. Two men could not have been more different. The shining god-like creature, physically perfect and with a natural dignity and grace, a man as many said born to be king and who looked every inch of it, and his poor misshapen servant. It might have been this contrast which attracted Richard's attention. In any case he soon discovered the mental brilliance of his servant and began to take notice of him. Soon Longchamp was making Richard see how clever he could be and the King took him more and more into his confidence.

So firm did Richard's patronage become that when he was King of England and planning his crusade he decided that Longchamp should be his Chancellor and share with Hugh Pusey, Bishop of Durham, the office of Chief Justiciary in the commission he was appointing to govern England during his absence. What did it matter if Longchamp was ugly? He was going to show Richard that he had not misplaced his confidence and to flaunt his wealth and position in the faces of those who had jeered at him for his lack of social grace. It was not long before he quarrelled with Hugh Pusey; they were both ambitious and each saw in the other a rival to power. Longchamp was the more wily, always one step ahead; and in a short space of time he had completely overcome Pusey, bringing charges against him which justified imprisonment and then taking from him, in exchange for his liberation, his office and some of his possessions. Thus Longchamp became the sole justiciary, the man in whose hands lay the means and the power to govern England during Richard's absence.

Of course the people hated him. He was a Norman and insisted on unfamiliar customs in his household. Then there was his love of ostentation. It was natural enough that one who had been despised must find it necessary to show continually how rich and powerful he had become. Every extravagance was a gesture. See how the King loves me! he seemed to be saying. But the more gestures of this nature there were, the more the people hated him. He in his turn hated the English. He was constantly trying to show them how inferior they were. If he were an astute statesman he was no student of human nature. He blindly revelled in

Richard's favour and cared nothing for the enmity of others, forgetting that Richard was far away and that his enemies were all around him.

The crusade swallowed up great wealth. More was constantly demanded. If he were to serve his master well he must see that taxes were levied and paid; it was ironical that the people of England should not blame their King whose activities made it necessary that the money should be raised but his Chancellor whose duty it was to see that the money was collected.

There was murmuring all over the land about the upstart Norman, the nobody who dressed as richly as a king and travelled in great state wherever he went. When he went about the country and rested at religious houses as became a man of the church, for besides being the King's Chancellor he was also the Bishop of Ely, there were complaints that to house him and his splendid retinue cost them several months' revenue.

Longchamp heard the sly allusions to his humble origins and this only made him the more extravagant; he was determined to show them that however he had begun he had climbed to the pinnacle of success at this time. He insisted that his servants kneel when serving him, a fact which was noted and circulated throughout the kingdom. The arrogance of the man was unendurable. The King himself could not live more regally.

It was inevitable that his enemies should see that the King heard of his growing unpopularity. Queen Eleanor had become disturbed and when in Sicily had advised her son to send Walter de Coutances, the Archbishop of Rouen, over to England, ostensibly to assist Longchamp in the Regency, but in fact to watch events carefully and if Longchamp became too unpopular, and that might cause the people to rise against him, to take over the reins from him.

Longchamp was suspicious of the Archbishop. He misconstrued the reason for his coming, and had an idea that he was doubtless hoping to attain the See of Canterbury which was vacant. As he himself had his eye on this prime plum of the Church he was antagonistic towards the Archbishop.

But his real enemy was Prince John. Longchamp smiled to himself to imagine John's wrath when he heard of how the Chancellor roamed the country in as royal a fashion as any

king. He did not fear him. What was the Prince but a lecherous profligate? He had no stability. The people would never
support him. King Richard was however inclined to be lenient regarding his brother's peccadilloes. 'John would never
succeed in taking a kingdom,' he had once said. 'And if by
some strange chance he did he would never hold it. He is not
of the stuff of which conquerors are made.'

Richard had communicated that contempt to Longchamp,
so when he heard that John was fulminating about him the
Bishop merely shrugged his shoulders and ignored him.

It was at this time that he became concerned with the affair
of Gerard de Camville who was the sheriff of Lincoln. He
believed that man to be a troublemaker because he was
friendly with Prince John and he suspected him of urging
that the Prince rise against the Chancellor. Gerard de Camville had in fact sworn allegiance to John as though he were
already King or at least heir to the throne. Longchamp was
determined that the next King would be Arthur of Brittany,
which would suit him very well. If Richard died while the
boy was a minor then he, Longchamp, would continue as
Regent until Arthur was of such an age to govern. He would
bring him to England and have him educated there under his
guidance. It would be an excellent arrangement. The fact
was, though, that Richard was by no means old, had married
the Princess of Navarre and might well have heirs which
would put Arthur out of the running. But with Richard's son
being brought up by the Chancellor or—failing a son of
Richard's his nephew Arthur—the prospect was good, although there was one who could put it in jeopardy: John.

Therefore it was disconcerting to have men like Gerard de
Camville swearing allegiance to the Prince and when it was
brought to his notice that de Camville had sheltered robbers
in his castle and allowed them to go free even though they
had taken the goods of a band of travellers passing near
Lincoln, this seemed too good an opportunity to miss. The
late King's laws against robbery had been very severe and
Richard had not altered them. It had been made clear that if
the country was to be safe for travellers, drastic penalties
should be meted out to offenders. This had been proved over
more than a hundred years. William the Conqueror had
made England law abiding and the people had seen that it
was to their advantage. Only during the reign of weak

Stephen had it lapsed, and then robber barons had waylaid travellers, to rob, torture and kill them. No one wanted a return to that.

So Longchamp had a very good reason to reprimand Gerard de Camville.

He sent for Gerard, who refused to come himself and sent a messenger in his place. This was an insult in itself.

Longchamp demanded: 'Where is your master?'

'He has other business to occupy him, my lord,' was the answer.

'I summoned him here,' replied Longchamp, 'and when I summon a man if he is wise he comes.'

'My lord bids me ask you to state your business to me and he has furnished me with some answers for he guesses you wish to speak to him concerning the guests he recently entertained at his castle.'

'These men were robbers. They should have been dealt with by the law.'

'The men they robbed were Jews, my lord.'

'What of this?'

'The people do not love the Jews. Nor does the King. Many were killed at his coronation.'

'Go and tell your master that he has offended against the laws of this land and he is summoned to the courts.'

'My lord answers only to one master during the absence of the King. He is the liegeman of Prince John.'

'Pray go and tell your master that he is summoned to the courts and it will go ill with him if he does not obey this summons.'

It was this matter which was giving Longchamp anxious thoughts on this summer's morning of the year 1191.

* * *

When Gerard de Camville asked for an audience with Prince John he was received at once.

'This insolent Norman flouts you, my lord,' cried Gerard. 'I have told him that I obey only one liege lord: my Prince. His answer is that that will not serve. He ignores you, my lord and your authority.'

'By God's eyes, 'tis so,' cried John. 'We'll show the knave. I'll drive him from his office. You will see. I am the King's brother. I am in fact the rightful King, for you know full well my father wanted me to have this kingdom.'

Gerard was silent. He was with John at the moment but one must be careful not to utter treason. There were too many who could overhear a carelessly spoken word.

'As your liegeman,' said Gerard, 'I maintain that it is only in your courts that I can be tried.'

'Leave this to me,' said John. He was excited, seeing here a chance for open conflict with Longchamp. He wanted to think what trouble could grow out of this incident.

He whipped himself up to a fury. It was an indulgence he could never resist. Anger stimulated him. He liked to feel it rising within him to such heights that he had to let it out. Now he felt he could indulge in righteous anger.

'Am I a king's son or am I not?' he demanded.

'You are indeed, my Prince,' answered Gerard, soothingly. 'Any who denied it would lie in his throat.'

'And one denies it. This low-born peasant, this serf who gives himself the airs of a King. Would I had him here, Gerard! What would I do with him? No torture would be too severe. It would please me greatly to listen to his screams for mercy.'

'He is indeed an arrogant upstart, my Prince.'

'Aye, and living like a king. His servants ... *English* servants mark you! ... kneeling before him when he eats. I should like to make him kneel ... kneel to the humblest man I could find. That would amuse me. Strip him of his silks and jewels and have him mother naked in the streets and the lash descending on his peasant's back till the blood flowed.'

Gerard was wondering what reasonable action the Prince would take.

He said cautiously: 'That will come, my lord Prince, but first it will be necessary to warn him.'

John scowled. Warn him! He didn't want him warned. He wanted him to go on making such mistakes that the whole country would rise against him.

'I shall take up arms against him,' growled John, 'and there'll be many to follow me. The people hate him, Gerard ... even as I do.'

He shouted to a messenger. 'Come hither. Go at once to upstart Chancellor William de Longchamp and tell him this from me. He is to stop persecuting Gerard de Camville. If he does not he will wish he had never been born, for I shall come against him in battle with such forces that will drive him out of this land.'

When Longchamp received this message he knew that he must take speedy action. Only by force could he reason with John. It was deplorable. The King would be displeased; but Longchamp could see nothing for it. He could not allow John to dictate to him.

He summoned the leading ministers, but before they arrived news was brought to him that the castellans of Tickhill and Nottingham had handed the castles to John.

Longchamp was horrified.

'There must have been threats,' he said. 'These men would never have given up their trusts otherwise. They have been holding the castles in the King's name and now to hand them over to his brother is an act of treason against Richard.'

'And Richard,' his ministers reminding him, 'being far away...'

'Aye, 'tis a sorry state of affairs, for as Regent I must do as the King would do. I see that Prince John has his eyes on the crown, and that I must hold at all costs for my master.'

'This will mean open friction with the Prince,' Walter de Coutances, Archbishop of Rouen, warned him.

'If that is so then it must be. John should never have been allowed to come back into the country. The King forbade him to for three years.'

'But the King later gave permission for both John and his base-born brother Geoffrey to return.'

'So 'twas said. I cannot believe the King would have been so unaware of their trouble-making propensities to allow it. We must take bold action. It is the only course when dealing with men such as Prince John. I am going to summon him to appear before courts to investigate the manner of his return to England when the King banished him for three years. If the King indeed gave him leave to come back, it must be proved.'

The Archbishop of Rouen agreed that while such action was taking place it might give those who were seeking rebellion time to brood on what this would mean and it was a way of reminding people that although the Prince, as the King's brother, was becoming a powerful force in the land he like everyone else was a subject of King Richard and must obey his laws.

'My lord Archbishop,' said Longchamp, 'only you are of sufficient rank to take the summons to Prince John.'

The Archbishop nodded ruefully. He could imagine the Prince's wrath when he realized he was summoned to appear before the courts.

It was as he anticipated. He had never seen such fury except in the old King Henry II. The Prince's skin was livid, his eyes ablaze with fury; he foamed at the lips and clenched and unclenched his hands.

'By God's eyes,' he shouted, 'if I but had that devil here. He'd never limp again. I'd slit that big belly right up ... I, with my own knife. He'd not die easy ...'

The Archbishop allowed him to go on and his very calmness cooled John's temper. The Archbishop showed no fear; he stood rather like someone who was patiently waiting for the storm to be over.

It irritated John for it spoilt the excitement his fury always gave him. He liked to see people cringe before him. This calm dignified man in his robes of office, which must always inspire a certain respect, disconcerted him.

He stopped suddenly and looked full at the Archbishop.

'And what say you, my lord, to see a Prince so treated?'

'I say this,' answered the Archbishop: 'You should offer to meet Longchamp and find a solution to your differences.'

'Do you think there will ever be any solution?'

'We must pray for peace, my lord, until the return of our sovereign lord the King.'

Sovereign lord the King! Where was Richard now? Why was there no news? He was in constant danger. Why was God so perverse that he continued to protect him from that poisoned arrow?

*   *   *

The opposing parties met at Winchester both supported by armed followers. The Archbishop of Rouen however was successful in advising a peaceful solution. The two castles which had been surrendered to John were to be given up, for they were after all the King's castles, and those who had surrendered them had been but custodians. John agreed that they should be given back but, if the King died or Longchamp did not keep his side of the agreement between them, the castles should revert to him. Wilily he arranged that the castles should be put into the hands of two men who were his friends. Longchamp was aware of this and insisted that the greater strongholds of Winchester, Windsor and Northampton were to be guarded by his own supporters.

John was disappointed. He had believed that more of the barons would be ready to support him on account of the unpopularity of Longchamp. It was true that the Chancellor was disliked but the barons could see that John was not strong enough to stand successfully against him. He was weak, self-indulgent and that violent temper augured no good. They longed for a strong King. If Richard would return they were convinced that all would be well.

However, the meeting could be considered successful because it had not resulted in open warfare and a compromise, however shaky and insecure, had been reached.

John was seething with disgust. He had hoped many would rally to him. He was determined though to seek the first opportunity to make trouble.

*   *   *

He did not have to wait long.

The Chancellor's supporters saw in the recent agreement with John victory for Longchamp and those connections who had benefited by his rise to fame were convinced of his ability to get the better of Prince John.

Roger de Lacy, a member of the Chancellor's family, quarrelled with the castellan of Nottingham castle who had handed it over to John, accused him of treason to the King, and hanged him. He then did the same to the custodian of Tickhill. This was arrogance in the extreme.

'The great Chancellor William de Longchamp, my respected kinsman has been avenged,' vowed Roger; and riding with his friends he took them to that spot where the body of the custodian of Tickhill was swinging on its gibbet. One of the victim's menservants was attempting to drive the crows from his master's body and take it away for decent burial.

'Hi there,' cried Roger, 'what do you?'

The man answered that his master should be decently buried.

'This man is a traitor,' cried Roger. 'Should traitors be

decently buried? Any who defend traitors is himself a traitor. Take that man,' he ordered, 'and hang him beside the one whom he calls master.'

This foolish, arrogant and cruel action gave John the chance he needed. He came with a troop of soldiers and laid waste Roger de Lacy's lands.

John was now ready to make war on the Chancellor but his friends advised him to hold back for a while for another incident had occurred which they saw as causing far more disquiet to Longchamp and enraging the people against him to a greater extent than John could do by marching against him.

They managed to make John see that if he were to succeed he needed the people behind him. The Chancellor was fast becoming the most unpopular man in the realm and John only had to wait a while and public opinion would do what he was planning to do with arms.

Geoffrey, John's bastard half-brother, who had been forbidden by the King, with John, not to return for three years, now returned, declaring that Richard had given him permission to come back when he had done the same for Prince John.

Longchamp immediately sent him orders to keep away from England.

*   *   *

It was a September morning when Geoffrey landed at Dover. Geoffrey was the son of Henry II and his one-time mistress Hikena, who was a woman of loose morals and had managed to captivate the King for a while—at least long enough for her to persuade him to care for their son. Henry had always looked after his bastards. He delighted in them and had often said that they had been more faithful to him than his children born in wedlock, which was true.

Geoffrey had been brought to the royal nursery by the King and had shared the tutors of the princes and princesses, much to Queen Eleanor's disgust. Indeed the coming of Geoffrey to the nursery had been the beginning of the rift between her and her husband.

King Henry had doted on Geoffrey who had loved his father as none of his legitimate sons ever had. When they had been conspiring against the King, Geoffrey was the one who had remained with him and had been at his side at the time of his death, and the King's dying wish had been that Geoffrey should be given the Archbishopric of York. Richard had respected his father's wishes and complied with this request.

Geoffrey was a great soldier as well as a man of the Church and had commanded troops under his father. He was the son Henry would have liked to have been his heir; as Geoffrey was a bastard that was out of the question but he had done all he could for him.

Richard suspected that Geoffrey might have ambitions for the crown; he was friendly with John; and for this reason Richard had imposed the ban on his going out of England for three years.

When he had taken his farewell of Richard before the King left for the crusade, Geoffrey had paid Richard a sum of money in exchange for his promise to be allowed to return to England. Richard's crusade was in constant need of money and the King was ready to do almost anything to obtain it. However to allow Geoffrey to return to England seemed wise when rumours of the unpopularity of Longchamp reached Richard. A good strong Archbishop of York would be a restraining influence.

So Geoffrey set out for England.

Longchamp had had no notification of the fact that he had bought his way back and sent him a message to the effect that he was not to return.

This Geoffrey ignored and when he arrived at Dover and was met by a company of men who told him that the Chancellor had ordered them to meet him and conduct him to Dover castle, he said that first he would take refreshment at an inn.

It was not refreshment that he took but the clothes of one of his humble followers and he rode out to St Martin Priory where he asked for sanctuary.

The Chancellor's sister, Lady Richenda de Cleres, who lived in the neighbourhood, took it upon herself to attempt to arrest him. Her brother had stated that Geoffrey was not to come to England and he had deliberately disobeyed. All the Chancellor's family were devoted to him, and when he rose they had risen with him. They could never forget it nor could they be grateful enough. His command was their will.

And how could a grateful sister show her gratitude more than by having arrested a man who was her brother's enemy?

She sent soldiers to the Priory to take Geoffrey of York. He was at prayers at the altar when the soldiers burst in.

'You are our prisoner,' they cried. 'You will ride with us to Dover Castle.'

Geoffrey looked calmly at them and stated: 'I shall not ride to Dover castle. What right have you to arrest me?' he asked.

'We are the servants of the Chancellor,' they said.

'Forget not,' said Geoffrey, 'that I am a man of the Church and a brother of the King.'

'Brother of the King maybe,' was the retort. 'Begot in the bed of a whore.'

'By a great King,' said Geoffrey.

'You have sworn not to enter this country for three years.'

'I have the King's permission to return.'

'Tell that to your judges.'

They seized him and dragged him out of the Priory.

People crowded into the streets demanding to know what was happening and when they saw the Archbishop of York being taken to a prison in Dover castle many crossed themselves in horror. Geoffrey's father, King Henry II, had done penance once because it was believed he had ordered the murder of another Archbishop. Nothing had gone right for England after Thomas à Becket was murdered, until the King did humble penance for his part in the murder. And who was this low-born Chancellor to give orders to a holy Archbishop, son of a King?

Geoffrey was taken to Dover Castle and there made a prisoner but the news spread rapidly and the name of Thomas à Becket was repeated again and again. The murmurs against the upstart Chancellor grew and Longchamp realized that his sister, in her attempts to show her loyalty to him, had acted without wisdom. He sent word to Dover that Geoffrey was to be immediately released.

Prince John was at this time in his castle of Lancaster when the Bishop of Coventry called upon him.

'Your brother Geoffrey has arrived in England,' he told him, 'and been imprisoned in Dover Castle by the low-born Norman.'

'By God's eyes,' cried John, 'he gives himself great powers.'

'Is it not time, my lord, that they were wrested from him?'

'How dare the serf's son arrest a king's son—albeit a bastard one! 'Tis time he were himself put in a dungeon. I'd like to deal with him with my own hands.'

' 'Twould be better, my lord, to let your servants do that. This last may not be such an ill matter, for surely others who have so far been reluctant to take action against him will now see that this must be.'

John nodded. 'My good Hugh,' he said, 'I believe you to be right.'

Hugh Nunant, Bishop of Coventry answered: 'I feel sure of it, my lord. Why do you not call together the most important barons to meet you and decide what should be done about the fellow?'

'I will. We will ride south at once. I'll have messengers sent. William the Marshal must be there. Men trust him.'

'The Bishop of Lincoln has already declared himself ready to excommunicate all those who were party to the arrest of the Archbishop of York.'

'Then let us send for the Bishop of Lincoln to join us.'

John, with Hugh Nunant, immediately set out for the South, messengers riding on ahead of them to invite the barons to join him at Marlborough Castle.

*   *   *

Longchamp was disturbed. It had been a rash act of Richenda's to order Geoffrey's arrest. He knew of course that it was done for love of him, but it was going to make trouble.

John would hold it against him. The Prince was already his enemy. This would not help.

He let it be known that he had meant no harm to Geoffrey. The arrest had been the work of his over zealous friends and he himself had had no thought of making a prisoner of the Archbishop of York. He had known that the King had sent him into exile for three years and as he was acting on behalf of Richard and had not heard that his order had been rescinded he considered it only right to ask Geoffrey to go back to France which was in fact all he had done. He reiterated that the arrest had not been on his orders and reminded everyone that as soon as he had heard of it he had set Geoffrey free.

He wondered what was happening on the crusade and

whether Richard would come safely through it. It was certain
that he would be in the thick of the battle. Could he possibly
avoid death? Many did; on the other hand many fell; and
soldiers of the Cross were apt to be reckless, seeing in death,
when engaged on such a mission, a certain and quick way to
Heaven.

And if Richard did not return from his crusade, what of
William of Longchamp? It would go ill with him if John
ever came to the throne.

Perhaps John never would. Hadn't Richard named Prince
Arthur as his successor? When Richard returned, *if* Richard
returned, he would do his best to persuade him to bring
Arthur over to England. The boy should be educated as an
Englishman and then when he was of age the people would
accept him. After all, as the son of John's elder brother, he
had more right to the throne than John.

Longchamp wrote a letter to the King of Scots asking him
if he would support Arthur of Brittany as heir to the throne
of England in the event of Richard's death without heirs. If
he would, he would make a pact in Richard's name, with the
King of Scotland. This was the time for if it were known that
Scotland supported Arthur that fact must influence a number
of people below the Border and they would become accustomed to the idea that Arthur had the prior claim to the
throne.

The messenger was sent off but on his way to Scotland he
was waylaid and his papers stolen. John's spies had caught up
with him and it was not long before John was reading the
message to the King of Scotland asking him to support
Arthur's claim.

John foamed with rage.

'By God's eyes and teeth,' he cried, 'I'll kill the Norman
with my own hands.'

*   *   *

The Archbishop of Rouen conferred with the Bishop of
Lincoln and William the Marshal, that staunch supporter of
royalty who had saved Henry II's life when he had disarmed
Richard and indeed had Richard at his mercy; he had spared
Richard's life and had expected to lose his own when Richard
came to the throne; but Richard was wise enough to know a

good and loyal man when he saw him and guessed that he would serve him as well as he had served his father. In this he had made no mistake.

The fact that the Archbishop of York had been arrested in the name of Longchamp and now he was unmasked as attempting to negotiate with a foreign power with regard to the succession of the throne of England had roused reasonable and worthy men such as the Marshal against him.

In a small chamber at Marlborough castle these men gathered together with Prince John to discuss what must be done.

William the Marshal said: 'We have to bear in mind that King Richard gave power to William of Longchamp. What he does, he does in the name of the King and therefore it seems we must act with caution.'

'Even when he conspires against me?' cried John.

'My lord Prince,' replied the Marshal, 'it is a matter of his conspiring against the King.' The Marshal was never one to mince his words. He would speak against the King himself but only in his presence; and he saw it might well be that Longchamp had had secret instructions from Richard to sound the King of Scotland about the succession of Arthur. The news was that he had made a pact with Tancred of Sicily and had offered his daughter Arthur as a bridegroom, which was significant.

'Am I not the King's brother?'

'You are,' answered the Marshal. 'None could dispute that.'

'And heir, in the event of the King's having no issue?'

'Prince Arthur is the son of your elder brother Geoffrey. It will be a matter for your brother the King to decide.'

John scowled, but he realized how much weight the Marshal carried.

'It would seem to me,' said Hugh Nunant, who could always be relied on to support John, 'that Longchamp has exceeded his powers in arresting Geoffrey of York.'

'That is true indeed,' said the Marshal, 'but he has released him and declares the arrest was made without his knowing.'

'A likely tale!' cried John.

'He released him immediately,' the Marshal reminded him.

'When he knew the people were against him and were talking of Becket.'

'If we but knew the will of the King...' began the Marshal.

Then the Archbishop of Rouen spoke. 'There is a matter I must lay before you. The King having heard that all was not well in the realm and hearing of the unpopularity of Longchamp sent me to govern with him and if the occasion should arise to depose him and take the reins of Regency into my own hands. I can tell you this: There has been no instruction from the King to prepare the King of Scotland to accept Arthur as his heir. He is newly married. It seems likely that he will get a son of his own.'

'If a Saracen's arrow does not get him first,' murmured John.

William Marshal cried: 'Is this indeed so? Then my lord Archbishop of Rouen is our Regent and we can indeed proceed against Longchamp. The people have never accepted him gladly. He is unpopular. He has exceeded his powers. We will summon him to meet us at the bridge over the Lodden between Reading and Windsor and there we will ask him to give an account of his actions. Do you agree with this, my lord of Rouen?'

The Archbishop declared that he thought it the wisest way to act.

*   *   *

When Longchamp received the summons he was so terrified that he had to take to his bed. He was too ill, he said, to meet his accusers. It was an alarming discovery to realize that he was not merely facing John and his friends, for whom he had no great respect, but others such as the Archbishop of Rouen and William the Marshal; and the fact that the King had given such special powers to the Archbishop of Rouen was very disconcerting.

He could not evade the meeting entirely and promised to be at the Lodden Bridge the following day. Just as he was about to depart one of his servants came hurrying to him with the news that his enemies were marching on London where they intended to take possession of the Tower. So instead of going to Lodden Bridge, surrounded by his troops, he set out for London. On the road he encountered the soldiers of his enemies and there was a clash but Longchamp and his men managed to fight their way through and proceeded with all speed to London.

They reached the Tower and shut themselves in. He was, after all, Longchamp reminded those about him, custodian of the Tower of London in the King's name.

For three days he remained in the Tower but could hold out no longer.

His enemies then forced him to give up the keys not only of the Tower but of Windsor Castle. There was no help for it; one false step now could cost him his life. He must get out of England, back to Normandy and there begin to reform his life. He was not to leave England was the order, until the castles had changed hands, but he was determined to get away.

The best method seemed to be to disguise himself as a woman; and this he did. A woman pedlar would attract little attention and the fact that she had goods to sell would be a reason for her travelling.

He set out with two of his faithful servants and counted himself fortunate to reach Dover without mishap. Afraid to go near any town or hamlet they slept under trees and by great good fortune when they reached Dover they found that a ship would shortly be sailing for France.

Longchamp, burying his face in his cape and cowering beneath the skirts and petticoats was congratulating himself that he would soon be able to discard them when a group of fishermen came by.

One among them cried: 'But see what a fair wench this is! What is she doing sitting here alone? I would fain share her company.'

'You will go away,' said Longchamp in a muffled voice.

The fisherman nudged one of his companions. 'What airs she gives herself, this saucy wench, and what sort of wench is she that travels the country so ... selling her wares? What wares? Tell me that, wench. Pray don't play the coy virgin with me for I'll have none of it.' He seized the hood and tried to pull it off. Longchamp clung to it in terror. But they were too many for him, for the three companions of the fisherman had joined with him. 'Such a coy creature must be immediately relieved of her coyness.' They would every one of them be her tutors.

They were tearing at his clothes. Any moment now and he would be revealed. He could have wept with dismay. Desperately he fought back, but they were too much for him.

'Why 'tis no maiden then!' cried the first fisherman. 'Look you here, what we have. A man ... in disguise!'

They had made such a noise that others had gathered to look and one of them cried: 'I know that face. It cannot be!'

'He has the look of a monkey.'

''Tis Longchamp the Norman.'

So the secret was out.

They set three men to guard him while someone went to the castle.

Within an hour he was taken there, a prisoner.

*　　*　　*

When John heard the story of the amorous fishermen he roared with laughter.

Poor Longchamp! In danger of being raped. And to have got so far and then to be discovered ... and by a fisherman!

It was the height of indignity. He could picture the ungainly little man.

'His just deserts,' he declared. 'Let him go to France. We have no further use for him here.'

And so at the end of October of that year 1191 Longchamp left England for France.

The Return of Eleanor

MEANWHILE Philip had returned to France. He had done the wise thing in coming back, he was well aware, but it was necessary to justify himself and he lost no time in doing so.

He smiled cynically as he ruminated on the new state of affairs. How fickle were human relationships, particularly it seemed such as those which had existed between himself and Richard! He had loved Richard passionately when they were young and Richard had been his hostage; now all sorts of emotions had mingled to change that love into hatred. His feeling for Richard was as strong as it had ever been and always would be. Richard obsessed him. He kept going over in his mind how Richard had allied himself with Tancred. How he had been bemused—as Philip expressed it—by Saladin. Wherever Richard was there was drama and excitement and when he was absent life became less colourful. There was an aura about the King of England which attracted not only the King of France but everyone who came into contact with him. It seemed one must either hate him or love him.

How could the King of France love the King of England? It had been different when Richard had been a Prince; they had not met on the same footing then and Philip, less handsome, less spectacular had been in the superior position. Now they were equals in power.

Philip had realized the state of his feelings when he had had an audience with the Pope on his way home. He had had

to make excuses for his defection and he had been surprised
by the vituperative storms of abuse which flowed from him.

Pope Celestine had been somewhat taken aback.

'Holy Father,' Philip had said, 'it was imperative that I
return. If I had not I should have died. I was so beset by fever
that my hair fell out and my nails flaked off. I was delirious
and a burden to my men. I could not lead them.'

'I believe, my son,' the Pope had replied, 'that the King of
England was similarly afflicted.'

'His was a recurrent fever. It comes and passes. It was
different with him.'

'And you wished to return to the comforts of your court?'

'I had my duties to my crown. My son is but a child. There
could have been civil war in France had I died.'

'The King of England is without an heir.'

This harping on the King of England had maddened
Philip. Wherever he went there was no escape from Richard.
Was he going to be haunted by him for the rest of his days?

He had cried out: 'It is partly because of Richard that I
found it necessary to go. His arrogance was causing strife
throughout the armies. Leopold of Austria will bear me out
and so will the Duke of Burgundy. Even the men were dis-
gusted by his recklessness and extravagance. His severity to
the men was without parallel.'

Philip had stopped suddenly. Celestine was looking at him
with astonishment. Philip muttered: 'I had to return because
I have sworn an oath to protect my kingdom.'

'Let us not forget,' replied the Pope, 'that this recklessness
of the King of England may have been one of the reasons why
Acre is now in the hands of the Christians and that we are a
step nearer towards the Holy City.'

Philip bowed his head. He was glad when the audience was
over. He knew he had not made a very good impression on
the Pope. Richard seemed to cast his spell over everyone.

And he had returned home, brooding.

There was no need to justify his return in France. His
ministers made it clear that he had acted wisely in coming
back; and as some of them pointed out it was not a bad thing
for the King of France to be in his dominions when the King
of England was far from his.

He was warmly welcomed in Paris. Not that he had come
back covered in glory. It would have been wonderful if he

could have returned as the man who had brought Jerusalem back to Christians. Instead of that he must be content with the conquest of Acre, which he had achieved with Richard, who was certain to get the greater share of the glory.

The Cardinal of Champagne who had been regent in his absence assured him when they were alone that it was time he came back. He had shown his piety by going to the Holy Land; now France claimed his attention. Little Prince Louis was so young and with the King far from home there were certain to be those ambitious men who would seek to govern a child and rule a country.

Even to the Cardinal Philip must make his excuses.

'I was close to death,' he said, 'and Richard was not to be trusted.'

His conscience smote him then. Richard might be arrogant, reckless, cruel ... but untrustworthy, never. Hadn't he teased him about his forthrightness, his lack of cunning?

'An uneasy situation,' agreed the Cardinal. 'The King of France can never be on terms of real amity with the kings of England while they hold Normandy.'

'He arranged the murder of Montferrat hoping that his man Guy de Lusignan might be King of Palestine, and then let it be rumoured that the Old Man of the Mountains was responsible.'

'But Henry of Champagne now holds that post.'

' 'Tis so, for Richard was able to give his favourite Cyprus. He has a great fancy for this Guy,' he added bitterly.

'Suffice it, Sire, that you are back in France and with the King of England far away opportunities might arise.'

'By God,' cried Philip, 'I would seize those opportunities.'

'They are at hand, my lord.'

'Is that so?'

'We learn that John has his eyes on the throne.'

'John! I was led to believe that his thoughts were all for extravagance and sporting with women.'

'He still has time to dream of a crown. There is conflict between him and Longchamp.'

'He's a clever fellow, this Longchamp. I hear he rose from very humble beginnings to be virtually King of England.'

' 'Tis so, but his birth goes against him. He is not accepted by the people. He is ill-favoured—short of stature and malformed. Not a figure to win the acclaim of the people. Moreover he is a Norman and they prefer to be ruled by an Englishman. John is making much of the situation and particularly so since Richard made his compact with Tancred.

Philip's face darkened. He remembered well his jealousy of Tancred and Richard. Richard had spent some time in Tancred's castle and there they had made plans together.

'Richard has offered Prince Arthur of Brittany to Tancred's daughter and that means Arthur is heir to the throne of England—if Richard dies without issue, that is.'

'Which is likely,' said Philip smiling slowly. 'He scarcely lived with Berengaria.'

'Being most of the time with his army, I'll swear.'

'There were times when he could have had her with him, but he did not. He is not over fond of the company of women.'

'He must realize it is necessary for him to get an heir.'

' 'Tis my belief that the matter is distasteful to him and therefore he consoles himself with the fact that Arthur can follow him. There is also John.'

'It seems strange for a King to name another man's son as heir when he is of the age to beget sons himself.'

'But in a position to meet sudden death.'

'All the more reason why he should spend much time with his wife.'

'Ah, Richard is no ordinary man. What of this conflict between Longchamp and John?'

'John wants Longchamp out of the country. It's easy to see what he is after. He wants the throne. It would be good for France if he were to take it. He is weak; he is no soldier; I hear that his rages are terrible. With such a King on the throne of England ... who knows what good could come to France?'

'You are suggesting that I should form an alliance with John ... against Richard?'

'It would be the greatest good fortune for France. You could send for John. Offer him help in securing the crown. Why, Sire, trouble in England ... in Normandy ... is that not exactly what we have been praying for?'

Oh Richard, thought Philip, my love, my friend, I hate you now. John will take your kingdom from you. You will do your noble deeds in the Holy Land or perhaps meet your end. And it may be that one day you will come to me supplicating, humble, as it was when you were a hostage Prince and you and I were together as we have never been since.

'There is your sister the Princess Alice,' said the Cardinal.

'Richard has treated her shamefully,' cried Philip.

'She is no longer young. It is an insult that Richard should put her aside that he might marry Berengaria although he had been betrothed to her in his youth.'

'We came to an agreement that this should be,' said Philip.

'It does not alter the fact that a Princess of France was slighted. Why should she not even now be the Queen of England?'

'How could she be that?'

'If John were King and she married him.'

'John is already married to Hadwisa of Gloucester.'

'There is a blood tie. The Pope has never given them a dispensation. To set her aside would present no difficulty.'

Philip clasped his hands together. 'It is a project which gives me great amusement.'

''Twould give more than that, Sire, were it to bear fruit. Richard deposed by John! We could do anything with John. In due course we could bring Normandy back to the French crown. Who knows we might even make England a vassal of France.'

'I can scarcely wait. I shall send messengers to John without delay.'

Philip was excited. Richard could still dominate his life even when they were far apart.

*   *   *

John, in his castle of Lancaster, received the messengers from the King of France. When he heard what they had to say he was amazed and delighted.

The King of France was offering to be his ally. Glittering prospects stretched out ahead of him.

He sent at once for Hugh Nunant, the Bishop of Coventry, who, having received no favours from Richard, was eager to see John on the throne. Hugh looked for great advancement should this event come about and he was as excited as John.

'With Philip on your side,' he declared, 'you cannot fail. This is a Heaven-sent opportunity. Richard must have offended Philip mightily to bring about this happy state of affairs.'

'Such friends can become enemies and then the enmity between them exceeds the love they once had for each other. Philip hates Richard now and longs to bring about his downfall.'

'Would you accept Alice?'

'Yes, I would.'

'She is no longer young.'

'There will be young girls to comfort me for that I doubt not.'

'I doubt it not either,' laughed Hugh. 'But she was your father's mistress remember.'

'He had a great fondness for her. She must have been a worthy mistress to satisfy him. There was never a more lusty man than my father.'

'She was young then.'

'What care I! She is still the sister of the King of France.'

'And bore him a child.'

'Then she is fertile.'

'*Was* fertile.'

'Oh come, what is the marriage for but for the sake of Philip's favour?'

'It will be one of his conditions.'

'And I'll rid myself of my whimpering Hadwisa. That will not grieve me, as long as I keep a tight grip on her lands.'

'We will arrange for that. And since you see the advantages that are being offered, it would seem we should set out for France without delay. Normandy will be yours and you will swear fealty to Philip. Do that and then I doubt not you can talk with him of how best to acquire the throne of England.'

'Imagine Richard's fury when he hears what is happening.'

'It will madden him so much that he will doubtless return home.'

'If he is not drowned on the way which I must confess would save a great deal of trouble. No matter. We will be ready for him. I will prepare to leave for France.'

Just at that time Queen Eleanor arrived back in England.

*   *   *

Having come, she was filled with misgiving. She had worked so hard to see her beloved son Richard King of England; in fact the greatest differences with her husband, which had resulted in those years of captivity, were in some measure due to him; and now that he had the crown he had left it for this romantic adventure abroad.

Thank God for allowing her to return safely; she dreaded to think what might have been happening during her and Richard's absence. At least, now that she was here she could do her best to hold the kingdom loyal to him. But during her journey she had often thought how unwise it was to leave it, particularly as he had so recently attained it. She had hinted this much to him but she had quickly seen that it was impossible to turn him from his purpose. The lives of most people were strewn with unwise actions and looking back one could see what effect they had had on events. But being old at least one acquired a certain wisdom and sometimes she thought that acquisition was worth all the high adventures and excitements of youth.

A terrible doubt had come to her in that she had acted unwisely in advising Richard to allow his brother John and his half-brother Geoffrey to return to England. She loved her son John. She was after all a mother and he was her youngest and her inordinate love for Richard did not prevent her caring for her other children. John would be contented, she tried to soothe herself. Richard had been generous and John was rich, for his marriage with Hadwisa of Gloucester had brought him rich lands. He would not make trouble. She knew him well. Pleasure loving he most certainly was but could she blame him for that? When she had been his age what a glutton she had been for excitement. It was said that John was a profligate, that he indulged in lascivious orgies, that no woman was safe from him. She could not expect a son of hers to live like a monk and because she was saddened by rifts in the family she had persuaded Richard to give him permission to come back to England if he wanted to.

Did he want to? He had come immediately.

Now she wondered what was happening and after she had been ceremoniously received in London she travelled to Winchester and asked William de Longchamp and the Archbishop of Rouen to meet her there.

The Archbishop came. Where, she wanted to know, was

Longchamp? She believed there had been some trouble between him and Prince John.

The Archbishop explained that there had indeed been
great trouble, that Longchamp had been guilty of indiscretion in arresting the Archbishop of York and quarrelling
with Prince John.

Eleanor was alarmed.

'What was Prince John's grievance?'

'That Longchamp had asked the King of Scotland to support Prince Arthur as heir to the throne, for news had
reached us that the King had made an agreement with
Tancred and had given Prince Arthur to Tancred's daughter.

There was a great deal of news which Eleanor had yet to
learn. She asked the Archbishop to let her know at once all
that had happened while she was making the journey home.

What she heard gave her no comfort. She saw that her
worse fears had some foundation. John was too mischievous
not to try to make trouble during his brother's absence. Oh
yes, indeed it had been a mistake to allow him to come back
to England. Her only consolation was that had he not come
he would have attempted to make trouble in Normandy.

When she heard that the King of France had invited John
to visit him she realized how deep was the danger.

'My lord Archbishop,' she said, 'my son John must not go
to France.'

'I agree, my lady,' was the answer, 'but how can we prevent
him?'

Eleanor's eyes flashed. The old vitality was still with her.

'Know this,' she said, 'that my youngest son would wrest
the crown from his brother. It seems to him a heaven-sent
opportunity with Richard away. There is only one king of
this country while Richard lives and that is Richard. We
must take firm action.'

'He is due to embark next week,' said the Archbishop. 'I
have made myself aware of his movements.'

'It would seem,' said Eleanor, 'that I have come home just
in time.'

'What do you propose to do, my lady?'

'We will travel with all speed to Southampton. Let us take
with us William the Marshal and Hugh of Lincoln. These
men and ourselves will convey to the Prince that he must
take note of what we say. I myself will speak to him and let

him know that if he attempts to make terms with the King of France he will lose everything he possesses in England.'

'Can you make him accept this, my lady?'

'You will see,' she answered.

*   *   *

As he came into Southampton John was surprised to be met by members of his mother's household.

The Queen wished to see him, he was told, and would he go to her with all speed.

John grumbled that he was on the point of departure but he could not, of course, refuse to see his mother.

When he came into her apartments she greeted him with affection.

'It is good to be in England with my son,' she said, her eyes watchful.

'Indeed yes, Mother. It has been an anxious time. I dared not think how you might be faring on the seas.'

'Travel is perilous,' she said. 'I fear for the King.'

She could not fail to see the cunning lights in John's eyes. He was hopeful, she thought ruefully. It was indeed fortunate that she had come home in time.

'He has conquered Acre,' said John. 'Doubtless by this time he is setting the Christian flag over Jerusalem.'

'I pray God that he has done that and is on the way home. The kingdom misses him.'

' 'Tis true,' said John smiling wryly.

'There are always those who would take advantage of a sovereign's absence. It is good fortune indeed that I am here to watch over Richard's rights.'

John nodded.

'Never forget, John, that Richard is strong. It would go hard with any who sought to take advantage of his absence.'

'He would be a brave man who dared do that,' said John blithely.

'Nay, only a foolish one.'

'How so?'

'Because when Richard returned he would have to answer to him.'

'What if Richard did not return?'

'That is a matter I will not consider.'

'Then you should, my lady, for the chances are that he never will.'

'Is that why you plan to see the King of France?'

'What mean you?'

'Philip has invited you, I believe.'

'We are his vassals for Normandy.'

'*We.* The King holds Normandy under the King of France it is true but he stands his equal as King of England. Philip has made propositions to you, has he? He has promised you great glory if you will be his tool. That is so. He will give you Normandy? Make you its Duke? Is that what he has promised? Let me tell you this, John, he has no power to do that. The dukes of Normandy are the rightful heirs of Normandy and there is already a Duke. He is Richard your King and your brother.'

'Who cares more for fighting the Saracen than holding his throne.'

'Because he has made a holy vow, because he is a soldier of the Cross, that does not mean he is not a great King.'

'Of a country he has scarcely seen?'

'What have you in your mind, John? To take it from him? Is that why you go to France? He has made you rich here, given you great lands; he has allowed you to marry into Gloucester although there is consanguinity there. He has given you a great deal and you would play the traitor to him. You will not go to France.'

John's temper was rising.

'Madam, I am merely waiting on the wind.'

'Very well, go to France. Play traitor to your brother with the man who once was his friend. See how he will treat you. Remember this, though, as soon as you set sail for France all your lands in England will be confiscated and held under the crown.'

'Who would dare do this?'

'I would dare, John. I am your mother and during the King's absence I rule this land. If you wish to hold what you have in this country then stay here, and keep what you have intact, for with God's help I will strip you of every possession you have if you dare conspire with your brother's enemies against him.'

She left him then. John bit his lips and foamed with anger. He would show her who was master. He had men to follow him. He was going to set sail for France. He was going to see Philip, work with Philip, and together they would rob Richard of his crown.

But to lose everything in England! She meant it, and she could do it. Suppose he lost everything in England—and Normandy not in his grasp! Could he trust the King of France who had been so friendly with Richard but recently?

His schemes were crumbling. How could he take the risk?

He gave way to temper. He tore at his clothes; he lay on the floor and kicked. He gnawed the rushes as his father used to do in his outburst of fury.

No one dared approach him.

* * *

John and his mother were on uneasy terms. She had shown so clearly whose side she was on; and responsible men of the country ranged themselves beside her.

Several months passed and there came news that the King was sailing for home. John was angry and frustrated. Richard had not after all captured Jerusalem; this crusade had achieved the capture of Acre and three years' truce—not much for all the expense that had been incurred, pointed out John; but few listened to him. The King was coming home. It was not the time to range themselves about his young brother. John might talk of the perilousness of journeys, but no one listened.

Christmas came. Some pilgrims arrived in the country, with the news that they had seen the King's ship at Brindisi but that Richard was not there.

Speculation was rife. Where was the King? What would the next news be? John's hopes were high. It was time the King returned. If the pilgrims were in England so should he be.

'He has met some disaster,' he said to Hugh Nunant. 'Depend upon it.'

'Alas, we must depend on nothing,' answered Hugh. 'We must walk very carefully now that your mother is here.'

'Richard was always her favourite,' said John sulkily. But he was full of hope. He was sure Richard was dead.

Messengers came to him from the King of France. The news they brought was startling. Philip enclosed the copy of a

letter he had received from the Emperor of Germany. King
Richard of England was his prisoner, ran the letter; he was to
be held for ransom. The whereabouts of his prison was unknown but it was somewhere in the Emperor's territory.

It was impossible to keep such news to himself. Moreover
travellers coming into England reported that they had heard
of the King's capture.

Eleanor was in despair. She conferred with the Archbishop
of Rouen. She raved against the injustice done to the man
who had done more for Christendom than any other living at
the time. He had sacrificed a great deal, he had placed his
kingdom in jeopardy for the sake of the Holy War, and what
had happened to him, he was imprisoned, not by a Saracen,
which would have been understandable, but by those who
should have been his friends.

She was desperate. She prayed that God might overlook the
wickedness of her youth and not visit her sins on her innocent
sons. She spent hours on her knees calling to the virgin.
'Mother of Mercies, help a miserable mother.' But she was
not of a nature to rely on prayer alone.

First she considered going in search of him; then the possibility of what might happen in her absence if she did deter-
red her from this action. She must stay here. When he was
released there must be a kingdom for him to govern.

But what could she do? Would the Pope help? He could
demand Richard's release immediately if he wished. But why
should he go against the wishes of powerful Henry?

She was desperate and uncertain and as she passed one of
the rooms she heard the mournful strumming of a lute.

She looked inside to see who was there and saw Blondel de
Nesle, one of Richard's favourite minstrels. He was seated on
a stool and as he played a sorrowful dirge the tears ran down
his cheeks.

'What ails you?' asked Eleanor.

'My lord's absence, my lady.'

'I believe you were a favourite of his. He loved you dearly.'

' 'Twas so, my lady. I would have fain stayed with him and
begged to do so, but he wouldn't have it and sent me here.'

'Do not weep, pretty boy. He will return.'

When she had left him Blondel continued to weep.

He must return, he said to himself, or I shall die.

Blondel's Song

THE frustration which had overwhelmed Richard when he
was first brought to the Castle of Dürenstein had given way to
resignation. He had endured hardship during his campaigns
and had never complained on that score, so that now he
found himself a prisoner in an alien land, he could shrug
aside any physical inconveniences.

That it should have been Leopold into whose hands he had
fallen was indeed galling and that Leopold's overlord should
be the Emperor Henry VI of Germany was a further ironic
twist. During the first weeks of his captivity he had asked
himself what could possibly happen next; and now it seemed
that fate might decide to allow his brother John to succeed in
making himself King.

But his resilience had never failed him yet. There was that
in him which could overawe those about him. Even when he
had faced Leopold and been obliged to hand over his sword
the Duke of Austria had quailed before him. He might be a
prisoner but he was still Coeur de Lion, the greatest and most
renowned soldier in the world. No one could forget that and
when they stood before him and he drew himself to his full
height and gave them his cold stare their stature seemed to
decrease and they trembled. It was amusing. He had no fear
of them. That was the secret. That was his great quality.
Whatever the situation, Richard was the one who struck fear
into his opponent not they into him whatever their advantage.

He had seen that when the Duke of Austria brought him here he was uncertain what should be done with him, and had immediately despatched messengers to his Emperor for instructions because he feared the responsibility of holding King Richard. Poor Leopold, he had always been a braggart and braggarts were notoriously men of straw, crowing like cockerels in a farmyard to call attention to their strength lest it should be suspected that they had none.

So Richard had passed his first weeks in Dürenstein speculating on the possibility of escape. It might seem remote and it was clearly because his captors feared they could not hold him that they had chosen such a spot as Dürenstein. It seemed impregnable with iron bars set across the narrow window which was cut out of the thick stone wall. The natural rock formed part of the castle wall on one side and below were the craggy rocks and the River Danube. Escape that way seemed out of the question. There might be other ways. His custodian Hadamar von Kuenring feared it, and he was a very anxious man. But during his first days in the castle von Kuenring had come to him being most anxious to impress on him that he was well aware that the King was a very special prisoner and he had no desire to show disrespect; indeed he was eager to do everything possible—providing he did not go against the wishes of his master Leopold—to make Richard's stay at Dürenstein comfortable.

'Such a situation as that in which I find myself could scarcely be expected to bring me comfort,' said Richard. 'If you can do that you are possessed of supernatural powers.'

Richard smiled wryly as he spoke but there was little humour in this officer of Leopold's guard. He went on: 'Your page who betrayed you is here in the castle. I will send him to you that he may serve you. We hold another of your men, William de l'Estang, and I shall put nothing in the way of your enjoying the companionship of your friend.'

This was indeed good news. William de l'Estang was a man Richard had always liked and his company would be very welcome.

His young page was brought to his cell and fell on his knees before the King who raised him up and embraced him.

'My lord, Sire,' cried the boy and began to weep.

Richard stroked his hair. 'I understand, little one. The cruel men threatened you.'

'To tear out my tongue and to put out my eyes.'

'And would have done it too, God curse them. All is well. Have no fear now.'

'But, my lord, I led them to you.'

'Nay, they would have found me. Dry your tears. Serve me well and it shall be as it ever was.'

The boy fell once more on to his knees and kissed Richard's feet.

It was pleasant to have him.

The days began to pass. Richard was allowed to walk out on to the ramparts as long as he was surrounded by guards. William de l'Estang came and spent the hours of daylight with him; they played chess together and sometimes von Kuenring would play against one of them while the other looked on. Von Kuenring gave Richard a lute and while they played chess the page would play softly. Richard himself often played it and the three of them would sing together.

Richard's voice which was powerful could often be heard in the castle and it was marvelled that one who was a captive could so forget his woes in such songs, many of which were gay.

In fact they marvelled at Richard who did not seem to resent his captors. He liked to test his physical strength with his guards in the courtyard where he would wrestle with them much to the amusement of the onlookers. He selected the tallest and strongest looking men for his opponents and the rest of the guards would watch in amazement, for invariably Richard proved himself the stronger.

Then he would go to his cell and play chess or sing. He was composing a *sirvente* of seven stanzas which he said would tell the world—if it ever heard it—how he felt about his prison.

Sometimes he would talk to William de l'Estang of escape. Was it possible? Could they scale those rocky walls? The guards were ever watchful. Every night special men came to his cell. They were the biggest and most powerful soldiers in the Duke's army, and that was why they had been chosen to guard Richard. They placed themselves about his bed and through the night sat there, their great swords at their sides.

'If we were to escape,' said de l'Estang, 'where should we go? We should be discovered in a short time and put in an even stronger fortress.'

Richard agreed.

'If we could but get a message to my mother ...'

'But how? We are watched day and night.'

'I know not,' said Richard. 'But help must come from somewhere.'

When he was most desperate he turned to his music. It comforted him more than anything.

He sang the first verses of his *sirvente* to William. Poignantly it expressed the plaintive lament of the prisoner.

'It is a little like a song I composed with Blondel de Nesle some time ago. Do you remember Blondel, William?'

'I do, Sire. A handsome boy and devoted to you.'

'He wished to come with me. If I had allowed him to he might well be here with me now. I wondered whether he would have lost his eyes or his tongue for my sake. I would not have had it so. Our poor little page lives in perpetual remorse. Comfort him, William. Make sure he knows that I understand.'

'You yourself with your usual generosity have conveyed it, Sire.'

'I hope Blondel reached England safely. He is a good boy and a fine minstrel.'

'I doubt your brother will appreciate that.'

'Let us hope so, William. Send for the page. Let him sing for us. You and I will go to the chess board and get a game while daylight lasts.'

*　　*　　*

The news was spreading through Europe. Richard a prisoner and none knew where. But there was a firm belief that he was in the hands of Leopold of Austria and that meant that Henry of Germany would have jurisdiction over him.

John was gleeful. The news couldn't have been better. He chuckled over it with Hugh Nunant. Philip of France was sending secret messages to him. Nothing could have suited them better. Philip was amused. He remembered the altercation between Richard and Leopold on the walls of Acre. Was Richard regretting his hasty action now? No, the answer must be. Richard would remain aloof and dignified implying that he would do it again even if he had pre-knowledge that later he would be the Duke's prisoner. There was something fine about Richard. Would to God, thought Philip, that he were my prisoner.

And here he was trying to form an alliance with John. It was all for the good of France. He sent a message to the Prince. 'If Richard is in the hands of Henry of Germany, a fact on which all rumour seems to agree, it is our good fortune. The longer he remains there the better.'

They should offer Henry money to keep him a prisoner until the end of the year 1194. He, Philip, would be prepared to pay fifty thousand marks of silver to Henry of Germany if he would hold Richard until that time and keep his place of captivity a secret. Philip thought John should offer the Emperor another thirty thousand. 'Of course,' added the King of France, 'it might be wiser to pay the Emperor month by month, for if we paid a large sum in advance and Richard escaped the money would be wasted. One thousand pounds of silver say for every month the Emperor held Richard.' They might add that they would jointly be prepared to pay the large sum of one hundred and fifty marks of silver if the Emperor would give the prisoner into their care.

Philip's eyes shone at the idea. He could picture Richard's riding in the centre of his guards, coming to him, to be his loving hostage as he had been once before.

John was excited by all this intrigue and he believed it could not be long before he was on the throne of England.

Queen Eleanor was deeply distressed. She who had never been pious now spent long hours on her knees reproving herself, asking God if he were punishing her son for her past misdeeds.

'What can I do?' she demanded of the Archbishop of Rouen. 'My son's dominions here and in Normandy are threatened on all sides. I must go and search for him, but if I do what will happen here and in Normandy? You know how he suffered from his fevers. I greatly fear he may not survive the life of a prisoner.'

The Archbishop soothed her by recalling Richard's fine physique. 'There is no man to compare with him,' he insisted. 'He has the strength of twenty men.'

'If I but knew where he was...'

'What should we do then?'

'Bring him back.'

'It is certain that they would want a ransom.'

'Then they must have a ransom.'

'Who knows what terms they will insist on.'

'Whatever the terms, they must be accepted. Anything ... anything is preferable to the death of the King.'

Then she began to talk of her sins in the past and to cry out in her wretchedness that she believed she was paying for them now.

The Archbishop sent one of the minstrels to attempt to soothe her with his music. Blondel de Nesle crept silently in and seating himself in a corner started to play.

She listened, charmed by music as she ever was.

'It was beautiful,' she said. 'Who composed it?'

'My lord the King and I together,' answered Blondel.

'You harmonized well I believe.'

'He said so,' replied Blondel. 'There is another song we made together. We have never sung it except when we were alone. He said that was how he wished it. It was our song.'

Eleanor nodded. 'I grieve for him, Blondel. How I grieve for him.'

'Can nothing be done, my lady?'

'We do not know where he is. His captors will not tell us. Until we know how can we do anything to save him?'

'It is said he is in Austria.'

'It is said so. Would we could prove it. His Queen Berengaria saw a jewelled belt for sale in Rome and she knew it for his.'

'How could it have been in Rome, my lady?'

'He might have given it to someone who travelled there.'

'Surely that person would have treasured a gift from the King?'

'It could have been stolen from him. Oh, Blondel, my child, we cannot know what has become of him. I am filled with foreboding.'

'If someone could but find him, my lady...'

'I would go and seek him ... were it not for the state of the Kingdom.'

'His captors would be aware of you, my lady. It would seem to me that one should go who would not be recognized.'

'You are a wise boy, I see. Come, play to me. Play Richard's song.'

And as he strummed Blondel thought of the King and his

many kindnesses towards his minstrel; and he yearned to see his face again.

The next day when the Queen asked that Blondel come to her to soothe her with his music, Blondel could not be found.

*   *   *

It had been a long journey to Austria. Blondel had sung his way across the continent. He had stood in the market places of many towns and so sweet was his voice that people had paused to listen and drop a coin into his hat. He was so handsome that many took pity on him. Often some mother would be reminded of her son and bring him in to her cottage and make him cut wood or perform some such service for his supper and a place to sleep under her roof.

He asked questions about the castles and those who lived in them and whether it was possible that if he called and asked to sing for them he would be allowed to do so.

He invariably was. A minstrel was always welcome, especially one with as fine a voice as Blondel's.

Arriving at a castle he would humbly ask that he might rest a while and play his lute for the company. He would be taken to the great hall and there would invariably be many who were eager to hear the songs of a wandering minstrel.

He would make a point of being friendly with those of the kitchen. They would give him titbits to eat and smile at what they thought was his cunning. Cunning it was, but his motives were not what they thought.

'The youth has not seen a good meal for many a long day, I'll trow,' said the cooks. ' 'Tis small wonder he wants to fill up while he be here.'

But it was gossip he wanted. He would sit by the great fires turning the spits and singing as he did so. In the kitchen they would know perhaps if there was a stranger in the castle whose presence was not generally known. Such a stranger would have to eat and the cooks must be aware of it. There would be a certain ceremony about a king's meals surely.

He asked searching questions and every time it seemed he came away disappointed.

There must be a castle somewhere which was an impregnable fortress. Perhaps on a hill, its thick grey walls a challenge to any invader, it would be formidable. A fortress, thought Blondel, and a prison.

When he came to Dürenstein he went into the square to talk to the traders and sing for his supper and a bed.

There was one woman who had brought her eggs to market and because he thought she had a kindly face—his adventure had made him quick to assess character at a glance—he took his stand near her and sang for her. Tears filled her eyes and she begged for more and as he sang she thought how young he was.

She beckoned him to come nearer and this he did singing and attracting customers with his songs and helping her to sell her produce.

'You are travelling alone?' she asked.

He told her that he was.

'And you sing for your living. Where will you sleep tonight?'

'In the forest, beneath a hedge ... I will find somewhere to sleep.'

'My son has recently married a wife. He no longer lives with me. You may have his bed if you will sing again for me and mayhap come to market with me one other fine day.'

It seemed that she was suggesting he stay for a while and he answered that he was a wanderer, but he would gladly accept her offer for the night and would be willing to do any work for her providing it was not beyond his powers.

He went home with the woman and as they sat at table he asked her who lived at the grand castle on the hill and what was the name of it.

'It is Dürenstein,' she told him. 'It belongs to our Duke Leopold.'

Blondel remembered him at Acre and wondered how he would have behaved if by some chance he was Richard's jailer.

'A very important officer is now the custodian. They say he is of high rank. He came to the castle some time ago. We see him riding in the town now and them.'

'I shall ask if I may sing for them. Do you think I may?'

'I know not. You can but try. And if they will have none of you, you may rest here for a while.'

Blondel thanked her. He did not go to the castle the next morning but waited until later in the afternoon. That was the time when men and women were more mellow. They had generally eaten well and often dozed at such an hour. It was then and at night that music sounded sweeter.

He presented himself at the castle gate.

'I am a wandering minstrel,' he told the serving men. 'I would I might sing in the great hall tonight.'

The men exchanged glances.

'Do you think...?'

One shook his head. 'Our master would not care for minstrels.'

'Who is your master, kind sir?'

'He is Hadamar von Kuenring and very important. The Duke himself comes frequently to the castle since...'

'Since when?' asked Blondel.

'Since it has been in our master's hands.'

'What think you?' asked one of the men. 'Wouldn't you come into the kitchens and sing for us?'

He would indeed, with the greatest pleasure. He chose gentle songs, songs of love to bring tears to the eyes of the women.

They gave him cold venison and half a loaf with ale to wash it down.

'I sing better when my throat has been moistened,' declared Blondel.

He sang some more and then he asked if he might stroll round the castle, for he had thought it quite the most impressive castle he had ever seen.

One of the serving men said he would take him round. He had quite clearly taken a great fancy to Blondel, and as they went Blondel sang.

All the time he was alert; he looked for windows—narrow slips with bars of iron across, the window of a prison. There high in the castle was one of them. A great feeling of excitement possessed him; he broke into song suddenly; he let his voice soar up throwing it with all his might towards that barred window; and then his heart seemed to stop beating, for someone was singing up there, singing in answer to Blondel's song. Blondel continued to sing and the voice answered him.

'I have never heard that song before,' said the serving man.

'Someone in the castle has. Who was that singing with me?'

'I know not,' said the man. 'I have heard the voice but I know not whence it comes.'

'Come,' said Blondel, 'let us return to the castle hall. Think you your master and mistress will allow me to sing to them tonight?'

'I know not, but it will please us of the kitchens if you do.'

What did it matter? thought Blondel. His one thought was to get back to England.

He had discovered Richard's whereabouts, for that was Richard's voice he had heard and the song they had sung was that one which they had composed together and which Richard had decreed should be sung by no one but themselves.

Release

WITH as much speed as he could muster Blondel made his way back to England and sought out Queen Eleanor without delay.

She was astounded when she heard his story and gave way to relief and joy. Richard was alive, albeit a prisoner, and she knew where. He must be brought home; his kingdom must be set in order, his enemies scattered.

'And you, Blondel, have done us this great service,' she cried. 'Rest assured you shall be rewarded.'

'All I ask,' replied Blondel, 'is to see my lord home safe and well.'

Eleanor lost no time. She sent for the Archbishop of Rouen and they called ministers and barons together at Oxford where they discussed what should be done. The news had seemed that Richard alive and well was a prisoner of Leopold in the castle of of the Cru-

story of which love

of the times. He was a legend. They wanted Richard back. There was wild talk of going to war with Germany with an army, of scouring the country, putting it to fire and sword out of vengeance for this treatment of the Lion-heart. They planned grand processions through the land with Richard at their head while they proclaimed to the world the sort of treatment which would be given to those who dared insult their great King.

All dreams, of course, for how could England invade Germany? But it was good for the people to feel thus, reasoned Eleanor, and they should be encouraged in it.

John was furious. He wished he had cut out Blondel's tongue before he had gone off singing round the castles of Europe. He gave vent to his rage in the usual manner but chewed rushes were small consolation for power.

With her usual energy Eleanor set about taking action. An embassy should be sent without delay, not to Leopold of Austria but to his overlord the Emperor of Germany. Terms for Richard's release would no doubt be suggested. They must consider them and if the only way of freeing him was by paying a ransom then that ransom must be paid.

The Emperor received the Embassy courteously. It was indeed true that Richard was a prisoner of his vassal Leopold, and when it was pointed out that he could command Leopold to release Richard he agreed that this was so but added that there were charges against Richard which must first be answered.

Like most rulers Henry was in need of money and he believed that the English would be ready to pay a high ransom for their King. Moreover he had a personal grudge against Richard. Henry's wife Constancia was the sister of the late King of Sicily and in Henry's opinion th........................ to that island. Ric...........................
made agreem..................
to his da.................
promise..........

He........
that........

enemies could no longer let it be presumed that he was dead, was in high spirits. His stay in Dürenstein had not been uncomfortable, merely restricting; and his health had improved a little. There had been no attack of the recurring fever which had so sapped his strength and from which it took time to recover. He was therefore in excellent health.

Arrived at Haguenau he was permitted by Henry to meet members of the embassy from England.

He plied them with questions. The answers were not very comforting.

He heard what had happened to Longchamp, how John was raising supporters and that Philip of France had become an ally of John and it seemed that their motive was to put a crown on John's head.

Richard did not seem greatly surprised.

Philip hates me now, he thought. Strange that once we were such friends. But such friendships are sometimes not of the heart.

And John! My own brother!

He smiled wryly. 'There was ever conflict in our family,' he said. 'Sons against father, brother against brother. Perhaps it is why we are known as the devil's brood. It may well be true that my ancestress was a witch. As for John he is not the man to win a kingdom by force of arms, if he meets the slightest resistance.'

'It would seem, my lord, that you will come home just in time.'

'How are the people? How is the King of Scotland? He has always seemed to be a good friend of mine.'

'The people are with you, my lord, and the King of Scotland your friend. There were bonfires in the hamlets and songs of joy in the streets when news that you were alive was let loose.'

'Then there is nothing to fear from John ... nor from the King of France.'

'Nay, my lord, not now that you are found.'

' 'Twas young Blondel. I shall never forget this.'

'It is reward enough he says that he had the honour of serving you. He says it will never be forgotten and that he is the proudest minstrel in the world. He will be the happiest when you are free.'

'God bless the boy,' said Richard.

But the Emperor was determined that he should not be

easily released. He had paid certain moneys to Leopold of Austria for the captive and he wanted to get that money back with interest.

Meanwhile Eleanor had sent messengers to Pope Celestine begging him to intervene in the unlawful detention of Richard. The Pope, always anxious not to favour one side when the opponents were as powerful as the Emperor of Germany and the King of England, gave his verdict that it was indeed wrong to imprison in secret a ruling monarch unless of course there were good reasons for doing so.

Thus challenged the Emperor declared that he had his reasons. Several people had brought charges against Richard and justice demanded that until these had been satisfactorily answered it was just for Richard—King of England though he might be—to remain a prisoner.

The Emperor then summoned an assembly and the charges against Richard were stated clearly in his presence, so that he could answer them in person.

The first charge was that he had supported Tancred to the detriment of the Emperor whose wife was the true heir to the island of Sicily.

Richard replied that the island had needed a strong king and Tancred was there to provide it. Richard himself had been on his way to a crusade and the most important thing was to proceed with all speed on his mission. By making terms with Tancred he had been able to do this and to make sure that other crusaders on their way to the Holy Land would not be prevented from making the journey. The same applied to Cyprus where he had set up his own ruler so that it could now be a haven for pilgrims and crusaders.

The serious charge of having brought about the murder of Conrad Marquis of Montserrat was the next.

This he utterly refuted.

It was well known, he replied, that the Old Man of the Mountains was responsible for that deed because Conrad had intercepted his ships and robbed them off the coast of Tyre. It was only slander which had brought the charge against him because he had supported Guy de Lusignan as candidate for the crown of Jerusalem. He had however agreed to accept Conrad. Why should he then murder him, for his murder had not put Guy on the throne, for Henry of Champagne had that honour.

This seemed reasonable and the assembly was swayed in favour of Richard.

The French representative in the assembly rose to declare that Richard was guilty of treason against his feudal lord, Philip of France.

Richard laughed so loudly that his laughter echoed through the hall.

'I ... accused of treason!' cried Richard. 'My lords, if there is one guilty of treason that is the King of France. He has sworn friendship with me. We vowed to go together to the Holy Land. He broke his vow. He could not endure the hardships. They brought him near to death, he swears; and he returned to France and planned to rob my kingdom and my dukedom while I continued to act in accordance with the vow I took with the King of France. Is this treason to Philip? Nay, my lords, Philip is the one who is guilty of treason, of breach of friendship, of broken vows and promises. He has taken advantage of one who believed himself to be his friend. Think of his actions during my absence. Is he a man of honour? Come, my lords, search your consciences and do not speak to me of *my* lack of loyalty to the King of France.'

There was murmuring in the hall. They must agree with him. He was right. The King of France had betrayed him and what sort of man was it who attacked another's dominions while he was away engaged in a holy war?

There were followers of Leopold of Austria who related that Richard had insulted their flag. He had torn it down from the walls of Acre and stamped on it. Was this not an act of treachery against a good friend who had fought side by side with him in the conquest of the city?

'My lord,' said Richard, 'this was no single triumph. This was the triumph of the Christian army. In such an undertaking there are certain to be conflicts between nations. As commander of the army it was my duty to suppress this. The Duke of Austria was arrogant, not ready to work with the rest of us. When I myself repaired the walls of the cities with my men, the Duke of Austria declared himself too noble to work with us. I am the son of a King, my lords, yet I could work side by side with my men, share their hardships, show myself to be one of them. It is necessary in an army. It is not good for that army to see among them those who are too proud to share in the task and then would take the glory.

I did what you accused me of and, by God, I would do it again.'

It was not only his words, it was that aura of nobility and almost superhuman power, his exceptional good looks, his tall commanding figure, which made Henry realize it had been a mistake to bring him to face his judges. The accusations should have been made in his absence.

But Henry was shrewd. He knew he had lost so he went to Richard and embraced him.

'I see,' he cried, 'that the King of England has been falsely accused and I believe this assembly to be in agreement with me.'

There were cries of agreement and cheers.

Now I shall go home and set my affairs in order, thought Richard.

*   *   *

But Henry was not going to relinquish his prize so easily. Richard might be innocent of the charges brought against him; Pope Celestine might declare it was not right for the Emperor to detain him, but the Emperor saw that there was money to be gained and he shook his head over Richard and murmured that it was only proper that if the English wished their King to return they must be prepared to pay for the privilege.

Richard was therefore conducted to the castle of Trifels, a suitable place for a King to be held to ransom. Trifels had been built on a hill surrounded by wooded mountains; there was no town within miles, the nearest dwellings being in the village of Anweiler. Richard was treated with respect; comforts were provided for him; he had his page to sing and play to him and William de l'Estang as a companion. But he was surrounded by an even stronger guard than he had had at Dürenstein. At least, however, thanks to faithful Blondel it was known where he was and he could rely on his mother to do everything within her power to bring about his release.

*   *   *

The bargaining began and went on for months. Philip was urging the Emperor not to release Richard. He wondered what they would say to each other if they were to come face to face again. How Richard would revile him! He would never understand that he reviled himself. What was it, this desire to destroy that which in a way he loved and yet he hated? Richard would never understand the complex feelings of the King of France.

Meanwhile Henry of Germany was determined to make the best of his bargain.

He visited Richard and they talked together.

Richard was his prisoner, he pointed out. He had bought the right to hold him from Leopold of Austria who had good reason to hate him; and he must have something for his pains. What would Richard think of handing him the crown of England in exchange for his freedom?

'I'd rather you took my life,' retorted Richard.

'You should have the crown back,' temporized the Emperor, 'and hold it as my vassal.'

Richard laughed at the thought.

'What of seventy thousand marks of silver?'

'That's a great deal,' said Richard. 'Dost think my people would consider me worth as much?'

'They would seem loyal at this time. They regard you as the hero of the crusades. They might think it worth the price to have you back and so avoid the crown's going to John.'

'Then let us see if they will raise it.'

'The daughter of the Emperor of Cyprus is detained by you. She is the niece of the Duchess of Austria and should be given to her aunt to be brought up.'

'That can be done,' said Richard.

'To show friendship with the Duke of Austria whom you insulted on the walls of Acre his son should have for wife your niece the maid of Brittany sister to that Arthur whom you have named your heir.'

'That should also be done,' replied Richard.

'Then all that is left is to raise the money.'

'It will take time,' said Richard.

'That is to be expected.'

'You cannot hold me here for years. Let us say that when the first instalment is made I am allowed to go.'

This was agreed on and Richard in his chamber at Trifels waited eagerly for release.

*   *   *

Eleanor was indefatigable. How could she raise the first instalment of the ransom which was necessary for Richard's release?

Nothing and no one must be spared. Every knight must contribute twenty shillings. Every town and hamlet must pay its due. Every man who had anything to give must give it. The abbeys and churches were to give their silver plate but Eleanor swore it would only be as a loan and the articles should later be restored to the churches. The monks were to give the wool from their sheep. No one must be spared.

Once the King was back there would be prosperity in the land. But the King must return.

The money was paid and there was no longer any excuse to keep Richard prisoner. He set out from the Castle of Trifels on his way to England.

William de l'Estang was uneasy, as Richard himself was.

'I'll not feel safe,' said Richard, 'until I am free of the Emperor's domains.'

Even so he refused to show any sign of haste and paused in Cologne to receive the Mass which was given in his honour.

He did not linger though. Something told him that Henry was already regretting his agreement to let Richard go.

'Let us go with all speed without seeming to,' suggested William, and Richard agreed with this.

When they arrived at Antwerp it was to find English ships waiting to take them home, but their progress was slow as the sandbanks were notoriously dangerous and skilful navigation was necessary to avoid disaster. A sudden storm drove them into the port of Schouwen where it seemed wise to rest until the sea was calmer. However news came that the Emperor, reconsidering his decision to allow Richard to go, was sending a troop of his best soldiers to bring Richard back to him. The thought of being once more a prisoner decided Richard. He would face the storm rather than that. He was fortunate and managed to weather it, and in due course landed at Sandwich.

As soon as he knew that his brother had landed John lost no time in going to France.

The Reconciliation

So he was back in England. It was four years and three months since the day he had left and now he was landing at Sandwich on this April Sunday.

It seemed that the whole of England had come out of their homes to welcome him. He was content to have his mother beside him, his good friends around him and his loyal people making him aware of their pleasure in his return.

First to Canterbury to prostrate himself at the shrine of St Thomas and to thank God and the saint for bringing him safely through so many adventures. Then to London where it seemed the citizens, wild with joy, were determined to make feasts for him and bestow rich gifts upon him.

And after London to St Albans to kneel before the shrine there and offer to God the banner of Cyprus that his conquest of that island might be blessed.

Winchester should be next but there were one or two matters to be set right before he went there. Certain of his castles had defected to John and he must show the inhabitants of these that he was determined to take back that which was his by right.

Nottingham was the chief of these and it only needed him to appear for the citadel to surrender and those who had held it in John's name to come on their knees and beg his clemency. He was in a forgiving mood. He was so pleased to be free and to know that his kingdom was once more in his hands and his subjects loyal to him.

At Winchester he enjoyed a second coronation, carrying the regalia as he had done when he was crowned king.

His mother, who had been beside him during his triumph-
ant progress, was deeply moved. But she it was who reminded
him that the life of a King was not all pageantry.

'You have regained England, my son,' she said, 'and methinks you returned just in time. But John has gone to
France and you know who your real enemy is.'

'Philip,' he murmured.

'Aye, the King of France. He has encouraged John to act
against you and I believe to be true the rumour that he
bribed the Emperor to hold you prisoner longer than he
might have done.'

'Why, Mother? Why?'

'Because he is the King of France, Richard, and you are the
King of England. You hold Normandy and he wants Normandy. What better reason than that?'

'But I had thought Philip was my friend.'

'Always an uneasy friendship, Richard.'

'Aye, so it would seem.'

'What of Berengaria? It is long since you have seen your
wife. You should send for her as soon as we reach Normandy,
for to Normandy we must go at once. England will be safe now
but not so Normandy.'

' 'Tis true that we must go to Normandy.'

'And Berengaria?'

He was silent.

'You do not love her,' said Eleanor. 'Does she not please
you as a wife?'

'She is well enough.'

'Ah, my son, I understand. You do not want a wife. But it
is necessary for you to produce an heir, you know.'

' 'Tis the duty of all kings I well know.'

'Get her with child and then pursue your own way of life.'

Richard did not answer and Eleanor shook her head sadly.
It seemed strange to her that a man such as Richard should
not love women. He must be induced to go to Berengaria for
a while at least. She, Eleanor, must live long enough to see
them produce the heir to the throne.

Before May was out they set sail for Normandy. It was
imperative to do so as there was no time to lose. Richard set
up a Regent to act for him until he and Queen Eleanor returned.

*   *   *

In their apartments in the castle of Poitou the Queens of England and Sicily with the Cypriot Princess, who had been their constant companion since Richard had sent her to them, heard the news of the King's return.

They knew then that the life which had been theirs since they came to the peace of Poitou was coming to an end.

During that time Berengaria had often said that she felt they were living in a dream from which they would have to awaken sooner or later. Life seemed to have stood still. There had been the years of waiting for Richard, then the adventure of going to Sicily, Cyprus and the Holy Land, marriage, the perilous journey to Poitou followed by the quiet life when every day seemed like the one before and nothing seemed to happen.

'Nothing?' Joanna had cried when Berengaria had spoken of this to her. For to Joanna something had happened. Ever since the handsome knight had been bidden to escort them from Marseilles she had begun to change. Joanna and Raymond of Toulouse had ridden side by side on that journey; they had laughed and talked together, becoming so absorbed in each other's company that any attempt to join them on the part of Berengaria seemed to spoil their pleasure.

And since they had been at Poitou the Count had visited them frequently, and when he came Joanna was gayer and younger than Berengaria had ever seen her before. In the beginning Berengaria had hoped that the attachment would fade away. The Count of Toulouse had brought them in safety to Poitou and there his duty ended; if he had not returned to them again and again Joanna might have begun to forget their charming escort and those pleasant hours which flew by with such speed as they talked together and discovered so much in common with each other.

But it seemed that Raymond of Toulouse found it impossible to stay away from Joanna.

Berengaria talked of the matter with the Cypriot Princess. 'It goes too far,' she said.

'It is too late to stop it now,' replied the Princess.

'I fear Joanna's heart will break when she has to give him up.'

'Need she?'

'Richard's family and his have always been in conflict. Why even during the crusade the Counts of Toulouse invaded

Guienne. Had my brother Sancho not fought in Richard's defence Guienne would have passed into the hands of the Counts of Toulouse.'

The Princess shook her head sadly. 'It is all fighting,' she said, 'and we must suffer because of it.'

'I trust Joanna will not suffer too deeply,' replied Berengaria.

There was about Joanna a defiance. She said that if a Princess married once for state reasons she should be allowed to choose her second husband.

But all of them knew that the days of dalliance were coming to an end, and the climax which they knew was inevitable was moving nearer.

Joanna and her lover talked together, as they walked in the castle grounds.

'Now that my brother is free I will send a message to him,' she said. 'I will send one to my mother also. Who knows, they may allow us to marry.'

Raymond was less sanguine. 'There has always been enmity between our houses.'

'Then, my dearest love, I will point out that a match between us will mend the rift.'

He kissed her tenderly, loving her vitality, her enthusiasm. Then he said: 'And if they should refuse?'

'I am not a child,' she said. 'I have done my duty once. This time I will have my way. I will go with you wherever you take me.'

He pressed her hands.

'It could mean death to us both,' he told her.

'I would face death for love,' she answered, 'and whatever the future held we should have had some time together.'

'You are reckless, Joanna.'

'Let us be reckless. I will if you will.'

'Then be ready.'

'First though I will send to my brother and to my mother also. I have hopes, for Richard has never been vengeful. I believe I was always his favourite sister and I know he would wish to see me happy. As for my mother she knows what it is to love. Let us hope, Raymond.'

So Joanna sent messengers to Richard and Eleanor and, at the same time, being uncertain of what their reaction would be, prepared herself for flight.

Each day she and Berengaria were at the turret watching for riders.

Berengaria thought: Richard will send for me. He must now that he is in Normandy.

During the years of his captivity she had forgotten his neglect of her in the Holy Land; she made excuses for it. He had been so deeply involved. His purpose was to regain Jerusalem. He had no time for the society of women. But there had been occasions ... She shut out such thoughts and memories of the rumours she had heard about his nature. She thought only of the knight in shining armour whom she had first seen at the tournament of Pampeluna. The dreams of an idealistic young girl were superimposed on the bitter truth of experience.

'Richard will come to me soon,' she told herself.

The Cypriot Princess was growing out of childhood. She still thought of her father and dreamed of the day when she had heard that he was a prisoner. That had been so difficult to understand at that time. He the mighty Emperor whom all men feared, a prisoner in chains—silver chains she was told, as though that would console her.

She had been frightened then but she had not fully understood the possibilities of what could happen to an unprotected princess. Since the fall of Cyprus she had lived closely beside Joanna and Berengaria; she had seen Berengaria's unhappiness through the neglect of her husband and Joanna's delight and fears as the prospect of marriage with Raymond of Toulouse or of parting with him for ever loomed up before her.

Why could not life be simple as it had seemed to a child in her father's palace? she wondered. But to enjoy the simple life one must be simple oneself. As one grew older and knew what was happening in the world one realized the awful possibilities.

She knew why the Queens watched eagerly. Joanna was waiting for a messenger from King Richard and Berengaria was waiting for King Richard himself.

At length it came. Ironically no one was watching at that time and the messenger rode into the courtyard while they were at table.

Joanna stood up, all the colour drained from her face. Berengaria was trembling.

Letters. The royal seal. Not for Berengaria. Of course he will come in person, thought Berengaria. But letters for Joanna.

She seized on them and carried them to her own chamber. Berengaria felt limp with disappointment. She knew in her heart that she had been foolish to hope.

She went to the chamber next to that of Joanna. She wanted to be alone. Is it that he dislikes me? she asked herself. Can the rumours be true? Are there some he loves?

Joanna was at the door. Her cheeks flushed, her eyes shining.

'Wonderful news, Berengaria. Richard is the dearest and kindest of brothers! He wants me to be happy, he says. I have suffered a great deal. He loves me dearly.'

'They are permitting the match with Raymond?'

'They are ready to make arrangements. Concessions will be asked doubtless. But what do we care for that? Raymond and I are to be married.'

She threw herself into Berengaria's arms. 'I'm so happy, Berengaria. Princesses are rarely so happy, I know. When I think of my last marriage ... a little girl going into a foreign land to a stranger ... And now Raymond! Oh what a good brother Richard is to me! And there is my mother. She writes that there has always been conflict between her house and that of Toulouse and that the Counts of Toulouse have always believed they had a claim in Aquitaine. She will give up her rights to Aquitaine to me so that in this way the claim will be settled.'

'So, my dear Joanna, you are the most fortunate Princess alive. You can mend a quarrel between states and marry for love at the same time.'

Joanna paused and looked at Berengaria, her delight momentarily dimmed. Here am I rejoicing, she reproached herself, when Berengaria is so sadly deserted.

Oh Richard, how can you be so good to your sister and so cruel to your wife!

'I doubt not,' she said, 'that Richard will be here. He will want to be with you as soon as he has made Normandy safe.'

Berengaria turned away.

She knew the truth.

*   *   *

As Richard moved across Normandy recovering all that had been lost, John was terrified. All his dreams of power had evaporated. Richard was home safe and well and likely to live for a good many years. He gave way to his violent rages but of what use were they? He had to face his brother sooner or later and what the outcome of that would be he dared not think.

There was one hope. His mother was with Richard. If he could talk with her in secret, if he could get her to plead with Richard ... there might be a chance. But would she? She was on Richard's side absolutely. Her greatest mission in life was to keep him on the throne. What would she think of one—even though he were her son—who had tried to take it from him?

She was softening in her old age. Look at this affair of Joanna's! She had always been fiercely against the house of Toulouse. There was the perennial quarrel about their claim on this and that. Yet she had talked with Richard and Joanna's happiness and been a factor in their decision. She was a mother as well as a Queen and she was his mother.

Richard had power to send him to prison. The fate which befell prisoners would not bear contemplation. To be shut up in a dungeon for years, to have jailers who might treat him with cruelty or at least without respect, was something he could not endure. Yet he had played the traitor. He had to admit it. He had intrigued against the King and even though his father had named him his successor Richard was the eldest son and accepted by the people as the true King. One only had to remember how they had drooled over him when he had returned. The great hero, the Saviour of Acre, the man whose name was a legend throughout the Christian world. The Lion-hearted King! They forgot he had deserted them. had taxed them to pay for his crusade, had cared little for his native land and had offered to sell London if he could get enough money for it to spend on his Holy Wars. Yes, they forgot that. He had come home covered with honours; he was romantic; he had been imprisoned in a German schloss; he had been discovered by his minstrel boy and they had had to pay a vast sum for his ransom. This did not add up to a good king but they loved him none the less. And there was no doubt that he was strong. None it seemed could stand against him. Philip was less friendly now that he was back, inclined to be contemptuous of John and speaking of his enemy Richard as though he were some kind of god.

John knew when he was beaten and he was beaten now. His only hope was his mother.

He would go to her quietly, secretly; he would plead with her to speak for him to Richard as she had for Joanna. He would remind her that he was her youngest son.

There was no time to lose. If Richard captured him ... He shivered at the thought.

Taking with him a few of his attendants he rode to Rouen where he knew Richard and Eleanor were; and he managed to find a way into the Queen's apartments.

He threw himself at her feet and begged her clemency.

'John,' cried Eleanor. 'So you have come then!'

'Yes, Mother,' answered John, 'and in most wretched state as you see.'

'Oh, John,' cried Eleanor, 'what have you done?'

'I have been foolish, Mother. Do not reproach me, for your reproaches could not match my own. I have been wicked. I have been wrong. I have been led astray by evil counsellors. How can I face my brother?'

The Queen replied: 'You have in truth been wicked, John. You have plotted against the finest man in the world.'

'I know it. I know it now. Would to God I had not listened to those evil men.'

'Aye, would to God you had not.'

'Mother, you are wise, you are good. I want you to tell me what I must do. Shall I take a sword and pierce my heart? I think that would be best. First though, I would wish to prostrate myself before my brother. I would wish to show him my contrition. I want him to know how miserable I am, how I hate myself, and perhaps to ask his forgiveness and that of God before I take my own life.'

'You are talking nonsense,' replied Eleanor sharply. 'Put thoughts of taking your life out of your head. I would not wish any son of mine to act in such cowardly fashion.'

'But I have offended...'

'Deeply,' she cried. 'Your God, your King and your country.'

'I must be the most hated man alive. There is no reason for me to live.'

'Stop such talk! I am your mother and I could not hate you.'

'You hated my father when he worked against Richard. You have always loved Richard and hated those who worked against him.'

'I love all my children,' she answered, 'and I never truly hated the King, your father. You could not understand what there was between us. But that is of the past. It is the present that matters. You have proved yourself a traitor and there are few kings who would not condemn you to the traitor's death. But Richard is your brother. He is by nature tolerant. I am your mother and whatever you have done you are still my child.'

'What should I do then, Mother? I beg you tell me.'

'Leave this with me. Go away quietly. I will speak to your brother and mayhap he will send for you and perhaps he will find it in his heart to forgive you. If you should be the luckiest traitor in the world, then remember what great fortune is yours and serve him with all your might and heart for as long as he shall live.'

'Oh, my mother, I would. I swear to God I would.'

'Then go and leave this matter to me.'

When he had gone Eleanor was thoughtful. She knew him well. He was avaricious; he was weak; he wanted the crown. But he was her son. She could not get out of her mind what a pretty baby he had been and how she had loved him—the youngest, the baby. It had been one of the tragedies of her life that she had not been able to keep her children with her.

He deserved death or imprisonment, but he was her child.

Richard would forgive him if she asked it, she knew. And if he were forgiven, there must be an heir to the throne. Richard was not an old man: he had many years ahead of him. She wanted to see some healthy sons before she died.

Richard might pardon John and if he did he must call Berengaria to his side. He must live with her. It was imperative that he have sons to ensure the succession.

It would be a tragedy for England if John ever came to the throne.

* * *

It was Eleanor who brought him to the King.

Richard looked at his brother and thought: As if he could harm me!

John ran to him and threw himself at his feet.

'You tremble?' said Richard.

'My lord, I have sinned against you. I deserve any punishment you should give me. I cannot understand myself. I was possessed by devils. How otherwise could I have gone against the brother whom I revere as does all the world?'

' 'Twas not devils,' said Richard, 'but evil counsellors, Come, John, do not fear me. You are but a child and you fell into evil hands.'

He rose and drew John to his feet. He kissed him. It was the kiss of peace and pardon.

'Come,' he said, 'we will go and eat and from now on there shall be harmony between us.'

All those who were present marvelled at the King's generosity or simplicity. The fact that he had returned and was in power could by no means have diminished John's ambitions. But Richard seemed to be of the opinion that it did.

One of his servants brought in a salmon which had been presented for the King's table.

'A fine fish,' said the King. 'Cook it and I will share it with my brother.'

John was relieved but at the same time resentful; he knew that Richard's leniency meant that he had little respect for him.

Well, he must be quiet for a while. He must watch his actions and wait for the day when the crown would be his.

*   *   *

Eleanor expressed her pleasure that the brothers had been reconciled.

'You are magnanimous, Richard,' she said. 'I do not believe many kings would have been so.'

'Bah,' said Richard. 'What is John but a child? He could never take a kingdom. His only chance of getting one would be if it were handed to him without a fight.'

'Is that what you intend to do ... to hand it to him?'

'I am not dead yet, Mother.'

'Nay but you are ten years older than John. It is thirty-six years since I bore you. You must get an heir or there will be trouble, Richard. Why do you not send for Berengaria?'

'There is much yet to be done. I don't trust Philip. I shall be engaged here in Normandy for some time.'

'She could be here with you as I am now.'

'Mayhap,' he said; and she knew that he did not intend to have her.

The next day he said: 'I shall send for Arthur. He should be brought up in England.'

'That you might make him your heir?' replied the Queen.

'Is it not wise to have him brought up in the country he may well govern?'

'He would only be the heir, Richard, if you did not have sons.'

'It is well to be prepared,' replied Richard. 'If he should be displaced it will have done him no harm to have had an English upbringing. Why, Mother, what ails you? You are thinking that it would go ill for England if John were King. That is why we send for Arthur.'

Eleanor understood. Richard meant that he was not going back to Berengaria.

Reunion with Berengaria

THE King was riding to the hunt in the Normandy forest. Like his ancestors he loved this sport and found greater relaxation from it than in any other way.

It was a year since he had been released from captivity; it had been a year spent chiefly in fighting, subduing those who would rise against him, regaining those castles which had fallen into other hands while he was away.

He had not seen Philip in that time but there had been opportunities when they might have met. Neither wanted it, certainly not Philip. He could never have faced Richard after all his perfidy; he could never have explained what had prompted him to betray him, to seek an ally in John when Richard was in prison. He thought of him constantly though; and if Richard could not be his loving friend, he found some consolation in being his enemy.

A great deal had happened. Joanna had married and had given birth to a child. She was happy with her Count and Richard was glad of that. The Princess Alice, who had once been betrothed to him and had been the mistress of his father, had been returned to her brother after a treaty he and Richard had made. Poor Alice, she had not had much of a life since the death of King Henry. Perhaps there would be a change when she went to France. And so it had proved to be, for Alice, now thirty-five years of age, was married to the Count of Ponthieu who evidently believed that alliance with the royal house of France was worth while even if it meant taking a princess who was no longer young and about whom there had been scandal in her youth.

Richard hoped Alice would at last find peace.

His sister-in-law Constance had refused to send Arthur to him. Clearly she did not trust him. What a fool the woman was! Surely she wanted Arthur to have his rights and there was no doubt that he was the heir to the English throne. Had he lived Geoffrey would have been pleased to see his son so elevated. But an English king should know the English and the best way of doing that was to be brought up among them.

Yet Constance had sensed some intrigue. She did not trust her brothers-in-law. That she did not trust John was understandable as Arthur would displace him, but why not Richard? She had even sought the aid of Philip to help her against Richard, and he had heard that she had sent her son to the Court of France to avoid his being taken by the English.

Richard shrugged his shoulders. If that was what she wanted let her have it. It could well lose her son the throne. John was at least known to the English. Oh God in Heaven, thought Richard, what would happen to England if John were King!

His mother would say: Get heirs of your own. All that is needed is a son of yours.

No! he cried, and tried not to think of Berengaria lonely in the castle at Poitou. Joanna had gone now and even the little Cypriot Princess had been returned to Leopold's wife in Austria who was her kinswoman.

Leopold had died recently. He had fallen from his horse and broken his leg which mortified to such an extent that amputation was necessary. Knowing that if it were not removed it would corrupt his whole body he himself held the axe while his chamberlain struck it with a beetle. He had courage, that Duke, thought Richard; but after his leg had been cut off he died in terrible agony which many said was Heaven's retribution for his treatment of Richard the Lion-hearted who enjoyed favour from above on account of his having brought Acre to the Christians.

One day, thought Richard, I will go back to the Holy Land.

Saladin was dead. His intimate, the Saracen Bohadin, had told how nobly he had died. He was both brave and humble and talked of the perishability of earthly possessions. He told those about him to reverence God and not to shed blood unless it was necessary for the salvation of his country and to the glory of God. 'Do not hate anyone,' he had said. 'Watch how you treat men. Forgive them their sins against you and thus will you obtain forgiveness for yours.'

Oh Saladin, thought Richard, would we could have met in different circumstances! But how could it have been otherwise than it was? I a Christian, you a Saracen; yet I would have trusted you as I could few men and I knew that you felt thus towards me.

Thinking of these matters he had ridden a little ahead of the party. It was often so, for he liked now and then to be alone; and as he came to a clearing in the woods a man ran forward and stood before him.

'Who are you, fellow?' demanded the King.

'None that you would know, sir. But I know who you are.'

'Who am I?'

'A king and a sinner.'

Richard laughed aloud.

'And I would say you are a bold man.'

'You too, sir, for you will have need of your courage when you are called on to face a King far greater than any on earth.'

'Oh, you are calling me to task for my wayward life, is that it?'

'Repent, while there is time.'

'Am I not a good king?'

'The life you lead is not a good one.'

'You are insolent, fellow.'

'If truth be insolence then I am. Remember the Cities of the Plain. God moves in a mysterious way. Repent, lord King. Turn from your evil ways. If you do not you will be destroyed. The end is near ... nearer than you think. Repent, repent while there is still time.'

A sudden rage seized Richard. He drew his sword, but the man had disappeared among the trees.

He remained in the clearing staring ahead of him. Thus his friends found him.

'What ails you, Sire?' asked one of them.

''Tis nought. An insolent fellow ... a woodman mayhap.'

'Dost wish us to find him, Sire?'

Richard was silent for a few moments. Find the fellow. Cut out his tongue. Make him remember to his dying day that on which he had insulted the King.

Nay. It was the truth. He had reverted to the wildness of his youth. The manner in which he behaved was truly not becoming to a king. A man should not be smitten for speaking the truth.

'Leave him,' he said. 'Doubtless he was mad.'

*   *   *

It was but a month or so later when he was plagued by an attack of the tertian fever. The ague possessed him more firmly than ever before. He felt sick unto death and as he lay on his bed he remembered the man of the woods.

Pictures of his past life kept flashing before his eyes: Rearing horses, showers of arrows, boiling pitch falling over castle walls, the lust of battle which had sometimes overcome his sense of justice. Now and then he had killed for the sake of killing. He thought of the Saracen defenders of Acre whom he had caused to be slaughtered in a fit of rage because Saladin had delayed keeping to the terms of their agreement. Thousands slaughtered on the whim of a king—and not only Saracens, for Saladin had naturally been obliged to retaliate and slaughter Christians. He had always wanted to be just and honourable in battle. So often he had been lenient with his enemies. Why must he forget those numerous occasions and remember the isolated few when he had lost all sense of honour in order to appease his temper? And there was one other to whom he had caused great suffering. Berengaria! He remembered her at the tournament at Pampeluna, a fresh innocent child. Her eyes had followed him with adoration and he, knowing then of his father's relationship with his betrothed Alice and determined to have none of her, had decided that he would take Berengaria. Yet he wanted no women and none knew that better than he. He had married her though. Kings must marry whatsoever their inclinations. They must get heirs. If they did not there was trouble. John ... Arthur ... what of the future? If he were to die now with his sins upon him...

One of his servants came into the room.

'My lord, there is one without ...'

Before Richard could answer a man had come into the room. He stood over the bed, the servant cowering in the background. Richard saw him through a haze of fever.

'Who are you,' he asked, 'the angel of death?'

'Nay, Sire,' was the answer, 'he has not come for you yet. It is Hugh, your Bishop of Lincoln.'

Richard closed his eyes. That old man whom many thought a saint; one of those churchmen who was not averse to acting against his own interest in what he believed to be right. Uncomfortable people! His father had found the leader of them all in Thomas à Becket.

Recently he had quarrelled with this man over a priest whom Richard wished to install in Hugh's See and Hugh had objected to the King's choice. Richard had told the Bishop that as he did not want this priest, he, Richard, would be prepared to allow things to remain as they were if the See would make him a present of a fur mantle at a cost of a thousand marks. Hugh had replied that he had no knowledge of furs and could not therefore bargain for a mantle but if the King wished to divert the funds of the See to his own use and there was no other way of settling the matter, Hugh had no alternative but to send him one thousand marks.

This incident had created a coolness between them and the King reasoned that Hugh had come to crave his pardon.

'Why do you come?' asked Richard.

'I come to ask that there be peace between us, my son,' answered Hugh.

'You do not deserve my good will,' muttered Richard. 'You have stood against me.'

'I deserve your friendship,' answered Hugh. 'For hearing of your sickness I have travelled far. In what state is your conscience?'

'Ha, you have decided to kill me off. I tell you this, prelate: my conscience is very easy.'

'I cannot understand that,' was the disconcerting answer. 'You do not live with your Queen whom the whole world knows to be a lady of virtue. You pursue a life which cannot give pleasure to your people. It is becoming notorious throughout the country. You have no heir and you know full well that were you to die there would be conflict in this realm.'

'I have named Prince Arthur as my heir.'

'A boy who has never seen this country! Do you think the people will accept him? What of Prince John? Were you to die tonight, my lord King, you would be loaded with sin. The friends you choose, the life in which you indulge, these will never bring you an heir. You have taken money from the poor to buy vanities for yourself; you have taxed your people...'

'That I may fight a holy war and set my kingdom in order,' Richard defended himself.

'Think on these things, my lord. Life is short and Death is never far away. If you were taken tonight would you care to go before your Maker weighed down with sin as you are?'

The old man had gone as suddenly as he came.

Richard lay staring after him. He thought: It is true. He is a brave man. I could cut out his tongue for what he has said to me this night, but I would not add that sin to all the others. I must rise from this bed. I must mend my ways. I must subdue my inclinations ... Oh God in Heaven give me another chance.

Within a few days the King's health had so much improved that he was able to rise from his bed.

* * *

He rode to the castle of Poitou.

Berengaria, sitting at her embroidery, her only consolation now that Joanna and the little Cypriot had gone, was wondering whether this was how she would spend the rest of her life. Few came to the castle; the days followed each other one so like the others that she lost count of time. The excitement of Joanna's romance was over; there was no longer the little Princess to talk to. Sometimes she wondered whether she could ask to go back to her brother's court. Her father had died some time before and Sancho would welcome her, but that would be to let the whole world know that Richard had deserted her.

And then there came visitors.

She went down to the courtyard to meet them and at the head of them looking as noble as he had that day at the tournament in Pampeluna was Richard himself.

He leaped from his horse and as she would have knelt he lifted her and embraced her.

'Come into the castle,' he said. 'I have much to say to you.'

Bewildered, her heart beating with a wild emotion she was led into her chamber and there he took her hands and said simply: 'Berengaria, we have been apart too long. It must be so no more.'

She did not understand why he should so suddenly have changed towards her, but what did it matter? He was here and in the future they were to be together. He had said it.

The Saucy Castle

So they were together at last and now it was only war which separated them. Richard was constantly engaged in it, for Philip had made the most of his absence and his alliance with John to take possession of much of Normandy. Richard was going to bring it back to the Dukedom.

He was not sorry—war was his life; and the conflict with Philip gave him a satisfaction which Berengaria never could, not even the talents of his beloved Blondel. Philip was the one who dominated his thoughts; and he knew that Philip felt the same about him. Philip might marry and beget children—he was more successful in this field than Richard could be—and yet it was hatred of Richard, his determination to beat him in conflict that was the major force of his life.

Now on the banks of the Seine where the river winds through the valley past the towns of Les Andelys—Petit and Grand—he was building a castle and he was determined that this castle should be the finest, the most beautiful castle in France. It was to be set up in defiance of France; it was to be the defence of Normandy; it would stand there proclaiming that Richard the Lion-hearted was invincible and that Philip of France could never pass beyond that spot to take Normandy. Every moment Richard could spare he was at Les Andelys watching the building of his castle.

Before it was completed, he had named it the Château Gaillard—the Saucy Castle—and saucy it was, perched on a hill overlooking the Seine, commanding the countryside, in-

viting the French armies to come and see what they would get
if they attempted to invade the Normandy of Richard Coeur
de Lion.

He had gloated over his prize with its ten feet thick walls
except in the keep where their thickness was twelve feet. It
was said that it was built on French blood and to give this
credence Richard had actually thrown French prisoners from
the rock of Les Andelys on to the stones which were the
foundations of the castle.

He loved this castle. There was not another to compare
with it in France. Men marvelled at it—impregnable, standing at the gates of Normandy; it was built with all the skill
gleaned from experience of defensive warfare in Palestine. It
was the wonder of the times.

In France a new saying passed into the language: 'As
strong as the Saucy Castle.'

Philip boasted: 'One day I will take it, were it made of
iron.'

Richard responded: 'I would hold it were it made of but-
ter.'

When the castle had been completed one year Richard
celebrated its anniversary with a great feast to which he summoned all his knights and barons.

'See how beautiful she is, my child of one year old,' he
cried.

He delighted in the castle. He had failed to win Jerusalem
but he had built Château Gaillard.

He continued his wars with Philip and so successful was he
that the time came when Philip was obliged to sue for peace.

What peace there could be between them would be temporary and both knew it, but Philip was asking for it and
Richard laughed to himself to contemplate the humiliation
the French King must feel.

'The King of France believes that a satisfactory peace can
only be made if there is a meeting between himself and King
Richard,' was the message Philip sent to him.

A meeting! They had not seen each other since they had
parted at Acre. Richard remembered him then—a sick man
Philip had been, for it was true that that pernicious climate
had impaired his health. His thinning hair, the pallor of his
face, the flaking nails ... he had not been like the arrogant
Philip of their youth.

And now ... what had the years in France done to Philip? All that time when Richard had been imprisoned Philip had been living his luxurious life in France. Nay, he had been fighting, with John as his ally and only those loyal Norman seneschals had kept Normandy for its Duke.

To see Philip again. Yes, he wanted it. He wanted to remember long ago days when they had been young and had meant so much to each other.

He would meet Philip. Where? He, Richard, would choose the place since it was Philip who sued for the meeting. It should be on the Seine with the Saucy Castle as the background of their meeting place. Not too near; he was never going to allow the French very near his darling. But just so that Philip could see those mighty towers and bastions and realize through them the invincible might of Richard of England.

He would go by boat from Gaillard to the meeting place. He would not leave his boat. He would not go too near Philip. He wanted hate to be uppermost not love. Love! They were enemies. It was true, but once there had been love between them, a love which neither of them had been able to forget throughout their lives.

*   *   *

Philip was on horseback close to the banks of the Seine; Richard was seated in his boat.

'It is long since we met,' said Philip, and there was a faint tremor in his voice.

'I remember it well. You were in a sorry state. You had broken your vows; you were creeping back to France.'

'It was that or death,' answered Philip.

'Your vows broken.'

'My health was broken.'

'You have recovered now, Philip.'

'And you look as healthful as ever,' replied Philip.

'War suits me, victorious war.'

'We were born to fight against each other ... more's the pity. I would rather be your friend, Richard.'

'You have said that before.'

' 'Tis true. I remember ...'

'It is not good to remember. We have business to talk. You

took advantage of my absence. You worked with my enemies against me. You bribed the Emperor to hold me in his fortress. This I can never forget. It has made me your enemy for life.'

'If we could talk together...'

'We are talking together.'

'Alone...'

Who could trust perfidious Philip? he asked himself and he answered: 'You could, Richard, as once you did.'

Richard hesitated just for a moment. He thought of past pleasures. Those youthful days when they had ridden together and lain in the shared bed and talked of crusades.

But Philip was King of France, the proven enemy of the King of England. They did not meet now as friends and lovers—though in their hearts they might have been so—they met as the Kings of two countries who must ever be at war with each other.

The Pope's legate was on his way to mediate between them. Their wars were devastating the land. There must be a pause in their hostilities. There must be a treaty of peace between them.

If we were at peace, thought Philip, we could be friends. Why should we not be? But the needs of France must be his main concern. Private feelings must not come between him and that. And how beautiful was Richard, seated there in his boat, a little arrogant against the background of his Saucy Castle.

They talked of terms. A marriage between a niece of Richard's and Philip's son Louis. Her dowry to be Gisors, that important fortress built by William Rufus and which was always a cause of concern to the side which did not own it.

They came to an agreement. The treaty should be drawn up.

'We shall meet again for the signing,' said Philip.

The Crock of Gold

RICHARD returned to the Château Gaillard, nostalgic with memories of other days. They would sign their treaty and perhaps when they had done so they would meet in a more friendly fashion; perhaps together they could find a way to a true peace between their countries.

Into the courtyard rode a troop of his soldiers who had come to join him lest he need help against Philip. They would dine together off roast boar, said Richard, which they did.

During the feast the Captain of the guards related a rumour that he had heard. A peasant ploughing the land for his master who was Achard Lord of Chaluz had turned up a wonderful treasure. This was in the form of a great block of gold which had been cut into a group of figures representing an emperor and his family and dated back many years to when the emperor was presumably the ruler of Aquitaine.

'A figure of gold!' cried Richard. 'Why it must be worth a fortune!'

'It must indeed, Sire, and if one piece were found why should there not be many more?'

Richard was deeply impressed by the story; he asked innumerable questions and in the morning when he arose he announced his intention of going to Chaluz to see the treasure.

Such treasure was surely the property of the sovereign lord, he reasoned, in which case the treasure was his. The thought of augmenting his depleted coffers excited him so much that he had forgotten temporarily the treaty with France. There would be time to sign that later.

He sent a message to Achard to tell him that he was on his way and that he was to guard the treasure until he came to claim it, for Achard would agree that his sovereign rights proclaimed him the owner of it.

He was close to Chaluz when the messenger arrived from Achard to say that the find had been grossly exaggerated. There were no golden figures; all that had been found was a jar of gold coins. The value was not great and Adamar of Limoges, whose vassal Achard was, had already claimed the treasure and had no intention of handing it over to Richard.

Such defiance infuriated Richard. He vowed vengeance on both Achard and Adamar and advanced through Limousin laying waste to the land and pillaging the hamlets.

As he approached the castle of Chaluz, Adamar sent out a messenger to ask Richard to put the dispute before the King of France, for as Duke of Aquitaine and Normandy he was a vassal of that sovereign.

It was a suggestion to arouse Richard's fury and he went into action against the castle, determined to bring about its destruction.

The defenders pleaded that it was the Lenten season and no time to indulge in a battle for gold.

Richard laughed aloud at that. Give him the treasure, he said, and he would abandon the fight and not before. It was a bitter battle. The castle was not well defended, but both Achard and Adamar knew that if they surrendered they would have to face Richard's fury. They preferred to die fighting and would not give in.

There was one among them, a certain Bertrand de Gourdon whose home had been destroyed some years before by Richard during the wars in Aquitaine. He had lost his father and brothers in the battle and had hated Richard ever since.

He was ready to fight desperately against the King and had joined Achard for this purpose.

He was in the keep when he saw the King. Richard would always stand out among his men, and Bertrand watched the King take an arrow and shoot it at the keep. It lodged there in the wall close by Bertrand. The King's arrow! Bertrand reached for it. He fitted it into his bow and let it fly towards the King. It struck Richard below his neck and penetrated under his shoulder blade.

His knights called out in dismay but he shouted that all was well.

The castle had fallen to the King's men, but the King was in agony.

*   *   *

He lay on his sick bed. He had tried to pull the arrow out and in doing so had broken it. It needed an operation to remove the barb.

The days began to pass and the wound was festering. The pain was agonizing. It was with horror that he realized mortification had set in.

This was the end, and he knew it.

*   *   *

Eleanor came to his bedside from Fontevrault, the Abbey where she had been finding a certain peace now that Richard was in command of his kingdom.

Her grief was terrible.

'It cannot be,' she cried. 'Not you ... not Richard! My beautiful son!'

''Tis so, Mother,' he said. 'This is the end for me. An arrow shot at Chaluz—and all for the sake of gold treasure which they tell me is very little. I might have died fighting for Jerusalem and they will say of me now that I died fighting for a vessel of gold coins.'

'They will say of you that you are the bravest soldier of the Cross that ever lived,' cried Eleanor fiercely. 'And you are not going to die. *You* cannot die.'

'I am mortal, Mother. See how weak I am.'

'I have seen you weak before with the fever on you, but you always recovered did you not?'

He shook his head. 'You and I should speak the truth together. We always did and we must do so now. I am dying, Mother. You know it.'

She could not speak, so choked was she with her emotion; she could not look on the beloved face for her eyes were blinded by her tears.

'Mother,' he said, 'what will happen when I am dead? Arthur should have been here. The people should have known him. They would have loved him. The young are so appealing. But his mother refused to allow him to come and now there is only John.'

She could not answer him; she could only think of him in all his youthful beauty—her beloved, her Lion Heart.

'John is English,' he said. 'The English know him. They will accept him as they never would accept Arthur. It must be John, Mother. God help England.'

She clung to his hands; she kissed them.

She said: 'You see, you *must* recover, my beloved. What will England do without you? What shall *I* do without you?'

But she knew, as he did, that there was no point in deluding themselves. The bitter tragic truth must be accepted.

'Send for the Archbishops and the Bishops,' said Richard. 'My brother John must be proclaimed King on my death. It is the only way for peace in the realm.'

There should have been an heir he was thinking.

My poor Berengaria, you should have been the mother of my sons.

'I will have them brought to you,' said Eleanor. She rose to her feet.

'Farewell, my mother,' he said. 'There has been much love between us.'

She could not answer him. She wanted to cry out in her misery. She wanted to curse God for taking from her the only one she truly loved.

*　　*　　*

Richard asked that the man who had shot the fatal arrow be brought to him.

Richard looked at Bertrand de Gourdon steadily and said: 'What have I done to you that you should slay me?'

'You slew my father and my two brothers. You would have killed me and all for a pot of gold. I am ready for revenge. Inflict on me what tortures you can contrive. I care not. I have had my reward. I have seen you on your deathbed.'

'There is a brave man,' said Richard. 'Let him go free. I forgive him what he has done to me and I trust he will forgive me what I have done to him. Send my Queen to me.'

He must not die until she came. He wanted to ask her forgiveness. He wanted to convey to her somehow that it was not his dislike of her personally which had kept them apart.

She came—sad and pale, a tragic queen who had rarely known real happiness.

She knelt by his bed and wept.

'It is farewell,' he said. 'Forgive me, Berengaria. I would I could have been a better husband.'

She shook her head and her tears fell on to his hand which she held in hers.

He looked at her sad fair face until his eyes grew glazed and he thought he was on the walls at Acre and that Saladin was beckoning to him.

JEAN PLAIDY HAS ALSO WRITTEN

BEYOND THE BLUE MOUNTAINS
(A novel about early settlers in Australia)

DAUGHTER OF SATAN
(A novel about the persecution of witches and Puritans in the 16th and 17th centuries)

THE SCARLET CLOAK
(A novel of 16th century Spain, France and England)

Stories of Victorian England
{ IT BEGAN IN VAUXHALL GARDENS
LILITH

THE GOLDSMITH'S WIFE
(The story of Jane Shore)

EVERGREEN GALLANT
(The story of Henri of Navarre)

The Medici Trilogy
Catherine de' Medici
{ MADAME SERPENT
THE ITALIAN WOMAN } Also available in one volume
QUEEN JEZEBEL

The Lucrezia Borgia Series
{ MADONNA OF THE SEVEN HILLS } Also available in one
LIGHT ON LUCREZIA } volume

The Ferdinand and Isabella Trilogy
{ CASTILE FOR ISABELLA
SPAIN FOR THE SOVEREIGNS } Also available in one
DAUGHTERS OF SPAIN } volume

The French Revolution Series
{ LOUIS THE WELL-BELOVED
THE ROAD TO COMPIÈGNE
FLAUNTING, EXTRAVAGANT QUEEN

The Tudor Novels
Katherine of Aragon
{ KATHERINE, THE VIRGIN WIDOW
THE SHADOW OF THE POMEGRANATE } Also available
THE KING'S SECRET MATTER } in one volume

MURDER MOST ROYAL
(Anne Boleyn and Catherine Howard)

THE SIXTH WIFE
(Katherine Parr)

ST THOMAS'S EVE
(Sir Thomas More)

THE SPANISH BRIDEGROOM
(Philip II and his first three wives)

GAY LORD ROBERT
(Elizabeth and Leicester)

THE THISTLE AND THE ROSE
(Margaret Tudor and James IV)

MARY, QUEEN OF FRANCE
(Queen of Louis XII)

The Mary Queen of Scots Series	⎰ ROYAL ROAD TO FOTHERINGAY ⎱ THE CAPTIVE QUEEN OF SCOTS
The Stuart Saga	THE MURDER IN THE TOWER (Robert Carr and the Countess of Essex)
Charles II	⎧ THE WANDERING PRINCE ⎫ ⎨ A HEALTH UNTO HIS MAJESTY ⎬ Also available in ⎩ HERE LIES OUR SOVEREIGN LORD ⎭ one volume
	THE THREE CROWNS (William of Orange)
	THE HAUNTED SISTERS (Mary and Anne)
	THE QUEEN'S FAVOURITES (Sarah Churchill and Abigail Hill)
The Georgian Saga	THE PRINCESS OF CELLE (Sophia Dorothea and George I)
	QUEEN IN WAITING ⎱ (Caroline of Ansbach) CAROLINE THE QUEEN ⎰
	THE PRINCE AND THE QUAKERESS (George III & Hannah Lightfoot)
	THE THIRD GEORGE (George III)
	PERDITA'S PRINCE (Perdita Robinson)
	SWEET LASS OF RICHMOND HILL (Mrs Fitzherbert)
	INDISCRETIONS OF THE QUEEN (Caroline of Brunswick)
	THE REGENT'S DAUGHTER (Princess Charlotte)
	GODDESS OF THE GREEN ROOM (Dorothy Jordan and William IV)
	VICTORIA IN THE WINGS (End of the Georgian Era)
The Queen Victoria Series	THE CAPTIVE OF KENSINGTON PALACE (Early days of Victoria)
	THE QUEEN AND LORD M (Victoria and Lord Melbourne)
	THE QUEEN'S HUSBAND (Victoria and Albert)
	THE WIDOW OF WINDSOR (Last years of Victoria's reign)
The Norman Trilogy	THE BASTARD KING
	THE LION OF JUSTICE
	THE PASSIONATE ENEMIES
The Plantagenet Saga	THE PLANTAGENET PRELUDE
	THE REVOLT OF THE EAGLETS
	THE HEART OF THE LION
	THE PRINCE OF DARKNESS (*in preparation*)
Non-Fiction	MARY QUEEN OF SCOTS: *The Fair Devil of Scotland*
	A TRIPTYCH OF POISONERS (Cesare Borgia, Madame de Brinvilliers and Dr Pritchard)
	THE RISE OF THE SPANISH INQUISITION
	THE GROWTH OF THE SPANISH INQUISITION
	THE END OF THE SPANISH INQUISITION